Engn II

The Clockwork War

SIMON KEWIN

STORM
CROW
BOOKS

ISBN: 978-1-9993395-9-3

For Carole

To find the clock-winder they needed to find a clock.
He'd been looking for some high tower like the one
near the Valve Hall, but instead there was a small,
round clock on a building wall up ahead, its thirty-six
digits picked out in gold. Two incandescent bulbs
flickered beneath it, the clock's single hand casting a
long shadow up the wall…

- Engn

CONTENTS

I	1	XIII	122	XXV	222
II	10	XIV	130	XXVI	226
III	17	XV	134	XXVII	233
IIII	30	XVI	146	XXVIII	244
V	41	XVII	159	XXIX	257
VI	53	XVIII	165	XXX	267
VII	66	XIX	169	XXXI	275
VIII	78	XX	178	XXXII	283
IX	90	XXI	186	XXXIII	295
X	92	XXII	189	XXXIV	301
XI	102	XXIII	200	XXXV	307
XII	113	XXIV	212	XXXVI	314

I

One hundred and seventeen years before the destruction of Engn...

Aivan was tinkering with one of the broken clocks in the Director's workshop when the iron-clad guards of the Ironmasters Guild came for him.

"You are needed at the Hub. Come quickly." Three of them stood in the doorway, voices muffled, faces invisible behind leather and metal masks. Strictly speaking, they weren't allowed in the workshop, or in any of the Director's private chambers. And yet here they were.

"What is it?" asked Aivan, annoyed at being interrupted but also alarmed at the intrusion. In his hand, he held a pair of tweezers, and in the tweezers, a tiny cog from the clock he was repairing. The cog glimmered as it caught the light. His hand was shaking. "What has happened?"

"You must come now," said the Ironmaster. "There is no time to lose."

Aivan set down his tweezers and stood. He didn't want to follow the Ironmasters. Could they force him to come if he refused? Perhaps, perhaps not. They always left the Director – and therefore Aivan, his apprentice – alone. But they also wouldn't obey direct orders. Or answer questions. The Director, despite his title, apparently wielded little control over the individual guilds. It was another thing that troubled Aivan. Another Engn mystery. Was the Director in charge, or wasn't he? Why was everything arranged like this?

One day, when the current Director died or retired and Aivan took over, he'd find out. Find out everything. The purpose of the machine. The secret at its heart. The truth about what the Director actually *did*. The prospect of it all sent a familiar thrill of anticipation through him. It was just a shame the Director was so young and fit. It would be years – decades – before Aivan finally got to know the truth.

"Come now. We must hurry," said the iron-clad guard. "An engine awaits at the terminus. You are needed at the Hub."

The guards stood in the doorway, as if a barrier prevented them from coming inside. Aivan looked around at all the clocks. The cogs and pendulums of the broken mechanisms. The faces of the functioning clocks, ticking their way through the hours. He liked it in here. He felt safe. The air hummed with the purposeful whirring of all the tiny machines. The world made sense in this little room. Everything was ordered. He could refuse to go with them. Couldn't he?

Still, for them to visit him was unheard of. It was an inversion of the natural order. Something serious had happened.

"Very well," he said.

The guards turned and left in a hurry, pacing across the expanse of the pendulum floor of the Western Grand Tower. *Clock seventy-two*. As Aivan stepped from the room after them, the array of timepieces behind him awoke and began chiming the hour in a coordinated cacophony of clangs and alarms. It was, he thought, as if they were trying to warn him about something.

Aivan had visited the Hub numerous times while shadowing the Director. There were clocks controlling each of the six steam-powered rams that met in the heart of the great cube, and the Director always paid these special attention. Checked their time every day. It was another mystery. The Hub was central, that was clear. Central to Engn physically, but also at the heart of the *purpose*. The secret. From what Aivan had managed to glean, Engn had been destroyed at least twice over the centuries. Rioters or invaders had wrecked the machinery, sending fires raging through Engn, triggering cascading explosions, levelling everything. Everything except for the Hub and one or two other important locations. It was the Hub the guards rushed to defend when conflagrations flared up. Always the Hub. Yet even they didn't seem to know why. He'd quizzed them, more than once, but had been met with shrugs and silence.

But it was from here they always rebuilt Engn, working their way outwards, connecting everything back together. This was the foundation. The centre.

So much in Engn was confusing and baffling that he'd long ago concluded it was deliberately built to be so. An attempt to confuse and dazzle, to obscure the true purpose. A baffling array of incomprehensible devices and meaningless customs. A machine so vast and all-encompassing people stopped seeing it, stopped asking why it was there. But he'd seen through that. Perhaps that was why he'd been picked out those years ago, plucked from his pointless hours of labour assembling valves to shadow the Director.

On at least one occasion, he knew, the machine had been deliberately dismantled and rebuilt. An older, smaller Engn replaced with a new one: bigger, taller, more powerful. But even through *that* the Hub had remained untouched, the machine growing greater and greater around it, feeding more and more power into it.

A thought came to him as he climbed from the moving engine whose rails had swept him across the machine at such eye-watering speed. Perhaps this, unexpectedly, was the day? Perhaps the Director had chosen *this* moment to pass on the secrets of Engn. Was it possible? The prospect was delicious and suddenly alarming. Was he ready for the responsibility? Was he ready for the truth? He suddenly wasn't sure. Aivan took a moment to look around, to calm his breathing. The familiar wheels and towers of the great machine gleamed. From the Hub, their arrangement was clear. Axles and belts and timing chains from all across the machine led here. *This* was what they were for. These six vast rams. Except, they didn't do anything so far as he could see. They just *were*. He was obviously missing something. And now, perhaps, he would find out what.

Steeling himself, Aivan turned to follow the guards. They hurried underneath the axle of the eastern ram, its smooth metal shaft vast and shining above his head. He could *feel* the power thrumming through it, the concentrated force in that great piston up above him. If you stopped and studied them closely you could see the rams jerking backwards and forwards, almost too quick to discern. The power required to push each piston in and out was titanic. He'd never been able to work out what was doing the pushing, let alone why.

His gaze followed the shaft towards the cube. A small crowd of people stood around the eastern entranceway. He faltered as he walked closer, seeing who they were. Not just iron-clad guards but those wearing gleaming silver, too: the soldiers of the Silversmiths Guild. Did they take orders from the Director or was it the other way around?

There were three masters there, too. The Clockmakers, the Ironmasters, and the Silversmiths Guilds. The trio who ruled the Inner Wheel. And all of them waiting there. Waiting for *him*. Dread lurched within him. The three watched him as he approached, suspicion clear on their faces.

The iron-clad guards stopped as they arrived at the group. Aivan wondered what he would say, how he would explain himself to these powerful and terrible people. But to his surprise, as he approached, they parted. Without anyone saying a word, they stood aside, granting him passage into the Hub. Looks passed between the masters, looks full of meaning he couldn't understand.

Not looking at them, keeping his eyes fixed firmly ahead of him, Aivan the apprentice Director of Engn, strode inside.

Light filtered into the cavernous space from the five openings in the walls and the one in the roof. Diagonal shafts of sunlight slanted through the western port, providing more shadow than light. Still there was no sound, save for the clacking of his own footsteps as he strode to the centre. The sense of suppressed, concentrated power was overwhelming in here. As it always was. The thrumming air was thick with it. The six steel shafts – one through each wall, one from the beam-engine above them and one thrusting up from the buried engine beneath their feet – glistened like a grounded star in the middle of the echoing chamber. The shafts tapered as they stretched towards each other, giving the room a confusing sense of scale, as if it contained vast distances.

And at the very centre, where they met at a point and all that terrible power was focused there was – what? He had studied it from below often, craning his neck upwards, trying to understand. A small cube of some rock or metal, held there for no apparent purpose. Doing nothing, achieving nothing. The Director always refused to talk about it, dismissing him with a wave of his hand whenever

Aivan asked.

Up ahead he saw something that shouldn't be there. On the floor in the very centre of the chamber stood a clock. A wooden casement clock, one he knew well. What was it doing there? The Director never let it out of his sight, carrying it with him all about Engn as he checked the accuracy of all the timepieces and control mechanisms. Sleeping beside it so the gentle ticking sound was with him every second of the day. Yet there it was, abandoned, an oblong wooden box quietly counting out the seconds to itself, standing like a tombstone in the middle of the floor.

Aivan slowed as he neared, trying to make sense of the sight, expecting some unnamed, terrible *thing* to happen at any moment.

"Aivan. You are here at last."

The quiet voice seemed to come from nowhere, from beneath his feet. The steps down to the underground engine. The Director must have set his regulator clock on the floor before descending. Wary now, suddenly not wanting to reach the centre, Aivan shuffled forwards. The concentrated atmosphere of the room seemed to press down on his shoulders.

"Aivan."

There, at the foot of stone steps, head and arms cramped against the walls, lay the Director of Engn. There was blood on his bald head, but the familiar glint in those eyes was bright.

"What has happened?" asked Aivan, hurrying down the steps, the sight of his master filling him with alarm.

The Director didn't speak for a moment, as if he was trying to remember how to make his mouth and throat work. "Fell," he said finally, his voice little more than a whisper.

Aivan put his ear close to the Director's. He couldn't escape the notion this was all some test, another part of his initiation. But the blood was surely real, and the Director's limbs and neck lay at very wrong angles.

"You fell down the stairs?" said Aivan. "We can lift you up; take you to the Infirmary."

The Director shook his head, the movement almost imperceptible. "No. Too late for that. It's my heart."

"Your heart?" said Aivan, as if he didn't know the word.

The Director nodded. "Ironic. Spent all my time worrying about the clocks in Engn. Never thought about the one ticking away in my own chest."

"You had a heart attack?"

The Director grimaced as some agony cut through him.

"Pain like you wouldn't believe, lad. Crushing my chest. That's why I fell down the stairs."

"But we can lift you up," repeated Aivan, not knowing what else to say.

"No. My heart's hammering away too fast. Stuttering like it's about to stop. That's why I sent for you; sent the others away. There isn't much time and a lot to tell you."

"Tell me? Tell me what?" But, of course, he knew. The day Aivan had long hoped for was here. And he suddenly wasn't ready. Wasn't ready at all.

"You need to know the secrets," the Director continued. "You're young, but there's no one else. Only the Director knows..." He stopped as more pain lanced through him, his face contorting into ugliness.

"Secrets?" said Aivan.

"The purpose of Engn. What it's all for. You must have wondered. Only I know, and now I must tell you."

"But there have to be others. The masters. There can't just be you."

"The knowledge is too dangerous. No one else must know the truth. They wouldn't stand for it, you see. If they knew what we'd done, they wouldn't stand for it. That's what we do, you and I. Director to Director, over the centuries, keeping the secret until the day it's needed."

"Tell me, then," said Aivan. "Tell me what I have to do. Tell me the secret."

"Engn is…"

Another spasm of pain. The Director clutched at his chest, his face creasing up in lines of agony. For a moment, Aivan thought he wasn't going to open his eyes again, that he was gone.

"Director! Tell me. I don't know what to do!"

The Director twitched. His mouth moved, whispering something inaudible. Aivan put his ear to the man's lips. "I didn't hear! Say it again."

"Engn," whispered the Director. "Engn is … a weapon."

"A weapon?" said Aivan. "How can it be a weapon? I don't understand!"

The Director spoke slowly, as if forming each word required the deepest concentration. "The ultimate weapon. Kept ready all these years for the final battle. The Clockwork War."

It made no sense. "But the war ended centuries ago. Everyone knows that."

"No, no. Not won yet. It's all still here. Ticking away. Counting down. People carry the war around in their heads, waiting to fight it again."

"But … how can Engn be a weapon?" said Aivan. "I don't understand. Is it something to do with this place? The Hub?"

There was no reply. Aivan shouted now, shaking the Director, wringing the truth from him. "You must tell me! I can't be the Director without knowing. The secrets must be passed on. What does it do? How is Engn a weapon? Why is it needed?"

Aivan's only reply was silence. The Director – the previous Director – didn't move or speak again. Aivan kneeled there for five minutes, ten minutes, trying to make sense of what he'd heard. But there was no sense to be made. Only scraps and glimpses. And what would he do, now, when his own time came? When he had to pass on the terrible secrets of Engn to the next Director?

There was nothing he could do. The secret had been lost. And that, Aivan saw, had to become *his* secret. The secret he would carry instead. No one else must ever know. Everything had to go on as before. Anything else was unthinkable. The lie had become too large. Engn was life for so many people and he had to maintain the illusion. Play the part for the rest of his days.

Finally, Aivan, the Director of Engn, stood. He climbed the stairs one by one back to the surface. At the top, he hefted the regulator clock onto his shoulders. The weight of it surprised him. It was a burden. He could feel the ticking clock kicking against his spine.

Looking straight forwards, he strode towards the eastern doorway to confront the knot of waiting masters.

II

Three years after the destruction of Engn...

Booming explosions shook Finn awake. For a moment, he lay unmoving in bed, slick with sweat, not sure what was real and what was dream. He'd been back inside Engn as the towers and wheels collapsed and bloomed into flame. He'd been in the dormitory as Graves or Croft or Bellow tipped his bed over and began their machine-like kicking. He'd been falling, falling down clanging metal chutes leading to the mines.

But no. He was back home and Engn was long gone. He'd lived in the valley for three years since the destruction. He was safe. Everyone in his family was safe. And yet his bed was lurching as if being shaken by some furious giant. He was fully awake, but the shaking hadn't stopped. This wasn't another nightmare; it was real.

On the shelf opposite, the small wind-up clock his parents had given them as a house-warming gift shuddered into life. It marched its way sideways, twisting around before toppling off and smashing to the floor. Badger, lying curled up on the end of the bed, whined in alarm. Her features blurred as Finn looked at her, as if something was wrong with his eyes.

"What's going on? What's happening?"

Diane's voice beside him was shaky, as if the two of them were rattling along the lane at high speed in a cart rather than lying in bed. Scraps of plaster and dust rained down from the ceiling above them, scratching into his eyes.

"Come on," he said. "We have to get outside!"

Helping each other, staggering across the swaying room, they blundered their way to the stairs. Badger led the way, more stable on her four legs despite her age, clattering down the steps before them. Finn and Diane followed. Downstairs, their little kitchen had come alive. Pots and cups and cutlery rattled and tinkled as if possessed. Finn stood for a moment watching it all, trying to understand. Diane, still in her thin nightshift, grabbed him by the arm and hauled him through the door.

They ran from the cottage they shared, Mrs. Hampton's old place, and stood looking back from the garden, both panting, holding each other's hand. Badger cowered behind them. It was barely light, the low winter sun just peeping over the line of the hills. Frost gilded every surface. The grass of their little lawn sparkled, but it was sharply cold on Finn's bare feet.

He'd thought, somehow, it would only be their house being shaken to pieces. But, no. The whole world was moving. The ground was suddenly no longer solid; it flowed and bucked beneath them like the sea in a storm. The trees all up the valley sides danced, scattering the last of their leaves as if being blown by a strong wind.

Then, in an instant, it all ceased. A huge silence rolled through the valley, as if every living thing was standing in stunned disbelief. Finn shivered, his clenched jaw muscles hurting sharply. He didn't move, waiting for something to happen, waiting for the world to start making sense again. Diane put her arm around his waist. Her body was warm against his. Relief and shock played across her face as she stared around.

"Finn!"

His father came careering down the lane, still clad in his own nightgown, sandals on his feet he kept slipping out of. In other circumstances, the sight would have been comical.

"Finn! Diane! Are the two of you okay?"

"Yes, yes," said Diane, her teeth clenched against the cold.

"What's happening?" asked Finn again. "What's going on?"

His father bear-hugged the two of them. His chest was heaving heavily from his sprint down the lane. He replied only when he'd released the two of them. "An earthquake."

"An *earthquake*?" said Finn.

He knew what it meant, of course. Still, it was hard to relate such a little word to the power of the real thing. The whole world had shaken. It was like the day Engn fell. The ground had cracked and broken then, too. But there'd been a reason for that – it hadn't just *happened*. It made sense. "But we don't get earthquakes," he said.

"No," said his father. "Not these days."

There was worry in his father's voice. For some reason, hearing that was worse than the shaking of the solid ground.

"Is mother all right?" he asked. "The house?"

"She's fine. A few plates smashed. These old houses were built to survive a little shaking."

"Have you heard from Shireen?"

"Your mother's gone up there to see if they're all right."

"Why didn't you use the line-of-sight?" asked Diane.

His father shook his head. "No good. Everything goes out of alignment when something like this happens. It'll take days to get it all running again. The quake probably heaved up a few roads and power lines, too. Flane is going to be busy getting everything straight. We all are."

Finn studied his father. What did he mean, *something like this*? *Something like this* never happened.

"Is it safe to go back inside?" asked Diane. She was trembling visibly in the freezing morning air. Her hair was long now, flowing and golden. When she'd been on the run, she'd kept it hacked short, so it didn't get in the way. It smelled good as Finn held her close. It was contact with a world that made sense.

"No," said his father. "There can be aftershocks. Sometimes they last a day or two. It's best not to go in."

"But we'll need warm clothes and blankets to sleep outside this time of year," said Diane. "I mean, we can manage, but not the older ones."

His father nodded. "In the old days folk used to gather together in the Moot Hall. It has deep foundations to withstand the tremors. The wooden walls sway rather than falling over. We'll gather there until we're sure there are no more quakes."

"I need to find out about my village," said Diane. "It may have struck there, too."

"It's a long way off," said his father. "Perhaps they'll be safe. We can leave a message at the Switch House as we go past. Rory will tell us as soon as we get word from down the valley."

Now Finn put his arm around Diane, offering her his warmth. The ice on the road sparkled in front of them. Everything was so peaceful, so right. It was too hard to believe what had happened. They started walking, but then Finn remembered something.

"Wait. I *have* to go back inside, just for a moment."

"Why?" asked Diane. The suspicion in her voice was clear. She knew very well what he was going in for.

"Connor's image spindle."

"Finn, no," said his father. "I told you, it's not safe.

Especially not for *that*. It doesn't matter."

Finn caught the look passing between Diane and his father. They'd discussed this before. Discussed him and his obsession with the silvery shaft of metal Connor had given him just before they'd destroyed Engn. He knew they didn't understand.

"But it might get damaged if the house does fall down," said Finn. "The spindle is delicate. Then there's the reader; it barely works as it is. It's taken me months to get it to show any images at all and now it could be smashed to pieces."

"Then it won't get any more smashed," said his father.

"I…" But before Finn could reply fully, another deep boom tolled through the air, heavy and solid in the still morning air, the sound rebounding off the stone sides of the mountains. For a moment, none of them spoke, looking around as if for an explanation.

"What was that?" said Diane. "Another earthquake?"

"Nothing shook," said Finn. "The ground didn't move."

"It sounded like an explosion," said his father. "A big explosion, far away."

They looked at each other, each thinking the same thought, none of them saying it. They'd all heard sounds like it before, although not for three years. But how was that possible? Engn had been destroyed. He had seen it destroyed. They all had.

There'd been rumours, of course. But people liked rumours, liked to make up stories to fill what they didn't actually know. Travelers passed through the valley with wild tales of being pursued by ironclads and the stories grew from there.

Besides, even if the concussion had boomed across the great grass plain, it didn't prove anything. Perhaps some surviving fragment of the machinery had finally corroded or collapsed. Shaken loose by the earthquake, maybe. Or some buried tank of oil had been ignited by a chance flame. That was all it was.

Still, the look of anxiety of the faces of his father and Diane was clear.

"Okay, look," said Diane. "I can see you're not going to come without the spindle. You go inside the house and grab it. I'll get the reader from the workshop. Then we can get to the Moot House."

"No," said Finn. "I don't want you risking yourself."

"And I don't want *you* risking yourself," said Diane, "but you're going to whatever I say, aren't you?"

She was right, of course. She thought he was obsessed with the object Connor had given them. Her meaning was clear. Risking himself meant risking her, too. Risking *them*. Just as it had before, back in Engn. Risking her was the price he would have to pay.

"Okay," said Finn. "Just … be careful."

His father looked troubled, but he didn't say anything. He would have, once. Now, since their return to the valley, he treated both Finn and Diane as grownups. Sometimes, Finn actually wished he wouldn't. Sometimes he wanted to be told what was best, what to do, what everything meant.

"You be quick, both of you," said his father. "If there's any sign of another quake, come straight out, you hear?"

Finn nodded. "I'll grab some more clothes, too."

His father held Badger while Finn and Diane ran back to the cottage and the little stone outhouse they used as a combined workshop and wood store.

At the door, Finn slipped on the outdoor shoes he'd left there the evening before, then stepped inside. He trod carefully, as if the slightest footstep could bring the whole house crashing down around his ears. He crossed their kitchen, shards of shattered pottery and glass crunching beneath his feet. On the mantelpiece, over the smoky old iron stove they cooked on, was the stone pot he kept the spindle in, as if it were their most treasured possession. Thankfully the pot was undamaged.

He lifted the slim metal spindle out, holding it carefully

by its tip to examine it in the morning sunlight. It looked intact. The tiny etched lines spiralling around it were unblemished. He exhaled with relief. All the answers he sought; they were still there. Still, literally, in his grasp. If only he could read them.

For months after their return to the valley, he hadn't even understood what the spindle was. Connor had given it to him just before he died. *It will come in useful. Remember what it was all for.* Finn had assumed it was some key or token he hadn't, in the end, needed. Then one of the tinkers passing through the valley, selling broken fragments of Engn machinery to anyone who would buy, had told him what it really was. A memory spindle. Used to record the images from the seeing orbs.

Finn recalled drawers full of the tinkling metal sticks. And Connor had gone to the trouble of giving him *this* one in the control room. Clearly it was important. Vital. He had only to construct a reader and all his questions about Connor and Engn would be answered. Soon, soon, he would uncover the truth.

Spindle grasped in one hand, he threw warm coats over his arm and picked up shoes for Diane, then crossed back to the doorway. The rising sun dazzled his eyes as he stepped outside, blinding him for a moment. His father was nothing more than a shape, Badger beside him, whining and scrabbling. Then Diane was there, standing in front of him.

"Finn, I'm sorry," she said. "There was nothing I could do."

Finn shielded his eyes and squinted to see what she meant. In her arms, she carried the smashed fragments of the memory spindle reader.

It was shattered beyond repair.

III

"How do you know all this about earthquakes?" Finn asked his father as they walked together towards the Switch House. "We don't get earthquakes."

"I just ... know the old stories."

Finn caught his father's momentary hesitation. "The old stories don't say anything about aftershocks and gathering at the Moot Hall," said Finn. "They're just children's tales about mad giants throwing rocks at each other in underground caves. Fireside stories for winter nights."

His father shrugged. "My grandfather told me other tales. Earthquakes used to be a lot more common in the old days. He always took some coaxing; he didn't like to talk about it. None of the old people did."

"Why?" asked Diane, walking along behind them. "Back home, we all knew about them."

"I think it was too painful," said Finn's father. "People died. It's worse up here in the mountains. My grandfather wasn't afraid of anything but talk of earthquakes made him go pale. Winter was worst, he said. Big tremors could bring down avalanches right through the valley."

Finn caught the glance of anxiety. His father didn't like to talk about that distant day; the day when Finn and Connor had survived an avalanche by climbing into the branches of an old oak tree. His father had admitted years later he'd been sure Finn was dead. That they were searching for bodies. A terrible day, but also the start of Finn's friendship with Connor. A terrible day and a good day. He thought back, trying to remember. Had there been an earthquake? A tremor to trigger the avalanche? He couldn't recall. It was all too long ago.

His father glanced across Finn, stroking his snowy beard as he did when he was thinking. Remembering those distant events. Some moments stayed with you however long you lived.

They found Mrs. Megrim on the ground at the foot of the spiral path up to the Switch House. The sight of her there, as they rounded the bend, took Finn to another memory. The day the old woman defied the ironclads and the master who led them. The day she slipped Finn the secret line-of-sight encryption key. She'd never really recovered from the injuries she'd sustained in performing that simple act, although it wasn't something she ever mentioned. She'd never walked straight again, limping awkwardly as if something inside her was no longer properly connected. And here she was once more, a heap of black on the ground.

"Don't just stand there gawping, boy," she called, seeing Finn and the others approaching. "Help me up."

Mrs. Megrim, at least, still treated him like a foolish child, chiding him constantly about the tasks he'd failed to complete to her satisfaction. Once he would have complained about it to anyone who would listen. Now he wouldn't have it any other way. Everything in the world could change, people could come and go, but Mrs. Megrim would still be there, telling him to stop dawdling like an idiot and hurry up.

"Sorry, Mrs. Megrim," said Finn. Standing over her, he could see the pink of her scalp through her wispy grey hair. She wore her usual dark-as-night black coat, but underneath there were woollens of purple and even red. Something she had taken to since Rory's return. She had lost Tom, along with a large part of both her sons' childhoods, but she had set aside her loss that much. He understood, now, that her habitual black had been a symbol of mourning. A prolonged, drawn-out grief that would never truly end. It was hard to believe Mrs. Megrim had once been the wild, fun-loving girl his mother described. Except, every now and then, he caught a flash of her sly sense of humour and saw the woman she might have been if things had gone differently.

Finn squatted down to lever her back up to her feet, cradling her elbow. "What happened? Why are you sitting here on the ground?"

Mrs. Megrim couldn't keep the grimace of pain from her face as her body unbent. "I'm not *sitting on the ground*. I fell over when the earthquake hit. Can't you work anything out for yourself, boy?"

She stood unaided, a little wobbly, leaning heavily on her stick. The stick that had been waved at Finn many times in his childhood. These days she needed it much more. These days it was a crutch rather than a weapon. Mrs. Megrim didn't leave her cottage often and rarely made it up to the Switch House. When she did venture out, she crept along, her stick rather than her legs doing most of the forwards movement.

Now Rory ran the line-of-sight network, with occasional help from Finn and Shireen. None of them were immune from the endless stream of reminders and instructions she flashed their way: recollimate the lenses, maintain the logs, watch the bank wall. If anything, the frequency of the messages had increased since she took to staying indoors.

And she'd also finally shown them, one dark night when the rain hammered down on the Switch House roof and no sensible person was out and about, the *other* message log she'd kept all those years. The secret log of communications to both the wreckers and the other Switch House operators she trusted. And also, of all the messages she'd deliberately failed to route through to Engn over the years. It was clear, documented proof of her many crimes. Mrs. Megrim had shown it to them with pride, unfolding the log from swathes of white cotton as if it were some sacred text. Finn had run his finger down the list of encrypted messages from Matt Dobey, sent over many years. He'd wondered what they'd all said. Whether they'd been about him or Connor or Diane. It didn't matter now. Matt was long dead. Matt and his masters in Engn. The log was no longer updated. There had been no need to add any entries to it for three years.

"But I don't understand, Mrs. Megrim," said Diane. "If you were here when the earthquake struck, you must have left home an hour ago. How did you know you'd be needed today? Did you know all this was going to happen?"

People still grumbled about Mrs. Megrim knowing everything, knowing their own business before they did. Even that she employed dark powers to uncover people's secrets or see into the future.

"No, no, girl, of course not. I'm not the witch Finn here says I am. I came because of the urgent message from Rory."

"What message?" asked Finn. "What did he want?"

"I haven't the faintest idea, have I? He told me to come to the Switch House, and this is as far as I got before the ground took it upon itself to start throwing me around."

Finn held his arm out to her, offering his support. Once she would have refused such an indignity. Now, with only a *hmmph*, she hooked her arm through his and they set off together, moving slowly.

The Switch House didn't appear to have been harmed by the earthquake. They climbed the spiral path and knocked three times on the door: the signal to the operator to shield their eyes from the light. This time it was unnecessary. Before they touched the door handle, Rory burst out. Behind him, a white incandescent bulb flickered away. A bulb Finn had never seen used in all the years he'd been coming there.

"Excellent, you're all here," said Rory, as if he'd arranged the whole thing. He looked warily around and back down the path as if afraid more people would be turning up. "You weren't harmed when the earth shook?"

"Obviously not, or we wouldn't be here, would we?" said Mrs. Megrim to her remaining son. "Now, tell us what you've dragged us all the way up here for."

"Come inside," said Rory. "I'll show you."

Badger snuffled around in the grass while the rest of them filed inside. In the bright light of the bulb, the Switch House looked smaller than usual. Strange to think of all the hours and days Finn had spent in the little square room. But of course, it wasn't just a room. In a way, the whole valley was in there. The valley and the wider world beyond, everything brought there on flickering beams of light.

It was immediately obvious none of the 'scopes were in use at the moment. Some were canted at wild angles, as if awaiting messages from up in the sky. Other tripods had crashed to the ground, where they lay in tangled heaps. His father was right; it would take days to get the connections up and down the valley working again.

"Well," said Mrs. Megrim. "I leave the place for one day and look at the mess you make of it."

Rory paid his mother no attention. He shut the door

and turned to face them all. He looked troubled. In his hand, he held a scroll of paper, a line-of-sight message, which he handed to Mrs. Megrim. Silence filled the room while she studied it. An unidentified sense of dread gripped Finn as he watched the deepening frown on her old face.

"What is it?" he asked at last. "What does it say?"

Mrs. Megrim held it out for them to see.

"But it's empty," said Finn's father. "It doesn't say anything. I don't see what the fuss is about."

"It's a timing signal," said Finn. "See, it has the header with all the sender information on it."

"So? We get timing signals like that every day."

"We get timing signals every day, but never like this one," said Finn. "We haven't had one of these for three years now. Look at the address. See where it's come from."

Understanding dawned on his father's face. He grasped what the rest of them had already seen. "1A11. That's Engn?"

"It is," said Mrs. Megrim. "This is a master timing signal, sent from the central clock. Used to get one first thing every day. Strange this should come through on the same day the quake struck. At almost the same moment." She took the sheet of paper again and examined it, holding it up to the light as if that would make it reveal its secrets. "This is the first we've had?"

"I would have mentioned it if there'd been others," said Rory.

"Did you reply? Did you route it to anyone else?"

Rory shook his head. "Didn't get chance. I sent you a message and then sat here trying to think what to do. Then the earthquake struck and knocked all the 'scopes out."

"So Engn is working again," said Finn. "The rumours are true."

"We don't know that," said Diane. "You know better than most messages can be intercepted or altered. All we know is someone has sent a message claiming to be from

Engn. It could be from anywhere along the line."

Mrs. Megrim shook her head. "It's too good a fake. It's exactly like the ones they used to send."

"It still might be from someone who knows what they used to look like," said Diane. "Any Switch House operator could have produced it."

Finn wanted to believe Diane, but dread had gripped him and wouldn't let go. He had taken these early morning messages often enough in the past. He stood and studied the square of paper for long moments, looking for some mistake in the wording, some clue it was a fake. But there was nothing.

"Engn was levelled," said his father. "We saw it. This is some joke, some fake. It's not important. We need to get to the Moot Hall; another tremor could hit at any moment."

Rory shook his head. "You all go. I'll start getting these 'scopes lined up. We're going to need to know what's going on elsewhere."

"Was there anything from down the valley?" Diane asked. "From home?"

"I'm sorry," said Rory. "As soon as it hit, we lost everything. But I'll send word as soon as I hear anything, I promise."

"Chances are they'll be fine," said Mrs. Megrim. "It hasn't brought any houses down here."

Diane nodded but looked doubtful.

"We'll stay and help," said Finn. "Get all these 'scopes lined up again."

Rory picked up the toppled tripods. "No. I could do with you at the Moot House. We need to get that 'scope lined up so I can communicate with everyone there. Then I can start directing you around the valley to fix the repeater mirrors. Okay?"

"And what about the timing message?" said Finn. "What are we going to do with that?"

"Hand it here," said Mrs. Megrim. "I'll burn it. There's

no need to go worrying folks, is there? Probably someone's idea of a jest."

She didn't look like she thought it was funny, though, as Finn handed her the message.

A crowd of people had already gathering at the Moot House. Some were well prepared, clutching blankets and baskets of food as if they'd been secretly expecting an earthquake all along. Other stood shivering in thin night clothes, their eyes wide. The sun was fully risen over the mountaintops now, but it brought no heat with it.

It was alarming to see everyone in this state. Finn knew each one of them, of course. They'd been there every day of his life in the valley. He'd joined in with their celebrations as babies were born or the old year turned into the new. He'd mourned with them at each loss of a loved one. He'd laughed along with them at summer feasts and winter games. Many of them had been there the day of the avalanche, joining in with the search for him and Connor. They would help each other in the days to come. They would survive this together.

Flane, the lengthsman, ticked off the names of each new arrival. Once, perhaps, Connor's father would have assumed the role, coordinating everyone and telling them what to do and where to go. But not anymore: he had left the valley two or more years ago and hadn't been seen since. Lost in grief for Connor, it was said. Now there was no *king* in the valley. The name had only ever been used in jest, nothing more than an echo of older days, but at times like this people needed someone to turn to for direction. It was a role Flane, and also Finn's parents, often played now.

More people arrived, and Finn saw not everyone had

escaped unscathed. There was Elidh the weaver with a bandage wrapped crudely about her head, blood already soaking through. Alongside her, Matilda from the old forge. In her eyes was a look of disbelief Finn recognized. He'd seen it the day Engn had come down, and often enough before that. A gaze into an unseen distance.

Flane went to meet them, enfolding Matilda in one of his powerful arms and lending support to Elidh. Meanwhile, Finn and Diane helped Mrs. Megrim climb the short set of wooden steps into the Moot Hall. It was already busy in there, people marking out where they would sleep with blankets on the ground, even erecting makeshift walls out of sheets. Whole families were setting up in corners. It reminded Finn a little of the mines of Engn; the way they'd pegged out their squares of cloth to claim their little patch of ground. Except, here people were smiling and laughing, despite everything. Helping each other, sharing what they had. For the youngest among them, the whole thing was a wonderful adventure. Small boys and girls jumped around, delighted at the break from their usual routine.

While Diane worked on the Moot Hall's line-of-sight 'scope, Finn and his father went back outside to see what needed to be done, who needed help to make it to the hall. The woods flanking the mountainside blazed with golden light, a mist drifting off them as if they were on fire. Here and there, a gap had opened in the dense canopy where trees had toppled over in the earthquake. Shielding his eyes, Finn gazed up the slope, picking out the lip of rock where, once, he and Connor had lain and looked down. The day the moving engine had first arrived. It seemed like a lifetime ago.

His mother, Shireen, and Nathaniel arrived together, all uninjured. Finn and his father went to meet them, hugging them close. It struck Finn, as it always did, how thin his mother felt in his grasp these days.

"You managed to get out of the cottage?" she asked.

"We're both fine," said Finn. "A few things smashed in the house. How about you?"

"Tiles down, a couple of broken plates," said his mother. "Nothing that can't be mended."

"Same at ours," said Shireen. "Nathaniel's a light sleeper. We were already getting out when the quake hit fully. A chimney pot crashed to the ground near us, that was all."

Shireen held Nathaniel's hand tight in hers. In many ways Nathaniel was still getting used to his new life, still getting over the delusions of his years in Engn. His face had the haunted expression it often bore, especially when he was outside. He'd found the wide expanses of the great grass plain deeply unsettling on the trek across. He much preferred the valley, with its high mountains like towering natural walls. Still, he preferred to stay indoors if he could.

"Put your stuff next to ours," said Finn. "There's plenty of room. We can sit and talk later."

Nathaniel squeezed Finn's arm in thanks. He and Shireen climbed the stairs to go inside.

"It looks like everyone is here," said Finn to Flane, looking around.

"Everyone apart from Connor's mother up at the farm."

"Oh, she wouldn't come," said Finn's mother. "You know she never leaves her room."

"Even so," said Flane, "we should check on her. In the summer, there'd be a few laborers helping out on the farm, but not this time of year."

"I'll go up and see if she's okay," said Finn. He had never, in fact, visited Connor's childhood home. Had never spoken to Connor's mother or even seen her. He'd often wanted to. Wanted to tell her everything that had happened at Engn, tell her in his own words what wonderful things Connor had done. There were matters that still puzzled him, too. Connor had risen through the ranks of the masters with such ease to become the

Director's apprentice. More than one person had mentioned Connor's contacts at Engn, but no one had explained what they were. Now only his mother could shed any light. But she, bedridden and reclusive, saw no one.

A look passed between his parents as they considered the wisdom of Finn's plan.

"I'll go," said his mother. "She might talk to me."

"No," said Finn. "You're needed here. And I can get her 'scope lined up while I'm there."

His father studied him for a moment, then nodded his head in assent.

Back inside the hall, Finn found Diane helping a young family with baby twins set up their temporary home. He touched her lightly on the arm. "I'm going to check on Connor's mother. Want to come?"

Diane brushed a stray curl of hair from her eyes. "There's a lot to do here. I'd best stay and help. Where's Badger?"

"Helping to greet everyone who arrives. She's having a wonderful time."

Finn and Diane embraced, holding on to each other, absorbing the welcome reassurance of each other. He was still shaking slightly, shaking as the valley had shaken, but Diane's closeness calmed him.

"Take care up there," she said. "You know what they say about the farmhouse. It's already half falling down. Don't go inside if it looks dangerous."

"I promise," said Finn. He held onto her for a moment more, then turned to leave.

He walked between high stone buildings into the central courtyard of the farm. The place was a sea of mud.

Crumbling wooden carts sagged in corners, never to move again. Stable doors gaped, their inhabitants long gone. Grass and one or two small saplings sprouted out of cracks in the stonework. There was a smell of damp and decay and a sullen, watchful silence about the whole place.

Once the place would have rung with the noises of activity: the stamp and bellow of the cattle, the rattle and clank of the machinery, the cries and laughs of the hands who worked the land. Now nothing moved, except for the odd scrap of rusting metal, lifted briefly back into life by the gusting wind.

Finn looked back at the track he'd taken across the fields up to Three Tree Hill. He could see a lot of the valley, all the familiar buildings and trees and lanes. Yet it was all different from the unusual perspective, as if someone had come along and jumbled everything around. Or as if he had never really known his home properly. Strange to think he didn't know the farm. He and Connor had roamed the whole valley in a childhood that had seemed, at the time, unending. They knew each tree, path, pool, bush, bank. Yet, every night, Connor had returned here, to a place Finn was never allowed to enter.

He had some idea why. Connor's parents fought – over what Finn didn't know – but enough to make Connor wary of bringing back friends. Shireen had mentioned it more than once. She'd come to read to Connor's mother when she was young and, without spelling it out, gave the clear impression Connor's home had never been very happy.

The arched door of the farmhouse in front of him was limed with green. This close, he could discern a diagonal crack running right up the wall, feeling its way through the stones. It reached from the floor up to the second story. Was it fresh damage, a wound opened by the earthquake, or had it been there for years? Was it safe to step inside this decaying old building? It must have been grand once. Window frames and lintels were finely carved, cut into the flowing shapes of animals and birds. But all was weathered now, all worn away, fine features blurred. The eroded heads of beasts adorned the door post, but it was impossible to tell what the carver had intended them to be.

Finn knocked and then, when no one replied, pushed the door open. He expected it to creak and groan, but it merely budged forwards a few inches then stopped, wedged against something on the floor. From inside, a damp-smelling darkness breathed out at him. There was no sound save for the slow, patient ticking of a distant clock. Someone had obviously been there recently. He called out again, as loudly as he could, but there was still no reply. Was Connor's mother dead? Knocked over or crushed in the earthquake? He suddenly didn't want to go inside. But he had no choice. He couldn't go back and say he hadn't looked.

Barging the door a little wider with his shoulder, he stepped forwards into the waiting darkness.

IIII

Finn stepped through the echoing halls of Connor's boyhood home, drawn by the ticking sound of the clock. Each time he stepped into another new room he thought he would find it, but each time he found only abandoned rooms, tattered furniture, moth-eaten curtains.

The house was huge, and Finn soon lost track of how many halls he'd crossed through, how many shadowy corridors he'd walked along. He wondered why anyone would need all this space. A family could live there and never meet each other from one day to the next. It must have been grand once, a sight, but now everything was abandoned and fraying. A smell of dust and damp rose from the faded carpets and the wood panelling. A smell of age. It seemed no one had been there for years. And yet, there was the ticking sound. He could feel it in the walls when he touched them, as if he was inside the mechanism of a giant clock. A clock that had been recently wound.

He crept through a long, echoing room, the walls lined with paintings. Even the pictures were dim and faded, their details lost in a mud of greys and browns. Here and there he could make out the disembodied face of someone long dead, eyes peering out through the mire. In one big picture, he could see a building, a tall metal clock tower. It stood upon a wide plain and there were lines of people all around it, although what they were doing, he couldn't tell. The tower looked like it could have been part of Engn, but he was sure he'd never seen it before.

Finely carved stone was everywhere, the lines sharp inside the house. Doorways, fireplaces, pillars, all beautifully sculpted. Finn brushed his fingers over the smooth, hard surfaces, taking pleasure in their clean lines.

He came to a wide oak staircase leading up into the darkness. There was another whole floor above him. The staircase groaned and complained as Finn ascended. The clock sounded nearer, the ticks more distinct, as if encouraging him on.

At the top, it took his eyes time to adjust. The windows were shuttered, only the thinnest slivers of sunlight sliding in. The air was a fog of dust and cobwebs. Feeling his way with outstretched arms he crept around. The old floor creaked sharply beneath his feet with each step.

In each room he entered it was the same story: shuttered windows, bed and chairs draped with white sheets, the air a fug of must, the floors thick with dust. He wondered which room Connor's had been. There was nothing in any of them, no toys or books or carvings, to suggest his friend had ever slept there.

Eventually he found the room the ticking was coming from. Putting his ear to the door, the sound became immediately louder. He was about to knock when a voice called from within.

"Connor? Is that you? Where have you been all this time? I told you I wanted to see you hours ago."

Finn's hand froze on the doorknob. Once again, he considered bolting, out of this crumbling house of ghosts and back into the light. A few years ago, before he went to Engn, he might have done so. But not now.

Turning the handle, he pushed open the door.

Connor's mother – it could only be her – sat on the floor amid the flowing folds of her white nightgown. Her hair was long and grey and straggly. All around her were the remains of broken clocks: a jumble of cogs and springs and dials. She held some of the pieces in her bony hands as if she'd been trying to connect them together.

By the shuttered window stood a line-of-sight 'scope on a brass tripod. It was old, a design Finn didn't recognize, the tube held in place by an elaborately decorated brass mount. By the look of it, it had been knocked completely off-kilter by the earthquake; it now pointed in completely the wrong direction for the Switch House. Thanks to some trick of the light, the lens glowed red. Near it, in a shadowy corner, stood a tall clock in a coffin-like wooden case. This was where the ticking sound came from: this clock picking its way through the seconds with its *whirr* and pause for thought and *clunk*. The heavy sound filled the room. How did she sleep in there with it? How did anyone sleep in the house, with that constant sound in the walls? Connor must have grown up with it: the seconds of his life being counted through. Perhaps he'd stopped hearing it after a while.

All around the walls were more of the sombre portraits, their details hard to make out through the grime. One large painting over the bed had been kept clean, though. From it stared a dour-looking man in ancient robes, a gold chain around his neck from which dangled a small clock. He had to be some forebear; the similarity to Connor was quite clear.

The woman, meanwhile, looked up at Finn with startled eyes. "You? What are you doing here? Where is Connor?"

What should he say? He saw, now, the real reason Connor had never brought him here. His friend had never talked about his mother much. The whole valley knew she wasn't well, stayed in her room, rarely saw anyone.

"Connor isn't here, I'm afraid," he said. It was a ridiculous thing to say. Connor was dead. Was it kinder to say that or not? He didn't know. Diane would know. He wished she'd come with him.

The woman looked puzzled for a moment, examining the clock pieces she held in her hands as if she'd never seen them before, or as if piecing them back together would clear the confusion in her mind. When she looked back up at Finn, a sudden rage burned in her eyes.

"And see what you've done! You've smashed all my clocks. They're ruined. Now I can't make any of them work. I don't know what the time is any more."

Finn thought about pointing out the tall clock in the corner. There was no way she couldn't see or hear it. "I … I just came to check if you were okay," he said. "I haven't touched your clocks."

"No, you've ruined them," she replied, half shouting now, her anger burning. "They were all safe on their shelves, ticking away together, keeping perfect time. Then the earthquake came and knocked them off and now they're all smashed. It's all your fault. I knew this was going to happen as soon as I heard what you did."

"I haven't done anything," said Finn. "I know the earthquake was frightening, but they're just something that happens. They're no one's fault." He found himself talking as if to a child.

"Of course, they're someone's fault," said Connor's mother. "They're your fault. You disabled the machine and now the earthquakes are starting again. Don't people understand? I told them this would happen and now it has. People don't *listen*. And there'll be more coming, you'll see. This is just the start."

Finn tried to make sense of her words. "You think destroying Engn caused the earthquake?"

"Isn't it obvious? What else did you think the machine was for? Used to be lots of tremors in the old days, before the beginning of time. Then we built Engn to stop them, didn't we?"

She was mad, that was clear. Unhinged. Finn had to get away. Get out into the light where there was air he could breathe. He'd done his duty, made sure she was okay. No one could expect him to do more.

He was about to make his apologies, turn and leave, but then he stopped. Something she'd said puzzled him.

"You said *we*."

"Hmm?"

"You just said *we built Engn*."

"Yes, of course. The Clockmakers, the Ironmasters, the Silversmiths, the Switchers, the Steamwrights, the Lensmen and the rest. The twelve Guilds. We constructed Engn between us. Don't you know anything?"

"But Engn was ancient, centuries old. You can't have been involved." He regretted saying it. It wasn't fair to challenge her delusions. But perhaps underneath all her ramblings she would reveal something useful.

The woman waved her hand. "Not *me*, obviously. Are you mad? I mean the twelve city-states. The Mechanical Guilds. Obviously."

He was about to reply, ask her what she meant, when the floor lurched beneath his feet. Another earthquake or an aftershock? Finn grasped the doorframe for support, half expecting the great old house to collapse on top of them both. Connor's mother shrieked and clutched the broken mechanisms to her as if to protect them. The great clock in the corner rocked forwards. For a moment, Finn thought it was going to topple over and crush her beneath its weight. He saw it all happening, imagined her pinned beneath it, the pooling blood. He called out to her in alarm. She watched the clock, not making any attempt to scurry out of its way. For a moment, balancing there on a corner of its case, it stopped its ticking, as if it, too, were waiting to see what happened.

Then the room ceased its dancing and the floor became solid once more. After a moment, the clock settled back and began ticking through the seconds. An accusing look came into Connor's mother's eyes. "See?" she said, as if the tremor confirmed all her explanations.

Finn kept hold of the doorframe. He had to learn whether she really knew anything useful.

"So, your family, you were part of this Guild?" Finn asked.

"We were the guildmasters. My forebears, generation before generation." The rage had all gone from her voice now, to be replaced with pride. "We constructed the machine. We and the others in the alliance. Many years ago. Many, many years ago. We fought the war, too, against those trying to stop us. All the crazy people wanting to turn back time."

"The war?"

"The Long War. The Clockwork War."

A phrase from old story books. Was she so deluded she thought she was living back then?

"That was centuries ago," he said. "The Twelve Guilds lost. Everyone knows that."

She looked delighted for a moment, as if she knew a secret he didn't. "Sometimes in war it isn't clear who has won and who has lost for a long time afterwards. We lost those battles, you're right. And yet here we all are with our clocks and calendars. Talking to each other with the line-of-sight network and lighting the darkness with electricity."

"That's not much of a victory. The old guilds took what was useful from those they defeated."

"Or perhaps that's what people were supposed to believe, eh? There are those who'd say you can't tell who won the war because it hasn't ended yet."

"But it was all so long ago. No one goes off to fight and die anymore."

She studied him for a moment, as if unsure how much to tell him. "You're sure of that, are you?"

Finn regretted getting into the whole argument. Whenever he tried to pin her down with his questions she danced away on some other stream of thought. He tried to make sense of her words. "You're saying Engn was built to stop earthquakes happening?"

Connor's mother shook her head, as if this was a troubling idea, like a buzzing fly was stuck inside her skull. "No, no. That's not it. That's not right at all. You mustn't say that."

"So why did the Guilds build it?" asked Finn.

She glanced around, as if people would be listening in. "You don't know?"

He thought back to Mrs. Megrim's history lessons. He should have paid more attention. "It was built as reparation for all those who suffered and died in the war, wasn't it? Some say there was no great purpose. Or, if there was, it's been forgotten. People stopped wondering about it, stopped asking questions, the way they do. They stop seeing the really big things and accept the world as it is."

The woman snorted, as if this was a ridiculous idea. She whispered conspiratorially. "We mustn't tell people the truth, must we? No one must know. That's why it all had to be kept a secret, wasn't it?"

"What did? What was the secret? Stopping the earthquakes?"

"No, no," she said. "Not that. Obviously not that."

"Then what?"

"Unlimited power," she whispered, savouring the words.

"Engn … gave you unlimited power? To fight the war?"

"No! Shh! Of course not. No, it was built to keep the whole world working. That was it. Those vast waterwheels generating electricity, powering the whole world. And then, later, the great steam engines. Such a glorious achievement."

"But … Engn didn't do that. I mean, there were wheels and engines, but they didn't send out power. They didn't *do* anything."

She ignored him. "A network of wires spreading across the plains, bringing light to all the lands." She stared into the middle distance, as if she could see the lines spanning the world. "Before Engn everyone lived in darkness and confusion. Engn brought order. That was what we gave them. So *they* thought."

"Who?"

"The old guilds. The Temple Guilds. The Twenty-Four."

"And Connor's father. The Baron. His family were on the other side." The words were out before he'd realized what he was saying. The idea had only just occurred to him.

Her expression changed immediately, from elation to sadness. She looked down at the shattered clocks surrounding her.

"Such a beautiful man, he was. So strong. He was on the wrong side, the other side, yes, but what could we do?" She looked back up at Finn. "It was love, you see. The ancient resentments still burned, smouldering deep, and sometimes we strayed into them together. Then the flames raged, and the days were bad, but still we loved each other. Our families disapproved, disowned us, but that wasn't our fault. Our differences were irrelevant because we were in love." She sighed, reliving happy memories, seeing things in the distance he could not.

"I'm sorry," said Finn. "I didn't know. I mean I … didn't think."

"Well, it doesn't matter now. He's gone for good. He was quite mad, you know."

She'd become suddenly matter of fact. He couldn't keep up with her changes of mood.

"He was?"

"Oh, completely. We used to have terrible arguments. He thought Engn threatened everyone. He hated the machine, said it endangered the whole world. Can you believe it? It was once a common superstition. I tried and tried, but I'm afraid he couldn't be convinced of the truth. It wouldn't have applied to him, would it? I wouldn't have let it."

"What wouldn't?"

"He was old guild, yes, but I was new. He'd have been spared it when the war resumed. Connor, too, of course."

She was making no sense. Perhaps she hadn't for a long time. "Do you know where he is now? The Baron?"

"Oh. He's dead. When Connor took my side and went off to Engn, it was too much for him. Poor man. It's just a good job I stayed here to hold everything together."

"You're saying Connor *wanted* to go to Engn?"

"Of course. Our Guild is still very powerful, you know. Very important. They still need us to run the place, don't they? Thinking they've won all this time. Ours is an important name among the masters. Connor went to assume his rightful place."

Finn thought back to the day Connor had left. No, *been taken*. He'd been shackled to a horse. And as he'd left, he'd shaken his finger to remind Finn of their pact. A tiny act of defiance that meant his mother had it all wrong. She was clearly deluded. Still, her story explained Connor's rapid rise in Engn. He must have played on his family name. Made use of it so he could get to the centre and destroy it all. That had to be it.

He decided not to say anything more. There was no need for her to be told what had really taken place. There was comfort in delusions.

"Look," he said. "Everyone is gathering at the Moot Hall. Until the earthquakes stop. Will you come?"

The woman didn't reply. She studied some delicate piece of clockwork in her hands. Her head was bowed as if she herself were a mechanism that had wound down. Her pale shoulders rose and fell as she sat there slumped in her heap of white cloth.

"Will you come?" Finn asked again. "We'll be safe

there. Just for a few days."

She shook her head without looking at him. Could he just leave her? He didn't see what else he could do. He couldn't drag her away. But he also didn't relish the thought of having to come back there all the time to check on her.

His gaze fell on the 'scope at the window, peering through the shutters. He'd seen another device downstairs; it appeared she had her own private line. He wondered whom she talked to. He didn't recall ever seeing any messages from her.

"The line-of-sight," he said. "If we get it working again, line it up with the Switch House, we'll be able to talk to you. You'll be able to tell us if there's a problem. Would that be okay?"

This time she didn't reply, as if she'd fallen asleep there on the floor. Finn stepped into the room and made his way past her, making very sure not to tread on any of the tiny cogs strewn around. He was about to touch the 'scope when she snapped back to life.

"No! Don't touch it!"

"But it will never work pointing up there."

"I said leave it alone!" She sounded furious once again, a flush of anger on her face.

"But you won't be able to get any messages. There are timing signals now, you know. You won't be able to receive them."

"Timing signals?"

"Yes. They started coming through again today. The start of day timing signal from Engn. Or at least, from someone pretending to be Engn."

Excitement and alarm chased each other across her features. "And was there another signal? Has the Clarion been transmitted too?"

"The Clarion?" said Finn. "I don't know what that is."

"Of course, you do. The signal for the end. The muster."

Finn shook his head, trying to make sense of her words. "No. No, I don't think there's been anything like that."

She stood, suddenly full of energy. "Very well. At last they're rebuilding it! Now everything is going to be all right." She babbled like an excited child, the flow of words unstoppable. "Now we'll all know what time it is again. Know *properly*. Now the mechanism is ticking again, I must get these clocks fixed so I can set them all. Oh, this is wonderful. Wonderful! I knew he would do it. *Knew* it."

She grabbed at handfuls of cogs and wheels, dropping more than she picked up.

"If you bring all the pieces to the Moot Hall we can help," said Finn. "My father, everyone. Perhaps between us we can get the clocks working again."

But she was ignoring him again, holding up delicate flywheels to the shuttered light from the window as if counting their tiny teeth. Finn picked his way back across the room to the door. She paid him no more attention, didn't even seem to see him. She scrabbled around for more and more pieces, trying to fit them together, her movements urgent as if every second counted.

There was nothing more he could do there. He stepped back from the room and turned to leave.

"Oh, and Finn?"

She still wasn't looking at him, her attention caught up in the coiling of a spiral spring. It was the first time she had used his name.

"Yes?"

"When you see Connor, tell him I said to hurry home, won't you? He should have been back hours ago."

He nodded, although she didn't see. "Yes," said Finn. "I will."

Quietly, he shut the door behind him.

V

Diane breathing quietly beside him, Finn lay awake thinking about everything that had happened. The things his father had said, and the things Connor's mother had said. He tried and failed to make sense of it all. He kept coming back to the unrestrained glee in Connor's mother's eyes when he'd told her the timing messages were being broadcast again. As if she'd been expecting it.

When he got chance, he would talk to Mrs. Megrim. She'd be able to make sense of it all. Either that or tell him to stop wasting his time worrying.

A low murmur of voices and coughs and the occasional whimper drifted through the air in the Moot Hall. Everyone was there, gathered from up and down the valley, lying side by side in the darkness of the night. Families from farther afield had continued to turn up throughout the day, some carrying nothing, others hauling carts laden down with supplies. The hall was now full. So far as they knew, only one person had died. An old man from way up in Ironoaks who'd been crushed by the falling beams of his house as he lay in bed. *It could have been worse*, everyone said. *It could have been a lot worse.*

Three more aftershocks had struck: brief grumbles rather than full quakes. Some people had fled the Moot Hall in panic, afraid it was going to collapse and crush them beneath its spars. But each time the old hall swayed and then settled back down, with perhaps a brief cascade of dust from the eaves. Just as his father had promised. They were as safe here as anywhere. A few days and maybe they could all go home.

At least the children were finally asleep. Worn out by excitement, they now lay strewn around the floor as if tiredness had come upon them mid-stride. For them, still, it was all an adventure. Finn envied them. He'd been like them once, he supposed, before he went to Engn. He missed living in an eternal *now*, free of worry, free of fear. Except, thinking back, it hadn't been like that, had it? Fear of the ironclads, fear of Engn, had been there since his earliest days.

An hour or so earlier, to get the children to sleep, one of the women had gathered them up and told them a bedtime story about the ironclads. How the unstoppable machines came for the children one night, intent on dragging them away never to be seen again. But they were foiled when a young girl threw water over them, rusting them in ridiculous poses. It was a variant on a story Finn remembered well from his own childhood. One Shireen used to tell him. The children squealed with delight at the story, although some of the younger ones hid under their bedclothes when the ironclads turned up.

The story was a way of laughing at fear. It was obvious now. One or two older people scowled at the tale, thinking it inappropriate. Real events too fresh in their minds. Finn found it amusing. They had nothing to fear from the ironclads now. If the soldiers of Engn had been reduced to ridiculous monsters in a children's story, he was happy.

He drifted off to sleep with visions of story ironclads

and smashed clocks and collapsing houses whirling around in his mind.

A banging on the door awoke him. He sat up with a gasp. He'd been lost in some nightmare of his time in Engn, real ironclads pursuing him, chasing him down endless corridors. There was no clock in the hall, but he knew it had to be long after midnight. One or two of the older people sat around candles, playing cards to pass the time. Their faces were lines of anxiety as they looked up at the door, eyes hidden in shadow. Everyone had been accounted for. Of those who had survived, only Connor's mother wasn't there.

Finn climbed to his knees to peer out of one of the hall's slit windows. A gibbous moon lit the scene outside, the hard light etching everything in deep shadows. It was hard to make detail out; the window was all misted up. He could see *something*. A cart and a figure, he thought. He wiped a swirl clear with his palm and pushed his face against the cold glass to peer out.

"Who is it?" asked Diane, sitting up beside him, a blanket wrapped around her body for warmth. "Who's out there?"

The scene shifted as the cart moved. Shadows and shapes clicked into place and became identifiable. A figure swathed in a long black cloak standing next to a black horse. The horse stamped one great foot in impatience, steam billowing from its nostrils. Behind them was the cart. Except it wasn't a cart. He recognized those spoked iron wheels, the curving shape of that outline. It was a moving engine.

A moving engine with a master in control had come to the Moot Hall.

Diane caught the look of shock on his face as he glanced down.

"What is it?" she said. "Let me see."

There came another rap on the door, a gruff call from outside. Was it possible? Was Engn sending out masters and ironclads once more, to harvest the land for fresh hands? But they had destroyed it. He had seen it collapse into its own pit. It couldn't be happening again.

Finn's father stood up, wrapping a gown about himself, a scowl on his face. He caught Finn's alarmed glance. Mrs. Megrim, over by the door, lay unmoving, but Finn could see she wasn't asleep. The candlelight glinted in her black eyes.

Diane stood and picked her way between the blankets towards the door. Finn followed, not wanting to go, but knowing it had to be done. It was warm and safe in the Moot Hall and opening the door was letting the world back in. But a master of Engn was out there whether they liked it or not.

It was only then it occurred to Finn he hadn't heard the moving engine. He remembered the machine's rushing, huffing roar only too well. This one had been silent. The thought gave him hope. Standing beside Diane he watched as his father unbolted the door.

"Mind if I come in? It is seriously freezing out here."

Finn recognized the stranger immediately, although he'd last seen him the day he'd first arrived at Engn. Master Whelm, who'd taken Finn from his home, forced him into a moving engine, then transported him across the great grass plain to abandon him in the machine.

"You," said his father, the threat clear in his voice. He'd recognized Whelm, too. Whelm that had given the ironclads instructions to strike his father when he tried to stop them taking Finn.

Whelm held up his hands as if to show he was unarmed. "Please, all I want is shelter for the night and perhaps some food for the horse. She's pulled a long way today." He looked from Finn to Diane to Finn's father. Did Whelm recognize them? Or had he taken so many people he'd forgotten all their faces?

Finn stepped forwards. "Hello, Whelm."

A look of confusion flashed across the stranger's face, along with a clear twist of fear. His gaze darted between them as if he expected them to attack him. He spoke quietly, warily. "Ah, I thought I recognized this place. It's years since I've been this way."

"You remember?" asked Finn.

"Of course," said Whelm. "Of course. Believe it or not, it's good to see you. I'm glad you survived."

"You shouldn't have come back here," said his father. "Alone, now, are you? No ironclads to protect you and carry out your orders?"

Whelm shrank back, a hunted look on his face. Finn could see the change in him. He was thinner. His face was scratched and bruised in more than one place. All that arrogance had gone. The Whelm who had taken him to Engn had feared no one except the higher masters. Now Whelm was a shivering, bedraggled tramp. Life as a former master of Engn would be hard; he'd be welcome nowhere. Yet Whelm hadn't tried to hide his former identity. It was brave, in a way.

Whelm had been cruel, it was true, but also friendly at times. In his own way. More than once he'd been on the point of confiding in Finn. His resentments. His fears. He'd been alone with only his ironclads to talk to. He'd loved Engn, but hated it too, so it had seemed to Finn. Fate had made Whelm a master, but Finn knew well that meant little. Being a master was better than not being a master, but it was still a role. A *part*.

Peering over Whelm's shoulder, Finn saw why he hadn't heard the moving engine. It was no longer a living machine. It was just the carriage and shell of one of the old vehicles. A cart made of rusting iron pulled by the horse. That was all.

"Come in," said Finn. "We can find room for you."

Whelm hesitated for a moment, remembering, perhaps, all he'd done to Finn on the journey to Engn. Or perhaps he didn't remember any of it and he'd simply learned not to trust people.

"No, I'll leave you in peace," said Whelm. "My horse and I, we've slept out in the open often enough. One more night won't kill us. I'm sorry I woke you. Perhaps it's safer out of doors anyway with all these earthquakes."

"You can sleep here," said Finn. He glanced across at his father, who clearly disapproved. "You can pay for your lodging with news. And then tomorrow you can help us start to repair the damage."

"Have you come down the valley or up?" asked Diane. There'd still been no word over the line-of-sight about her own village.

"I crossed the plain a week ago," said Whelm. "I've been making my way up the valley ever since."

"You passed through the villages near the plain?"

"I did. Although some I've learned to avoid."

"And the earthquake?"

"I was much further up the valley when it struck. Every place I've seen today was hit by it. Most buildings survived, but one or two…"

He tailed off, reliving sights.

"I'll help you with the horse," said Finn. "Then we'll find room for you." He looked at Diane and his father, unsure if either would accept this. Diane shrugged. She'd never met Whelm, although she'd heard Finn describe him more than once. After a moment, with a dismissive grunt, his father nodded and turned away.

While Whelm unshackled his horse from the iron cart, Finn strode around the ruined engine. It was tattered with ragged holes where the metal had flaked away. He couldn't resist peering inside, recalling long days spent in one of the machines. Suffocating heat and the smell of burning coal still made his stomach heave. Was this the very machine perhaps?

Moonlight peered in through the holes in the engine's casing, allowing him to make out details within. A roll of bedding lay up the middle of the engine. Whelm, clearly, slept in there. Finn recalled a day of lashing rain, when Whelm had taunted him for being dry and warm inside the moving engine. The irony that the ex-master now lived inside one of the machines wasn't lost on Finn. For some reason it wasn't a happy thought. If anything, he felt sorry for Whelm.

There were piles of other articles in the engine, too, stacked around Whelm's bed like a nest. Broken fragments of machinery: cogs, cams, chains, cranks. Even, he was amused to see, a self-governing valve. Finn picked it up, hefted it, his hands remembering the weight and shape of the iron valve. The useless iron valve.

"They don't do anything, you know," said Whelm, now standing behind Finn. "They could be used as thatch weights, maybe. Or ornaments. They're quite beautiful in a way."

Finn considered his former tormentor. "So, this is what you do now?"

Whelm shrugged. "Not much else I can do since the wreckers struck and destroyed Engn. No one takes orders from me anymore. I scrape a living here and there, selling bits of the old machinery to any who will buy them."

"So, you're free now? Free of the masters who gave you your orders."

"Sure. Free to starve. Free to freeze. Wonderful. A real step up for me."

"But you've been to Engn? Recently? You said you'd come across the plain."

Whelm nodded. "I was there two weeks ago, scavenging for parts to sell. It gets harder each time to find anything useful."

"But … it's all still there?"

"The ruins are. Lots of people still live among them."

"Who?"

"People with nowhere else to go. Tinkers and tramps. People like me. People fighting each other."

Was it Finn's imagination, or wasn't Whelm telling the full story? "Who? Who is fighting?"

Whelm shrugged and combed a hand through his unkempt hair. "I try to avoid them all. When Engn was destroyed and the old order broke down, the old rivalries bubbled up to the surface. All the old resentments. People who don't seem to have noticed it's all over. People who want revenge."

"You mean the wreckers?"

"Partly them."

"And who's on the other side? The masters?"

Whelm shrugged. "Maybe. Who knows? It's crazy there. It's not safe for anyone. I only visit when I have to, to find more things to sell. I get out as soon as I can, believe me."

"But who's in charge? Is there a new Director controlling everything?"

"Do we have to talk about this now?" said Whelm. He sounded exhausted, spent. "It's late and I'm freezing."

"And I don't want the others to hear it," said Finn. "Tell me. Is there a new Director?"

Whelm studied him for a moment, puzzled. "I don't know. Some say so. If you ask me, it's just a few ironclads too stupid to realize Engn's gone."

"You haven't seen a Director?"

"People say crazy things, invent wild stories."

"What stories?"

"What does it matter? They're just fantasies."

"Tell me what they say."

"Oh, you know. Engn was destroyed so they could make it larger, more powerful. Or Engn wasn't destroyed, it was just a story people invented. Or there's a machine in charge now, trundling around giving orders to the remnants of the ironclads."

"A *machine?*"

"Sure. A steam-powered machine like an old moving engine but with a person's head. That's the way it is now. No one knows what's going on and rumours and fantasies fill the void. I met someone down the valley the other day who swore blind the wheels of Engn were turning again. You only have to go there to see they aren't."

They stood together beside the bulk of the moving engine, the night air sharp with cold. "Did you know the timing signals had started up again?" Finn asked.

The look of surprise flashing across Whelm's face was genuine enough. "When was this?"

"Just today. Do you know who would have sent them?"

Whelm shook his head. "I have no idea. Like I said, I keep my head down when I go there."

"And yet you go about looking like a master. At least, not hiding the fact you once were one."

Whelm sighed and looked around, combing his hand through his hair again. A nervous tic he hadn't had before. "I do, it's true. It's good for business. If people know I was once a master, they think I'll have better items to sell than all the other tinkers. People will pay for genuine Engn machinery. Some of it *is* actually useful."

"But you're playing a dangerous game. Out here on your own among the people you once terrorized."

Whelm didn't reply for a moment. The hunted look was back in his eye. "It can be difficult. Lots of people have scores to settle, I understand. But what can I do? All I had was Engn and that was destroyed."

Did Whelm know about Finn's role in that? He'd known of Finn's plans, of course, but he'd said everyone taken to Engn had plans to destroy the machine. Even Whelm himself, once. And only a few people in the valley knew the truth. The people who had been there. People he trusted absolutely. They'd kept it quiet in case anyone from Engn wanted revenge. Whelm seemed to think the wreckers had been responsible. Best to say nothing now. If Whelm discovered the truth, there was a good chance the ex-master would blame Finn for everything he'd lost.

"Come on," said Finn. "There's a shelter to hitch your horse in. Your stuff will be safe enough but bring your bedding. There isn't much to go around."

Whelm nodded. "Thanks. I will do what I can to earn my keep."

"Yes," said Finn. "You will." Then the ramshackle assortments of machine parts in the old moving engine gave him an idea. "Whelm? One more question before we go inside." He fished the memory spindle from an inside pocket. "You know what this is, yes?"

Whelm held out his hand. Reluctantly, Finn passed the slim metal rod across. The ex-master held the silvery shaft up to the moonlight, examining it.

"It's a memory spindle. Quite a rare item. Full, too, by the look of it. Where did you get it?"

Finn was fully prepared for the question. "I found it while I was in Engn."

"You found it?"

"The thing is, I'd like to view the images stored on it. I've been trying to build a reader. I was thinking you might have parts I could use."

"Why do you want to read it?" asked Whelm. He looked puzzled.

Finn shrugged, trying to look like he didn't really care. "No reason. Just interested. It's all I really have of my time there. How do you know it's full?"

"These tiny spiral scratches are the recorded images. A diamond-tipped stylus etches them on. You need something similar to read them again. Similar but the opposite, if you see what I mean. Then some electrics to project the images into an orb."

Finn held out his hand and, after a moment, Whelm returned the spindle.

"I've got an orb," said Finn. "Bought it off a tinker a

year ago. And the remains of a reader with some wires. But I can't make any pictures appear. Something's not connected right."

"I might be able to help," said Whelm. "They're tricky things. Delicate. I think I have some parts you could use. I used to work on the readers, years ago."

Finn thought for a moment then came to a decision. He should have talked to Diane first, but surely she'd understand. "Look, why not come and stay with us? Once the earthquakes have stopped, I mean. We can give you a roof over your head for a few days and food to eat. Give your horse chance to rest. In return, you can help me get my reader working."

Whelm looked wary. "I'm not sure that's a good idea. I'm not welcome here, that was pretty obvious just now."

"They'll change," said Finn. "If they see you're being helpful, they'll accept you."

"No offence, but I've heard that before. More than once."

"At least think about it," said Finn. "Please. I'm sure I can persuade the others."

Whelm looked thoughtful. "This spindle ... it seems very important to you. Why do you really want to read it so badly?"

For a moment Finn was tempted to tell him everything. His family thought Finn was obsessed with the spindle and the secrets it might hold. Whelm might be more supportive. Still, he decided against it. The fewer people who knew his role in destroying Engn, the better. Some things should remain secrets.

"Like I said, there might be places or people I remember on it. And it could be useful. The moving images could even replace the line-of-sights."

Whelm said nothing. Finn had the clear impression the ex-master didn't believe a word of it.

"Look," said Finn. "Come inside, then tomorrow we can see what parts you've got and try and get the reader working, okay?"

After a few moments of calculation, Whelm relented. "Okay, Finn. It seems this time I'm in your hands."

VI

Whelm screwed a brass-ringed lens into his eye and studied the tiny spirals etched onto the memory spindle.

"Interesting," he said after a few moments of scrutiny. "Yes, very interesting." He looked up at Finn, his left eye huge through the lens. "I've never seen a spindle like this. Where did you say you got it?"

They stood in the workshop attached to Finn and Diane's cottage. It was a week since the earthquake. There had been no aftershocks for five days. Only a few people with badly damaged houses remained at the Moot Hall now. Some would be fixed, and some would be pulled down and rebuilt. Each day, everyone went to work repairing broken walls and cracked roads. Whelm, true to his word, had done what he could, lending his horse to lug materials, bending his own back to carry stone wherever it was needed. People were wary of him, resentful, but they appreciated his help. People gave him food and water in payment, not smiling as they did so, but not scowling either. Mostly they were too tired for either.

Whelm slept in the workshop, his roll of bedding filling the narrow space between the benches. It was the only compromise Diane would put up with. She hadn't wanted Whelm to stay with them at all. She'd made it clear she wanted him out of the valley, out of their lives.

"You told me often enough what he did, Finn. He carted you off to Engn in that steam-powered prison. He was a brute, and you're inviting him into our *home*."

She'd been angry, and they'd argued, something they never did. He understood why she was angry, of course, but things were different now. And if Whelm could help him with the spindle it would be worth it. In the end, Diane had agreed to let Whelm sleep in the workshop for a few nights, just while they needed help to repair what the earthquake had wrecked. But she didn't speak to Whelm, and she barely spoke to Finn when the three of them were together.

The ex-master, meanwhile, had spent two evenings working on the smashed spindle reader and now claimed it was nearly workable. The damage it had received in the quake had puzzled Whelm at first, and he'd quizzed Finn about how exactly it had got so mangled. As he'd promised, he'd worked hard on the device late into each night. Now the contraption sat on the workbench, an exploded version of the devices Finn remembered from Engn. Wheels and lenses and cranks were held in place by clamps or were lashed together with wire. The whole assembly hummed and gave off the faint smell of burning dust as Whelm connected it to a junction board fed by the cables from the waterwheel.

Once again, Finn wished he could tell Whelm everything about the spindle. It would be so much simpler. But he didn't dare. He needed Whelm's help, and the ex-master wouldn't help if he knew the truth. Finn was to blame for destroying Whelm's life. Somehow, Finn needed to see the pictures on the spindle without Whelm doing so as well.

He glanced down at the ex-master, who waited for the answer to his oft-repeated question of how Finn had acquired the spindle. How much did Whelm know? How much had he guessed?

"I found it," said Finn.

"But where?"

The easiest way to conceal a lie was to tell the truth. Or part of it at least. "The Directory. Did you ever go there?"

Whelm looked puzzled now. "Of course, I didn't. You couldn't go there. It was sealed off. No one was even supposed to know it existed."

"But you knew?"

Whelm shrugged. "I heard rumours. I pieced things together. But how did you end up there? You were never even a master."

Finn hesitated, thinking what to say. "I worked in the Blueprint Hall. We had to go all over Engn to deliver plans. One day I went to the Directory." It was the truth, in a way.

"And you just found this spindle lying around?"

"Yes."

Whelm didn't say anything for a moment. He studied Finn, eyes narrowed slightly. Finn could see he didn't believe him.

"So why is it unusual?" asked Finn, trying to change the subject.

Whelm returned his attention to the slender metal rod. "See here. Normally you get one continuous line etched into the metal, enough for maybe two hours of pictures. New spindles had to be constantly put in and the full ones taken away. That's why there were so many; they got through hundreds every day."

Finn recalled a room in the Directory where he and Diane had hidden. The rows and rows of metal drawers, each filled with tinkling metal spindles. There must have been tens of thousands of them. What did they keep them all for?

"But this one is different?"

"See the marks on it. They keep stopping and starting. There are tiny gaps between each section."

"What does that mean?"

"It means someone has recorded some pictures, then stopped, then later recorded more. Like they were *collecting* images together onto this spindle."

A thrill fizzed in Finn's stomach at Whelm's words. He tried to keep his expression neutral. It was just as he'd believed all along: the spindle was special. Connor had gone to a lot of trouble to make it, then had made very sure Finn received it. He had to find out what it said.

"There's more, though," said Whelm.

"What?"

"Well, it's the scratches themselves. If you look very closely you can see they look … odd."

"You mean like damaged?" He'd always been so careful. His excitement was replaced by dread. If they couldn't read the spindle, he'd never have his answers.

"No," said Whelm. "I don't think so. I think they're encrypted."

"How can you tell?"

"The grooves look different. The little marks look random. Disjointed rather than flowing. It's subtle, but you can tell if you know what you're looking for."

"The images can be encrypted like the line-of-sight messages?"

"They can. The reader lets you punch in the key to view the pictures just like any 'scope."

A terrible thought struck Finn. "Which means, if you don't know the key…"

"Then there's nothing you can do," said Whelm. "There's no way to view what's on the spindle. You could try each number in sequence but that would take your whole lifetime. Probably several lifetimes. These seeing orbs use twenty-digit numbers, not ten."

Finn sat down. The sinking sensation overwhelmed

him. This was bad news, very bad news. Connor hadn't given him the key. He'd just handed the spindle to Finn. Finn thought back, trying to recall everything Connor had said and done. At no point had he made any mention of a twenty-digit number.

Had Connor intended to give him the key later? Or had he hidden it somewhere and Finn had failed to spot it? He'd never know. Most likely, Connor had taken the key with him when he died in the fall of Engn.

The spindle was useless. It took several moments for the news to sink in. What was he going to do? He'd depended on the metal stick to explain everything, make sense of everything. The secrets were all on there, but now he'd never be able to decipher them.

"How come you know so much about the spindles, anyway?" asked Finn. Perhaps Whelm was wrong. Perhaps it was all a story so Finn would sell the metal stick.

Whelm shrugged. "When I first went to Engn, I was given the job of making the blanks. Me and lots of other people in this big hall, filing and polishing them to a shine. Later, I was promoted to working on the orbs. Repairing them and testing new ones."

"Then you must know how they function, how all the mechanics and electronics work."

"Pretty much."

A glimmer of hope returned to Finn. "Then you *must* know a way to view the pictures without having the key. A way to bypass the mechanism."

Whelm shook his head. "I told you, it's not possible. The images are hopelessly garbled without the key. If you try to view the pictures, you'll get a snowstorm of noise. I'm sorry, Finn, there's nothing I can do."

Finn nodded. His glimmer of hope died. He had to get away, think about Whelm's words. They changed everything. Had he become too obsessed with the spindle? Maybe this was a sign to move on. Forget the whole thing, get on with his life in the valley.

"I should go," he said. "I promised I'd take Mrs. Megrim some food."

"Okay," said Whelm. "I'll finish work on the reader anyway. I think I can make it work. It's delicate though – it could break down at any moment, understand? Not that it matters much now. The moment you put the spindle in you'll see…"

He trailed off. Something had occurred to him. He stared into the middle distance, eyes narrowed.

"What is it?" asked Finn. "What have you thought of?" The glimmer of hope sparked again.

"Do you have another magnifying lens?" asked Whelm. "A stronger one?"

"I suppose. We could use the lenses from a line-of-sight. Why? What is it?"

Whelm was deep in thought for a moment. Then he replied. "Something we worked out once with a broken orb. It's not going to help much. It's most likely not going to work at all."

"What? Tell me."

"When we were repairing the etching mechanisms, we noticed the encryption components didn't always engage straight away. It was a flaw in the design. The arm that was supposed to move across sometimes got stuck."

"Meaning what?"

"Meaning the images got recorded unencrypted before the thing was properly warmed up. Sometimes it was only a second or so. Sometimes a few minutes, like maybe the operator didn't notice for a while and then engaged the encryption arm manually. Sometimes they stuck mid-recording, too, but that was rarer. You'd see a stutter of normal pictures among all the random fuzz."

"There could be visible images on there after all."

"Maybe, Finn. It's very unlikely. Only if the pictures were recorded on a machine with the design flaw. And if it hadn't been repaired. And even then, you might only get a few seconds."

"We have to try," said Finn, full of excitement once again. He rummaged around for an old 'scope. He'd seen one about somewhere, one of its lenses hopelessly cracked. "Would this help?"

"It might. If I unscrew the eyepiece and get the focal lengths right. I'll have to hold everything in place with clamps."

Whelm worked for ten, fifteen minutes, making minute adjustments to the spacings between the lenses, occasionally muttering to himself. He moved his head backwards and forwards to get the tiny scratches into focus. There was silence. Finn found he was barely breathing.

Finally, he could stand it no longer. "Anything? Can you tell?"

Whelm didn't reply, all his attention focused on the spindle.

"Whelm?"

The ex-master looked up. "You're in luck. Not all of them, but some of the tracks have been recorded with a flawed orb. Which means the pictures were recorded on different devices and collected together later, as we thought. There should be a few scenes visible here and there. But not many, Finn. Most of the spindle will be unreadable."

"But you can get something?"

"There's a chance. If I can get everything hooked up properly." Whelm looked up at Finn. "Leave it with me for a few hours and I'll see what I can do."

"Thanks," said Finn. "I'll see to Mrs. Megrim and be back as soon as I can."

Whelm nodded, his attention already turned to the nest of wires and metal arms on the bench.

Outside, Finn collected eggs from the chickens they had scratching around in the garden. Diane approached from down the lane. She'd been helping Flane rebuild one of the bridges over the Silverburn. She's been happier these past few days, having finally heard from her home village. All was well down there. Still, she looked weary, her face stained with mud.

She smiled as she saw Finn and hurried up to kiss him, deliberately smudging mud onto his face.

"Thanks for that," he said.

"You're welcome. Off somewhere?"

"I'm going to take these to Mrs. Megrim."

"That's good. And how is our guest?" The ice in her voice was subtle but clear if you knew her.

"He thinks he can get the reader working again."

"He does, does he?"

"Which is good, isn't it?" said Finn. "Once that's done, and now most of the buildings are fixed up, he'll be leaving soon."

"And you think he'll just go?"

"Of course," said Finn. "He doesn't want to be tied down here. He likes to be free. He knows he's not welcome, not really."

Diane didn't look convinced. She was sure he was up to something. "Which is hardly surprising, is it?"

"No. I know."

She stroked his hair, brushing it out of his eyes. "You need to get this cut. How can you even see clearly?"

"Will you do it for me?"

"I will."

"There's hot water for a bath," said Finn. "You've earned it."

She squeezed his hand, then picked her way through their little patch of garden towards the cottage. Finn watched her go, grinning at the sight of her, then turned to head down the lane.

Shadows were already gathering in the valley as Finn followed the familiar track past the Switch House and up to Mrs. Megrim's cottage. The rooks had ceased their squabbling and settled down into the treetops for the night, bringing a welcome peace to the familiar scene.

Lines of smoke filtered up into the clear air from the chimneys dotted here and there. It was hard to believe the earthquake had happened. The valley glowed in the fading evening light and everything looked as it always looked.

Finn stopped to take it all in, breathing deeply. A breeze made the leaves whisper around him. It was strange, but he hadn't noticed the beauty as a boy. The valley was just there. His playground, his world. Only now he'd been away and come back could he see how special a place it was. He knew he was lucky to be able to spend his life there.

Like Connor's mother, Mrs. Megrim sat alone in her room. Her window, however, was open to the evening air. She sat in her old leather chair, a woollen shawl around her shoulders, reading the reams of line-of-sight messages scrolling constantly from her 'scope. She might not get out much anymore, but she still knew everything taking place in the valley. And beyond. It came tumbling out of her device in a constant torrent.

"Ah, there you are at last, boy," she said, looking up at him over her half-moon reading glasses. "I thought you'd forgotten all about me."

"I brought eggs and bread," said Finn. "Shall I cook something?"

"As long as you don't burn it like last time."

Finn went off to prepare food in Mrs. Megrim's tiny, square kitchen. When he returned, she was frowning over some fresh scrap of readout, shaking her head and tutting.

"What is it?" asked Finn.

"Oh, youngsters," said Mrs. Megrim. "They're all idiots."

"Yes. You've mentioned that before."

"Well it's true. Don't know what's good for them, that's their problem. Think they know best." She dropped the piece of paper and turned to study Finn. Under her gaze the room seemed to shrink, gather around Finn as if leaning in to hear what he had to say for himself.

"So, Finn. Are you still giving that cruel young man a place to sleep?"

"You mean Whelm?"

"Of course I mean Whelm. Who else would I mean? How many cruel young men are you currently housing?"

"He's still staying with us, yes."

"I don't approve, you know."

"I know. You said."

"Neither does Diane. It's not fair on her. It's not fair on you, either."

"He's trying his best to help. He couldn't help becoming a master, could he?"

"Couldn't he? You managed to avoid it. You had your chance to play their ridiculous game and you turned away. That one revelled in it."

It had been Whelm, of course, who had dashed Mrs. Megrim to the ground the day Finn had been taken, leaving her in a broken heap by the side of the road. The fearsome Mrs. Megrim reduced to a pile of rags.

"He's helping me to fix the spindle reader," said Finn.

"And you know what I think about that, too, don't you?"

"If I recall correctly, you think I should melt it down in my father's forge and get on with my life."

"Nothing wrong with your memory, at least."

"You should eat your food before it goes cold."

"Trying to shut me up, eh?"

"Always," said Finn.

With a *hmmph*, Mrs. Megrim began to eat.

"Actually," said Finn. "There was something I wanted to ask you about."

"Oh, I'm allowed to speak now, am I?"

"It's about Connor's mother," said Finn, ignoring Mrs. Megrim's jibe. "You know I went to see her."

"What about her?"

"How well do you know her?"

"Not well at all. She's not from the valley, of course. Connor's father brought her here, away from her own family. I've never even spoken to her, not face to face, but somehow I don't think she was very happy here."

"Because she was bed-bound?"

"Perhaps. She wasn't always, though. I don't think she's ever really felt she belongs here."

"Because of her family? She said something about the old wars."

Mrs. Megrim nodded. "Her family's too stuck in their traditions and resentments, fighting ancient fights."

"To be honest what she said was all a bit … confusing. She kept contradicting herself."

Mrs. Megrim nodded and stared out of the window for a moment, as if looking for answers. "She's not well," she said finally, "and I don't just mean her legs. Her mind isn't always in the same room as her body, if you know what I mean. I think she's stuck in all that history. She's not always sure what is *now* and what is *then*. She was immersed in it as a girl, brought up to think it still matters."

"She said Engn had something to do with the war. And the earthquakes. And then how Engn was built to provide power. Or standardized time. Or the line-of-sights. To be honest, I'm not really sure what she was saying."

"No, well, she's been through a lot. Losing Connor and then her husband has tipped her over the edge. It's understandable."

Finn didn't say anything. He wondered how close Mrs. Megrim had been to that edge, with both Tom and Rory taken to Engn.

"She's right about the clocks, though," said Mrs. Megrim. "Engn did standardize time. And more besides. The names of the days, the length of the week, even what year it is. Before Engn, every little place had their own system, their own names. You could walk ten miles and suddenly find you were a hundred years in the past in a completely different month. It was madness."

"And that was what people fought over? It's ridiculous to have a war about what time it is."

"Oh, you'd be surprised how much people resent a little thing like that. They think the way they do things are normal and natural, and everyone else is deluded. No one likes being told what to do. Besides, there were other arguments, other resentments. They called it the Clockwork War, but I think the clocks were just the final straw. The excuse. There were already all these ancient rivalries going back years."

"The Guilds?"

She nodded. "Glad to hear you paid some attention in my lessons. The ancient city-states had been scrapping for centuries. They'd been keeping each other in check, I think, with all their intrigues and alliances. Then the upstart houses came along with their new ideas and clever mechanisms, and everything changed. The arguments came to a head over the clocks and suddenly it was all-out war. Ridiculous, really. But that's people for you."

More paper scrolled out of Mrs. Megrim's line-of-sight. The network was back to normal. He wondered what she did with all the rolls of paper. Somewhere she must have a room full of them.

"Here's one for you," she said, angling the sheet to the light so she could read it.

"For me?"

"From Diane. Or from that master, I suppose. It just says *Come home. Something you need to see.*" She looked up at him. "And what's that all about, I wonder?"

"I don't know," he said. But he did, of course. Whelm had got the spindle reader working. "I have to go. I'll try and get back tomorrow."

He rose and turned to the door.

"Finn, I don't like this. I don't like any of it. Whelm. That damn spindle of yours. No good's going to come of it, understand? No good at all. People will start going off again and getting themselves killed. If you want my advice you should leave it alone. Leave it all well alone."

Finn nodded but didn't reply. He closed her door quietly behind him as he left, but then broke into a run, back up the lane.

From her window, Mrs. Megrim watched him race off into the darkness. "Ah, Finn. You're not going to pay any attention to what I say, are you? You never did. Off you'll go, back to Engn. You haven't even admitted it to yourself yet. You're drawn to that place like a moth to a fire. It's been *destroyed* and yet look at you. You've got your master to take you and now you're going to find your excuse for returning."

Shaking her head, she watched him as he disappeared from sight.

VII

Finn's breathing was ragged, the stitch in his side sharp, by the time he reached home. He'd never really recovered from his ordeals in Engn. It didn't take much to wear him out, and some days he had no energy at all. Diane always assured him it would take time, that he'd get over it. It had been three years now.

He took a moment to let his heaving chest calm a little. He didn't want Diane or Whelm to see him like that. When he was ready, he pushed open the little wooden gate to their garden and made his way towards the workshop, threading between the vegetable beds. This time of year, with nearly everything harvested, they were little more than oblong mounds of bare earth.

"Finn."

Diane stood on their doorstep of their cottage. For some reason she was still in her stained work clothes. She should have been lying in a steaming tub of water.

"Whelm wants me," said Finn. "In the workshop. I think he's found something."

"It was me who sent the message, Finn. Not him."

He stepped closer to her. Something was wrong, he could see. There was a knot of anxiety about her eyes.

"What is it? What's happened?"

"Come inside. I'll show you." Finn saw her glance over at the workshop, as if she was afraid Whelm would overhear. The ex-master was still in there; he could see the flicker and glow of electric lights. Was the reader finally operating? Perhaps. The urge to go and find out was almost too much to resist.

Instead, he turned and followed Diane inside their house. Whelm would have to wait. Diane led him through the kitchen, all sign of the smashed glassware and crockery now swept away. Into the west-facing room they sat in together each evening. Their line-of-sight 'scope was there. Finn saw straight away this was what she wanted to show him.

"I see we've had messages," said Finn. "More news from home?"

Diane stooped to pick up the rolls of printout unfurled upon the floor. "No, not from home. And we've only had *one* message. The same message every ten minutes, repeated over and over. Someone really wants to make sure we get it."

"What does it say?"

Diane held out a sheet of the paper for Finn to see. "I don't know. It's encrypted."

"You obviously tried our key."

"Obviously. And your old one from your parents' house. And my old one from back home. Even the one Mrs. Hampton used when she lived here. I tried them all, Finn, but none of them worked."

"Who's sending it? Let's just ask them to switch to plain text."

Diane shook her head. "No, Finn. See." She handed him the piece of paper. Finn suddenly knew what the source address would be before he even looked. *1A11.*

And below it, before the garbled stream of random characters, a heading in clear text. *For Finn and Diane.*

He looked back up at her. The alarm was clear in her eyes now. Finn looked back at the message, but it was completely undecipherable without the key, of course. And it was a long message. Several pages.

"You're sure it's the same message over and over?"

"I haven't checked every character, but they look the same. I'm guessing they're giving us a chance to get the key right."

"How many times has it come now?"

"Five. It should come through again in two or three minutes."

Diane had already tried all the keys he knew. Except she hadn't, had she? He could think of two more. Two that had been stuck in his memory for years, numbers that would rattle around in his brain until the day he died. One was Matt Dobey's, the number Finn has tricked the old lengthsman into providing. The other was the one Mrs. Megrim had given him, scribbled on a scrap of paper before Whelm – Master Whelm – threw her to the ground.

"Let me try," said Finn. He dialled in Matt's old number on the little brass wheels beneath the 'scope.

"Whose number is that?" said Diane.

"Matt's."

"Matt's dead, Finn. We both saw it."

"I know. But maybe someone knows we'd know his number. It's…"

The lights flickered in the 'scope, then, cutting Finn off. They waited for the paper to start spooling out of the little slot in the bottom of the machine.

1A11. For Finn and Diane, it said. And then it came: line after line of meaningless characters.

"Okay," said Diane. "Not Matt."

"I've got one other number to try."

"You can change the key mid-message?"

"You can. It'll be garbled for a few seconds as the code

mechanism switches around, but it's perfectly possible."

"And what key is this? One you learned inside Engn?"

"The one Mrs. Megrim gave me." This one would work. He *knew* it. Someone must have found out about it, would have known Finn had memorized it. He dialled in the familiar list of ten digits with his thumb.

When he'd finished, they stood together again, watching the printout from the machine. It stuttered for a moment, paused as if confused, and then resumed. More lines of indecipherable nonsense spooled out. Finn watched it for long seconds, unable to believe it. He'd been so sure. He kept expecting it to begin printing out words he could understand. But it didn't.

Diane seized a sheet and studied it, as if she could wring meaning out of it by sheer willpower.

"We could just reply and ask them to send the key," said Finn.

Diane shook her head as she studied the printout. "They're hardly going to do that, are they? Anyone could intercept the key and read the message, and they've gone to a lot of trouble to keep it secret."

"I suppose."

"You know what I think we should do, Finn?"

"What?"

"I think we should burn these messages. And I think we should tell Rory never to route through any more claiming to be from 1A11."

He didn't say anything. The truth was he *had* to find out what these messages were. The spindle and the timing signals and now these. They were all vitally important. How could she not see that?

"You don't agree," said Diane.

"I don't think we can ignore all this," said Finn.

"I think that's exactly what we can do. Ignore it completely."

"And if we're meant to do something?"

"Meant by whom, Finn? We spent enough time chasing

cryptic trails when we went to Engn before. I don't want any more of it."

Finn looked down at the paper. If only they had the key. The words, surely, would be enough to persuade her.

"You know what's odd," said Finn.

"What?"

"It's addressed to us at this house. How did they know we live here?"

"Everyone knows we live here," said Diane. "It's hardly a secret."

"Everyone in the valley. But how does Engn know? Rory would have said if anyone had sent out any encrypted messages. If there was another Matt in our midst."

"Perhaps he missed a message."

"I don't think Mrs. Megrim's son would fail to notice an encrypted message being sent through. Especially one sent *there*. And obviously everything has to go through him to…"

He trailed off. A memory had been niggling at him for a few days now. Could it be? Was it possible?

"What, Finn? What is it?"

"It's … just something I saw at Connor's house."

"What?" She sounded wary, as if this was simply the latest in a long line of mad ideas. Perhaps it was.

"You know I said Connor's mother had her own line-of-sight? The completely misaligned one?"

"What about it?"

"Well, what if it wasn't misaligned? What if it was pointing *exactly* where it was supposed to be pointing? What if she has her own line directly to Engn that we don't know anything about?"

"Is that possible?"

Finn shrugged. Was it? He didn't see how. But why else would she have her own 'scope? And she'd been very clear he wasn't to touch it. "I don't know. Maybe. The messages would still have to bounce off mirrors to get around the mountains. Perhaps they're hidden all down the valley and out across the plain."

Diane shook her head. "You know what I think? Do you want a much easier explanation than secret mirrors and alternative line-of-sight networks?"

"What?"

"That Connor's mother is lost in her own fantasy world. And as for these messages, someone passing through the valley must have reported back to whatever remains of Engn. Told them everything about us."

"Who would do that?"

"Let's see. How about an ex-master pretending to sell useless scraps of machinery?"

"You think Whelm is spying on us?"

"Do you think he isn't?"

Finn didn't reply for a moment. The idea hadn't occurred to him. He knew Diane didn't trust Whelm, but he'd assumed it was because of what happened before Engn.

"Whelm's changed," said Finn. "He's not the person he was. He seems … broken somehow."

"Which means he'll be all the keener to fix things. Get Engn working so he can become a master again. Don't you see, Finn? This is the person you've invited into our *home*. He and all the others must have been reporting back all this time."

"But there's no one to report back to. Engn is in ruins."

"Is it? You're sure of that?"

"I thought you wanted to forget all about the place. Now it sounds like you think it's working again. I don't understand what you're saying."

He was half shouting. They both were. They realized it in the same moment, caught themselves. Finally, Finn looked down. He hated to argue. They both hated to argue. They'd seen too much fighting.

Finn stepped away to look out of the window. One thing was clear: Whelm was causing tension just by being there. He'd have to go. First thing tomorrow, he'd have to leave.

"You've had a message?" Whelm stood in the doorway. They hadn't heard him enter. How long had he been standing there? How much had he heard?

Finn shook his head, thrown by the ex-master's presence. "Yes. It's nothing. How's it going with the reader?"

Whelm grinned. "Come and see. I think I got it working."

"You've got pictures?"

"I haven't tried it yet," said Whelm. "I thought you might want to be there. The whole thing could blow up at any moment and never work again. That earthquake did a remarkably good job of bending the cogs inside the mechanism." He glanced at Diane as he said this.

Diane said nothing. She returned her attention to the garbled line-of-sight messages, a scowl on her face.

"Coming?" asked Finn. "Surely you want to find out what's on the spindle at least?"

"Not really. Sometimes you're better off not knowing things."

"Look," said Finn. "I'll tell you what. If there's nothing on the spindle, if it's just random old pictures, then I'll leave it, okay? I'll do what you said. Destroy it, ignore the messages, everything. Get on with my life. With our life, I mean."

She studied him for a moment. "And you can do that, can you? Just set it all aside. Or will you just find something else to get obsessed with? Some new, terrible secret you have to uncover?"

Finn didn't reply for a moment. *Could* he set it all aside? He'd never really thought about it properly, because he didn't believe he'd have to.

Eventually, he nodded. "If there's nothing on the spindle then I'll forget it all," he said. "I promise you. But if there is something there, if there is something we're supposed to do, will you do it? Will we do it together?"

Now it was her turn not to answer for a moment. Finally, she, too, nodded.

They had their agreement. Their new pact. One of them would be right about the spindle and one of them would be wrong, and whichever it was, they would each go along with it. Once they'd needed rings and blood and spoken vows. Now it needed only these two nods and the look of understanding passing between them.

Finn grinned at her and she gave him the look of exasperated indulgence she kept only for him.

"So, are we going to switch the reader on or not?" asked Whelm. "Because I can see there's more going on here than just one little picture spindle."

Diane set aside the sheet of paper she held and swept forwards, past them both and through the door.

"Come on," she called back. "We'll settle this one way or the other. Let's see what's on the damned thing right now."

Bare copper wires snaked from the electrical switchboard into the mass of valves and arms and cogs making up the dismantled spindle reader. Finn and Diane watched as Whelm gently pulled the brass lever opening the connection to the machine.

Immediately there was a smell of burning metal. A growing hum came from the mechanism. Finn could feel the sudden heat from it on his face.

"It'll take a minute or two," said Whelm. "Once the orb is warmed up, I'll engage the reader." He turned from the mechanism to look at the two of them, standing over him in the cramped workshop. "The thing is, I had a good look at the spindle when you were gone. Inspected it closely all the way along."

"And?" asked Finn.

"There are some quite long sections of unencrypted etching in the middle. It's as if, I don't know, whoever made this didn't know what they were doing."

"Or maybe they were in such a hurry they had no choice," said Finn. "They had to copy the pictures from another spindle and didn't have time to set up all the encryption."

Whelm nodded. His look of suspicion had returned. "Maybe. The question is, why? And why would they be doing it in secret?"

Finn shrugged. "I don't know. Just a thought."

"You think we should start in the middle?" said Diane.

"No, let's start at the start," said Finn. "Things will hopefully make more sense that way."

"There are some unencrypted pictures at the beginning of the very first section," said Whelm. "I'll start there."

"Will there be sound?" asked Finn. Thinking back to that day in the Control Room, he remembered only pictures, flickering silently away in the line of glass orbs.

"Could be," said Whelm. "At least, the orbs have the means of recording sound. It's impossible to say whether there's any on there. Perhaps a voice commentary added later. Like a diary of events."

Whelm turned to study the humming machine, peering inside. In the depths of the mechanism, something glowed red hot. Whether it was supposed to, Finn couldn't tell.

"I think it's ready," said Whelm. "The thing is, I've had to cobble together scraps and parts from a load of other mechanisms. I can't actually guarantee any of this will work."

"If it fails, could it damage the spindle?" asked Finn.

Whelm considered for a moment. "It's unlikely, but I can't guarantee it. Do you want me to engage it or not?"

"We have to try," said Finn, not looking at Diane.

Whelm turned a brass knob on the front of the

dismantled machine. Immediately something whirred and buzzed, the sound of a motor spinning up to speed. There was a *clunk* and a series of clicks and then a silvery light flickered in the glass orb, as if it was nothing more than a weak incandescent bulb. Finn found himself peering nearer, gazing into the misty depths. His own features reflected at him, weirdly deformed by the curved glass. Diane was there, too, all nose and chin as she studied the orb.

An image appeared. Faint and shaky, it shook and disintegrated into a blur of lines as if being blown to pieces in a high gale. Then it solidified again. A man standing in a room. Finn recognized him immediately.

Connor looked wary, glancing around him as if afraid of being interrupted. Behind him, unmistakably, was the Control Room. The lines of orbs and the panels of controls were just as Finn remembered.

The voice, when it came, was distant and hushed, as if shouted through a high wind, but the words were there.

"Finn. There isn't much time. This spindle will explain everything. Everything you must do. I'm told you're here in the Directory now. You'll understand it all when you see. We had it so wrong, Finn. I mean, we were right, of course, but we knew nothing. Everything depends on this, Finn. On you and Diane. *Everything*. What we're going to do is just the start. Engn is…"

The images abruptly ceased, replaced by a swirling fuzz of black and white dots. They watched for five seconds, ten, but there were only more dots, accompanied by a discordant squeal of sound. Finally, Whelm pushed the lever, and the light in the orb died.

Diane was staring at the orb with a frown on her face. "You heard?" asked Finn. "You heard what he said?"

She didn't speak for a moment, deep in thought. Finally, she seemed to emerge from herself to return Finn's gaze. "I heard."

"Do you believe me now? You see we have to do

something? Something important?"

"Perhaps. It doesn't really prove anything. Perhaps he was talking about something we were supposed to do years ago, when we were there."

"I don't think so. He said that was just a start." Finn turned to Whelm. "You heard, right? Connor said we have to do something."

Whelm didn't reply. He was considering Finn with narrowed eyes. "The Director's apprentice gave you this spindle? Your boyhood friend who became so high and mighty in Engn. You didn't *find it*. You went to the Directory and he gave it to you."

"It was … something like that, yes."

"Why would he do that, Finn?" said Whelm. "That doesn't make any sense at all. What's going on here?"

"Truly, I don't know," said Finn. "That's why we need to see the rest of the spindle. Connor didn't get chance to explain very much. Things were … rushed at the end."

Whelm didn't look satisfied. He was clearly suspicious. He didn't speak for a few more moments as he weighed up Finn's words. Finally, he said, "You'll need the key to see all of it. Connor *must* have given it to you. He went to a great deal of trouble to give you the spindle. He wouldn't just forget a thing like that. He wasn't stupid."

Finn looked up at Diane. "Do you remember anything? Anything Connor said about a key?"

Diane shook her head.

"Wait, wait," said Whelm. "You were there, too, Diane? All three of you in that room in the Directory?"

Now no one spoke for a moment.

"Yes," said Diane finally. "I was. We were all there. The three of us."

"How is that possible? I mean, why? Why were you there?"

"It's a long story."

"Which means you're not going to tell me, right?"

"Not right now, no," said Finn. "You said there were

longer sections of unencrypted pictures. Let's watch them. Perhaps they'll make things clearer. Clearer for all of us." He glanced at Diane, who nodded reluctantly.

"Okay," said Whelm. "Since you're obviously not going to tell me anything, I'll skip to the next readable section on the spindle."

As the machine crackled and buzzed once more, the three of them leaned in closer to the glass orb to see more of the indistinct images forming. It was a scene Finn recognized from his time in Engn. A voice spoke, too. No one Finn recognized. An older man, seeming to narrate the events portrayed by the flickering pictures…

VIII

Guildmaster Ven Adage of the Clockmakers and Timecounters walked into the echoing stone chamber of the Inner Wheel. Each step on the hard flags jarred through his knees and into his hips. As they always did these days. He was getting old. Still he, of all the guildmasters, had to accept the fact. Had to accept the passage of time. He had lived his life by the ticking of clocks, by the careful, deliberate measurement of each passing second. He could have no complaint time was catching up with him.

And he only wanted to live long enough to see their long plans realized. That would suffice. Oh, he would never see the final end of the Clockwork War of course. That was a distant prospect. But he might see the decisive battle won. The turning point reached; the moment when the clock started ticking for their enemies and their destruction became an inevitability. And the beauty of it was the great old guilds had no idea the battle was even being fought. They'd destroyed the great clocktower and they'd destroyed all the mechanicals sent against them in battle, and so in their simplistic way they thought they'd won the war.

The whole thing was an intricately crafted mechanism, as cunning as any of the miniature timepieces his Guildsmen laboured over. Yet it was a mechanism so vast it was, in a strange way, too big to see. Too big to understand. It became simply *what was*. And it was a mechanism that existed in people's heads as much as it did in the stone and steel of the real world. That was the beauty of it. Their hated oppressors thought the twelve mechanical guilds had been beaten back into their place. And it was being allowed to think those thoughts that would, one day, spell their doom.

Adage couldn't resist a smile at it all. Just so long as their enemies never learned the truth. Didn't grasp the Treaty of Enloth was a sham, a feint. Carried on thinking the upstarters were utterly defeated, their troublesome ideas crushed. Because, in truth, they nearly had been. But the old guilds' ignorance had been their downfall. They didn't understand, could never understand what was being built. Their brains couldn't think big enough thoughts, that was their problem.

So, they had accepted the stories about *reparations* and *compensations*, secure in their supposed superiority. They had accepted the assurance the great machine would supply free, unlimited energy to all the ancient city-states ringing the great plain. All those backwards bastions of inequality and superstition with their crumbling temples. And they would never know what was actually being built here in their heartland. They would never know until it was too late.

Adage reached his chair, carved into the very rock of the stone chamber. The twelve chairs were arranged in a circle, like the face of a clock. He liked that. Strictly speaking, of course, there should have been thirty-six thrones. Twenty-four for the old guilds and twelve for the new. One for each hour on the standardized time they used within the machine. But this was their inner sanctum, and the masters of the old guilds weren't welcome there. This was where Adage and the others could discuss their plans in safety. And, thinking themselves so superior, the old guilds simply let them get on with it.

He looked up at the towering stone walls around him. Across the circle, where the masters of the Silversmiths Guild sat, the likeness of old Agrion had already been carved into the bare stone. His old friend had been dead a month and now a new master sat in the throne. And that was the way it should be. Life was change. Time moved on. It was the old guilds that wanted everything to remain the same forever. One day soon, his own face would be carved above the Clockmakers' Throne. And there he would remain for decades and centuries to come, watching over each new generation of masters until the time finally came. He craned his beck upwards. The soaring walls of the Inner Wheel chamber rose into distant shadows high above him. Room for the many masters to come after them.

The others were filing in now: some old like him, some young and keen-eyed. The brightly coloured robes they all wore always amused him. Their ridiculous regalia, the decorated clock he wore around his own neck, and all the rest of it. But they'd deliberately mimicked the old guilds to maintain the pretence of defeat and compliance. Adopted their ceremony and archaism. It was a price worth paying.

Adage waited for them all to be seated before he began. "We are all gathered. Are the doors closed and guarded?"

Master Dragus of the Ironmasters hauled himself back to his feet with his iron stick and nodded his head, his shaggy grey hair falling over his face for a moment. "I have set iron-clad guards of my own guild upon the door. No one will enter without their say so. We may speak freely."

"And the seeing orbs?"

Now Enderby of the Lensmen bobbed to his feet. "The orbs are now fully functional in this part of the machine. Everything they see is being stored on the spindles."

Here was something that troubled Adage. People said he was too old, too cautious. Perhaps he was. But they were playing a long game, and even one small mistake could still ruin everything. Of course, the completed spindles were to be hidden away in an underground chamber, but could they remain a secret for all the decades and centuries to come? "Can we be absolutely sure our enemies won't see what the orbs see? They think they own the machine; that they control it. What would they say if they discovered what the orbs actually do?"

"They would probably think them magic and run a mile," said Enderby. A murmur of amusement rippled around the circle. "But there is no need to worry. Most likely our enemies think the orbs are mere incandescent bulbs we can't make work."

Another ripple of amusement.

"Even so," said Adage, "We must take no chances. Now the first stage of our plans is nearing completion there must be no possibility of our hosts discovering what we are doing. No chance whatsoever. Do we agree?"

"Oh, absolutely," said Enderby. "But we must also be sure those who succeed us understand everything we have put in place here. Everything we have set in motion."

"The masters of the old guilds will never be able to grasp the truth of the machine," said Dragus. "We have deliberately built it to be complicated and confusing. The very idea of it is so large they'll never be able to fit it into their crumbling brains. They look at it all and shake their heads in disbelief and walk away. We'll give them standard time and the telescopic conversation network and the promise of free power one day and they'll be content."

Master Trabat of the Railers stirred, a series of little coughs and exhalations indicating he was preparing to launch into speech. The word was he hadn't cut his hair for forty years. Looking at him, Adage could believe it. A look of amusement flashed between the younger masters as he hauled himself briefly to his feet before sinking back into his chair. Trabat was by far the oldest of the twelve and the one, if the whispers were to be believed, most sympathetic to the old ways. More than one wayward son or daughter from his family had married into the Wheelwrights or the Woodturners or one of the other Temple Guilds.

"And what of these cold northerners we have allied ourselves with?" Trabat rumbled. "How can we trust them? What do *they* see when they look at the machine? How do we know what they really want?"

It was an old argument, often repeated. "We do not need to trust them," said Adage. "It is a simple arrangement of mutual benefit. They get what they want from the arrangement and we get what we want."

Trilobite worked himself up to another sentence with a series of snorts and *hmmphs*. "Their wonderful technology failed us in the last war. All those clockwork soldiers and steam-powered carriages. Why should we trust this monstrous mechanism anymore?"

"The war started before we were ready," replied Enderby. "Another twenty years and the forces we were building would have been unstoppable."

"Besides," added Adage. "It is to their advantage to ensure this new marvel works."

"And," said Enderby. "It is us who will betray them. Eventually."

Trabat looked unconvinced. "If everything works as planned. It's a dangerous line to walk if you ask me. A very dangerous line. Many of us could be killed."

"None of our descendants will be anywhere near at the end," said Adage. "We will make sure of that. The Clarion call will ring out to warn them. Then, afterwards, they can return and reclaim what is rightfully theirs, all our enemies destroyed."

"And these Lords of the High Ice?" said Trabat. "They won't take very kindly to that, will they? When they realize what we've done. Who knows what they are really capable of?"

"They will hardly be able to complain," said Enderby. "They will have done very well out of the whole arrangement. We're the ones taking the risk."

Adage nodded. "Quite right. I believe we need not fear our friends from the north. Nor do we need to concern ourselves too much about the Temple Guilds. They are incapable of understanding anything more complicated than an abacus. I see only one threat to our plans. One group of people who might endanger us."

"Who?" asked Enderby.

"Us," said Adage. "The Inner Wheel."

"You think someone among us can't be trusted?" said Dragus, a look of outrage on his old face. A ripple of unease flowed around the circle like an electric current. Master glanced at master, as if suddenly expecting to see a traitor sitting there next to them.

"No, no," said Adage. "Not any of us, of course. We have all fought together, suffered together for too long. Slaved away under the yolk of the Temple Guilds. I would trust each of you with my own life. But it is the generations to come I am thinking about. Those who succeed us, as Enderby puts it. All those as-yet-unborn masters who must carry on the plans until the time comes. What of them? When we are all carved heads above these thrones, faded and worn into oblivion, can we really be sure that each and every master who sits in these seats is to be trusted? Because if any hint gets out about what we are really constructing here, the old guilds will rise up in rage and march upon us."

There was silence in the room, a heavy stone silence. The deep, distant rumble of the machinery thrumming through the floor seemed to wake to fill the quiet.

"So, tell us," said Enderby. "What new piece of mechanism do you have in mind? I know you. You only ever ask a question when you already know its answer."

"An outrageous statement," said Adage, letting the faintest smile play about his lips. "But it is possible I do have an inkling of an idea. This secret underground chamber of yours, where the memory orbs send their pictures and the spindles are stored. Where is it exactly?"

"North, far from here," said Enderby. "Well away from the Hub and well away from the Inner Wheel. I can show you the way."

"And you say the room is difficult to find?"

"As cryptic as any maze if you don't have the map."

"And should anyone manage to find this *sanctum sanctorum* there are, no doubt, dire warnings about the dangers of entering? Of, perhaps, delicate or deadly machinery within? Of the forbidden place that must not be entered?"

"Just so," said Enderby. "The best barriers are those people carry around in their own heads. The ideas they keep with them and whisper to their children so the lie is continued."

"Excellent," said Adage. "Then I think we should follow your lead, old friend. Except, I think we need to think larger."

Another heavy silence filled the room then as the gathered masters considered Adage's words.

Finally, Dragus spoke. "How much larger, exactly?"

"*Much* larger," said Adage, looking up as if to perceive distant vistas. "Much, much larger."

"Go on," said Darien, the new master of the Silversmiths. "Do, please, spell out exactly what it is you have in mind."

Adage paused for a moment, deciding where best to begin. Darien was young, ambitious. He rarely spoke when the Inner Wheel met, but Adage wasn't fooled. Darien was clever. Calculating. It was perfectly clear he was plotting ways to replace Adage and run the Inner Wheel himself one day. Which was exactly what Adage would have done. What he *did* do once, come to that.

"The best machines are those regulating themselves," said Adage. "Are we agreed? A mechanism requiring constant oversight will fail sooner rather than later. But a mechanism that governs itself without need for outside intervention will run and run."

"Just so," said Darien. "But I don't see how this relates to the machine we are constructing here."

"It's perfectly clear," said Adage. "We need our great device to govern itself, without outside control. Therefore, we need a self-contained, sealed system that understands and directs the purpose without the need for anyone to intervene."

"You are suggesting we cede control of the engine to another group?" asked Darien. "A wheel *within* the Inner Wheel?" The young master looked scornful.

"In a way, yes," said Adage. "Although simply creating another wheel won't change anything. We'd still have the same problem. I think we need a completely different approach. Something akin to Enderby's secret chamber, but greater in scope. A whole secret machine within the machine, cut off from the outside, immune to outside interference. A machine that can direct operations for the decades and centuries to come."

"And who will form this secret Inner *Inner* Wheel?" asked Darien, suspicion clear on his young face.

"We will," said Adage. "You, I, all of us. We will select the initial population from among ourselves and those we trust. When the population is large enough to be self-sustaining, we can seal them off and let them run everything, secure in the knowledge the great purpose is safe in their hands."

"But we tell no one about it," said Darien.

"Only those selected to go," said Adage. "Only them and no one else. The guards, the other guild members –

none of them must know. We will set the mechanisms up, so they are all controlled from in there. No one out here will take direct orders from them, but secretly everything will be directed by them. They will be the guardians of the sacred flame – the sacred furnace, I should say – at the heart of the machine."

"And the Inner Wheel?" asked Enderby. "What happens to all this? Do you just toss this aside?"

"Oh, it continues," said Adage. "In fact, it must. It is all a part of the show. The image we are presenting to the old guilds. Everyone will believe the Inner Wheel is running everything. And it won't matter how fossilized or ineffectual or ridiculous we eventually become, because really the secret group will be directing matters."

"This secret wheel would have to be huge to be self-sustaining," said Darien. "It would need hundreds of people."

"Just so," said Adage. "And we can perhaps allow one or two to join over time. Carefully vetted, of course. Fresh blood will always be needed. But no one here, outside, must ever know the truth. Must ever know the secret heart of the machine even exists."

"It will be difficult to miss something as large as that," said Darien. He sounded just a little like he was warming to the idea.

"That is true," said Adage. "But people are rather good at not seeing large things and focusing on the tiny and inconsequential, don't you find? I think we simply need do what Enderby has done with his secret chamber. No obvious way in and plenty of talk of dangerous machinery. It isn't safe to go near. People will soon accept it. It's amazing what people will overlook if they see others doing so."

"It will need many hands for the construction," said Dragus. "What of all them? How are we going to ensure they keep this thing quiet?"

"Simple enough," said Adage, as if it was of no

consequence. "We will have to keep the people building this new part of the machine isolated as well. Seal them off, wall them into villages of their own."

"Walled villages are hardly secure," said Dragus. "Some people see a wall and feel the urge to find out what is on the other side."

"Then a labyrinth of underground tunnels," said Adage. "A maze not connected to the rest of the outside world the workers are taught to navigate. Although nothing must be written down, of course. They'll have to keep the paths of the maze in their heads. But they can live their lives in subterranean caverns while they carry out their labours. It is hardly any different to what is taking place in the mines being excavated beneath the machine."

Darien still looked suspicious. "And what if – many years from now – someone from within this secret place becomes curious? As Master Dragus says, people see a wall and wonder what lies over it. We can't be sure they will remain trustworthy either."

Adage nodded. It was a good point, and one he'd given considerable thought to. "Ah, but by then it will be too late. We will bring up each successive generation to believe what we want them to believe. We can direct them, mould them. Take away their curiosity. Discourage questioning, instil loyalty. They will come to *know* a simple, quiet truth: that there is nothing outside the machine. Nothing at all. Nothing beyond the walls. That the walls aren't walls, but rather ... the edge of things. These will become sacred truths, passed from generation to generation. Don't you see? We all laugh at the old guilds and their ancient ways, but perhaps we can learn something from them. Use their superstitious ways against them."

"You wish to learn from the old guilds?" said Darien. It was dangerous talk to suggest anything good about their enemies. Adage knew this was precisely the sort of thing Darien would use against him if he could. He had to tread carefully.

"Let me enlighten you," said Adage. "Were you aware the Guild of Papermakers *know* anything written on paper not made by them is automatically and eternally wrong? No matter what it is, however obvious? That is why they take such delight in burning books and scrolls whenever they can. Their belief is clearly ridiculous, yet they would defend its truth to the death. As they have on many occasions. People are malleable, you see. They can be squeezed into shapes like ingots of lead. Or beaten into shape if necessary, like iron on an anvil. We must simply foster the myth in our chosen few that the larger world does not exist. In time, the inhabitants of this secret wheel will accept it. Give them a vital purpose, make them *know* they are superior, the elect, and they will even become proud of what they believe. I told you. Most people don't ask the big questions. Only the trivial ones."

"And when the work is complete?" said Enderby. "What of the hands living in the underground labyrinth?"

"Regrettably, we will have to kill them all," said Adage. "For fear of the secret escaping."

There were one or two frowns among the masters at that. They had all suffered at the hands of the old guilds. Their families had suffered and died for generations. They, the twelve mechanical guilds, were different. But sometimes a price had to be paid for a greater good. No one spoke up. As Adage had calculated they wouldn't.

"So, a secret group controlling everything, cut off from all outside influences," said Dragus. "And what should we call this place, this group? What name had you in mind, Adage?"

Adage shrugged, again as if he had given the matter no thought. "They will be directing the machine. I suggest the Directory or the Directorate, something along those lines."

"And is there to be a Director?" asked Darien. "A single person controlling everything; the true and ultimate power in the machine?"

"Well, yes, that does seem like a very good idea now

you mention it," said Adage. "The one individual who can pass between the secret heart and the rest of the machine, ensuring the smooth running of everything. I will, of course, be happy to put my own name into the hat for election to such a difficult and onerous position."

"Yes," said Darien. "I suspected you might."

No one spoke for a moment. The tone of threat, of challenge, was clear in the young master's words. Adage studied Darien. He would have to offer the boy something; otherwise, they would be mired in pointless arguments for years. Old masters pitted against young.

"Although, of course," said Adage, "there will need to be an apprentice to the Director at all times. A younger master who is taught the secrets and who is ready to take over at a moment's notice. Should the worst happen."

It was a dangerous road to take. If Darien became the apprentice, he would have a clear incentive to kill Adage one quiet evening. Darien would see that, of course. The risk was not so great; there were ways to manage it. It was simply a matter of eking out the secrets piece by piece. Ensuring the apprentice didn't dare act for many years for fear of missing something vital.

Darien was grinning now. A contented grin. He had taken the bait. Adage smiled back and nodded his head.

There would be interesting times ahead.

IX

"It cuts out there," said Whelm. "To be honest, I'm surprised we got as much as we did. It must have been a section from the master's personal diary, his recorded thoughts and recollections overlaid onto the pictures."

"It's amazing," said Finn. "That was the Inner Wheel, where I was judged. But it was ancient when I went there. I remember all those carved stone faces reaching up into the shadows. *Hundreds* of them. I knew Engn had been there for a long time, but that must have been centuries and centuries ago."

"I heard of people who spent their days copying spindles," said Whelm. "Just duplicating old ones onto new ones, one after the other for their entire lives. I suppose they must have been doing it to keep those ancient recordings readable."

"It's odd, though," said Finn. "That master. *Adage.* I thought I recognized him from somewhere."

"You saw his face carved above one of the thrones," said Diane.

"No, they were all worn away. And it's more recent than that. I've seen him somewhere else."

"Or it's just possible you've imagined it."

Finn nodded. Perhaps she was right. "But the recording: it proves it, doesn't it? All those secrets. The Directory. The secret purpose of the machine. Connor must have discovered all this and collected together the ancient recordings so we would know what we must do. You see, don't you?"

She looked troubled by what she'd witnessed. But he could see she wasn't yet convinced.

"Perhaps. Show us the next readable section, Whelm. Perhaps it will tell us none of this matters any more. That it's ancient history. Perhaps, I don't know, Connor did all this to make sure we came and found him when we were in Engn."

Whelm returned his attention to the machine. He held up a magnifying glass, turning a brass wheel on the machine with great care as he did so, lining up a fine metal tip to a precise point on the slim metal spindle. Finally, he sat back.

"Okay, here's the next section. Impossible to say whether we'll have something before the encryption kicks in."

Lights glowed and, once again, images swirled and flickered in the glass orb while Adage's crackly voice spoke from the machine…

X

The wind blowing off the plains whipped the tails of Adage's robes around. Reflected in the silvery walls of the Hub behind him, he resembled a black flame burning in the heart of the machine.

He pulled the robes more tightly around him. They needed higher walls around the machine, not just to keep the people in but to keep the damned wind *out*. When it blew from the north like this, it froze his ancient bones into rods of cold iron within his flesh.

His three silent companions didn't appear to feel it. Of course. Their home lay far to the north. Adage had never been to No, their distant city, but he'd heard much about it. Far beyond the plain, over unknown mountains. A place of permanent snow. A city built upon the ice of a frozen lake. Upon a frozen *ocean*, others said. Some even claimed No moved around, hauled along on enormous runners by titanic moving engines. Others said its buildings and walls were constructed from blocks of ice rather than stone. Or that there were in fact lots of cities, all fuelled by fire sucked from the ground.

Well, perhaps. Adage chose not to believe most of what people said about the Lords of the High Ice, but the undeniable truth was they troubled him. Despite all his public assurances. If there was one flaw in the great design, one speck of grit in the smooth running of the machine, it was their reliance on the cold, strange northerners with their incomprehensible arts and their secret machines. He reassured himself the contingency plans known only to a select few of the masters would be there if ever they were needed. The construction of Gargantua, the alternative containment engine, was a large draw on their resources and numbers but, they'd decided, a necessary one, in case the worst came to the worst.

For many years the Lords of the High Ice hadn't taken sides in the Clockwork War. They'd watched, aloof, while the armies of the old guilds and the new battled each other and slaughtered each other. Some whispered they were simply waiting for the two sides to wipe each other out so they could claim the lands for themselves; others, that they were secretly directing the entire war for purposes of their own. Adage doubted it. The Lords he talked to were uninterested in the affairs of others, seemed concerned only with their own ancient arts and practices. So Adage told himself, anyway.

And what those ancient practices might be, Adage had no idea. The Lords weren't a guild or a city-state. He had no idea what they made, what they did up there in the frozen north. What they *were*. He did, at least, know the reason for their sudden involvement. For their offer of mechanized soldiers and weaponry and all their mechanical marvels. From where he stood, he could see the power lines snaking across the plain into the distant north, carrying the electrical current the seismium containment engine generated. Vast amounts of free energy, safely generated far from their own lands where any accident wouldn't be able to harm them. That was the deal. They didn't need to know the truth, of course. Even if they did – and Adage sometimes wondered – the arrangement still made sense. Free electricity for decades and centuries to come, even if, one distant day, the flow inexplicably cut off.

"The engines are working?" one of the Lords asked him. "The particle is now fully contained?" It was the woman, the tallest of the three. She wore the robes of the Switchers Guild, but the disguise really didn't work. She was at least a foot taller than any Switcher he'd ever met. He also hadn't met any with blond hair braided with silver and plaited all the way down their back. Plaits that swayed and spat like serpents when they moved. And no one from the city-states ringing the great plain had such steely blue eyes, eyes that never seemed to blink as they studied you. Adage just hoped the masters of the old guilds were sufficiently foolish not to notice. Which, so far, they had been.

"All working," said Adage. "Containment pressure is at ten thousand pounds per square inch, as instructed."

"From all six machines?"

"All six."

The woman nodded. "Very well. We will go inside and see."

Sometimes he couldn't be sure if they were giving him orders or simply didn't know polite forms of wording. He preferred to believe the latter, but he fervently wished he understood the technologies they'd been given a little better. He'd asked for explanations, of course, for technical details, for calculations and projections. But the Lords of the High Ice would only smile and shake their heads. *Do you give away your guild secrets? No. You keep the hidden knowledge of how to channel electrical sparks, or how to build machines that know the time of day, to yourselves. You keep your secrets and we will keep ours.*

And there was nothing any of them could say to that, because it was true. Adage would defend the secrets of his own guild to the death. As they all would. Still, he wished he understood the details of what the vast machineries they were constructing actually did. And how they did what they did.

The four of them walked beneath the ram of the northern containment engine, the smooth steel of its vast piston as big as half the sky up above them. Adage could see no movement in the ram, but he could *feel* the raw power thrumming through it. It frightened him and delighted him in equal measure. The huge pressures the rams maintained were incredible. Thirty-six great steam engines powered the axles that in turn maintained this one ram in its state of unrelenting, straining pressure. The ram that was, at the same time, forced outwards by the particle, allowing it to capture the excess energy. The gearing to balance all that thunderous power onto the worm drive of this single ram took up a building in its own right. A building of roaring, screaming, furious metal always one moment away from explosion. And this was only one of the six.

The northern, southern, eastern and western rams were impressive enough. It was the engineering required to complete the underground and sky rams that dazzled Adage. They sky ram alone had taken five years to design. Now it towered above them, and all that pressure was brought to bear by the vast arm of the biggest beam-engine the world had ever seen. The arm was the single largest steel object ever cast. By some margin. They'd designed and constructed towering cranes to just lift it up there. And employed large cranes to erect the vast cranes.

The whole construction was truly a triumph, a marvel. And each time he looked at it, the unfocused anxiety flared within Adage's stomach. He knew in vague terms what everything did, but never with the intimate understanding he had of how a clock functioned. He could identify the precise purpose of each spring and cog and spindle in a timepiece. Why it was laid out as it was, how each component connected to each other in just that way. With the containment engine he had only his faith it would all work. And faith was a poor substitute for facts and equations and knowledge.

They walked past the three iron-clad guards protecting the northern doorway and into the echoing space. Each of the six compression rams penetrated one side of the cube, meeting in the distant centre high above their heads. To Adage, used to the minutiae of clock cogs and escapements, the sheer brute scale of this place felt oppressive, a weight bearing down on him. The rams tapered as they approached the centre, focusing the power, amplifying the pressure so they resembled some metal star, captured and caged in the great building.

Could steel really withstand such pressures? It had so far, but that didn't mean much. Metal failed eventually. Fatigue, rust, fractures. And although the current pressures were huge, they were nothing compared to those they'd see during the next Event. Would the rams work then? Or would they crack and fail? He was almost glad he wouldn't be alive to see it. Not for the first time he found himself regretting the whole thing. Regretting the terrible machine they had wrought.

They stopped beneath the tiny, dice-sized particle held between the diamond tips of the six rams. Adage peered upwards. His sight was weak these days, even with the eyeglasses the Guild of Lensmen had crafted for him. He could see a grey smudge, nothing more. Such a tiny amount. Yet this was the total amount they'd recovered from the huge pits excavated beneath the workings. A dice-sized cube. And he didn't like to play with dice, didn't like games of chance. He preferred cold, hard certainty.

"You're sure it's enough seismium?" he asked of his companions. "You're sure this is all it will take?"

The three Lords of the High Ice stood there with him beneath the particle, also gazing up, murmuring together in their incomprehensible language. Adage saw glances pass between them. Was it his imagination, or was there anxiety in those eyes of ice? Once again, he had the uncomfortable feeling they weren't telling him everything.

"It is enough," said one of the men. "We have calculated very precisely, constructed very carefully. So long as containment is maintained, all will be well. We will all have the electricity we need. The power will flow, and you will be quite safe."

There it was again, the language barrier. Did the northerner mean *quite* safe or completely safe? His blue eyes were impossible to read as he looked at Adage.

"The machinery must be maintained, yes?" the northerner continued. "The pressures will increase over time. There will be periods of calm and periods of convulsion. There will be minor surges all through the cycle, then a long dormancy before the Event. The exponential peak of the energy cycle every three hundred and seventeen years. This is how it works. You must ensure the machine holds even as it extracts the energy. As it contains the frozen explosion."

"We will make sure," said Adage.

"And contains it forever," said the woman, the note of warning clear even in her foreign accent. "Not for a few years or decades. *Forever.* An agglomeration of seismium this big. If containment was lost at the wrong moment…"

"Yes, yes," said Adage. "We understand. We will build the machine ever bigger and more powerful to hold the particle. You'll get your flow of electricity, have no fear."

"Very well." The satisfied look on her face troubled him for reasons he couldn't quite put his finger on. They *should* all be satisfied. It had taken them decades to get to this point. They should be celebrating. Everything was in place. Still, it gnawed at him.

"Well," said Adage. "I will leave you in peace. You will be returning home to No soon?"

The man who had spoken glanced up at the particle and then back at Adage. "Oh yes, we will be leaving very soon. The sooner the better, in fact."

Back outside in the chill of the wind, Adage stopped for a moment to collect his thoughts. He tried to push his lingering suspicions about the Lords of the High Ice to the back of his mind. This had all been sorted out years ago. The meetings and plots and pacts. Now all they had to do was wait. Wait and make sure the secrets were passed down the line of Directors in readiness.

And make sure, also, the secrets remained secrets until that day. By the doorway, a plaque had been bolted onto the stone of the wall, bearing the name of the building. *Seismium Containment Engine*. There were signs like it all around the machine, but this one suddenly seemed far too obvious. It was rare to see a master of one of the Temple Guilds there in the Hub, but they couldn't be prevented going where they pleased. This was supposed to be their machine after all, built for their benefit. It wouldn't do for one of them to start asking what this *containment engine* actually contained. They'd already had enough trouble. Machinery being attacked and wrecked by those who didn't understand it and were therefore afraid of it. It couldn't be allowed.

He turned to the three guards, standing in the chill wind. "You. I want this sign removed immediately. Then go around all the other entrances and remove the signs there, too. Understand?"

The guards nodded, looked to each other, then turned to examine the sign. It was a painted steel plaque, the letters embossed upon it and picked out in gold.

"We'll need tools," said one of the guards, his voice muffled by the adapted forge worker helmets they all wore.

"No time," said Adage. "It doesn't matter if you break the thing; I just want to see it removed. Immediately."

As well as their muskets, the guards carried steel staves with sharpened edges. They slid them behind the sign, attempting to lever it off the wall. They had to work together; the sign was well secured. They worked away for several minutes, buckling the sheet of metal before, with a ripping *clang*, sheering right through it. A section containing part of the name, some of the letters from *Containment*, hung loose. More minutes of twisting and flexing and the guards managed to work the fragment free.

"Good," said Adage. "Keep going."

He watched as they laboured to pull off more and more letters, ripping the metal sign to jagged shards. Despite the iron chill of the wind, Adage stood watching. In a few minutes there were only a few scraps of the original sign left.

"Wait," he instructed. "Stop there."

The guards stepped back, their chests heaving from their labours. Adage considered what was left behind. Four letters from *Engine. Eng n.*

It would do. Some sign was better than no sign. No sign at all might make the Temple masters suspicious. This, on the other hand, sounded plausible but didn't convey any of the dangerous meaning of the original. If someone were to ask questions, they could easily invent some story of what *Engn* might mean. An ancient spelling or an abbreviation. Some overcomplicated puzzle to dazzle and confuse them.

"Good," he said. "Talk to Master Dragus. We want new signs for all the entrances, each of them saying that. That and nothing more. Understood?"

Once again, the guards looked to each other, unsure, but none dared refuse. Adage wasn't their guildmaster, but Dragus, who was, would never dare ignore a direct instruction from Adage.

Satisfied, Adage turned and walked away.

Engn. Yes. He liked it.

Not far away, the newly installed steam-powered rail carriage stood waiting, sending billowing blooms of grey smoke up into the cold air. He turned and…

The sudden bang and flash of light made Finn, Diane and Whelm jump back from the seeing orb. A plume of grey smoke rose from the inner workings of the spindle reader. An acrid smell of burning filled the air, prickling Finn's nose and the back of his throat.

Diane reacted first. A can of water for the chickens stood by her on the floor. She picked it up and hurled it onto the smoking device. Seeing what she was doing, Whelm put his arm up to try and stop her, but it was too late. There was a crackle and fizz of electrical sparks, the sharp *crack* of glass breaking and then silence. The seeing orb went dark.

"What are you doing?" asked Whelm, the shock clear in his voice. "All the electrics will be ruined."

"It was on fire," said Diane. "It was going to burn the whole building down."

Whelm looked horrified. "It was just a bit of smoke. Now look at it. It'll never work again. The glass is cracked." He looked to Finn in exasperation, clearly expecting him to agree. Diane looked at Finn too, one eyebrow raised. They both waited for him to take their side.

Couldn't they see it wasn't important? The images they'd seen had made that obvious. That was the Hub, clearly enough. But something had gone wrong. Somewhere over the years, it had all gone wrong. The machinery had fallen into ruin, but it was still dangerous. Terribly dangerous. And Connor had seen that, understood that. He'd uncovered some surviving threat and he'd needed help to prevent it. He'd needed *their* help to complete the destruction. And he'd given Finn the spindle to explain everything.

"Finn?" said Diane. "Tell him. Tell him it's time he left. We're grateful for what he's done, but now it's time for him to move on."

Everything was a confused jumble in Finn's mind. Recent events in the valley. The visions in the orb. Like the old master in the moving images, he couldn't see how the parts connected. How they worked. But one thing was clear.

Finn looked at both of them. "No. Don't you see? It doesn't matter. Because we must go back. We have to go back to Engn."

XI

Finn sat in the nest of arching branches high up in his oak on Three Tree Hill. The oak he had climbed so often as a boy. It had always been the one place in the whole world purely *his*. No one else ever came here. For some reason he'd never even told Connor about it. He could still climb this wide, towering tree with his eyes shut, his limbs remembering the dance of movements required to reach each branch and fork. The words he had carved into the rugged flesh of the old bark were still there. His name. A series of dates, the earliest from when he was eight. No one else had ever added any.

He remembered the day, years ago, just after Shireen had been taken, he'd climbed up there to try and see over the mountain tops to Engn. He'd failed, of course, but he had seen Connor coming across the fields from the farm, killing crows with his catapult. Finn still recalled his alarm as Connor had started firing at *him*. His panicky escape across the branches of the three trees. Things were very different now. Finn longed to see Connor again, longed to see him wading through the high grass to stand underneath the tree and explain everything. Explain what Finn was supposed to do. Explain precisely the terrible secrets he'd unearthed in Engn.

They'd gone there to destroy it, and they had destroyed it, but clearly Connor had realized that wasn't enough. There was more to be done. This *particle* in the Hub was at the heart of it. Had that been destroyed? If not, it had to be. They had to make sure everything was annihilated, so completely it could never be rebuilt. That had to be Connor's message.

Finn sighed. Was that right? If only Connor was there to simply tell him. But his boyhood friend was dead. He survived only as a series of flickering, ghostly images in a glass orb. And now that, too, was broken. He had lost Connor forever. Everything had been left up to Finn. And Diane, if she could be persuaded.

It was still early in the morning. Light was beginning to fill the valley, colour washing over the sides of the mountains to bring the fields and houses back to life. Finn had crept from bed, leaving Diane still slumbering. He needed time to think. To make plans. He'd barely slept. He never did when they argued. He'd spent the night twisting and turning, knotting himself up in the bed sheets, anxiety a sharp lump of jagged metal in his stomach. There was only one thing they ever argued about. Engn. Connor. The memory spindle. It was all the same thing. They had done all they could already. She was weary of the whole thing. And, in truth, so was he. He had suffered enough in Engn to never want to go back. But he couldn't let it drop. Why couldn't she see?

They talked, sometimes, about having children. Not now, not any time soon. But one day. And because of that he understood why she wanted to stay in the valley, build their life there and not go chasing off across the plain again. But the thought of having children of his own just made him more determined to find out what was going on.

To make sure the pattern didn't repeat.

His father had once apologized to Finn for not trying to do what Finn had done. And if Finn didn't act now, he might end up saying the same thing himself one day. Apologizing to his own child as the ironclads came for them. He didn't want to bring up a family in a world where anything like that was possible. He wished, he really wished, he could put it all out of his mind, live his life with Diane, here among the people he'd grown up with, the people he loved. But he couldn't. He'd tried many times since coming home. Tried to lose himself in the daily routine, the simple things, but it wasn't going to work. Recent events made it clear. The earthquakes, the timing signals, Connor's mother, the encrypted messages, the ancient images on the memory spindle. He could see no alternative. They had to go back to the shattered ruins of Engn with work still to be done. Connor, even from beyond the grave, still needed them to do something. To complete the destruction they'd started.

And, somehow, he had to persuade Diane to come with him. Again.

And Whelm? Would the ex-master travel with them? He'd been there recently; he would be useful. But that wasn't going to make it any easier with Diane. He didn't see how he could ever persuade them both to come with him.

He rose to his feet in the crook of the curving branches, hoping to shake these troubling thoughts from his mind with activity. He hadn't climbed up there to mope. He'd come up to work something out. See what he needed to see.

The idea had occurred to him some time in the night, as he drifted in and out of confused nightmares. The ancient line-of-sight scope in Connor's mother's room had to be another piece of the puzzle. If it was possible she was able to use it without the messages passing through the normal network; it might help explain Connor's ascent to his position as apprentice Director. Perhaps she'd been secretly conversing with Engn all along. With people in power there. She had family ties to the old guilds, perhaps there'd been people at Engn who still listened to her. And if that was the case, perhaps they were still there, and perhaps Finn could find answers of his own from them. Answers that might help persuade Diane.

He thought back, trying to place in his mind where her room had been in the farmhouse. He hadn't seen through her shuttered windows, so it was hard to be sure. He'd become so mazed in those endless, echoing rooms he'd lost track of which side of the house her room was in. But – he remembered now – the sunlight had been slanting through the blinds when he entered, barred shadows lining the floor. Which meant her room had faced east. The 'scope had been pointing upwards and to the left, so that would mean it was facing perhaps northeast.

The farm buildings sat in a little dell; he could just make out the very top of them from his vantage position. With his outstretched finger he tried to trace the line of where the 'scope might be pointing. Up out of the dell, between those two stands of trees, directly over the rolling fields, across the lane and up into the woods and … there.

He pointed at a patch of trees on the steep slopes of the valley sides. A part of the forest he knew well enough, a place where large mossy boulders littered the floor, as if strewn there by giants. The trees seemed to grow directly out of them, their roots writhing across the stone in search of soil. A strange place. Why would a 'scope point there?

He shinned down the tree, unravelling the movements of his ascent and dropping the last five feet to *clump* to the ground. He moved at a half jog up to the tree line. Beneath the boughs it was still night. He could see only a few yards. He moved inside, weaving between the trees, his feet following the lines of the woodland pathways his eyes couldn't see.

Fifteen minutes later, breathing heavily, his side hurting

sharply, he sat upon one of the tallest rocks and gazed out over the world. There was a clear gap in the canopy there, where the scatter of too many rocks prevented the trees from growing. A wispy mist lifted off the canopy as if burning with a cold fire. He could see right across the valley, between the two distant stands of trees and directly to the upper story of the farmhouse. The windows in the rooms up there glinted as the rising sun caught them. There could be no doubt; this was where the 'scope had been pointing.

Skidding down the rock, he searched around in the undergrowth. But that made no sense. A mirror down there would get quickly overgrown. It had to be high up, on one of the tall boulders. He climbed each one, looking for anything out of the ordinary. Some were close enough for him to leap between, but with most he had to jump down to climb from ground level. He and Connor had done just that often enough, yet they'd never spotted anything. Perhaps there was nothing there, and the whole thing was another of Connor's mother's delusions.

Fifteen minutes later, just as he was about to give up and get back home, he found it. A mirror, concealed in a hollow carved out of the face of one of the tallest rocks. It was too high to reach from the ground, but by holding on to the top of the rock with one hand and feeling around with his other, stretching as far down the vertical face as he dared, he'd found it. The smooth surface could only be a mirror. It felt solid, like it had been cemented in. How long had it been there? And how often had he passed by it without knowing?

Holding onto the rock with just his fingers he leaned down to try and get a better look at the mirror. He needed to follow its angle, see where it pointed. He found a narrow foothold, little more than a diagonal crack in the face of the rock and swung his foot around into it. If he kept his foot sideways to the rock, he could just about support himself. He crouched down, balancing precariously by his toehold in the fissure, and leaned towards the mirror. At that moment, dim lights flickered in it. He pulled his hand away sharply, not wanting anyone to know he was there, interrupting the message. Was this a line-of-sight being sent directly to Engn? He crouched there, his right leg cramping from the strain of supporting him while he tried to read the pattern of flashes.

He got nothing. Probably it was encrypted. The light was also, for some reason, red, while normal line-of-sight light was white. The lenses in the 'scope in her room had been red, too, hadn't they? The tiny detail came back to him now. That had to be something to do with how this worked. Perhaps, somewhere, messages for this secret network were kept isolated from normal one by filters and prisms splitting off the red light. That could work if there were enough repeater stations to keep the signal amplified. Or perhaps they'd simply used red light in the old days.

When the message stopped, he leaned forwards again, trying to get his face as close to the mirror as he could. His leg and arms were shaking with the effort as he held himself there, looking at the slant of the small sheet of silvered glass, trying to gauge with his eyes where it would bounce messages to. *There.* Not back down the valley as he'd supposed, but directly back across to the far slopes. And much higher up, too, at the snow line capping the high hills from early autumn to late spring.

He held himself for a moment, puzzled. Was that what they did? Bounced the messages to and fro, higher and higher and then *over* the mountains to cross the plain? He'd never heard of anyone even climbing the high peaks. Nothing lived up there unless it was an occasional swan, flying impossibly high in the thin air, a distant white X in the sky. Was this the original line-of-sight route perhaps, built before the one they now all used?

He crouched there pondering for too long. His shaking foot suddenly slipped from the thin crevice and he was sliding down the face of the boulder, scraping skin off his hands and knees and cheek. He crashed into the ground, landing heavily on his shoulder, rolling over into a clump of ferns and nettles.

Groaning, he worked his way back to his feet. Both his hands bled, flecks of grit under flaps of separated skin. He'd have to get to the river, wash out his wounds. He peered upwards at the rock for a moment, then across the valley to the distant slopes. He had only a rough idea where the next mirror would be.

It took him five hours to find it. High up in the woods across the valley, the carpets of pine needles gave way to little cliffs of stone that were the start of the sheer rock faces of the true peaks. His breathing was laboured, painful in his chest as he worked his way up the slope. But he found the second mirror wedged into place in a sconce in the rocks, angled to receive the messages from the first mirror and relay them back across the valley once again. Across the valley and up. It was aimed at a notch in the distant line of peaks. There had to be another mirror up there. A mirror or a lens or maybe even a repeater station, angling the message back down and across the great grass plain to Engn, catching the light of the sun and using it to transmit the faint message stronger and brighter. From there the signal would find stations marching across the plains, its red light marking it out, keeping it separate. As he sat there, another message flickered in the glass. Outbound or inbound? It was impossible to tell. Was it Connor's mother talking to Engn? And if so, was anyone listening? Or was this a reply? A message from the machine coming in for her?

He didn't need to attempt those unreachable slopes. He'd seen enough. If he couldn't get answers from Connor, he could at least get answers from his mother. She, clearly, knew much more than she'd said. If he confronted her with what he'd learned about the red line-of-sight network, she'd have to tell him. He would go back there now. Demand answers.

He weaved his way between the reaching boughs of the trees, sliding sometimes in a mini avalanche of pine needles. He jumped over a chortling brook, realizing as he did so that it was the same one that he and Connor had often tried, uselessly, to dam.

As the ground levelled out, he reached the edge of the trees. He crossed the narrow gap to cultivation and climbed over the hedgerow marking the start of the fields. Once he wouldn't have dared trespass like that, but there was no one to chase him away now. No one worked the farm and people grazed their own animals without anyone stopping them. A few wary cows were there, watching him mournfully while continuing to chew.

He was in sight of the farmhouse when his legs wobbled beneath him. At first, he thought he'd run too much, or he'd injured himself in the fall. But there was no pain. He stopped, puzzled. The wobbling became a lurching and then a shaking. It was only then he understood what was happening. An earthquake. Another earthquake. The ground bucked and threw him to the grassy ground. The impact caused him to bite his tongue with one of his remaining teeth, filling his mouth with the taste of blood.

Cracking booms echoed from the woods behind him, the trees splintering as the shaking ground snapped them into pieces. The ground beneath him tossed him again and again into the air. He could see the field heaving in waves like a slow sea. More trees fell, crashing to the ground with a roar and an explosion of splintered branches.

From somewhere distant, up the valley or down the valley, he heard high-pitched screams. Screams of raw terror. He scrambled to his feet and staggered forwards. Again and again he was thrown aside, hurled to the ground. He headed for the farmhouse, although he knew it would be madness to go inside the old building. The reassuring, solid bulk of the stone walls pulled him in. Again, he was thrown to the ground, and he felt the earth beneath him subsiding, slipping away as if the ground had been hollow all along. The field was being sucked into a cavern. A crack was opening in the ground, wider and wider, tufts of grass and sods of earth tilting over and falling in. It was like the day Engn collapsed and they'd raced from the walls before it swallowed them. Finn tried run, lurching forwards as quickly as he could.

He was nearly at the farmhouse when the sound of thunder boomed around him. He stopped, confused, unable to work out where it had come from. The sky about him was cloudless, although a mist of dust filled the air.

Then, looking ahead, he saw what it was. The old farmhouse, Connor's farmhouse, was collapsing. The walls buckled and shattered, the upper floors crashing down to the ground with a rattling boom, throwing a great bloom of dust across the ground towards Finn. He threw himself down, covering his head with his arms and lay there, tasting grit, while debris rained down on him. He didn't know whether he'd be crushed by the falling walls or swallowed up by the ground. He lay where he was and waited for it all to stop.

Finally, after long, long minutes, a great stunned silence swept through the valley. The earth lay beneath him, solid again, as if exhausted from its exertions. Finn pushed himself to his feet, a thick layer of dust sloughing off him as he stood. He spat out dirt and tried to see through the blooms of dust filling the air what had happened to the farmhouse.

He soon saw. Where the old building had stood only minutes before there was now a miniature mountain range of rubble.

He ran to the ruined building and pulled on the nearest boulders, hoping to find some way in. It was no use. The jagged lumps of stone were far too large for him to budge. In any case, there was nothing to unearth but more rubble. If he wanted to find Connor's mother, he had to get to the top of the pile and burrow down from there. He climbed his way up the dusty, shifting pile of stone, again and again putting his foot through into some cavity within the pile. Here and there, blades of glass protruded from the wreckage, threatening to slice his feet open. Once the stones he was standing on collapsed inwards completely and he thought he was going to fall right down to ground level. Bare rafters, like the exposed ribs of some giant creature, caught him. He shouted into the dark interior, calling for Connor's mother, for anyone, but no one replied. Coughing with the dust, he called again and again.

Finally, he worked his way into the middle of the mountain, thinking perhaps some of the building might have survived. He pushed aside roof tiles and stones, sending them tumbling and crashing down to the ground. After half an hour, he'd worked his way down little more than a foot. Instead of the room he'd hoped to reach, he'd exposed only more stone. He stopped and stood there, panting heavily. The truth he'd been trying to ignore hit him. No one could have survived. Connor's mother wasn't down there waiting to be rescued. The collapsing building had crushed her as it had crushed everything.

From nowhere it occurred to him where he'd seen the face of Master Adage before. Not in Engn. The painting over Connor's mother's bed. The features were the same, and the gold chain with the clock. The meaning was clear. Adage was some ancient forebear of Connor's mother. And, therefore, of Connor.

"Finn."

He looked down through the plumes of dust still drifting in the air to see Diane. Grime coated her. His heart leapt with alarm as he saw she'd been cut on her forehead, the red gash clear even at this distance.

"Diane."

She ran forwards to the foot of the rubble. "Finn. We didn't know where you were. We've been looking for you everywhere. Finn, I'm … I'm sorry. You have to come."

Something had happened. He could see from her manner. He waded his way back down the shifting mountain of stone.

"What is it?" he called. "Is it the machine? Did the earthquake crush it?"

"The machine?"

"The spindle reader."

"No, no. Not that. But it was a bigger quake, Finn. More buildings have collapsed."

He half fell back down to ground level and staggered up to her. He could see she'd been crying now, the grime on her cheeks smeared. He put his arms around her and held her for a moment. Her body shook in his arms. Then he held her at arms' length.

"Which houses, Diane?"

"Finn, I'm sorry. Your father's workshop. It collapsed. We're trying to get him out now. Finn, you have to come."

XII

They spent most of the night pulling away the rubble of the ruined workshop. Once again, people came from miles around to help. Even Mrs. Megrim hobbled up to perch on a rock. She watched their progress in silence, a grim look on her face. Finn's mother did what she could, helping to roll away some of the smaller stones before retiring to sit with Mrs. Megrim.

When darkness fell, the people of the valley lit torches and carried on working. The smoke from the flames, the cries from the rescuers, all put Finn in mind of the day of the avalanche, when the whole village had come looking for him and Connor. Now it was the other way around: Finn desperately searching for his father.

Most of the time, he was too out of breath to talk, but every now and then he stopped to rest screaming limbs and exchange a few words with Diane. Neither talked about Engn and Finn's insistence they had to return. They had other matters on their mind.

"I have to go back home," said Diane at one point, a

simple statement of fact. "Find out what's happened there."

"I'll come with you."

She wiped the dirt from her face and looked around. "I think you're going to be needed here for a while, Finn."

She was right. Still, he didn't like the thought of her setting off alone. He returned to picking up stones and lugging them away from the ruins, slowly exposing what remained of the workshop.

Every half hour, Flane blew a whistle and they all stopped where they were. Listening intently, they called into the ruins, hoping to hear a response. For long hours they heard nothing and, each time no one saying anything, they returned to work. Then, around midnight, they finally got a muffled reply, faint but clear.

The forge had saved him, its stone bulk holding off the roof timbers and falling walls, creating a space for him to lie in. It was fortunate the forge wasn't running to consume all the air. He emerged, grimy and bleeding, like a part of the rubble coming to life. His left leg had been trapped under a fallen spar, and, unable to walk, he had to be carried away from the ruined workshop. They bore him down the lane to the Moot Hall, Finn's mother clutching his hand as they moved him. He nodded his head as they went, telling them over and over he was okay, he was okay, no need to fuss.

The six of them set up house again in a corner of the hall: Finn, Diane, Shireen, Nathaniel, and Finn's mother, all sitting around his father. Badger lay on the floor nearby, watching them with one eye. Finn's mother wiped grime from his father's face and gave him water to sip. His father grimaced whenever he tried to move his leg, but he was otherwise unharmed. The Moot Hall filled as once more the inhabitants of the valley took shelter, took comfort in each other's presence. They'd been fortunate; apart from Connor's mother, Finn's father was the worst casualty. There was no sign of Whelm, but he'd been there at the rescue. He was probably sleeping in his cart somewhere.

As Finn smiled along with his family's murmured recollections and jokes, he wondered if he could really do what he was about to do. They did need him more than ever. Many more houses would need to be rebuilt. But he couldn't ignore the possibility the earthquakes were something to do with Engn. The idea niggled at him. Connor had left him instructions, made it clear there was more to do. Maybe the tremors were Finn's fault for not acting sooner.

He hated to leave, not just his immediate family, but all of them. Mrs. Megrim, Flane, everyone. He belonged among them. But he couldn't settle, not yet.

It was fully dark when a lull in the conversation gave Finn his chance to speak. "Diane and I have decided to go to her village." Diane looked up in surprise at his decision to accompany her, but then she nodded in understanding. "The line-of-sight network is in pieces again and this was a much bigger quake. We must find out what is happening down there. If you can spare me."

Finn's father studied him from his bed. "And are you going anywhere else afterwards?"

Finn didn't reply for a moment. The darkness seemed to deepen about him as they waited for him to reply. He spoke in a whisper against the background murmur of voices in the hall. "Afterwards … afterwards I'm going back to Engn. To see if it is being rebuilt. To see if these earthquakes are connected in some way."

He glanced at Diane. She was staring at the floor and didn't look up. No one replied for a moment. Finn had the clear impression they'd all expected something like this. They had few secrets from each other.

"That master is leaving too, I heard," said Shireen. "Going all the way back to Engn to pick up more broken machinery. You'll be travelling with him, will you?" Her expression was hard to make out in the gloom.

"We'll travel together to Diane's village," said Finn.

"After that we'll see. Whelm can do what he likes."

"Once you watched me leaving the valley, riding off with a master," said Shireen. "Now it will be the other way around."

"It's hardly the same thing," said Finn. "No one is making me go. Whelm isn't a master. He's just a man. He's no threat to anyone."

Shireen didn't reply.

"While I'm away you could find that old glade in the woods and sit there and think of me," said Finn. It was a poor attempt at humour.

"I might just do that," said Shireen. "I might just have to do that." Unexpectedly, she reached out to stroke his face, like she used to when they were children.

"Finn." His father's grey beard wagged as he spoke. "We can't stop you going, I know, but we won't be able to come and rescue you this time. You understand that, don't you? Your mother can't travel much anymore. And I don't think I'm going to be running about any time soon with this leg."

Finn squeezed his father's hand and took his mother's in his other. "No, I know. You both need to stay here and look after yourselves. And I don't want to leave you, not now especially, but I think this is something I have to do."

"And we can't say anything to stop you?" his mother asked.

Finn shook his head.

"Then I can only sit uselessly and watch you leave. And tell you to look after yourself like I did last time, as if it will make any difference."

"I came back then, didn't I?"

"You did," she said. "Just about, you did." She didn't sound at all reassured.

They sat together for another hour, exchanging words, sharing the silences. Finn didn't want the time together to end, but they were all exhausted. As they rose to sort out bedding, Nathaniel stepped over to talk to Finn alone. He looked troubled.

"You're sure about this, Finn?"

"I am."

"You weren't completely right, you know."

"About what?"

"About the Directory. About the delusions I was under when I lived in Engn."

"What do you mean?"

"Oh, I know I was wrong," said Nathaniel. "It's embarrassing now to think back. Obviously, it was madness to deny the outside world exists. I mean, here we are. Still, there was sanity in it, too. A sort of sanity. Not in denying it, perhaps, but in choosing to ignore it. Or seeing only the small, nearby things. The things you can deal with. I know there is a great, wide world outside the valley but still, I don't want to go there. I can stay here and be content. Live my life here. I think … I think sometimes there's a lot to be said for having delusions. If they bring peace of mind."

"Perhaps you're right," said Finn. "And I'm glad you've found peace of mind here with us, Nathaniel. I really am. I envy you. But I need to do this for my own peace of mind. Does that make sense?"

Nathaniel sighed. "I suppose. Just make sure you do come back. Nothing will be the same with the two of you gone."

Finn tried to smile reassurance back at Nathaniel, but his face, dried out from the dust of the digging perhaps, didn't want to form the expression properly. "I will. And look after Shireen, won't you? Look after all of them."

"I will."

The following morning, Finn, Diane, and Whelm prepared

to set off down the valley. Their horses huffed out plumes of steam in the early morning air. Most of the village had come to see them off, although there was no sign of Mrs. Megrim. It took the best part of an hour to get ready and say their goodbyes. His father was up and about, hobbling around to help pack everything up, refusing all offers of assistance. Shireen held onto Badger. Few words were spoken; everything had already been said.

Finally, they were ready. Finn squeezed his parents tight one more time. His mother gave him a bag of honey sweets for the journey. It was clear from her eyes she'd been crying. Finn climbed onto his horse and Diane onto hers. All too soon, they were away. Whelm's horse towed the metal cart, trundling and squeaking along behind them. In the cart were all his worldly belongings, along with the lifeless remains of the spindle reader. Badger tried to follow them and whined when she could not. As they swayed forwards, Finn looked back repeatedly, waving until a curve of the lane took his family from him once again.

They plodded along in complete silence. Diane had always tried to ignore Whelm, and now her worry for her own family consumed her. Whelm, for his part, remained silent as well, keeping his thoughts to himself. Finn tried to talk to the two of them, make plans and arrangements for the days to come, but they only nodded and said nothing. He soon gave up. An early morning mist threaded through the valley. Finn's thoughts strayed to another day when he'd left the valley on horseback. The taste of honey sweets filled his mouth, although he hadn't eaten any of them yet.

As he knew she would be, Mrs. Megrim waited for them at her cottage gate. She leaned on her stick as they approached.

"Sneaking off without saying a goodbye, eh, lad?"

"I wouldn't dream of it, Mrs. Megrim."

They stopped. Finn dismounted while Diane waited

astride her own horse, eager to be making progress. Whelm, wisely, stayed out of Mrs. Megrim's way, pretending to tighten straps and check the axles on his cart.

"Hardly worth saying goodbye, anyway, is it?" said Mrs. Megrim. "You'll be back in a week or two."

The look in her eye made it very clear she knew he wouldn't be. She, like everyone else, had worked it out. Perhaps she was the one who'd told everyone.

"I'll be back as soon as I can," said Finn.

Mrs. Megrim *hmphed.* "Think you're so clever, don't you, boy? Going off to save the world again."

"Diane's family is all that matters. Making sure they're safe."

"Of course, but what then? You'll be heading off with your new friend, will you? Him skulking behind his horse for fear I'll knock his head off with this stick." She spoke these last words deliberately loud so Whelm would hear.

"He's not my friend," said Finn. "I know what he is. What he was. He's been helping us, nothing more. We're traveling together for a time."

She spoke in hushed tones once more. "Traveling all the way to the Engine you mean." She was painfully thin now, the contours of her skull visible beneath her drawn skin. There was no point lying to her. She always knew everything.

"I have to," said Finn. "The timing messages. Everything Connor's mother said. The earthquakes. I have to be sure."

"Connor's mother was crazy; you can't believe anything she said. It's sad she's gone, but it doesn't change the truth."

"So, you think I'm wrong to go? I thought you at least would understand."

"I understand you're going to get yourself killed. It was a miracle you survived last time."

Finn shrugged. "If I stay here, I could get killed. Any of

us could at any moment. The last week has shown us that."

"You're a lot more likely to get killed if you go back there, aren't you?"

"So, the timing messages, you're not worried about them? You don't want to know where they're coming from? Who's sending them? You don't want to know who Connor's mother has been communicating with all this time?"

Mrs. Megrim snorted. "If she's been talking to anyone. I've checked with all the people I could reach about these red line-of-sight messages. You know Henri?"

"She's one of the Switch House operators, downriver."

"Lives at the foot of the valley, not too far from Diane's, where the two lines arrive across the plain. Half the messages come north up this way; the other half are switched south to the villages down there. I've known her for donkey's years, although we've never met. But if people think *I* know everything, they should speak to her; she sees the world clearly, always knows what's going on, understands people's problems before they do. And she's never heard of these red messages, either. Connor's mother had probably been imagining voices in the static for years."

"Perhaps. Perhaps not. But I have to go and find out what Connor wanted me to do."

Mrs. Megrim studied him for a moment, then sighed. "There's no stopping you, I can see. But of course, you've never listened to me, have you, boy? Just you make sure you know who your friends are." She glanced over at Whelm again. "And who they *aren't*, you hear me?"

She reached out and clutched him. Her hand was all bones and sinews. Finn felt the scrap of paper she concealed. The scrap she passed to him. "This might help you with the wreckers," she whispered. Then, out loud, "Just make sure you come home safe, understood? Once the network's running again, I'll be telling you every day.

Wherever you are in the world."

"I'll look forwards to reading your messages," said Finn, not glancing at the piece of paper. What was it? Another encryption key? Clearly, she didn't want Whelm to know anything about it. He would study it when it was safe to do so.

"And Finn, if you should happen to end up near those mines you mentioned. Where Tom was, I mean. I don't suppose there'll be any flowers growing there or anything as useless as that. But perhaps you could stop and say something. Or just think about him for a moment. It won't change anything, but it would help. It would be good to know he'd been remembered."

Finn nodded. "I will. If I can, I will. I promise."

"Good. Thank you, boy."

"Now we'd really better go," said Finn. "The sooner we leave the sooner we can get to Diane's."

"Off you go then."

Mrs. Megrim turned and tottered her way back to her gatepost.

Finn hauled himself back onto his horse. He didn't ride much; it already felt like he had a nice collection of bruises forming. Still, it was better than being inside a moving engine. He glanced at Diane, who smiled a weak smile. Soon, Mrs. Megrim was a stationary sliver of black in the distance behind them.

XIII

They had to detour around the trees that had crashed to the ground as they made their way down the valley. On more than one occasion they were forced to manhandle Whelm's cart through the mud. The line-of-sight was dark at each house and hamlet they came to, but they saw few collapsed buildings. Some communities had escaped the quake unscathed, and Diane's spirits rose. She and Finn chatted as they swayed their way southwards, although neither talked about what they would find in her village. Nor about where they would go afterwards.

People regarded Whelm with open hostility when they saw him. Each night when they stopped, Whelm took himself off to sleep in his moving engine, away from everyone else. More than once Finn tried to get him to stay but Whelm only shook his head and disappeared into the darkness for the night.

Finn and Diane, meanwhile, would sit near a communal fire or in someone's home and share what stories they'd heard. With the line-of-sight network not functioning people were desperate for news of friends and family. Finn and Diane accumulated more and more messages to pass on: questions about family members or reassurances someone had survived. When he manned the Switch House, Finn always felt like a spider at the centre of its web, but now all the messages were loose threads flapping around, connections broken. He and Diane gathered up as many as they could and tied them up as they went.

"Why do you never stay in the villages we come to?" he asked Whelm one day, as they skirted the woods. No trees had fallen there, and no collapsed buildings were in sight, making it possible to believe the earthquakes had never happened. Diane was in the lead, twenty or thirty yards ahead.

Whelm shrugged. "I learned long ago I wasn't welcome. People want to buy what I sell, but that doesn't mean they're glad to see me."

"People have more important things to worry about than everything that happened back then."

"Perhaps. I'm still not going to risk it. It's best I stay out of everyone's way, especially in places I visited when I was a master. People don't forget."

"You came into our village when the first earthquake struck."

Whelm didn't reply for a moment. He looked uncomfortable. "I wasn't sure if anyone would even have survived. And I didn't want to be on my own, I suppose. Out in the wilds it was pretty alarming when the quake started."

For some reason Finn had the impression Whelm wasn't telling him everything. That he'd made the explanation up. Perhaps Whelm had simply learned to be wary of giving people the truth.

"Do you think you'll be able to get the memory reader working again? Once you get the parts in Engn?"

"Maybe," said Whelm after a moment's thought. "It's

pretty wrecked. Depends what I can scavenge. But I thought you were coming as well?"

"I don't know," said Finn. "We'll see what we find at Diane's village."

"And what will Diane do if you do go?"

"I don't know that, either."

"Haven't you asked her? That's how it's supposed to work."

"There hasn't been the right moment yet."

"She doesn't think you should go, does she?"

Finn didn't reply. Whatever they found at Diane's village, he hoped to set off across the plain for Engn at some point, and he had no idea what Diane would do. Come with him? Wait for him? Or, perhaps, insist he choose between her and Engn.

They rode along in silence after that, Whelm occasionally flicking at the flies gathering around them.

"Those old images we saw in the orb," said Finn, eventually. "Those *Lords of the High Ice*. Did you ever meet any of them?"

"Me? No. Never saw anyone like that. As far as I know they died out years ago. Centuries ago."

"What do you know about them?"

"Not much. They told us some history when we became masters. They were great engineers; they basically built the original machinery at the heart of Engn. That place we saw."

"I thought the masters built it. The twelve guilds."

"Oh, they did, but it was the Lords of the High Ice who showed them how. Gave them the knowledge to construct on such a scale. Drew up the blueprints. So we were told."

"How do you know they're not there anymore? In the far north?"

Whelm shook his head, something like the old, mocking Master Whelm reappearing for a moment. "I think we'd know if they were. I've never seen any messages from the mysterious frozen wastes."

"Perhaps you weren't allowed to read them," said Finn.

"Perhaps."

"Did you ever see those power cables? Heading north from the Hub?"

"No, there's nothing like that."

"Then perhaps they're underground now. Out of sight."

Whelm sighed. "More secrets? You know, the simplest explanations are usually right, Finn. It's much more likely there is no one living in the far north anymore. That they died out years and years ago."

Finn didn't reply. Maybe Whelm was right and maybe he wasn't. Just because you couldn't communicate with a place didn't mean it wasn't there. Just because he couldn't talk to Mrs. Megrim didn't mean she wasn't alive. Or at least, he couldn't say for sure whether she was alive or not. It was true people believed in many things that weren't actually there: ghosts and gods and giants. And sometimes they didn't believe in things that clearly were there. Like Nathaniel in the Directory, insisting the outside world wasn't real. The problem was knowing which was which. Telling the difference between reality and fantasy.

These thoughts looping around in his head, Finn rode on in silence once more, and Whelm seemed content to do the same.

Finn and Diane stayed that night in a small hamlet of ten or twelve houses. Once again, Whelm couldn't be persuaded to join them. He rumbled off to sleep in the woods, out of sight of the lane.

The houses of the hamlet clung to the bank of the river, each standing upon thick wooden stilts, so their ground floors were roughly at eye-level. Such buildings were common enough down the Silverburn, allowing people to live and work on the river while protecting them from floods. The design also, Finn now saw, made the houses earthquake-proof. The wooden stays would sway rather than snap when the tremors struck. None of the houses had been damaged and life was going on as normal. Still, the inhabitants were eager for word of the outside world. They gladly offered Finn and Diane food and shelter in return for news.

"Have you heard anything from downriver?" Diane asked as they sat with a group of villagers on a wooden platform built over the water. A crackling, smoky fire set upon a ring of stones kept the midges away.

"Only one boat has passed upstream since the second quake," an old man said. "They'd seen some damage along the banks, but nothing terrible. A roof down here, trees across the lane there. So far as we know, your village has escaped unscathed."

The words raised Diane's spirits even more. That night she slept well, finally waking long after it was light. Knowing how exhausted she was, Finn didn't wake her. He spent the time realigning the lenses flashing messages up and down the valley. There was no traffic from the south, but word came through from home. All was well, his father was recovering. The news filled Finn with hope, too. It was a bright, sunny morning. Everything was going as well as he could have hoped for. Perhaps after a few days at Diane's village, she could be persuaded to join him on the crossing to Engn before they made their way back home.

Whelm wasn't waiting for them on the lane when they returned to it. "Perhaps he's gone on without us," said Diane. "Got sick of waiting and left." She didn't sound displeased at the idea. But there was no sign of wheels in the dust of the lane, other than those of the night before. Whelm had wheeled his cart into the woods but hadn't come out again.

"Perhaps he's slept in, too," said Finn. It seemed unlikely. Whelm was usually the first up.

In a small clearing, out of sight of the lane, they found him. He was bound to a tree, bruised and bleeding, head slumped forwards. The cart stood some way off, Whelm's horse tethered to it, patiently waiting. The grass all around Whelm was trampled as if by many feet. The ex-master wasn't moving. But when Finn and Diane rushed up to him, he lifted his cut and swollen face to look at them.

"What's happened?" Diane asked. "Who did this?"

Whelm's voice was rough and slurred. "Travelers on the road. A rabble from the wreckage."

"But why?"

"You know why. It happens."

Finn worked at the ropes lashing Whelm to the tree. "They left you here to die?"

"I think they planned to come back tonight for another go. And to take all my stuff."

Finn caught Whelm's eye as he worked. The ex-master looked away, ashamed.

"I'm sorry," said Finn. "We should have stayed with you."

"It's not your fault."

"Actually, it is. In a way."

Whelm looked puzzled. "Why do you say that?"

Finn unravelled the blood-stained ropes. "You haven't worked it out?"

"Worked what out?"

Diane cast a worried look at Finn. But Whelm would have to know the truth sooner or later.

"That we destroyed Engn," said Finn. "Diane and Connor and me. Isn't it obvious? We're to blame for you not being a master anymore. I don't regret it, not at all, but still I'm sorry for what's happened to you."

Whelm stood on shaky legs. "Don't be ridiculous, Finn. Of course you didn't. It blew up by itself. The machine went wrong. Everyone knows that."

"No. It was us. Truly. You saw the images on the spindle. That was the control room. Between us, we set off the explosions from there. That was why I was in the Directory."

Whelm looked from Finn to Diane. His expression was hard to read through his broken features. "Is this true?"

Diane looked like she was going to deny it. Then she relented. "It is."

Whelm staggered towards his horse and cart. Finn reached out to lend him a hand but Whelm swept his hand away. "Just get away from me, Finn."

"Whelm, come on. I told you what I planned when you took me there. We had to do it."

"No!" Whelm's face was livid when he turned to face them. "No, you didn't have to. Do you have any idea what you did? You ruined everything. I was only a low master, but at least I was somebody. People did what I told them. Now they punch me and kick me. And they laugh as they're doing it. Look at me! Now the whole world's falling apart. And you're to blame. You know, Finn, I felt bad about what I did to you. I felt guilty. But you've already got your revenge, haven't you? You've paid me back a thousand times over. I should never have come to find you."

"Whelm, I…"

"Just go away, Finn. I don't want to hear it. You can find your own way to Engn. Thanks for releasing me, but now it's time to say goodbye."

"You're injured," said Diane. "You're in no state to travel. And it's safer in a group."

But Whelm was already tightening the harnesses on his horse, grabbing his belongings where his attackers had scattered them. Rage was clear in every motion. "I managed perfectly well before," he said over his shoulder.

He climbed onto the moving engine and, with an angry lash of his reins, urged his brown horse forwards. The cart lurched around in a wide circle to head out of the woods. Whelm wiped the blood from his face with an oily rag. He didn't look at Finn or Diane.

"Whelm!" Finn shouted.

"Let him go," said Diane. "He was never going to stay

with us once he found out."

The ex-master didn't stop as he trundled away. The squealing of his wheels faded as he headed down the valley to find a path of his own across the plain. It was several hours before it occurred to Finn that he had taken the remains of the spindle reader with him.

XIV

Diane and Finn rode together all that day, and the next. Diane, at least, seemed happier now Whelm was gone. They came across very little destruction, and she talked excitedly about seeing her family again. Despite all his gloom about losing Whelm and the reader, Finn had to smile at the sight of her. It was good to see her laughing again as she recounted tales from her girlhood. He'd visited her home several times and always received a warm welcome. He couldn't help wondering about Whelm, though. Would the ex-master be pursued? Would they ever see him again? If not, how was Finn ever going to assemble another spindle reader? Perhaps he couldn't. Some of his hope from the day before ebbed away.

The light was fading to grey when they rounded the foot of a round hill and saw fires blazing in the distance. They looked welcoming, but the sight of them stopped Diane mid-sentence as she recounted another of her tales. The shock on her face was alarming to see.

"What is it?" he asked.

"Those fires are coming from my home," she said. "I know what they are. Finn, there are funeral pyres burning."

A day later, Finn sat with Diane on top of a hill overlooking the remains of her village. It was a height she had scaled often as a girl. A place to sit and think, above the world, separate from it. A place for perspective, something like his tree. Maybe she'd been up there once, looking down, while he'd been up the oak on Three Tree Hill, the two of them enjoying their separation from the world without knowing about each other. Now they were together, arm in arm on the springy grass, the wind tousling their hair, blowing the cries of birds at them. Below them, the place that had once been her village lay in ruins, as if some giant had come along and trampled it to pieces.

Diane sat with her head resting on his shoulder, both of them lost in their thoughts. The pyres were still burning down below. One for each person lost, including the one for Diane's mother and the one for Diane's father.

The plumes of smoke from the fires rose vertically into the evening sky. Thirty or forty feet up, the breeze catching them, the grey columns merged into a single cloud. The sight pleased him, as if the smoke were their souls reuniting. Some said the sparks from the pyres were people's spirits spiralling upwards to join the stars. He knew that wasn't true, but still it was a comfort. Sometimes you told yourself things like that to try and make some sense of what was happening. They were stories, nothing more, but stories could make you feel better even if you knew they were just stories.

"Do you think it's true?" said Diane, breaking the silence. "What Connor's mother said about the earthquakes? How we caused them by destroying Engn?"

"I don't see how," said Finn. "Her mind was tangled up in itself."

"But you're still going to go, aren't you?"

There was only one answer he could give. "I am. I think there's something that still needs to be done, I really do." He kissed her on the top of her head. Her hair smelled of wood smoke. "But I don't want to leave you, especially not now, especially after all this."

She didn't speak for a moment. Then she slipped a thin knife from inside her boot. She handed it to him.

"Cut my hair."

"What?"

"Cut it. Long hair is useless in the wilds – it gets matted and tangled. It gets in the way when you fight. Cut it so it's how it used to be."

"Why?"

"Because I'm coming with you," she said.

That threw him. He desperately wanted her to come, but he hadn't been prepared for her wanting to. For some reason, the unexpected change of heart troubled him.

"But why? You've said often enough you don't ever want to go there again."

She didn't reply for a moment. At the foot of the hill, a single figure crept from one of the ruins towards the wide river. One of the few survivors.

"There's nowhere else to go, is there?" said Diane. "There's nothing here for me anymore. And if you're off to Engn, I don't want to head back up the valley alone."

"My whole family is there," said Finn. "They're your family now. My parents and Shireen and Nathaniel. Mrs. Megrim. All of them. You'd obviously be welcome there even without me."

Diane nodded. "I know. But I don't want you going alone. And I need to *do* something. If it is all starting up again, if those timing signals are from Engn, if the earthquakes are somehow caused by it, I want to make sure we destroy it properly this time. Destroy it for good. This thing with the spindle and the secret trail – I don't see it, to be honest. I think you're wrong, and I think you're a bit obsessed, my love. But we do need to make sure the machine is properly destroyed. And Connor's dead and Whelm's gone, so it's up to you and me, isn't it?"

Finn put his arm round her and held her tight. "I thought you were going to tell me to go and not come back. I thought I might not see you again after today."

"You really thought that?"

"I did."

She sighed and stared off into the distance. "If anyone from my family had survived, I would have wanted to stay, for a while at least. To help. But now everything is different. Now I'm coming with you."

"When do you want to leave?" asked Finn.

She considered for a moment. "In a day or two. I'd like to stay that long at least. Make sure I've done everything I can. Say goodbye to things. To people."

"Take as long as you need," said Finn. "When you're ready, we'll leave for Engn together."

"Okay."

When he'd finished slicing through her golden hair, the pool of it on the grass around her, they sat in silence together once more. The shattered world lay peaceful in the evening light.

XV

A valley between two mountains allowed access from Diane's village onto the great grass plain. A year previously, a wooden barricade had been erected by the villagers, a distance of nearly a mile. The plain was lawless and troubled, and the barricade had been an attempt to keep out marauding bands of looters. Looters and worse.

But now, after the quake, no one manned the wooden gates standing in the middle of the barricade. Diane and Finn lifted the heavy bar that kept the gates locked at night and pushed them wide. Beyond, the plain stretched into the hazy distance. In the wind from the mountains, the grass had become a sea, waves sweeping through it. The track leading to Engn cut through it in a straight line to the horizon.

They closed the gates behind them and stood for a moment. Taking the first step felt like crossing a line.

"Do we stick to the track?" said Finn. "Or cut across country?"

"The road will be quicker," replied Diane. "If we see

someone coming, we can always try and find somewhere to hide."

"And you're sure you want to do this?"

She glanced at him, then back to the road ahead. "I'm sure."

"Let's go then."

Climbing back onto their horses, they set off.

Around midday they neared the first of the relay towers. Finn watched it approaching, remembering doing the same from within the choking heat of the moving engine. It soon became clear the timing signals hadn't come that way. The tower was a ruin, canted over to one side like a giant caught in the act of striding drunkenly across the land. By the look of it, someone had tried to set fire to it, one of its four legs burned right through.

"Does this mean the signals couldn't have come from Engn after all?" Diane asked. She sounded hopeful.

"Not necessarily. They might have crossed the plain on another line, going to some other valley, and been routed up to us from there. Thanks to people like Mrs. Megrim, messages find their own way through the network."

Diane nodded but didn't reply.

They slept in a bowl-shaped dip in the ground just about deep enough to conceal the standing horses from anyone traveling on the road. Even so, they took turns to keep watch. Finn slept first and was roused by Diane in the depths of the night. They exchanged groggy smiles but no words. Huddling in his blanket for warmth, Finn sat and tried to stay awake, listening in the darkness for anyone approaching. Occasional rustling in the grass nearby sent alarm shooting through him, but he saw nothing, and nothing came near them.

Despite all his efforts, he must have slipped into a doze, because he awoke suddenly to the sound of shouts nearby. Shouts and cries of pain. It was already light, the sun detaching itself from the line of the mountains. He crawled to the lip of the dip and peered towards the road.

After a moment, Diane joined him.

A group of people, maybe twenty, stood on the road. They were outlandishly dressed, some like masters, some more like ironclads. But they were such a ragtag assortment, their clothes patched and tattered, that it was clear they weren't real masters or real ironclads. One or two wore tall, chimney-like hats, a style Finn had seen a few times in Engn. Others appeared to be an amalgam of master and ironclad, wearing both grey armour and black cloaks. At first it wasn't clear what they were doing standing in a huddle. Then the agonized yelps came again, and Finn saw they had someone surrounded. A man lay curled up on the ground, arms covering his head while the circle kicked and kicked at him.

"We can't just let them do this," Finn whispered. Perhaps these were the same people who had attacked Whelm.

Diane put a hand on his arm to stop Finn moving. "No. We'll only get ourselves attacked."

"But they'll kill him."

She nodded. "We can't stop them. We have to stay hidden."

After a few minutes, the cries of terror faded and stopped. The ring of ironclad masters parted to reveal their victim, now just an unmoving heap on the ground. One of the group, the leader perhaps, stood over the figure, laughing. The left side of his face was badly burned, the light from the rising sun lighting up livid red wounds. He shouted some order and the others began to rummage through the clothes and possessions of their victim, handing anything of interest to the leader. Once they'd picked the carcass clean, they rolled it to the side of the road.

The leader with the ruined face looked around, and Finn and Diane ducked down. Had they been seen? Diane's face was so close he could feel her breath tickling his nose. Not daring to move, they listened for sounds of the attackers approaching. He just had to hope the horses didn't whinny. There was a low conversation from the group, words Finn couldn't hear. Then they moved, armour clinking. For a moment Finn thought they were coming nearer, and his hand went to the knife he carried at his belt. Diane did the same. But then he heard someone in the group laughing. A few moments later, slightly farther away, the laugh came again. The group was heading away, up the road towards Engn.

Finn and Diane waited for the best part of an hour. Before they left, they checked on the man waylaid by the mob, but there was nothing they could do. He'd been kicked to death, his face purple and alarmingly bloated. They left him there and moved off, avoiding the track and cutting across the green expanse, trying as much as possible to walk within the dips undulating across the plain. They saw no more of the ragtag ironclad masters.

That night, with Diane on guard, Finn tried to sleep. But all he could think about was the traveller on the road being kicked and kicked. One more death that was his fault? If Engn hadn't been destroyed, would that solitary figure, whoever it was, still be alive? It was impossible to say. Still, he lay there agonizing over whether they'd done the right thing in destroying the machine. Uselessly, he ran through the calculations again, trying to weigh lives saved on one hand and lives destroyed on the other. Trying to measure the amount of misery on each side of the scales. It was futile. Still, scenes such as the one they'd witnessed made him doubt what they'd done a little more. He couldn't get the vision of the unmoving shape on the road out of his mind. Despite his tiredness he tossed and turned restlessly until Diane roused him for his turn to take watch.

They reached the Halfway House two days later without encountering anyone else on the road. A heavy rain poured down as they approached, turning the ground to mud, soaking Finn and Diane as they surveyed the building from a safe distance.

The great yew still stood, its gnarled and misshapen trunk writhing out of the ground, branches draped over the white walls as if to shelter them from the rain. Everything else was very different. The building had survived the earthquakes but looked as if it could fall at any moment. Fires had clearly raged within them at some point, blackening the walls with fronds of soot. The glass in the windows was all gone, as were many of the roof tiles.

From within, voices shouted and roared. It was hard to tell if people were singing in there or fighting. As Finn and Diane watched, two figures appeared in one of the upper windows. At first, Finn thought they were lovers embracing. Then he saw they tore and punched at each other. They lurched their way towards one of the gaping window frames but continued to grapple. Then, with a cry, one toppled out and plunged to the ground with a crash. The other peered down from the broken window and roared with delight.

"That does not look like a safe place to stay," said Diane.

He'd hoped the Halfway House might be a haven from marauding bands on the plain. It didn't look like it was. "There was a relay tower not too far away," he said. "If it's still there, we could shelter for the night." It was a risk. The towers were clearly visible for miles around. But perhaps they'd be safe so close to the Halfway House. Who'd sleep in a leaking wooden hut on stilts when they could be inside those stone walls?

Water dripped from Diane's nose and chin as she considered. "Okay." The shiver was clear in her voice. "We'll die anyway if we stay out in this."

This relay tower at least was largely unscathed. A rope, green with rot, hung down from the trapdoor. It seemed to be strong enough to hold them. They tied the horses to one of the legs, hoping once again no one would spot them. Then Diane shinned up the rope, followed by Finn.

Inside the tower, the 'scopes were smashed and useless, but most of the wooden planks of the floor and walls were intact. They laid out their blankets in the driest corner and changed into what dry clothes they had. Perhaps by morning their soaked things would be dry enough to wear again. Finn peered out through the round holes in the walls that, once, line-of-sight 'scopes had pointed through, relaying messages to and from Engn. He could see little out there. The Halfway House was a flickering glow in the distance. Beyond was a paler but much wider glow in the sky. It could only be the lights from the ruins of Engn. Fires burning in the wreckage perhaps. Apart from that, the whole world was darkness and rain.

They ate more of the supplies they'd brought with them from Diane's village: crusts of bread now as tough as leather; apples and pears from the recent harvests; rubbery wedges of yellow cheese. They lay down to sleep, arms around each other for warmth. Diane soon slept. She was good at sleeping whenever the opportunity arose, something she'd learned to do in her years of fleeing the ironclads. Finn, once again, lay awake, listening to the patter of the rain on the roof of the tower, feeling the whole structure sway beneath him as the wind gusted. Occasionally one of the horses whinnied. He wondered once again whether they'd done the right thing those years ago. And whether they were doing the right thing now. He was still thinking these troubled thoughts when sleep finally overcame him.

Sometime later, the rain awoke him again. It roared on the hut with renewed urgency. Except it wasn't rain. He sat up, suddenly alarmed. He'd been dreaming about the fire in the Blueprint Hall that day. The reek of the burning oil and the roar of the blue flames as they engulfed the shelves.

There was fire again now. The smell of oil and burning wood. Smoke roiled around within the tower as if trapped and seeking a way out. From somewhere outside he could hear the crackle of the flames. And then a babble of voices, shouts and cheers and laughter. The tower tottered to one side suddenly, as though one of its legs was giving way.

Diane was already on her feet, fingers through the ports to hold herself upright. "We need to get out of here!"

Finn pulled aside the trapdoor they'd climbed through, and then wished he hadn't. Flames licked at the underside of the tower and a plume of acrid smoke billowed in. Silhouetted figures, details impossible to make out, stood around the fire as if for warmth. He slammed the door shut again. He thought about crying out, telling them there were people trapped inside. But their evident delight in the destruction of the tower stopped him.

Diane kicked at one of the walls of the hut, the one farthest from the ground if they fell. The smoke was thick, making them both cough, the oily stench prickling the back of his throat. It was suddenly hard to see anything. The floor lurched again, and Finn thought they were going to crash to the ground. Somehow the tower remained upright. He too kicked at the wall, now sloping above them like an angled roof. They had to hold on with both hands to kick. They were trapped in a burning wooden box, and their only thought was of escape. Escape before the whole thing crashed to the ground in an inferno of blazing spars.

The rotten planks of the wall gave way to their blows, the wood soaked and soft. The sodden timbers up here hadn't yet caught fire. Their attackers must have soaked the legs in oil to start the fire but hadn't been able to reach that high. Between them, Finn and Diane tore and kicked open a hole big enough to peer out of. The night sky above was clear now, the stars looking quietly down. Smoke and dancing sparks filled the air all around. Sparks from their own funeral pyre.

"Jump!" said Finn. "We have to jump clear!"

They kicked their way through the broken wooden wall and stood on the lip of the drop. The ground was a long way down, but anything was better than burning to death. Perhaps, somehow, they could land safely and then get away without being seen. Another cheer came as the tower lurched again, dropping several feet.

Holding hands, Finn and Diane leapt into the darkness.

The ground met them with a jarring thump. Pain shot through one of Finn's knees with the impact. The stench of burning oil was strong down there. He pulled himself to his feet. He'd have to limp but all that mattered was getting away. Diane was already up, hauling Finn away from the flames and the ruined tower. In front of them lay the welcome safety of the night.

"There they are! They're running!" someone shouted over the roar of the flames.

"Take them!" shouted a deeper voice. "Bring them to me."

Finn lurched forwards, not looking back, sharp pains shooting through his left knee each time he put any weight on it. Diane ran on ahead of him a short way. She, at least, wasn't injured.

They ran five steps, ten. He thought they were going to make it. Then a whirling, whistling sound flew towards them. Finn ducked. A weight struck his legs. He looked down to see it was a chain with round weights on its ends, wrapping itself around him with furious delight, locking his limbs together to pitch him forwards from his own momentum.

"Run!" he shouted to Diane. "Keep going!"

But then two more metal chains whistled through the air. Diane dodged one, but as she swayed out of the way the second caught her, locking her legs in a tight embrace. With a cry she, too, crashed to the ground.

Desperately, they tried to free themselves, tearing at the chains in panic. The weights on the end were brass spheres, heavy enough to coil tightly around their legs. Like the grapple an ironclad had once caught him with, the links of the chains had little teeth locking them together.

They half freed themselves and managed to stagger to their feet. But they were too late. The pretend ironclads and masters from the road stood around them, calmly waiting for Finn and Diane to disentangle themselves.

They truly were a motley assortment. Some wore rags, tattered assortments of scraps scavenged from somewhere and anywhere, faces filthy and scarred. One or two had ears or hands missing. Others in the throng were as well dressed as any master in Engn. All carried weapons – throwing-chains, metal clubs, swords. One of the masters whirled a large watch around on a chain as if he intended to fling it at them at any moment.

"Who are you?" said Finn. "What do you want?"

"We are the masters," one of them said.

"There are no masters anymore," said Diane. "Engn has been destroyed. Didn't you hear?"

A ripple of amusement circulated among them. One of the group, a man who'd been silent so far, strode towards them. He wore one of the cylindrical hats on his head and a black cloak flowed around his shoulders. He held his torch up to Finn's and Diane's faces, studying them. The heat of it made Finn's eyes hurt, but he could see immediately it was the burned man. Half his face was melted, as if it were made from wax. His left eye was milky and useless. But the other half of his face was normal. His one good eye peered sharply out. A grin curled up the good half of his mouth and Finn saw in that moment who it was.

"Graves."

"Well, well," said Graves. He spoke in a whisper, close to Finn's face as if he didn't want the others to hear. "Finn Smithson. What a very fortunate meeting. I thought you were long dead."

"And I thought you were,'" said Finn.

"Oh, nearly, nearly, but I clung on. No thanks to you. Do you remember all the tricks you played on me? All your little games? The way your lured me down into the mines, just so you could use me in your escape plan. The way you left me to die down there while you got out. Do you recall all that, Finn Smithson?"

Finn didn't reply. None of that was right, but it wasn't going to help to say so.

"I'm afraid I had the bad manners not to die," continued Graves. "When the roof caved in it was terrible. The world falling in. Everything was crushed. Everything and everyone except for one or two mangled wretches who managed to crawl out through the wreckage, hauling their useless limbs along behind them."

"I'm sorry," said Finn. "I'm sorry about what happened to you."

"This?" said Graves, stroking the ruined half of his face. "Oh, this didn't happen in the destruction. I already had this. Do you want to know how? Shall I tell you?"

"Yes," said Finn, although he didn't want to hear. But anything to keep Graves talking, buy more time. Perhaps, somehow, they could trick him again and get away. He was cruel but stupid.

Graves spoke more loudly so his band of followers could hear. "The masters thought I was in league with you. They thought I knew where you were going, what your plan was. Oh, I swore I didn't, but they wouldn't listen. I pleaded and begged, but it was to no avail. To encourage me to talk, they put my face to one of the braziers. Held me there while the hot coals ate away at me. So, you see, I have you to thank for all this, too."

"I didn't mean that to happen," said Finn. "I had no choice."

"Oh, it doesn't matter," said Graves. "It doesn't matter at all. Because now I can return the favour, can't I? I thought you were dead, but here you are. A gift from the universe. And, see, we have a nice fire going already. We are the masters and we do as we please. I wonder how much you'll scream when the fire starts to consume you? We can take it nice and slowly. Start with your arms and legs. We have all night."

"I'll kill you if you touch him," said Diane. She pulled a thin blade from somewhere and held it up to Graves. Graves laughed, looking around at the gang surrounding them.

"Oh! She has a little knife. We'll have to be careful; she might kill us all with it."

Laughter rang around the ring. Graves frowned with the good half of his face and now peered closer to Diane.

"And it's you, isn't it? The girl who was there, who escaped with him. Well, well. This gets better and better. The happy couple. How touching. Now we can really have some fun." The half-grin reappeared on his face. He was clearly enjoying acting out the scene to his audience. "I'll tell you what, Smithson. You're clever. You're just the sort of person we'll need to build the new Engn. I'll make you a deal. Despite everything, I'll spare you. But we're going to take it out on *her* instead. Join in with us while we have our fun and I'll let you become a master afterwards. Think of it as a little … initiation. What do you say?" Graves seemed delighted with his idea.

"You were always an evil bastard," said Finn. "Right from the start you had it in for me, from that very first day in Engn when we waited at the gates. You hated me for no reason. I know you were just a frightened kid like I was, but you know what? I don't care. You've brought all this on yourself by your own stupidity and cruelty. You lay a finger on her and I'll kill you."

Graves laughed at Finn's words. He turned to Diane. "Then I'll make you an offer, girl. I'll let you go. Yes, I will. Let you scurry off to the hills or wherever it is you come from. I give you my word. All you must do is help us give him the punishment he deserves. Hold him down in the fire to show us you mean it and then you can leave unharmed. What do you say?"

Diane didn't speak. Finn could see from her eyes she was planning something. Trying to see a way they could both escape. Weighing ideas. Perhaps she could outrun their attackers at least, but with his knee he couldn't move fast enough. Hopefully she'd see that and make a dash for it. At least she might get away. Could he, somehow, hold them back while she fled?

Graves, meanwhile, assumed from Diane's hesitation she was considering his offer. Delighted, he stepped back to play to his audience. "See, she's tempted! What do you think, shall we let her? Shall we watch as she pushes him into the fire? Or shall we start slicing parts off both of them?"

Graves laughed while the mob bellowed and cheered their approval. There was a moment while he stood there, face upturned in triumph, the happy smile clear on the good half of his face.

Then a gunshot roared from somewhere in the night, a flash of red in the darkness beyond the ring. Something stung Finn's cheek, sharp like a wasp sting. And, three yards away, Graves' face dissolved into red pulp. In place of his features, a strange assortment of machine parts had suddenly appeared, as if they'd burst out of him: cogs, bolts, scraps of jagged metal.

It made no sense. Finn stepped backwards, trying to understand what he was seeing. Screams came from somewhere. In front of him, Graves folded and crumpled to the ground.

XVI

"I have two more muskets loaded" came Whelm's voice from the darkness. "I can't kill all of you, but I can take down another two. Who will it be?"

Nobody from the ring of masters moved. On the floor, Graves twitched, his feet working as if he was trying to run away, like a dog dreaming of the chase.

"Take their weapons," called Whelm.

Finn watched their attackers warily as he reached for their blades and staves. "Don't get too close," said Diane. "Make sure he has a clear shot."

"Throw your weapons on the ground," Finn said. "Then step back. Let us go and no one else will be harmed."

Faces in the circle glared with fury and hatred. But also, with fear. There was more than one among them who hadn't been shouting and laughing. More than one who was there, most likely, for their own safety. Better to be hunter than the hunted. One threw a crude sword to the ground and stepped backwards into the darkness, face down. After a moment the others followed, metal weaponry clattering to the earth. Soon there was a jumbled pile on the ground. Beside them, Graves lay unmoving.

Whelm threw a coil of rope to the ground. "Tie them up so they can't follow us." He stepped into the ring, holding two of the wide-mouthed muskets, one on each arm. Diane helped Finn uncoil the rope and between them they wound it about their attackers, yoking them together. Several of the masters in the group resisted at first but were persuaded by the sight of the muskets. Finn had to push aside the troubling thought he was helping a master – or at least an ex-master – hand out punishment. It was all different now, wasn't it?

There was no sign of their two horses. They'd either been released or had fled in panic when the fire started. Diane took the muskets while Finn and Whelm lugged the pile of weapons away to Whelm's cart. The line-of-sight tower was a burning hulk, the heat from it still intense.

"We should kill them," said Diane. "Shoot them all so they don't come after us. It's the sensible thing to do."

Whelm took one of the muskets from her. "You're right. Only way to be sure."

"No," said Finn, stepping in front of them. "No more killing. We can be far away by the time they get free."

Whelm didn't look convinced. "We might regret it. And they were going to kill you, you do know that don't you? Kill you slowly."

"I know," said Finn. "Even so, I don't want this on my conscience as well."

Whelm lowered the two muskets. "Just as well. I used all my shrapnel in the first shot. And this gun hasn't worked for years. If they had attacked, I wouldn't have been able to stop them anyway."

"You tell us this *now*?" said Diane.

Whelm grinned. "I was hardly going to mention it before, was I?"

"Why are you even here?" asked Finn. "Why have you

done this?"

Whelm climbed up onto the cart. His face was still swollen from the beating he'd taken, and he moved awkwardly, muscles stiff with pain. "Several reasons. Do we need to go into them now?"

"Yes."

"Can we at least get moving?" He offered them a hand. After a moment Diane took it and hauled herself up onto the cart. Finn followed.

Leaving the tied-up masters by the smouldering tower, they headed into the darkness. The iron wheels of the cart squeaked as they rumbled over the rough ground.

"So, why?" said Finn. "I thought we wouldn't see you again. I thought you blamed us for everything."

"I'm here for revenge, partly," said Whelm.

"Revenge on us?"

Whelm indicated the tied group with a backwards nod of his head. "On them."

"Those were the ones who attacked you?"

"The burned man was the worst of them. Took great pleasure in what he did to me."

"Even though you were once a real master?"

"He said I was a traitor to Engn."

"But why rescue *us?*" asked Diane. "You didn't have to do that."

The cart bumped and rattled over the ground for a good minute before Whelm replied. "You know, Finn, when you let me sleep in your Moot Hall, you were the first person since the day Engn fell to show me any kindness. The first person since long before that, if I'm honest. I was angry back there in the woods. Humiliated. But I shouldn't have taken it out on you."

"We were to blame for destroying everything," said Finn. "That was the truth."

"Maybe so," said Whelm. "And perhaps that ruined a lot of things for me. But perhaps it set me free, too."

"Are you're going to come with us to Engn?"

"I'm going that way. Might as well travel together again if you'll have me." He chuckled under his breath. "Plus, there's the money."

"What money?" asked Diane. Her usual hostility to Whelm was clear in her voice, despite the way he'd just rescued them.

Whelm shrugged. "Okay, since we're telling each other our secrets, I'll be honest with you. I was offered money to bring you back to Engn."

"What?" said Finn. "By whom?"

"I truly don't know. A figure dressed as an ironclad in the wreckage. Could have been anyone. But they were very clear. The two of you were to be brought together. Alive and unharmed."

"So that's why you were in the valley," said Diane. She sounded like all her suspicions had been confirmed.

"Yes. I thought I might have to drag you away, tied up or drugged. I didn't expect kindness."

"But now you're taking us there as agreed, to claim your reward?"

"If I were doing that, I wouldn't be telling you, would I? No. I want to know what's going on. The images on that spindle and the earthquakes – I need to know what it all means. Believe it or not, being a master wasn't always easy and it wasn't always pleasant. I want to know why any of it happened. What we were doing there. And that spindle of yours is the only way I've got of finding out."

When Whelm had first taken Finn to Engn, the master had seemed ill at ease at times, troubled by what he'd become. It seemed possible he was telling the truth now.

"You think you can get the reader working again?" asked Finn.

"I have got it working again. Just about. The whole thing is lashed together with frayed wires and rusted valves and cracked glass, but it should function. I've been trading for parts while I waited for you. It's in the cart. If you've got the spindle, we can take another look."

"Surely you don't have power out here?" said Diane.

"I have a little electricity," said Whelm. "Stored in voltaic cells in the cart. I charged them up at your house. Without telling you, I'm afraid. There's not much juice in them, but it should be enough for a few minutes. If we can find any more scenes on the spindle. You have it here?"

"I have it," said Finn. "Where do we go? Is there somewhere safe?"

"Nowhere is safe out here. Nowhere is safe anywhere. Maybe we can find cover. Then we can rest, and I'll show you." He paused, glancing across at the two of them. "So, anyway, there's my terrible secret out in the open. Anybody else want to share anything while we're talking?"

"What do you mean?" asked Finn.

Whelm looked back to the way ahead. "Oh, nothing. Just wanted to be sure we were all being completely honest with each other. Now we're traveling together again."

"No secrets," said Finn. "You know as much as I do about what's going on."

Finn's words seemed to amuse Whelm, but the ex-master said no more.

They stayed away from the road, cutting across country once again. Behind them, the sky shaded from black to purple, then glowed with oranges and pinks as the sun rose. They pressed on until it was fully light, keen to put as much distance as possible between themselves and the Halfway House. Finn glanced back repeatedly, looking for signs of being followed. They were leaving a clear trail across the grass of the plain, the twin lines of the cart's wheels crisp. He just hoped the knots they'd tied would keep their attackers from pursuing them for a while.

"How did you even find us?" asked Finn. "How did you know we were here?"

"I figured you'd pass by the Halfway House at some point. Didn't see you, but I did see the flames from the tower, so I came to investigate. Fortunately, the sound of the fire covered the noise of the cart. I crept as close as I could and saw it was you and *them* together. Pretty lucky, really."

"It was a good shot," said Diane. "A musket isn't a very accurate weapon."

Whelm shrugged. "It wasn't that good. I was trying to hit him in the legs. I…"

A metallic sound cut through the morning light. A discordant trumpeting, as if someone was blowing through some cracked and battered horn. It made Finn's heart pound; it was a sound he knew well. A sound he still heard in his nightmares. Diane knew it too, of course. She'd heard it often enough while being pursued, echoing through the trees to find her. She looked at him now with clear alarm on her face.

A master's hunting horn.

Whelm stopped, too, and stood listening, head cocked on one side, a frown on his face.

"It's coming from back there," said Finn. "They're after us. They must have got free."

"It could be anyone," said Diane. "Anyone could have found one of those horns in the ruins." She didn't sound convinced.

With a practiced leap, Whelm hopped onto the wheel of his cart, using it as a steppingstone to leap on top of the moving engine. He stood there surveying the scene, pulling out an old brass 'scope from a coat pocket and sweeping it around the plain.

"Can you see them?" asked Finn.

"Nothing," said Whelm.

"They'll be able to track us easily," said Diane. "It's obvious where we're going."

Whelm looked the other way now, scanning all about as if they were on a boat in the middle of some vast body of water and needed to find the safety of land. "There's a cobbled road half a mile or so farther on. One of the old trade routes heading north into the mountains. If we hit that, they won't be able to follow our tracks."

"They'll know we've gone way or the other," said Diane. "If they split in two, they can still follow us."

"There's a whole network of tracks, laid out when Engn was first being built. Or, I don't know, before that even. Most run north south, but there are crossing tracks, too. There must have been lots of traffic into the far north once, but they're not used much these days. They're broken and overgrown in places, but we can use them. Zigzag around. They can't keep dividing their forces. Sooner or later there'll be only one person following us."

"Then let's go," said Finn. "If we stand here, they'll see us sooner or later."

They hit the cobbled track half an hour later, just as Whelm had said. A strip of smooth, rounded stones running straight across the plane, directly north to a distant horizon that was part white mountain and part white cloud. Here and there, tufts of grass and clumps of moss grew from the cracks between the stones. Enough for someone to spot a mark and track them? They had to hope not.

"Let's heard north," said Finn. "South is more obvious. The main road to Engn is that way."

At Whelm's instruction, the horse heaved forwards again, hauling the metal cart up the gently curved side of the ancient road. Whelm manoeuvred the carriage backwards and forwards so both wheels were on the road. There were ruts there, ruts the ancient stonemasons had lain so the wheels of a cart would ride within them, like the rails of the steam shuttles of Engn in reverse. To Finn's surprise, the wheels of the moving engine fit the span of the ruts exactly.

"I thought you said these roads were ancient," said Finn.

"They are," said Whelm. "Back then, cartwheels had a standard width and the roads were built to match them. When they built moving engines, they copied the gauge of the old carts."

They trundled along the road, the iron wheels much louder on the hard stones, grinding and rumbling. Surely their pursuers would be able to hear. For the twentieth or thirtieth time, Finn peered backwards, looking for signs of pursuit. He could see nothing. They didn't hear any more from the horn.

Despite the ruts in the road, the cart lurched and bucked around as it rode the cobblestones, but progress was a little quicker than through the soft grass of the plain. Normally, Whelm rode on the footplate of the moving engine, steering the horse with leather reins, but now he didn't need to. The ruts kept the cart moving in the right direction. He leapt back on top of the machine and stood there gazing backwards, swaying nonchalantly as the cart moved around beneath him. He had clearly done so many times before.

"No sign," said Whelm.

"How far until the next junction?" asked Diane.

Whelm considered. "A mile or two. We could throw them by heading back east when we get there, then cutting west again further north. It'll make the journey longer, obviously."

"Let's do it," said Finn. "Anything's better than being captured."

It was early afternoon when they finally stopped. They'd turned four times onto crossing roads, Whelm working the horse to and fro each time to point the cart in the new direction. Once or twice they'd crossed sections of road that had crumbled away, or else been consumed by the slow invasion of the grass. At these points, their trail became briefly clear again. They just had to hope their pursuers – if there were pursuers – didn't come that way to see.

Whelm led them off the road and down into a dip in the ground he'd spotted. They'd seen more and more of these depressions over the past few hours. Diane had suggested they might once have been entrances to tunnels.

They'd searched one or two but hadn't found any sign.

"I doubt they'll track us all the way out here," said Finn. "We're miles out of our way."

Diane peered around, as if still expecting attack at any moment. There was only the hissing of the grass in every direction, a sound so familiar you soon stopped hearing it when traveling on the plain. She nodded. They were all tired. The horse, especially, needed to rest after her exertions. Her brown flanks glistened with sweat.

Whelm tethered her to a stake he hammered into the ground while Finn and Diane prepared food. All theirs had been lost, left to burn in the line-of-sight tower, but Whelm was well-provisioned. They ate salty, dried meat and crisp red apples, none of them talking.

"Shall we look at the spindle now?" said Whelm once they'd eaten and drunk some of the water he carried.

"It's not safe here," said Diane. "We should move on."

"There's no sign of them," said Finn. "I don't think they were ever even chasing us. And resting for half an hour won't make much difference." He looked at Whelm. "I think we can risk it."

"It's darker inside the engine," said the ex-master. "The images will be faint, but we should be able to see them in there."

Finn and Diane exchanged glances. Neither of them wanted to get inside the moving engine.

"We should leave the hatch open a little," said Finn. "For the fresh air. And to keep watch. Just in case."

Diane consented with a nod of her head. Whelm removed the numerous contraptions and metallic scraps he kept strapped to the walls of his iron cart. Then they crawled inside. The airless, rusty smell was immediately familiar to Finn. He tried to ignore it. The three of them sat together in the gloom while Whelm wound up something electrical, then took cables and clamped them to contacts on the reader. Lights glowed within the device. The smell of burning dust wafted over them.

"Do you have the spindle?" Whelm said.

Finn plucked it from the inside pocket he kept it hidden in. Whelm, holding it up to the light from the circular hatch, studied it with the cracked lens of an old eyepiece, frowning in concentration.

"Ah, here we are," he said after a few minutes. "Looks like a brief snatch of clear pictures. And then a longer section a bit farther down." He looked up in triumph at them. "Okay. Let's see what we can see."

Muddy swirls of light filled the glass orb, and, for a moment, Finn thought Whelm had it wrong. The section he'd lined the reader up on was encrypted after all. Encrypted or corrupted. There were lines and shapes in the fuzz, but it was impossible to make out any detail.

"Is that smoke?" said Finn.

"Rock, I think," said Diane. "It looks like the mines, but everything's lurching around so much it's hard to see anything."

The picture stopped swirling for a moment, and he saw she was right. They were looking down into the mines. Not the vast caverns he remembered, with their great pillars of rock holding up the machine. These were smaller delvings, the caverns only ten feet high. Perhaps the very first tunnels that later became the mines he'd laboured within.

They saw figures, then a band of ragged diggers pushing a low cart around a corner and directly towards them. They were all stick thin and covered in grime. They moved with the dogged determination of the exhausted. Two guards walked behind them, something like the ironclads they were used to but different, their faces visible, wearing less armour. The guards pushed at the figures wheeling the cart, urging them onwards.

The images blurred again, as if someone were violently shaking the orb taking the pictures. When they settled down again, the scene had changed. The cart was still there, but all the figures lay sprawled around on the floor.

Dust and rock rained down on them from above. At first Finn thought the diggers were all dead, but then they moved, hauling themselves back up to their feet, the guards kicking at them to make them stand. One of the figures didn't move, however much the guards kicked.

Finn understood what was really happening. An earthquake had just struck and the seeing-orb had captured it. Connor must have found the moment in history and added it to the spindle.

People ran in and out of the flickering scene, mouths open wide. There was no sound, but it was clear they were screaming. More rock crashed down, a huge boulder striking one of the figures and pinning them to the ground. The pictures shook again.

Then two more figures approached, running towards the cart, veering from side to side as if the tunnel were throwing them around. These were neither miners nor guards. Masters. Their clothing looked archaic, more like that worn by the masters in the other scenes they'd seen in the orb. He thought the masters were going to help the stricken miners, but when they reached the cart, they pushed everyone aside, dashing them to the ground. The guards joined in, keeping the miners back, preventing them escaping. Meanwhile, the masters unhooked one side of the cart and opened it up. Finn expected to see an avalanche of rubble fall out, but the cart was empty. Empty except for a single pebble, little more than a dot in the hazy picture.

The masters picked up the stone and walked back up the corridor. They moved with exaggerated care, as if the fragment of rock was incredibly fragile, or as if it might explode if dropped. One of the masters held a metal sheet over it to protect it while the other cupped it in his hands. Shuffling forwards, they moved towards Finn and Diane and Whelm. Behind them, as more rock showered down from above, the two guards stood, preventing the exhausted miners from following.

The masters had nearly reached the seeing orb when another tremor hit. This was a big one. Everything became blurred and confused again. Large amounts of rock and stone sleeted down, filling the tunnel. The shaking continued for long moments.

Then there was a single moment of clarity. The tunnel became visible again. It was filled halfway to the roof with boulders. The cart had gone, and the people had gone, all swamped by the rock fall. Here and there an outstretched arm reached from the rubble, bruised and bloodied. Incongruously, one of the masters' chimney-like hats sat upon the rocks, as if someone had gently laid it there. No head was visible beneath it. No one – miner, guard, or master – had survived.

Then more violent shaking came, and the pictures in the orb winked out.

In the gloom of the moving engine, Diane looked up at Finn while Whelm plucked the spindle from the machine and examined it.

She looked puzzled. "When you were down there in the mines, what were you actually digging for?"

"We weren't digging for anything," said Finn. "We just had to dig, deeper and deeper down. No one ever told us to look out for a particular sort of rock or anything like that. I assumed the whole thing was all one more pointless activity. Like the valves. It didn't make a lot of sense, but then not much did."

"There was no gold?"

"None that I saw."

"Whatever was in that cart, it was clearly precious. Even the masters risked their lives to get it."

"It must have been the seismium the other scenes mentioned."

"It seemed such a small amount, though," said Diane. "They risked their lives for that tiny speck of it. And why didn't they run when they had it? Why did they walk so slowly when they knew the roof could come down at any moment?"

"It must have been unstable somehow, I guess. Maybe it could have exploded – or whatever it is this stuff does." He turned to look at Whelm, who was still peering at the spindle through an eyepiece, turning it around slowly while he studied it.

"Can we see the other section you mentioned?" asked Finn.

Whelm continued to peer at the spindle. "I'll line it up now. Hopefully the cells will have enough power."

"I'll go check we're still alone," said Diane. She crawled through the hatchway. Finn and Whelm waited together in the darkness. The iron tank surrounding them *tinged* gently in the heat of the sun. Neither spoke.

After a few minutes she climbed back inside. "No sign of anyone."

Whelm nodded and, carefully, placed the spindle back into the reader. He lined up the tiny stylus that would read the next set of pictures. A scribble of lights flickered in the orb. This time there was a voice, too. A narrator. It was, unmistakably, Connor.

XVII

Baron Rankin stood with the assembled masters and generals of the Temple Guilds upon a rise in the ground, surveying the battle laid out before them. Gram, the Chevalier of the Ostlers Guild, stood directly beside him, holding a spyglass to one eye. Rankin didn't approve. They didn't need to employ the devices of their enemy in this war. He, Baron Rankin of the Guild of Stonecarvers, could see perfectly well how a battle was proceeding with his own eyes.

Gram's cavalry units were vital to their efforts, there was no doubt about it, but still Rankin disapproved of the younger master. Too ready to adopt the new ways, that was Gram's problem. Too ready to embrace change. Sometimes Rankin suspected Gram's loyalties were divided. The Ostlers were an ancient and respectable House, but the latest guildmaster seemed intent on throwing away all their fine traditions. It wasn't just the spyglass: Gram had also set up a seeing-orb on a little iron tripod, claiming it would allow them to record scenes of the battle and study them later. *To learn from their mistakes*, he had said. Rankin had even seen Gram slyly consulting a pocket timepiece, one of the thirty-six-hour ones the damned upstarters insisted on using.

Baron Rankin would have to keep his eye on Gram. Once this war was won and the pre-eminence of the twenty-four Temple Guilds was established, there would inevitably be some jockeying for position on the Council. That was the game. And it was a game he, Baron Rankin, thoroughly excelled at. There were plenty among the twenty-four who would side with him.

He returned his attention to the battlefield. Before them, across the fall and rise of the ground of the plain, thirty thousand Temple soldiers were amassed. They marched forwards in twenty-four precise squares, one battalion from the militia of each guild. Some of the others – Gram among them – had wanted to mix the soldiery up, arrange them according to some scheme of skill or weaponry rather than by guild. Rankin would have none of it. The soldiers would fight hardest for the men and women of their own city. That was as plain as his nose. A Woodturner wouldn't lay down his life to save a Flintknapper. At least, not readily. But a Woodturner would fight to the death to protect a fellow guildsman. It was common sense.

Beyond the twenty-four squares of marching soldiers, across a thin strip of grass, stood the lines of their enemies. The upstarters were heavily outnumbered. They would be crushed in the battle and it would be a decisive blow in the war. Perhaps an end to the twelve mechanical guilds and their wild ideas. They thought they could control the world with their damnable machines.

Beyond both armies, atop the rise on the other side of the valley, stood the Great Clock. A two-hundred-foot tower elaborately decorated with a metalwork mesh and struts and spikes. It reached high into the sky, visible for tens of miles around. He could hear its ticking despite the roar and stamp of the armies in the valley. They'd made it deliberately loud, he was sure: sending those vast, metallic *tocks* out through to air to batter the ears of anyone within hearing distance. Telling everyone they were there. Chopping up time into so many precisely calculated moments, as if a life was a piece of metal that could be measured out and cut up.

Them and their damned thirty-six-hour clocks. Who needed so many hours in the day? What made them think they could tie down time like that? You got up in the morning and went to bed when darkness came. If you were hungry you ate. The sun told you the time of day. These clocks were a tyranny. A way of controlling people; parcelling up their lives into little pieces. Little broken fragments. And he would have none of it.

Beyond the clock, curling around the whole battlefield as if embracing it in an arm, the river En flowed, sunlight sparking off its wide waters.

"They're sending out some sort of weapon," said Gram, still studying the enemy lines through his glass. "The forwards ranks are parting. Some sort of machine."

Them and their infernal contraptions. Was it true they had allies from elsewhere, providing these mechanisms? That was the rumour. "What manner of machine? Cannon?"

"Don't think so," said Gram. "I've never seen anything like them. Want to look?"

"Certainly not."

"But it's okay for me to look and tell you what I can see?"

"It was your idea to bring the glass, Gram, not mine. Just tell me what you damn well observe. If you think you can trust the thing. For all we know it's showing you something that isn't even there."

"They're machines on wheels," said Gram after a pause. "About the size of horses, moving under their own power. Clockwork by the look of it. I can't see any steam."

"Clockwork horses? They'll get ten yards and then explode into a thousand useless cogs. And are there clockwork soldiers riding them too? Firing clockwork guns?"

"No, no, nothing like that," said Gram. "There's no one on them at all. They're all being lined up at the top of the slope."

"Mechanical devilry!" said Rankin. He turned aside to the three buglers who stood with them on the rise. "Signal the attack. Let's take them now before they can wind their damned clockwork toys up!"

The horns blared out, echoing around the valley. There was a moment's pause, as if everyone was trying to work out what the sound meant, then the twenty-four battalions surged forwards. Their combined voices came to Rankin's ears as a swelling roar. The sight of it made his heart pound within his chest. If he'd been twenty years younger, he'd have been down there, leading the charge.

The great clock struck then, the clangs from its bells heavy in the air, like being hit by something solid. For a few moments the sound filled the whole world, drowning out the cries of the soldiers.

Then, as the sound shimmered away to nothingness, the upstart army attacked. Rankin could see the devices Gram had mentioned. They shot forwards, flashing with unearthly speed down the slopes. One veered wildly to one side, crashing into another and bringing both to a tumbling halt. Rankin smiled at the sight. The ridiculous contraptions were no match for proper soldiers. The guildsmen would smash them to pieces just as they would smash the great clock to pieces.

The wheeled devices were almost upon the attacking lines when the first explosions blossomed on the battlefield. A moment later, a whole series of rattling booms hit them up on the hill. Screams accompanied each one. They were bombs. The upstarters were sending clockwork bombs into the Temple ranks. Rage boiled within Rankin. This wasn't proper war. Machines to do the work of men – it was an obscenity. When this was done, he would make them pay. Make them pay tenfold for every act of savagery.

"Give me that spyglass," he said, and grasped hold of it while Gram still held the damned thing to his eye. He had to see what was going on down there, even if it did mean using upstarter devilry.

He saw only a blur of colours: greens and reds and browns. You had to focus the damned thing. Why couldn't the contraption do that itself if it was so clever? Rankin turned the brass knob wildly backwards and forwards until, suddenly, the scene down on the battlefield snapped into focus.

The clockwork bombs had certainly done their work. Where they'd detonated the ranks were decimated. Bodies and unattached limbs lay strewn around in a sea of red. Survivors milled around, dazed, some of them facing the wrong way completely. All discipline and order had been lost.

"Resound the charge!" he bellowed to the buglers. If they weren't careful the whole battle would crumble into chaos. The militias had to pull themselves together and attack now, before more of those bombs could be trundled out.

The horns sounded again. Baron Rankin stood watching the effect on his troops, breathing deeply through his nose as if he were down there with them, fighting with them. Nothing happened. At the foot of the clock, in the upstarter ranks, he could see more of the machines being prepared, one being cranked with some hooked metal bar, giving it the power it would need to reach the Temple soldiers.

"Resound!" he shouted.

The horns sounded the charge for the third time. Finally, they had the desired effect. The Temple soldiers surged forwards, scrambling over their fallen comrades.

Rankin watched as the gap between the two lines narrowed. Good. The upstarters wouldn't dare release more of their wheeled bombs now.

With a metallic crunch, loud enough to be heard up on the hill, the two lines collided. Rankin lowered the spyglass so he could see the whole battlefield. Sunlight flashed off swords and pikes and hammers. Roars and screams filled the air. Upstarters and Templers fought and fell.

This was it. Proper war. Now they would learn who was in charge. Now they would see who really ruled the world. And when the fighting was done, and that great clock was toppled and dashed to the ground, and all their devices and machines were wrecked and reduced to rubble, then the upstarters could be dragged to the negotiation table and the terms of their surrender given to them. They could do it that night, there at Enloth. The upstarters made to pay for every death and every act of destruction they had wrought.

Baron Rankin smiled at last. This truly was a glorious day.

XVIII

"That's it," said Whelm from beside the spindle reader. "Power's all gone. We won't be able to see any more."

Finn still stared at the empty orb, trying to make sense of what they'd seen. These had to be old images. Perhaps the oldest of all. Connor had surely included them because they showed another turning point. He must have found a journal of the Baron from somewhere and overlaid a transcription of the man's thoughts and observations.

"Will you be able to charge the cells up in Engn?" asked Diane.

"Perhaps. There's still power to be found if you know where to look."

"Maybe we can see more when we get there."

"So now you want to see the pictures, do you?" said Whelm. The exasperation was clear on his face despite his bruises. The tone of accusation in his voice was obvious, too. The two of them just couldn't get along.

"Of course she does," said Finn. "Why wouldn't she?"

"Oh, I don't know. I just thought, with everything

that's happened…"

"What do you mean? What are you accusing her of?"

"Me? Nothing. I'm not a master anymore. I don't get to accuse anyone of anything. It's none of my business, even if it is left up to me to repair everything afterwards."

"Look, if you have something to say, then let's hear it, Whelm." In the confined space, Finn's voice boomed off the metal walls. The air was suddenly hotter and heavier than ever. He was overreacting, he knew, but being inside the engine unsettled him. It was wrong to take it out on Whelm, but he couldn't stop himself.

"Finn," said Diane, her voice quiet.

"No," Finn replied. "I want to hear what he's got to say. Let's have everything out in the open."

"Finn, leave him," said Diane. "Please."

He turned to her. There was something in her voice that troubled him. "Why should I? Just because he rescued us doesn't mean he can go around accusing you of things you haven't even done."

"Finn … the thing is, he's not. Accusing me of something I haven't done, I mean."

The whole turn of the conversation threw Finn. He wanted to talk about the images, discuss what they might mean. "What do you mean?"

"He's talking about the reader," said Diane. "How I tried to destroy it. Twice."

"What?"

"I smashed it up when I rescued it from the first earthquake, and then later on when I threw water into it to short it out."

It took Finn a moment to take in what she was saying. "But why?"

"I didn't want you coming back here. Didn't want anything to threaten our lives in the valley. I was happy, don't you see? For years I'd been on the run, living wild, afraid of dying every day. And suddenly everything came right and fitted together, like the happy ending of a story.

And I didn't want anything to change. I didn't want to lose you."

"And now?" His voice was shaking as he spoke.

"Now I know the story hasn't ended. Or perhaps we're inside a whole new story. Now we have to see where this one takes us."

Finn stared into the darkness where Diane sat. "And you couldn't talk to me? I thought we told each other everything."

"I did tell you, Finn. I told you to stop being so obsessed with the spindle a hundred times. But you wouldn't listen."

"So, you decided to smash up the machine I'd been building all that time?"

"I did. I'm sorry. I thought it was for the best. For both of us. I thought you'd forget about the whole thing and we could move on."

"And I thought I could trust you."

"You can trust me."

"But I can't, can I? Not now. You lied to me."

"Please, Finn. You can. Of course, you can."

"It's too cramped in here," said Finn. "I need to get some fresh air."

Snatching the spindle from the reader, he clambered out of the moving engine, half falling to the ground. He stood for a moment on the grass of the plain, chest heaving, the pain sharp in his knee. Anger burned through him. His mind whirled with great, unfocused thoughts. How could she have done that?

Without looking back, he strode away from the moving engine, filled with fury.

"Finn!" Diane had climbed out too. She ran after him and put a hand on his arm. "Finn, come on. I shouldn't have wrecked the machine. I see that now."

Finn shook her free. "Leave me alone. I'm going."

"Going where?"

"To Engn. On my own. Don't try to follow me."

Not looking back at her, he limped away across the grass of the plain.

XIX

Finn slumped to the ground to ease the burning pain in his knee. Before him, stretching from horizon to horizon, lay the great machine. Where once there had been a city of shining wheels and smoking chimneys and roaring fires, there was now a mountain range of rubble. Mangled, twisted mounds of machinery rose in rusting piles over the broken and crumbling walls. The gusting wind moaned through stray wires, a chorus of haunting voices.

Here and there, by some miracle, a remnant of the former machine stood intact. A single stone tower festooned with cables, like a metallic maypole. A wheel from one of the beam-engines, rusted into immobility, frozen mid-action. A smokestack with its walls of curved, shining stone. But these fragments only emphasized how complete the destruction of Engn was.

He'd imagined coming here and finding the machinery functioning again, the wheels turning, the chimneys sending plumes of grey smoke billowing into the clouds. There was none of that. The devastation they'd brought was complete. These were shattered ruins. Engn, surely, could never be rebuilt. It would rust and rot away here until the end of time. Could there really be answers in this rusting desolation? Or was he simply chasing phantoms?

He glanced backwards. He was alone. His knee slowed him down, but he could still move quicker than the cart across the rough ground. He'd left them behind hours ago. Maybe they hadn't even tried to follow. His anger was burnt out now, spent by the wearying march. He still couldn't believe what she'd done. After everything, she'd betrayed him. He had to get inside the city urgently now. Find out what Connor meant him to do. Make sense of everything.

He turned back to study the walls. As he'd approached, he'd picked out a likely place for climbing inside. Deep cracks rent the stone, and he'd aimed for the biggest he could see. Even so, up close, it was obviously not going to be easy. He'd have to climb twenty or thirty feet before reaching the cleft. The walls had buckled and heaved, giving him one or two handholds and footholds, but the problem was his knee. He'd have to put all his weight on it to haul himself upwards, and simply walking along flat ground was agony.

He limped the last few yards to the broken walls of Engn. He had to skirt around another bowl in the ground, this one with a capped shaft at its centre, like the ones they'd used to escape last time. A rusting iron tripod stood over the shaft, as if water had once been drawn up from the ground. Finn toyed, briefly, with the idea of descending the shaft and trying to find a way inside that way. But he had no light and no map for the tunnels. The old man who'd shown them the way last time – Bran, Master Owyn's father – had said there were only song-maps, verses passed down over the generations and never written down. Finn could recall some snatches of the melody of the one he'd been taught, but not the order of the words. He'd have no chance down there.

He climbed, using his arms as much as possible to pull himself up. Even so, there were several places where he had to lean on his bad knee while reaching up with his right foot. Each time his leg shook as if it was going to fall to pieces and the shooting pain made him gasp out loud. Each time he had to stop, all his weight on his right leg, while the agony subsided.

He was halfway to the cleft in the wall when the hunting horn blared. Holding on with his fingertips he tried to peer over his shoulder. In the distance he made out a group of black dots. Masters, coming for him. He had to be visible for miles. Were they the same ones led by Graves? It barely mattered. He had to climb the wall and get inside before they came for him.

Gritting his teeth, he reached up with his left hand, found a notch in the rock and pulled himself up. The V of the great crack in the wall was only a few yards above him. The masters' horn trumpeted again, nearer. Finn's breathing came raggedly as he readied himself for another push. He'd have to put all his weight on his left knee again, but he had no choice. He reached up. His knee trembled, then buckled. Finn fell, sliding down the wall. He skinned his hands as he tried, uselessly, to stop himself. He seemed to slide a long way before thumping into the ground, the impact on his left leg making him cry out in pain.

The horn sounded again as he pulled himself back to his legs. He stood with his back to the walls of Engn. There was no way he was going to climb back up before they reached him. He could think of only one thing to do. Crouching over in the hope they wouldn't see him over the rises and falls in the ground, he lumbered to the well shaft. He would climb down and escape into the tunnels. If he went carefully, remembered each turning he took, then he could wait a while and retrace his steps. Perhaps emerge at night when they wouldn't see him. Or he might find another shaft he could ascend, far away from this one. It was all he could do.

As before, the shaft had rusting iron rungs embedded in its wall. He sat on the lip and swung himself round. Damp, chilled air rose up from the depths. He could see nothing down there and had no way of knowing how deep the shaft was. It might even stop after a few yards. The walls were lined with stone, slick with green slime. He descended, supporting his weight with his arms each time he reached down with his good leg.

He'd descended twelve rungs when his pursuers reached the top of the shaft. He'd hoped, somehow, they might not realize where he'd gone. But clearly, they had. Peering upwards he could see their heads against the circle of the sky.

"Come back up, runaway," one shouted. "Come up and face us." The voice sounded strangely near in the narrow space, as if his pursuer was right beside him. Panicky now, Finn clambered down the shaft, desperate to get away. He could see nothing of the walls or rungs; the darkness about him was absolute.

A sharp weight smashed into his shoulder, almost dashing him from the wall. For a moment he couldn't understand what had happened. Looking up, he watched as a black shape was held over the circle. Held and then released. They were dropping stones to hit him.

Holding himself as close as possible to the wall, he continued to descend. Another stone clanged off the rungs above him. Finn clutched himself to the wall and the rock struck him on the back before falling into the darkness. He counted to three before the stone hit the bottom of the shaft. He still had a long way to go.

He climbed down one more rung before they dropped the next rock. Again, he heard it clanging off the rungs above him. Again, he hugged himself to the wall, hoping it would miss. The hard spike of pain on the back of his head made him gasp. There was a moment of disorientation, the rush of falling, and then darkness.

Finn was dimly aware of someone holding him close, hugging him. It was hard to think straight, his mind woolly and thick with pain. The pain in the back of his head. He'd been hit by a falling rock. He lay in cold water or mud, legs bent at an awkward angle where he'd landed. Someone was there with him, trying to pick him up.

"Diane?" he said.

But not Diane. Rough hands heaved his shoulders off the ground. A rope was passed around his back beneath his arms, then tightened against his chest. He tried to struggle, but he had no strength. He felt sick from the pain in his head. Someone hauled on the rope, bringing him upright in a series of short jerks. His feet left the ground. He swung around, crashing into the sides of the pit again and again as, inch by inch, they heaved him towards the distant circle of light.

The ascent took an age. The ropes cut into him, burning a line across his back with each tug, making it hard to breathe. At first, he tried to resist, hook an arm through one of the rungs and hold on, but he was too weak. They yanked harder and harder on the rope, and eventually he yielded. He swung around in the shaft, and in the darkness, it was hard to be sure if he remained conscious or kept passing out.

Long minutes later, they were hauling him out of the shaft like a fish pulled from the water.

Three of the half-ironclad, half-masters stood around him. Two he recognized from the group that had set the tower ablaze. Perhaps the third had joined in the hunt. The effort of hauling him up had clearly exhausted all of them. Finn thought about running but found he couldn't even get to his knees without the world lurching around him.

"Let's kill him now," said one of his pursuers.

"No," said another. "We'll wait for the others. They'll

all want to take part. They'll all want to see."

They bound his hands and feet together, then left him. Daylight was fading, the sun slipping behind banks of grey clouds billowing over the walls of Engn. A thumping sound banged through his head where it touched the ground, and he couldn't tell if it was the blood pounding through his arteries or the ground itself, thrumming with the motion of some buried machinery. It barely mattered. He wasn't going to escape. He'd failed Connor. He'd failed everyone.

Two more of the wasteland masters appeared over a rise in the ground. He couldn't tell if they were part of the original group or not. Both wore ironclad masks and had black master's cloaks wrapped around them. Both had iron swords at their belt. The horn must have been heard for miles around, summoning them all to the hunt.

One stopped to converse with his captors, talking in rough tones. The other walked across to stand over Finn. The new master kicked Finn hard, catching him on the arm. Finn cried out and the other masters laughed in appreciation. Finn tried to curl up in a ball. The master crouched beside him, and Finn flinched away from whatever fresh torment the man had in mind.

"Finn. It's me." There was no mistaking the whisper close to his ear. Diane. She'd come for him. "Finn, don't move. Don't react."

She stood and drew her blade. For a moment it looked as if she were going to prod him with it. Instead, with a cry, she spun around and swung at one of the three captors. At the same moment her companion – Whelm – drew his blade and struck. The three masters who had caught Finn were caught unprepared. Two fell immediately as Diane and Whelm's blades slashed through them, ugly wounds spraying blood wide. The third master staggered to his feet but had only a small knife to hand. He danced between them, but it was only a matter of time. Diane lunged, the master parried, and Whelm had a clear blow.

In only a few moments, the three captors lay in a neat triangle on the ground, none of them moving, the green grass beneath them stained red.

Diane and Whelm cut Finn's binds and then, between them, lugged the three dead masters to the shaft to drop them into the darkness. While they worked, Finn bound a strip of bloodstained cloth around his left knee, hoping it would help support him. Gingerly, he climbed to his feet.

"We have to get away from here," said Whelm when they were done. "Others will have heard that horn."

"Where's the cart?"

"About a mile away, south of here," Whelm replied. "There are easier routes inside that way. It's our only hope, we're too exposed out here."

Whelm unrolled a spare master's cloak and handed it to Finn. "Wear this. If we meet any others, we'll pretend we're part of the hunt." They set off, no one speaking, Finn concentrating on keeping his legs moving forwards, sometimes shutting his eyes to calm the throbbing pain in his head.

They reached the cart without seeing anyone else. Whelm's horse bridled as they approached, wary of them. Whelm removed his mask and whispered gentle words to the beast. "Sit inside," he said to Finn. "We'll move quicker that way."

Finn climbed in and Diane followed. She made him sit with his back to the light while she studied the wound on the back of his head.

"Look at you," she said. "You're a complete wreck, and you haven't even made it inside Engn yet."

His anger was gone now, burned out. He'd nearly died. "How's my head?"

"It's a nasty gash. It's still bleeding. I'll bind it, but it might need stitching."

"The pain takes my mind off my knee," said Finn.

"You're an idiot. You know that, don't you?"

"You came back," said Finn. "You came looking for

me."

She worked at his scalp for a moment, cleaning it with gentle dabs. "Of course. Finn, I'm sorry. Trying to wreck the reader like that – it was wrong. I truly thought I was doing what was best for you. For us. Please don't let one mistake spoil everything."

They swayed together as the engine trundled forwards. "I didn't know what to do without you," said Finn. "And storming off like that was pretty childish. I'm as bad as Whelm."

She crawled round in front of him and kissed him, gently, on the lips. "What you did was stupid, but we all do stupid things. It's allowed. Now let's get that wound bound up before you bleed to death."

Afterwards they sat together in the darkness of the moving engine, the squeak of the wheels and the stamping of the horse the only sound.

After a while Diane said, "We'll look for a power source inside for the orb. See if we can work out what Connor meant with it all."

Finn squeezed her hand in gratitude. "You didn't recognize him, did you?"

"Recognize who?"

"The Baron in those images. The one leading the assault. I suppose you never saw Connor's father, but the similarity was clear. The same squat, powerful build. The same nose."

"Connor was descended from him?"

"I think so. Related, anyway. When I went to look for Connor's mother, there was an old painting of that clock tower, too. Not in her room, in one of the hallways. I couldn't make the scene out, but perhaps it was the same battle, or when the tower had just been built. No wonder Connor's life was fraught at home. His parents from two sides in an old war, a war neither seemed willing or able to forget. They loved each other, I'm sure, but I don't suppose they ever agreed about much. It must have been hard for him growing up in that atmosphere at times."

She rested her head on his shoulder. "The wars were all so long ago. You'd think people would forgive and forget. Or, I don't know, just forget."

"People are good at keeping ancient resentments smouldering away, being slowly poisoned by them. If they're not careful."

She was silent for a moment, considering his words. Then she hooked her arm through his. "That battle we saw," she said. "Do you think it was before or after the other pictures?"

"Before, I think. Perhaps, I don't know, that was where they began to build Engn, after the clock tower was destroyed. Presumably the Temple Guilds won, and the Upstart Guilds constructed Engn as punishment or compensation. Or so it was claimed, at least."

"It all seems so ridiculous now," she said. "So unimportant."

"Like I said, some people let ancient disagreements dominate their lives. Not a good way to live your life."

Diane nodded, her head against his shoulder, and didn't reply.

XX

Whelm called a halt late that evening. The horse had gone as far as she could for one day. They'd seen no sign of pursuit. Finn stood outside the moving engine, testing his left knee to see if he could put any weight on it. Whelm oiled the bearings of one of the cart's iron wheels. Diane came to stand beside Finn, gazing up at the walls and the ruin beyond.

She slipped her fingers through his. "I don't see anyone in there. No defenders or anything."

"I guess it's the same as out here. People fighting over the scraps."

"You know," she said, "it's possible we won't find any answers now. We must be prepared for that. Perhaps we're simply too late. And, I think, sometimes there are questions that have no answers. Terrible things happen for no reason. And then people kill themselves trying to find an explanation. Drive themselves mad doing it. I'm just saying that might be how it is."

Perhaps she was right. Perhaps it was a mistake to try

and find answers in the wreckage, just as it had been futile amid all the complexity of the working machine. And yet, he *knew* there was something there. Knew it without being able to say why. There was something he was supposed to do. Was that a delusion? He'd met plenty of people who believed the craziest things. Perhaps he was crazy too. He didn't *feel* crazy. But perhaps you didn't.

He kneeled and put his hand flat to the muddy grass of the floor. The ground had been churned up by many wheels, as if people had been circling and circling the ruins, looking for a way in.

"Feel," he said. "There's still machinery running. Somewhere inside." The deep thrumming in the ground was unmistakable.

Diane knelt and put her hand to the earth. She looked up at him. "I can feel it. The machine. It's weak and broken, but it's still alive."

"Some of it at least. We have to go in there and find out what. And why. And we have to destroy it for good, as we said we would."

Whelm walked over to them, wiping oozing black oil from his hand with a stained rag. "Every time I come it's louder," he said. "Another piece of the machine brought back to life. The wrecked mechanisms combined to create new devices, new contraptions."

"By who?" asked Finn. "Who is doing this?"

Whelm shrugged. "People trying to rebuild the machine. People who think they can make the wheels turn again. Crazy people. They won't be able to do it in a thousand lifetimes, but that doesn't stop them. It's like Engn was the reason for their existence, and now they have to piece it all back together, cog by cog. And they don't know what they're doing. They have no design, no blueprints. They think they can rebuild Engn by simply connecting random parts back together."

"Perhaps they do know what they're doing, and you just don't see it," said Finn.

Whelm shrugged. "Maybe. If you ask me, they just can't accept what's happened. The world has changed, and they can't move on. They want to go back to a time when the world at least seemed to make sense."

"I thought you wanted answers, too?"

"Oh, sure. Always good to have answers. But about what it was *for* when it was working. Not about now. Now it's smoking ruins and mangled metal. Mile upon mile upon mile of it."

"How do you normally get inside?"

"You've seen the breaks in the wall. Elsewhere it's little more than rubble. People take stones for souvenirs, or to build new buildings. On some sections, you can pick your spot and go in wherever you like."

"So, if we wanted to go to, say, the Directory, we could?" asked Finn.

"There is no Directory anymore. There's no anything anymore. Broken fragments here and there, achieving nothing. That's all there is."

"What do we do?" asked Diane. "Where do we go?"

"We have to see everything on the spindle," said Finn, "and there might be a fully working reader in the ruins of the Directory."

Whelm shook his head. "You can look, but everything's been picked over a thousand times. A few years ago, you could still turn up items of value in the ruins. Now they're rare. Mostly it's scraps of rust and broken bones. And besides, I told you, we've been incredibly lucky to see fragments of the images on that stick. It was clearly put together by someone who didn't know what they were doing, but you need the key to see any more. The rest looks completely encrypted to me."

Finn said, "I've tried and tried to think what they key might be. But Connor just never told me."

"Then you'll never know what's on the stick," Whelm replied. "It's as simple as that."

"This ironclad who wanted you to fetch us," said

Diane. "How were you supposed to get back in touch?"

"There was a place I had to take you."

"That's where we should start then," said Diane. "Perhaps that will lead us to some answers."

Finn nodded his assent to the plan. Although a part of him couldn't help wondering if they were doing precisely what Whelm wanted them to do.

He put the thought out of his mind. Whelm had risked a lot to save the two of them. They had more pressing matters to worry about.

The sky was darkening now, the walls of Engn blotting out the fading western sky. It would be cold soon. There were no stars. More heavy lead-coloured clouds had filled the sky as they came south, following them it seemed, threatening more rain. The three of them were tired and hungry and thirsty.

"We need to light a fire," said Diane. "Find somewhere to shelter, either out here or inside the walls."

In the distance lay two of the settlements scattered around Engn, ramshackle collections of sagging huts. In the twilight, the first fires were being lit among them, the first coils of smoke rising into the air. Were there still messages in those plumes? Or had all that been lost, too?

Finn turned to Whelm. "What would you do? Stay out here or venture into the ruins?"

Whelm ran his hand through his lank hair. "I'd probably sleep out here by the wall, well away from everyone. I probably wouldn't light a fire. Then I'd go inside in the morning. We could…"

The blaring call of the horn cut him off.

They looked round in alarm, trying to place the sound. It came again from somewhere in the gloom, the mournful call echoing back at them off the walls, making it hard to place.

An answering horn came then: a lower, more raucous note, nearer by.

"They've found us," said Diane. "They've been

tracking us all this time."

"That decides it," said Whelm. "We have to get inside. We can lose them in the ruins. Out here we're too vulnerable." He reached into the moving engine for his muskets, handing one to Finn and Diane. The horse complained as Whelm led her forwards once more, but she relented and began, dejectedly, to walk. The cart lurched into life.

Diane jogged along beside the cart, wary of attack from the gloom at any moment. Finn, unable to keep up, climbed on top of the engine and sat scanning the plain, musket held ready. The ground was hummocky around there, long dips cut into it. They'd used them once to conceal themselves, they day they fled from Engn. For all he knew, their pursuers were using them now to surround the cart.

"Whelm?"

"Yes?"

"Which musket is the one that doesn't work?"

"Mine. Your two are loaded. If you must use them, make sure you hit. Why?"

"Just wondering."

There were cries from the darkness, then. Whistles, as if groups of people were communicating. The sounds came from all sides. Finn had the uncomfortable sensation of being herded.

"To the wall!" he shouted. "We have to get inside." In the shadows, it was hard to see whether there were gaps they could climb through or not. They had to take the chance.

Whelm goaded the exhausted horse onwards. They lurched over the rutted ground, the cart complaining with creaks and squeals as it was thrown around. More cries and horn blasts blared out of the darkness to find them.

The walls, when they reached them, were smooth and hard and unbroken, with no sign of a way in.

"Perhaps we can climb them," said Finn. "Throw up

ropes."

"I'm not leaving the horse and cart," said Whelm. "We have to stand and fight."

"How much musket shot is left?" said Diane. She stood with her back to the wall, peering into the gloom.

"None," said Whelm. "I've had to use more of the stock. Bolts, screws, washers. I'll give you everything I've got left."

"Not the reader," said Finn.

"What does it matter?" called Whelm, his voice muffled, head inside the moving engine. He turned to pass them handfuls of metal fragments. "If we can't fight them off, we're going to be killed here tonight. You do know how to fire muskets, don't you?"

Finn nodded, then wished he hadn't as the throbbing in his head flared up.

"If we can kill enough of them quickly the rest might run away," said Diane.

"Maybe," said Whelm. "Or they might just decide they really, really don't like us."

The three of them climbed on top of the moving engine, backs to the wall, waiting. The horse, unimpressed by any of the excitement, chewed what scraps of grass she could find with a loud munching sound.

Finn heard rustling and clanking noises. The sound of people approaching. Many people, from all around. He still couldn't see anyone.

A boom from inside Engn rattled the wall against his back. Finn looked up to see a fireball rolling into the sky. A ball of seething red in the dark. He could feel the heat from it on his face as it rose over the scene.

In the light from the fireball, illuminated for those few moments, their attackers became clear. A line of figures closing around them, their faces livid and distorted. The red of the fireball glinted off metal helms and the tips of swords. Some of the attackers had steel limbs, too: lengths of old girder or pipe replacing lost arms and legs. Many more had joined the hunt, a hundred stark faces twisted in rage or anticipation at what was about to happen.

"Get ready to fire," said Diane. She sounded weirdly calm. "They won't know how much shot we've got. Perhaps we can frighten them off."

One of the figures worked forwards from the line. For a moment, Finn thought it would be Graves. But, of course, it couldn't be. This was a rougher, older voice, not someone he knew. He looked to be wearing one of the top hats and black cloaks about a bulky, powerful body. He spun a chain in his hand, a chain with a spiked weight on its end. Then the light in the sky faded, and their enemies became rough, misshapen silhouettes once more.

"Time's up, runaways!" the figure called to them. "Time to receive your punishment for daring to oppose the masters."

"You're no masters," Whelm called, managing to make his voice mocking. "Look at you. You're ridiculous. If Engn was still running, you'd all be in the mines where you belong."

The words held them for a moment. Diane took the opportunity and fired, her musket roaring, a smudge of red flame in the darkness. The sound of metal pinging and zinging off metal filled the air. There was a cry from somewhere. Then, as if the gunshot had released them, the throng of masters roared and surged forwards.

Another ball of flame boomed into the sky. To Finn's surprise, the leader who had spoken still stood. He held aside his clock to reveal the rough metal armour he'd plated himself with. Scraps and corners of iron held together with leather straps. His hat, too, was iron, hammered out from sheets to form the rough shape. He roared with laughter. "Fire again, my friends! Send me more iron. A little more won't harm me!"

Finn fired. The leader's face was unprotected; perhaps if they could stop him the others would pause. The leader staggered back as he was struck, then stood upright again.

He turned to show the throng he was unharmed. The masters roared with delight and surged past him.

"Take them!" The voice roared from the darkness as the light from the second fireball faded.

"Stand up as long as you can," said Whelm. "Kick them down when they climb onto the engine."

There was no time to reload the muskets. Beside him, Diane drew one of the knives she carried. She handed it to Finn. "Take this. I've got others."

Finn took the blade. The three of them stood side by side as the screaming rabble of patchwork ironclads and masters converged upon them.

XXI

Finn kicked the first of their attackers in the face, sending him toppling backwards to land on two others climbing up behind him. The man laughed, even as others used him as a steppingstone.

Beside him, Diane's steel blade was darting backwards and forwards, slipping between gaps in their armour, through eye-slits in their helms. She handled the blade with practiced skill. She'd had to fight more than once in her time on the run, although it wasn't something she liked to talk about. Whelm, on the other side of Finn, was less clinical, swinging a metal club backwards and forwards in an arc, bashing several heads at once.

For a moment Finn thought they might survive. Four, five, six of their attackers fell back to the ground and still the three of them stood unscathed atop the moving engine.

But the horse, normally so placid, was bucking and thrashing in panic. She snorted and screamed, the edge of alarm clear in her voice. These clanking, shouting figures with their sharp metal and their strange smells were too much for her. She lurched forwards, desperate to get away.

Whelm had the brake on the moving engine, but the horse's panic was too great. The cart pitched forwards, tilting as the horse tried to haul it away. Finn half-slipped and fell to one knee. He managed to right himself, just in time to stab his knife through the hand of a top-hatted master who'd reached up to grab him by the foot. The master screamed, red blood adding to the black decorations tattooed on his arm. Finn stood for a moment, balancing on the bucking engine, ready for the next attack. Then the cart jolted again, and suddenly he was slipping, falling down the curved side of the engine. He jarred his back painfully as he fell. Diane called his name, tried to reach him with an outstretched hand, but it was no use.

Finn fell into a sea of attacking masters and ironclads. Something sharp pierced his side as he crashed onto their helmets and swords. He screamed. For a moment his fall was halted. The attackers bashed and slashed at him. He tried to fight back, but there was no room to swing his knife properly, no way he could reach even a fraction of them. All the breath had been knocked out of him. He fell again, twisting and spinning to land on the ground. Something metal cracked the back of his skull, banging the gash Diane had bandaged.

For a time, everything became distant. He welcomed it. Sounds came muffled, as if coming to him through deep water. It was good to close his eyes, let the pain and all those hard edges slip away. For a moment, he didn't know where he was or even who he was.

"Finn! Get up!"

Diane. So, she was there too. Of course, she was. They'd been fighting together. The two of them against the masters. Only there was a master with them, helping them. For the moment, he couldn't understand how that had happened. He looked up at her atop the iron cart, shouting down at him, face grimy and splashed with blood.

The master was with them. Whelm. Whelm who had taken him from his home in a moving engine. Twice now. Why was he there?

A weight thumped into Finn's chest. A booted foot. Someone was clambering over him, using him to climb up the engine to get to Diane. He tried to call to her, but he had no voice. Blood poured from the hand in which she held her knife. He couldn't tell whether it was hers or not. Whelm stood beside her, clubbing the arm of someone trying to drag him down to the ground.

All around Finn, like a forest being lashed in a wind, the legs of their attackers twisted and writhed. Again, he had the strange impression of being under water, of watching distant events, like glimpsing some ancient battle in the orbs. Another foot, and then another, stamped onto his stomach. He felt no pain, no pain. They would die there at the walls of Engn and there was nothing he could do.

He must have blacked out again, because the next time he looked up Diane was alone on the engine. She still fought, swinging her knife from side to side in a fury. She screamed at Finn again, but he couldn't make sense of her words. He waved through the throng of flashing limbs and swords above him to tell her he was still alive.

Something like rain streaked through the air then, a sudden downpour all about him. He watched it, confused. He wasn't getting wet. For some reason, the rain struck down the tall figures clambering over and around him. Three, four, five of them slumped to the ground. Then one landed directly on top of him, a shocked face suddenly filling his vision. The man didn't move or speak. A silver arrow had pierced his head, passing right through helmet and skull as if to pin his hat to him.

Not rain. It was a shower of steel from the walls. Marvelling at the strange workings of the world, Finn passed out one more time, even as another dead weight flopped on top of him.

XXII

Light flooded into Finn's eyes. Someone was holding his left eye open. A crackling torch was being held close to his face, the heat on his exposed eyeball alarming. Sounds came to him: an assortment of groans, the clank of metal, a babble of low voices, pleas for mercy and cries that ended abruptly. His stomach and knee hurt sharply, and his head throbbed with a heavy pain. He tried to blink through the light to see who was there. See where he was. He'd come back to Engn, hadn't he? Or maybe he'd never really left. Perhaps that was it. He was still in the mines, waking up from some impossible dream of life back in the valley. That had to be it.

"Finn. Are you okay? Can you hear me?"

Diane was there. That was good. Of course, she was in the mines as well. She'd been captured. Confused thoughts and memories swirled in his mind. He knew there were things he wasn't grasping, but he couldn't remember what they were. Then something like clarity returned. No. He wasn't back in the mines. They'd escaped Engn and then destroyed it, and now they'd come back to discover Connor's secret. They'd been attacked by a gang of makeshift masters and ironclads. They'd been about to die, there against the wall, and then for some reason they hadn't.

"Whelm?" he said.

"He's alive," said Diane. "Bruised and battered. Although I'm not sure they'll let him live; these people don't seem to like the masters. The horse wasn't so lucky. Our attackers cut her down so she couldn't escape just after you fell. She deserved better than that."

"Your face is covered in blood," he said.

"Don't worry. Most of it isn't mine."

He reached up to try and wipe it away, but for some reason his hand went wide, flapping around by the side of her head as if in a wind.

"What happened to me?"

"You fell. You bashed your head hard again, blacked out."

"How long?"

"Only a few minutes."

"But what happened? How did we survive? Who are these people?"

"I think they're the wreckers," said Diane. "The wreckers or what's left of them. It was them sending up the fireballs. They must have heard the horns and come to see. They shot down from the walls, killed all those masters."

"Wreckers?"

"I think so. They came from inside Engn. Once their arrows had done their work, they let down ladders and climbed down to finish our attackers off."

"Why? What do they want?"

"Beats me. Does it matter? I suppose they saw people dressed as masters and ironclads and attacked."

A woman he didn't know knelt over him, her face scarred with more than one healed wound, her eyes keen like a those of a bird of prey. Penetrating.

"We have to get back inside," she said. "Some of them escaped before we could kill them. There may be others around, too. We will be safer inside. Can you walk?"

Finn nodded, although he had no idea if he could. The woman and Diane hauled him to his feet. Pain thudded through his head, and his stomach felt like something sharp was embedded in it. He swayed from side to side for a moment while dancing lights filled his vision.

"Take it slowly," said the woman. "You can lie down once we get inside."

Finn mumbled thanks, as if she was responsible for making him better. He looked around, trying to understand everything that had happened. The wall of Engn rose dark in front of him, but now there were rope ladders dangling down. Did he have to climb up there? He wasn't sure he'd be able to. More figures like the woman flitted around, their movements swift and purposeful, checking the bodies strewn about on the floor. Many were dead, but one or two still lived, writhing in agony from some gaping wound or trying to pull themselves to their feet. One man, oblivious to everything going on around him, sat and stared at his left arm, which had been hacked off below the elbow. He held his detached forearm and turned it around and around, as if trying to work out how to fit it back on.

Their rescuers had some of the masters bound with ropes, tied in a line against the wall. More survivors were being added to the line, yoked together so they couldn't escape. Whelm was among them. The ex-master stood with his hands bound behind his back. Didn't they know he was with Finn and Diane? Surely, they'd seen. A weak smile passed across Whelm's face. It occurred to Finn he might be remembering another day: a day when it was Finn shackled in a line against the walls of Engn and Whelm who was free.

The woman who'd helped him up appeared to be in

charge. Runners darted up to speak to her, talking close to her ear. One or two pointed outwards onto the plain. Finn could see there were figures moving about on top of the wall, keeping watch or preparing to fight off more attackers.

Finn worked his way over to her and grabbed her arm. He pointed at Whelm. "He's with us. Set him free. They attacked him, too."

"We know him. He was a master once."

"Yes, but not anymore."

"And were you masters, then?" She looked suspicious. She still carried a blade in her hand. Not pointing at Finn, but not pointing at the ground either. Held ready.

"No, no," he said. "The masters captured me. I was sent to the mines."

"Then why were you traveling with him?"

"We were traveling together. It isn't safe on the plains."

She didn't speak for a moment, studying him. Did she know who he was, what he'd done? It didn't seem so. He thought about telling her. But he stopped himself. She surely wouldn't believe him.

"Why are you even here?" she asked. "Have you come to fight?"

"Fight? Fight who?"

"That depends on which side you're on, doesn't it? Which city are you from? Which guild? A mechanical?"

"We're not from any guild or any city. We're from the valley."

The woman snorted. "There are thousands of valleys."

"It doesn't have any other name. It's just the valley."

"And you've come to join in the fighting?"

"No, we didn't know there was fighting. We came back to find out what had happened to Engn since it was destroyed."

"Nothing more?"

"No."

She clearly didn't believe him. She didn't move for a

moment, deciding what to do with them. But he and Diane had been attacked by the tattered masters, and that seemed to count for a lot.

"We'll sort it all out inside," she said. "The Queen of the Desolation will pass judgement on you. Now let's go. More horns have been heard; they could be converging on us. Some of this rabble know the old song-maps, too. They could pop up out of the ground at any moment."

"We need to take the cart with us," said Finn.

"There's no time. And there's no way to move it."

"But we have to."

She looked troubled again now, as if he had said the wrong thing. "Why? It's just a wrecked old engine."

"Because … because there are some old bits of machinery in there I've been trying to get working."

"You like getting machinery working, do you?"

"Sometimes. If it's useful."

The woman laughed. "Well, don't worry. We've got lots of machinery inside. More than you could ever want. You can have years of fun trying to piece it all back together. Now come on. We have to go. Now."

The woman strode off, shouting orders. Diane put an arm through Finn's and supported him as they followed her. "The Queen of the Desolation?" she said. "Who's that?"

"Never heard of her."

"Hasn't Whelm mentioned her?"

"Not to me."

"Well, it looks like we'll find out soon enough."

They moved, the tied prisoners prodded with swords to urge them forwards. They left the dead horse where she was against the wall, her great body twisted awkwardly, still yoked to the moving engine. The bodies of all those who had died – masters and wreckers – were also left. Whelm glanced backwards at the scene until the prod of a sword tip goaded him into motion.

The rope ladders were hauled back up, leaving the tall

walls unclimbable once more. Sticking to the shadows, they made their way around the walls.

The first time he'd come there, vast gates had been hauled open by steam engines to admit him. This time, they clambered over piles of rubble to squeeze their way through a crack in the walls. They'd walked for ten or twenty minutes, no one speaking. Once or twice masters' horns sounded in the distance, but there were no more attacks. It was fully dark, stars occasionally peeping out from behind scurrying clouds overhead.

The woman with the scarred face stood by the crack in the fractured wall as, one by one, they filed inside the ruins of Engn. In the darkness it was hard to see details. Here and there, gas or oil flames burned, although whether they were flaming out of control or had been put there for illumination, Finn couldn't tell. The air was thick with their acrid fumes. Their flickering lights suggested the ragged outlines of shattered machinery looming in the darkness all around: the ghosts of the towering engines that had once filled the place. Here were the mountains of debris they had seen from outside: tangled wreckage amassed against the walls. But beyond them, in the interior of Engn, everything was different. He could see great distances now. The lights flickering in a ring stretched all the way around the horizon, but in the middle, there was only a gaping emptiness.

He limped forwards, making his way through a tangle of iron spars to get a better look. He crawled up the slope of a large clockface, embedded in the ground at an angle where it had fallen. Its rusting hand pointing nearly to XXXVI – 36 – recording the time of its own destruction. It had been about that time the night in the Control Room. Perhaps this clock had stopped there and then as its workings were smashed or its timing systems were interrupted.

Finn pulled himself up the clockface by the ornate metal hand to see what lay beyond. Weakened by rust, the hand sagged and then snapped, sending Finn crashing to the ground, awakening all his bruises. He levered himself back to his feet using the broken metal clock hand as a crutch, then attempted the ascent again, balancing on what was left of the movement and stretching with his fingertips to reach the rim of the clock and so haul himself up.

He was near the edge of the cliff. Far down below, more lights flared. It was hard to judge distances in the half light, but he appeared to be looking all the way down to the floor of the mines. Or to the wreckage that must now fill them. There was the abyss into which the machinery had collapsed. The thought made him step backwards, grasping for the solidity of the ironwork. Gazing down into that pit was dizzying; it was like looking up into the sky; a plain of darkness interrupted by constellations of flames. He had the strangest impulse to jump off and fly towards those distant lights. And were there people down there? Living among those mountains of wrecked machinery? It seemed the only explanation.

He looked again across Engn, trying in vain to pick out any details he might know. There was none, but now he saw there were floating islands of light in the far distance, seemingly hovering in mid-air. Finn tried to make sense of what he was seeing. The islands blazed with many lights, red and white. They appeared to be lit up by electricity as well as oil flame. But how were they hovering above the ground? He could see no lights or bridges connecting them to the walls in any way. They simply floated there, shining in the darkness.

Shouts and screams came from behind him. Some commotion near the walls. Hastily he worked his way through the wreckage to discover fighting had broken out in his absence. Some of the shackled masters had managed to break free and were swinging around what weapons they could grab from the ground, keeping their captors at bay. Angry shouts and screams filled the air. More than one person was down, clutching open wounds. Diane didn't seem to be among them but Whelm was there in the thick of it. He'd grabbed the clock hand Finn had broken off, an oversized metal arrow, and was scything it backwards and forwards in front of himself to clear a path. He was still tied to two others, and the three of them lurched towards the breach in the walls to get outside again.

More steel shafts lanced down. Finn shouted, but no one was paying any attention. One of those Whelm was tethered to went down, an arrow pinning him through his chest to the ground. Whelm was dragged to his knees. He sawed desperately at the rope binding him with the jagged edge of the clock hand.

He nearly made it when another bolt struck him. Finn heard Whelm's agonized cry as the steel shaft struck him somewhere in the shoulder, sending him spinning to the earth.

Finn fought his way through the melee to reach Whelm. The ex-master lay with his eyes closed where he'd been struck. The steel bolt protruded from his shoulder, blood pooling freely in the wound.

Finn shouted his name, shaking Whelm as if the ex-master had simply decided to fall asleep there. There was no response. He shouted again. *He'd* brought Whelm there. Brought him to his death, just as he'd brought death to so many others. There had been too much dying. The loss of Whelm, suddenly, was too much. Finn shook him again, angry, ordering him to come back to life.

To his surprise, Whelm's eyes flickered open. He winced in pain as he looked at the metal arrow piercing his shoulder.

"Wanted to get back to the cart," he said. "Get away. Best to run when the fighting starts."

"I thought you were dead."

"No, I don't think so. I'll be okay. It's not the first time I've been hit."

Finn was suddenly aware it had gone very quiet. He

looked around. The wreckers stood in a ring around them, the scarred woman nearest. She held her long, notched sword in her left hand.

"So, he's just someone you met on the road, is he?"

"No," said Finn. "I…"

"Tie them both," said the woman to those she commanded. "Make sure they don't escape. If anyone gets loose again, kill them immediately."

Rough hands hauled Finn to his feet and tied his wrists. He struggled. He'd done nothing wrong. And he'd been responsible for destroying Engn. They should be thanking him, treating him as a hero. Not this.

He kicked out, catching one of the wreckers in the face, sending blood spraying across his face. The man roared and stepped back, but two others took his place, smothering Finn, forcing him to the ground. He shouted and swore, but there was nothing he could do. They bound his hands, then lashed him in line with Whelm.

Lying there, face half in the trampled mud, Finn caught Diane's glance. She stood wide-eyed, looking like she would leap to his defence at any moment. Fortunately, she was restraining herself. They couldn't fight all these people. The woman appeared to think Diane wasn't really with them. That was good. Perhaps, somehow, it would help.

Finn, Whelm, and the other survivors were hauled back to their feet and, with many prods and curses, were pushed forwards through the tangled ruins.

They walked for another hour or more. They clambered through numerous collapsed buildings, metal girders wedged between broken walls above them looking like they could fall at any moment. Past a standing wheel, now a rusting skeleton, never to turn again, but still dizzying to see, the arc of its edge rising high into the night sky. Across gaping abysses in the ground, bridged by rusting iron walkways that swayed and sagged as they crossed. Finn looked in vain for something familiar from his first visit here. He saw only one thing he recognized. Lying half buried in the mud was one of the self-governing valves. He wondered if it was one he'd made. He would never know.

Eventually they reached a point where a finger of ground extended away from the walls out into the abyss. At its end was an iron walkway, something like those he had once used to cross Engn high up in the air. This one led to one of the floating islands.

Only they weren't floating islands. He saw, now, that they were the pillars in the mines. Some of those vast trunks of stone had survived the destruction, leaving patches of the old floor level still standing. Most of Engn was gone, fallen into the pit, but these few scraps of the old surface remained.

The wreckers headed that way. Torches blazed all around the edge of the island. Some large building stood there, but it was hard to make out the scale of the place. Was it where this Queen of the Desolation lived? Or were they about to be thrown from it into the pit below?

Iron barriers manned by numerous guards blocked the causeway. Shadows up on the makeshift battlements watched them approach. Finn knew there would be arrows trained on him and the other prisoners.

The scarred woman, leading the way, stopped before the gates and called out, speaking in a language Finn didn't know. Perhaps it was some sort of code. After a few moments, the gates creaked open. The woman stepped through, accompanied by her soldiers. Diane, he noted, walked a little way behind her.

Finally, Finn, Whelm, and the other captives were pulled through, roughly, so that they sprawled onto the ground. With his hands behind his back, Finn could do little to cushion his fall and he bashed his nose hard on the ground. Immediately, he tasted blood in his mouth.

Someone kicked him, turning him over onto his back. The scarred woman. She was smiling now.

"Get some sleep. If you can. You will attend the queen when the morning comes. She will decide what is to be done with you."

The woman laughed as if she had made some great joke and strode away into the darkness.

"This queen," Finn called after her. "Who is she?"

The woman stopped and turned. "You don't know?"

"No."

"She's the one who saved us. The one who destroyed Engn."

XXIII

Their laughing captors pushed Finn and Whelm into a cramped metal cage standing near the drop into the wreckage. Whelm sat down in resignation as soon as he was pushed inside, holding his damaged arm gingerly. But Finn struggled, bending his neck at an awkward angle to remain upright in the confined space.

"Let us out! We've done nothing wrong. We're on your side!"

The wreckers ignored him. One – a small, squat man with a red face, as if he was so furious he was about to explode – struck Finn's hands with the flat of his blade. Finn jumped backwards and the door was slammed shut, then secured with chains and padlocks.

Finn pulled on the bars of the cage, as if he could tear them apart with his bare hands. There had to be some weakness in the metal, some means of escape.

"Best not do that," said Whelm.

"Why?"

"Because of that." Whelm looked upwards. Finn

followed his gaze.

A huge metal hook was descending from the sky, a clanking chain paying out behind it. The hook swayed as it neared, as if it were sniffing Finn and Whelm out. Finn followed the line of the chain. It was attached to the broken arm of an old beam-engine high above them. The chain ran along the arm and then descended through some pulleys to a winch operated by three wreckers.

"What's that for?" asked Finn.

"Isn't it obvious? It's what they always do to people they take prisoner."

The hook clanged onto the top of the cage. With a practiced movement, one of the wreckers reached up with a metal pole and positioned the hook through an eye welded onto the top of the cage. The wreckers on the winch waited for the call, then began to wind. The cage jolted, then lifted into the air. Jerk by jerk, the ground fell away beneath them.

"See what I mean?" said Whelm. "Best you don't try and pull the cage to pieces while we're in it."

The cage stopped ascending and swayed to and fro in the night air.

"It's only a short way to the ground," said Finn, quietly so no one on the ground would hear. "We can work one of the bars loose and drop down. Or, wait. There's a hatch in the floor. This part levers upwards. We can escape that way."

"No, Finn," said Whelm. "No, we really can't."

The cage lurched again, then, but this time sideways. Puzzled, Finn looked up. Now the arm of the beam-engine was swivelling sideways, hauled around by ropes. It was suddenly obvious what was going on, what Whelm meant. Finn stopped pulling on the bars and clutched them tightly.

The spinning, swaying cage neared the edge of the drop, then continued out over the wreckage. Finn studied the hook above him anxiously. It seemed impossibly small and slender now. Patches of rust covered the ironwork of the cage. Would it all hold? The metal squeaked as the wind picked up and sent the cage swaying and spinning around. Finn took care not to stand on the hatch forming a quarter of the floor, imagining himself plummeting through as it gave way. Down below them – far, far below – distant lights twinkled. There was no doubt the drop to the wreckage would kill them.

The wreckers stopped hauling the beam-engine arm around. Finn watched with growing alarm as a single individual took hold of the chain. If she let go, the cage would plummet to that distant ground. Finn's heart pounded. The wrecker holding the chain walked forwards to the brick tower on which the beam-engine arm rested. The cage dropped and dropped again as she took each step.

Then the wrecker stepped back and there were her two hands, empty. For a chilling moment, Finn thought she'd let go, that this was all some elaborate punishment. But the cage didn't fall. She'd fastened the chain to a hook on the tower.

Without saying a word, the wreckers turned and filed away, some of them laughing. The cage containing Finn and Whelm swayed gently backwards and forwards in the air.

"See what I mean?" said Whelm.

"You've been here before?"

"Always avoided them. But I've heard all about it."

"That's why you were fighting back there?"

"Obviously."

"What happens now?"

Whelm shrugged. "Might as well try and get some sleep. We're not going anywhere."

"We could start the cage swinging," said Finn. "We might be able to get it over the ground if we work hard enough."

"And even if that was possible, which it isn't, and even

if I could help with my arm like this, which I can't, how would we get out of the cage exactly?"

"We could work some of the bars loose first."

Whelm shook his head. "You want us to start pulling the cage apart and *then* swing it backwards and forwards, hoping it all holds together long enough for us to time the leap so that we hit the ground and don't plummet to our deaths."

"Do you have a better plan?"

"Yes, actually, I do." Whelm closed his eyes and rested his head on the side of the cage. "We wait until the morning and see what happens."

"And what do the wreckers normally do to people they capture and put in here?"

"You really want to know?"

"I asked, didn't I?"

"If we're lucky, they'll send us down their wires into the underworld."

"And if we're unlucky?"

"Then they won't bother with the wires."

Whelm was soon breathing deeply, as if he was utterly used to sleeping in a metal cage swaying over an abyss. Finn stay awake for a long time. It was impossible to get comfortable. The metal bars dug into him however he sat or lay. His knee and head throbbed constantly. In the end, he took to sitting with his legs dangling over the drop, watching the twinkling of the distant lights. Now and then, screams and cries came to him from somewhere in the darkness.

He wondered where Diane was, whether she'd come to rescue them. They hadn't shackled her. She'd be somewhere in the darkness, coming up with a plan to get them out.

A clanging sound like some vast, cracked bell awoke him. His face was hard against an iron bar, digging into him, but a cool wind blew on his face, swaying him gently backwards and forwards. It took a few moments for recollection to come to him.

No rescue had come. At some point in the night he'd fallen asleep in the cage. He opened his eyes. The distant ground was far below. For a moment he couldn't make sense of what he was seeing. A jungle of tangled wreckage like a riot of overgrown vegetation. And, crawling all over it, tiny insects.

No, not insects. People. Hundreds of them. *Thousands* of them.

"There are people down there," he said. "Down in the underworld."

"Lots of people live down there," said Whelm from somewhere behind him. "Lots of people crawling among the wreckage."

"How do they get down?"

"There are ways. Ways back up, too, although those are rarer."

Finn pushed himself up to squat in the cramped cage. His limbs ached where he had lain on the iron bars. He was bruised and cold, his muscles stiff. He tried to work some life back into his body. Oddly, his knee felt a little better. His head still throbbed, but it hadn't bled any more.

He looked around. The sun was up already, filling the void where Engn had once stood with a hazy, glowing light. He could see what the torches and flames had merely suggested the night before. The scale of the wreckage made his head swim. He had to clutch hold of the bars of the cage for a moment as if he were in danger of falling. The mangled remains of the machinery spread for miles and miles, off to the horizon, filling the great pit into which Engn had collapsed. He'd thought he might recognize parts of it. In his memories it had shrunk down to the areas he'd known well. The Valve Hall. The

Blueprint Hall. The Directory. He'd forgotten how vast it was.

Many more of the islands were visible in the light, striding out across the void. Atop them, buildings and machines still stood, fragments of the great machine. There was movement there, too. More tiny black figures crawling around. But not only that. Here and there, quite clearly, machinery was working. Beam-engine arms pumped. Wheels turned. Electrical sparks arced. The mechanisms didn't go anywhere, weren't connected to each other, had no point he could see. Yet there they were, remnants of Engn. Was one of these broken fragments of the machine where the timing messages had come from?

The wind brought sounds, muffled by the distance but quite clear. Echoes of his former days in Engn. The explosive *humph* of a steam engine. The deep thump of iron hammers. The cycling squeal of turning wheels. He wished he had a line-of-sight 'scope to see more clearly what was going on. He'd done the right thing in coming there. Engn was being rebuilt, and Connor had foreseen it, given Finn a trail so he'd come back and complete the job they'd started. The final destruction of Engn.

He imagined felling one of those titanic pillars. If they did it right, it would fall and bring down the next. And the next. Perhaps they could bring them all crashing down with one well-placed explosion. Was that what he was supposed to do?

"Who lives on the islands?" he said.

"The islands?"

"On top of the pillars."

"Apart from this one, the remnants of the masters. The real masters, I mean, not that bunch of losers who attacked us."

"The masters are still there?"

"Some. Not many. Those who were lucky to survive when the machines came down. They try and maintain the old order. Pretend none of this happened."

"The masters are on their islands and the wreckers are here, all around the edge."

"Yeah."

"Then who is down there? Who are all those people living in the abyss?"

"They're just … everyone. Normal people. People trying to survive. People who don't know or care about masters or wreckers or any other title."

"You've been down there?"

"That's where the machinery is. That's where you have to go to find parts to salvage. But it's wild down there. Brutal. All the rusting machinery falling on you is bad enough, but it's the people you must watch out for. A lot of them are desperate. I've seen plenty of people go down and not come back. It's a battlefield, as often as not. The wreckers and the ironclads fighting over the scraps."

"But you've always managed to survive down there."

"I've been lucky. I don't take risks. I get out as quickly as I can."

"That's good to know."

Whelm laughed, sounding something like the old Whelm, when he still had ironclads to order around. "You think we can escape the wreckers?"

"Yes."

Whelm shook his head. "You don't get it, Finn. We had a chance before. Creep inside, get down into the underworld, maybe find my ironclad or a spindle reader. But we can't do that now. They're not just going to let us go. You do know that, don't you?"

"I destroyed Engn," said Finn. "The three of us did. Once we explain, they'll be on our side."

"Is that what you think?"

"It's obvious."

"Okay. Sure. That's what'll happen. They'll treat you as a returning hero and do everything in their power to help you."

The mockery in Whelm's voice was clear. But he was

an ex-master. He obviously wouldn't trust the wreckers. It would be different once Finn explained who he was.

He sighed and stared back out at the scene before him, the iron cage swinging slightly in the morning breeze. In the distance, the second or third island in line, some sort of bird had taken flight, a black letter T drifting stiff-winged in the air. Some sort of crow? He'd seen them often in Engn in the old days, flocking on the roofs. But no, this surely was no bird. The distance was too great. It had to be huge. Some part of the machine, although he couldn't see how that could possibly be. It left behind it a line of grey smoke in the air as it circled.

He cast a puzzled glance at Whelm, indicating the mysterious machine with a nod of his head. "What is that? That dot in the distance."

Whelm screwed up his eyes to see, then shrugged, seemingly past caring. "That? A machine."

"It's *flying*."

"Yes, so a flying machine."

"How can that be? What is it for?"

"No idea. Why does it have to be *for* anything? You need to stop trying to make sense of it all."

The flying T passed behind the distant island and was gone, and Finn was soon distracted by nearby shouts. The sound of chains rattling and metal scraping upon metal. He thought they'd come to haul the cage back in. But that wasn't it.

Further along the cliff was another broken beam-engine arm hanging over the drop. Smoke rose from its chain as it rattled and roared over the drum holding it. Something was being lowered down at great speed. Five or six wreckers were over there, but they stood well back from the crane, clearly wary of the screaming metal. The chain reached its end with a jarring crunch. For a moment, Finn thought the whole engine was going to be pulled into the abyss with the force of it. But the beam-engine arm withstood. Wreckers climbed it, out over the drop to peer down into the distant underworld.

Heavy horses were brought and attached to a capstan around which the chain was wound. Cries came from the wreckers on top of the beam-engine arm, and the horses were goaded into motion. They stamped forwards, winding the capstan, hauling up the chain from the underworld. Some great weight was clearly on the end. The chain swung to and fro as it rose, link by link.

Finally, after perhaps twenty minutes of effort from the straining horses, the burden lurched into view. Finn had expected to see another cage, people being hauled up to the surface. But it wasn't that. Instead there was a net containing a jumble of machine parts and broken mechanisms. The remains of some great tower clock were among them, its cogs and wheels turning no longer. He wondered which clock it had been, whether he'd ever seen it working.

"What are they doing?" he said to Whelm, who still sat with his eyes closed, head slumped forwards as if bored by everything around him. At Finn's question he opened one eye and peered out.

"Could have kept me in business for months, that little lot."

"They're collecting machine parts too?"

"To destroy them. That's what they do; melt down every piece they can get their hands on. Then they tip the molten metal back down into the pit and start again."

"Why?"

"They're *wreckers*."

"But it will take years to destroy all that. Lifetimes."

"They're not in any hurry, are they? They have all the time in the world. Each load they destroy is another victory for them. They are completely mad. Didn't I say?"

The remains of the clock and the other contraptions were lifted over a waiting metal cart. The ropes holding the net together were cut and the machine parts fell into the cart with the sound of thunder. More horses were lined up to haul the cart away. Finn watched as it passed by. He wondered if there was a spindle reader there.

Thirty minutes later another weight was hauled up to the surface by the heavy horses. This time it *was* people: another cage, but not padlocked or chained. Nine or ten wreckers sat or stood inside, all wearing leather armour and carrying a variety of weapons: swords, knives, clubs, flails. They'd clearly seen some heavy fighting. More than one had a bandaged head, and there were other wounds too, some serious. One woman's left arm ended at her elbow, although from her distant stare it was hard to know if this was an old wound or a fresh one.

The cage holding the soldiers was hooked and drawn onto the surface of the island. Slowly, many of them limping and grimacing, the wreckers returning from the underworld crawled out and away. One turned to look at Finn, a penetrating scowl on his face, as if Finn were responsible for all the injuries they'd received.

Three hours later, a group of wreckers came for Finn and Whelm. A grapple was swung over to their cage, and they were hauled back to sold ground. Finn and Whelm crawled out. It was a delight to stand on solid rock again. A delight to be able to stand upright. Finn hurt all over, his muscles bruised and cramped. His mouth was parched, and the pain in his head thundered. How long was it since they had eaten or drunk anything? At least he was able to put weight on his knee. The enforced rest had helped. There was no sign of Diane anywhere. He just hoped she'd been given better treatment.

The wreckers, led by the red-faced man from the night before, pushed and prodded them forwards. They walked along the edge of the drop for a way, past a line of twelve 'scopes pointing out at different angles down into the wreckage or across to the other islands. One of the 'scopes was in use: an older man was scanning the distant ground, peering through the eyepiece and then jotting notes down on a piece of paper. What was he looking for down there? He put Finn in mind of the masters, watching the workers toiling away in the Valve Hall from the safety of their high balcony.

The main building nearby was a round stone building, something like a clock tower whose top half had crashed to the ground. Now it was a ragged, windowless fortress. Many wreckers milled around the open ground in front of it, but three stood guard at the foot of a flight of steps which led up to the only doorway: an opening two or three stories up. It reminded Finn of the buildings around the Octagon, but that was surely miles away, if it even still existed.

The guards parted and Finn and Whelm were led up the stone stairs spiralling around the tower.

Inside, it took his eyes a few moments to adjust to the darkness. Shafts of light slanted down from above, lighting up one side of the walls, but the rest of the interior was lit only by torches set around the walls.

Finn's footsteps echoed as he strode forwards. He picked out detail of his surroundings. The room appeared to take up the entire floor space of the building. Ahead, a semicircle of chairs had been set around the room, chairs in which people sat, waiting for them. The similarity to the Inner Wheel was suddenly very clear, except there were many more thrones there. Instead of twelve there were – he counted quickly – twenty-four. Of course. These were the old guilds, the Temple Guilds, not the new.

Once again, he walked forwards to stand in the middle. Still no one had spoken. Once again, faces were hard to make out. The thrones were crafted from fragments of bent and broken machinery, each with a little canopy to hide the features of the individual sitting there.

The largest of the chairs was in the middle of the semicircle. Set upon a raised dais, it was welded together from the remnants of steam engines and clocks, its curving sides cut from some boiler. This had to be the throne of the queen the wreckers had mentioned. The Queen of the Desolation.

The woman sitting there stirred, then leaned forwards, the light of the torches catching her features. Finn saw immediately who it was. He'd last seen her on his final day in the Blueprint Hall, when he'd tried to start the fire and she'd refused to help him.

"So, it is you, Finn Smithson," said Maeve. "And Master Whelm of the Seventh Wheel. How good it is to see you both again."

XXIV

Finn peered warily around at the semicircle of guild leaders in their shadowy thrones. Here he was again, judged by another circle of masters. But it was different this time; he had nothing to fear from these people, not once he explained who he was and why he was there. They were on his side. They would welcome him. They might even help him find the answers he sought.

The woman he'd known as Maeve – and then as Lud, leader of the wreckers – smiled as if he was an old friend come to visit.

She clicked her fingers in the air as she studied Finn. An old man wearing a patched brown coat so long it dragged along the ground shuffled out of the shadows. He had pens wedged behind each ear. Ink dribbled down his neck and onto his shoulders. He appeared not to notice. He dragged along a long scroll of paper, which he stood on repeatedly, tearing the paper again and again. Each time he tutted and pulled the paper free from his feet with evident anger, as if he blamed the scroll for deliberately tripping him. He arrived at Maeve's throne with only a tattered section of the paper remaining, but he held it up for Maeve to see with satisfied delight.

Maeve studied what was written there. Finn could see her eyes flicking backwards and forwards, her thin lips moving as she read. Then she looked back up.

"So, Finn Smithson. Here you are. When we drew up the lists after the Wrecking, we assumed you had died. One of so many unfortunates crushed in the mines. But no, here you are, alive and well. It's quite remarkable. How on earth did you manage to survive the collapse?"

"I managed to get out of the mines just before the end."

"Did you? Interesting." Maeve nodded thoughtfully, as if judging his words. She turned to study Whelm. The ex-master stood beside Finn with his head bowed. He held his ruined shoulder with his left hand, as if holding his joint together.

"Now you, Master Whelm," Maeve said. "You are an old friend, aren't you? Always evading us down in the wreckage, always one step ahead of us. Clever, slippery Master Whelm. And here you are, too, in our clutches at last."

"I mean you no harm," said Whelm, his voice low and subdued. "I am no longer a master."

Maeve laughed an unconvincing laugh. A ripple of amusement rippled from around the ring of thrones.

"Even if that were true, do you think it would change anything?" said Maeve. "You think you can escape paying for all your crimes just because you've stopped committing them? If, indeed, you have stopped?"

Whelm shook his head but didn't reply. He glanced across at Finn. The look of desperation was clear in his eyes. Whelm thought he wasn't going to survive this.

"Where is Diane?" Finn asked. "The woman we arrived with?"

"She is safe."

"She … she wasn't with us," said Finn. "Not really, I mean. We met on the road. She…"

Maeve held up her hand to stop him. "Finn, Finn. Once again you underestimate us. We know Diane too. All those years while we waited and watched. We weren't simply doing nothing, as you once accused me of. We were laying our plans, keeping our records, making our lists. Preparing for the great day. We know Diane was never in Engn, except for a brief stay in the mines at the very end. She was never with the masters. She ran from them. Ran for years from the ironclads, living by her wits in the wilds, refusing to give in. Fighting back where others collaborated. We know also she lives a long way from you and that you met on the road and travelled together for safety. She at least has nothing to fear from us. Nothing at all."

That was good. Diane had done the right thing by pretending not to know him. It was a good job the line-of-sight network wasn't fully functional. Otherwise the wreckers could easily discover the truth.

"Where is she now?" asked Finn again.

Maeve shrugged as if it was of no interest to her. "How should I know? She is free to come and go. I do not control her. She's left for all I know. Gone back to her life in the wilds, her curiosity about the ruins of Engn satisfied."

Finn nodded, as if Diane's fate was of no great concern. He didn't like to think of her out there on her own. Although she could take care of herself, better than he could. Had she really left? Perhaps she'd had no choice. Well. By the sound of it she was safe, from the wreckers at least. That was something. If they could, somehow, escape, they could meet up again with her outside.

"The question is, though," continued Maeve, "what are we to do with you, Finn? Are you as guilty as your friend here, or as innocent as Diane? What side were you on when it came down to it? Who did you fight for when the battle lines were drawn?"

"You know very well I was on your side," said Finn. "I showed you. That day in the Blueprint Hall. When I tried to destroy the plans for Engn. You were there."

Maeve nodded her head, acknowledging the fact. "True, I was there. I also recall you disobeyed my direct instructions. Carried on with your small act of sabotage even though it clearly endangered us all. Risked our long plans."

"What plans? You weren't doing anything. At least I was trying." The injustice of this riled him still. He had destroyed Engn, he and Diane and Connor. Not her.

"Finn." Whelm's voice beside him was just a whisper. A warning. A warning not to antagonize the wreckers any further.

Maeve sat upon her chair of broken machinery, considering him. How much did she really know about what happened? Not much, he guessed. Engn had come crashing down around their ears one day, and she'd stepped in to claim responsibility. Maybe she even believed her own stories. So how could he show her he was on their side?

"Why are you here now?" asked a voice from the shadowed figures. "Why have you returned?"

"There were signals," said Finn. "Timing messages on the line-of-sight. I thought Engn had been destroyed, but it seemed to be starting up again. So, I came to see. Came to make sure it was all wrecked."

"And you travelled with Master Whelm?"

"We also met on the road," said Whelm. "We were attacked on the plain by people claiming to be masters."

"He saved us," said Finn. "He shot one of our attackers and got us away."

"Why would you do that, Master Whelm?" the man continued. "Tell us why you risked your life to save Finn."

Whelm glanced across at Finn again before replying. "I ... I felt guilty."

"Guilty?"

"Guilty for what I did to him."

"And what did you do to him?"

"I brought him in the first place. It was me. I took him from his home and transported him here in a moving engine. I didn't know he'd survived, but then I saw him on the plain. He was taking refuge in a ruined line-of-sight tower and the mob was burning him out. A mob dressed like masters and ironclads. I stepped in to help."

"These signals you mentioned." Another voice, off to Finn's right. A woman's voice with the croak of old age in it. "Tell us about them."

"They were timing signals, like in the old days. Sent from Engn."

"Messages sent from Engn and you come running. They don't sound like simple *timing messages* to me," said Maeve. "They sound like recruitment. A call to arms. It sounds to me, Finn Smithson, as if the masters summoned you and you came to fight for them. You and your friend Master Whelm."

"No. It wasn't like that."

"You knew full well the messages were sent by the Engneer, didn't you?" said the unnamed woman to his right.

"What? No. I don't know who that is," replied Finn. "I don't know anything about that."

"You claim you have come here to join us? Become a wrecker? Is that it?"

"I came simply to see what was happening, to make sure it wasn't being rebuilt. There were earthquakes, too, and I was told Engn had something to do with them."

"Earthquakes?" said Maeve with sudden interest, as if Finn had touched upon a delicate subject. "Who told you Engn was responsible?"

Probably best not to mention Connor's mother. Her connection to the Mechanical Guilds might well be known to the wreckers. "It was ... just a woman in my valley.

She's dead now, killed by one of the tremors. She didn't make a lot of sense, but I had to come and see for myself."

The woman off to his right persisted in her questioning. "Let me get this clear. You *haven't* come to join us?"

"No," said Finn. "I mean, I had no plan to. I just needed to find out what was going on. I didn't know you were still here."

"You know," said Maeve, "when there's a war on, you have to decide which side you're on. You can't simply wander around the battlefield claiming to be friends with everyone."

"I wasn't aware there was a war on," said Finn.

Maeve snorted. "And you expect us to believe that as well, do you? You arrived at the walls of Engn well-armed, in a moving engine, accompanied by a master. A master who has been here many times. And yet you know nothing about the battles being fought down there in the wreckage? Is that what you're saying?"

"I knew there was fighting, of course," said Finn. "I didn't know it was a *war*. I thought that was all ancient history."

There was silence around the ring as the assembled figures absorbed Finn's words. Why couldn't they see he was on their side? He thought about telling them about the spindle he carried. The glimpses of past events they'd seen in the orb. Surely, they'd understand then. See the need to help him find out the truth. But something stopped him from speaking. Fear of them seizing the memory stick and melting it down, perhaps. He couldn't let that happen. There were still secrets on there.

Someone else standing in the shadows behind Maeve's chair leaned into the circle to whisper in Maeve's ear. Maeve watched Finn as she listened. The whisperer glanced briefly at Finn before receding back into the gloom. It was enough to show Finn who this was. Ciara. Ciara from the Blueprint Hall. He had said things to her, hadn't he? Confided in her. He tried to recall his precise words. It hadn't gone well, that much he knew. The look passing across Maeve's face sent a chill through him.

"You knew Connor," said Maeve. It was a statement of fact, not a question.

"Connor?"

"The master who became the Director's apprentice. Don't pretend, Finn. You and he were boyhood friends. You swore Connor could be trusted. Said he was one of us, didn't you?"

"He *was* one of us."

"Yet he went on to become apprentice to the Director. He was next in line to be the ultimate power in Engn. The person in charge. And you still claim he was one of us?"

"He was, I swear it. He was playing a role all that time, so he could get close to the Director. It was all a plan so he could destroy Engn."

More than one of the assembled guildmasters snorted with disbelief at Finn's words. Muttered words passed around the semicircle of chairs, the undercurrent of anger clear in them.

"It's true," said Finn. "Do you even know who Connor's father was?"

"Why don't you tell us?" said Maeve.

Finn looked around the half circle of thrones. "Who here speaks for the Stonecarvers?"

The woman who had quizzed him replied from the shadows. "There is little left of that guild in these days. The upstarters have ground us down to grit and sand. The towers of Stonehavn were brought down many years ago, partly thanks to earthquakes and fires, but also because of depopulation, the loss of the young. The towers lie in ruins, and we are as scattered as the dust. But I speak for them. Why do you ask?"

"Because Connor's father was a descendent of Baron Rankin. The man who led the attack on the great clock tower all that time ago. And Connor was his father's son."

"How do you know this?" asked the woman.

He had to think quickly. "Connor told me. And in his house, there were all these pictures. Pictures of Rankin, pictures of the battle. Connor came here to complete the work his ancestor started. I swear it."

"And who was his mother, Finn Smithson?" asked Maeve.

"His mother?"

"Yes. His mother."

He couldn't avoid the question. It was suddenly clear Maeve already knew the answer. "Her family was from the Clockmakers Guild," he said.

A mutter passed around the circle. Maeve waited for it to subside. "Connor must have had an interesting childhood. And you claim he was his father's son? Despite all the evidence to the contrary he was his mother's?"

"I do. Connor was on our side all along. He and I worked together in secret for years."

"Worked together on what exactly? Tell us precisely what you did."

"Finn, don't tell them. It won't go well." Whelm's whisper was urgent. But Finn could think of nothing else to say. He only had to reveal the truth and they'd see. Realize they could trust him.

"We destroyed Engn. That's what we were doing. We made it to the Control Room and got the keys and codes necessary to disrupt the mechanisms. Engn didn't just implode or break down. It was us. Connor and me together. We brought it all crashing down. Connor died and I survived the collapse. And now I've come back to make sure we destroyed it for good."

There was silence in the room as the guildmasters absorbed his words.

Finally, Maeve broke the silence. "You are claiming you brought the great machine to its knees? Thousands of wreckers working in secrecy across Engn, laying plans for generations, but you did this thing? You and the apprentice Director?"

"Yes. It's true. I swear it."

"Centuries we've been fighting this war, Finn Smithson. Fighting these Upstart Guilds with their clever mechanisms that try to turn us all into machines. For generations they've fought us and killed us and mangled us in their engines. For generations we've clung on, fighting back where we could to stop the spread of their brutal ideas. And always with the distant plan, the hope, of finally levelling Engn, the machine from which the corruption spreads across the world. Generations of wreckers working away in secret to bring the machine to its knees. And finally, finally, after so much sacrifice, we achieved it. And yet you, a boy from the valleys, you say you did that? Won this great victory that has taken us so many hundreds of years to win?"

Finn nodded but didn't reply.

Maeve stood. "Take them back to the cage while we decide their fate."

"Wait!" shouted Finn. "Wait. It's true. I can prove it. I can prove I'm on your side."

"How?" said the woman, the Stonecarver guildmaster, her tone dismissive.

Finn took the folded slip of paper from his pocket. The one Mrs. Megrim had given him as he left. He glanced at it for a moment to remind himself of the words. He'd expected a line-of-sight encryption key like last time, but instead Mrs. Megrim had written, in her dense, spidery script, a series of seemingly random phrases.

The sun is setting in the west ... The great clock has stopped at one minute to midnight ... Fires burn where once there was peace.

They'd puzzled him at first. *This might help you with the wreckers,* she'd said. They could only be one thing: wrecker pass phrases. At least, he desperately hoped so. Perhaps she'd been told them, or perhaps she'd found them out by intercepting messages over the years. Or perhaps friendly operators from elsewhere on the network, someone like

Henri, had passed them along to her. If he ever got back home, he'd ask.

Finn handed the slip of paper over to Maeve. The look of alarm flashing across her features made it clear she recognized the words.

"Where did you get these?" she asked.

"A friend to the wreckers back home. She used the line-of-sight network to defeat Engn, stop messages getting through, communicate with friends."

"A *line-of-sight* operator?"

"I used to help her out. She was on your side. I mean, she *is* on your side."

"She was spying on us. The line-of-sight network was the tool of Engn. This friend of yours has intercepted our messages. Intercepted them and, no doubt, relayed them to her masters in Engn."

"No."

"Yes." Maeve motioned to the guards. "This condemns them utterly. This hearing is over. Take them away."

Rough arms seized them. Whelm gasped in pain as one of the guards grabbed his shattered shoulder. Finn struggled, but it was no use. There were too many of them. They were led away, back into the light, back into the iron cage dangling over the great drop into the underworld.

XXV

"What's taking the time?" said Finn. "What are they doing?"

It was evening again, the sky darkening to purple above them. Lights were beginning to sparkle all across the vast expanse of the wreckage below them. Distant clanks and a background roar filled the air. Finn was already not noticing it.

No one had come to deliver their fate. No one had come anywhere near them.

Whelm was slumped back in the corner, eyes shut again. "They're just stringing it out. Letting us suffer. I'm sure they decided what to do with us hours ago. I'm sure Lud made up her mind while we were still in there."

"To throw us into the underworld?"

Whelm nodded. "Obviously."

"I'm sorry," Finn said. "Sorry for involving you in this."

"You didn't force me, Finn. Not like I forced you to come last time."

"What you said about feeling guilty in there, about bringing me here – was that true?"

"Who didn't do things they regret when Engn was running? Things they had to do just to survive."

Finn nodded. He looked back to the ruined tower where Maeve and her wreckers held court. Figures came and went in the half light, but none came near. No one had even brought food or water. His mouth felt like sandpaper. His voice was a croak as he spoke.

"Maeve said something about an *Engneer*. Someone sending messages out. What did she mean?"

"A crazy story. The wreckers are full of superstitions."

"But what do they say?"

"They say there is this incredible machine built to take over the running of Engn in the event of catastrophe. A clockwork version of the Director that activates to coordinate the rebuilding. I think they just like to have an enemy, a demon to identify. Once it was Engn itself. Now that's gone, they've invented this story of the Engneer. Wheeling around on one of the islands issuing orders to the remains of the ironclad army, overseeing the reconstruction, a moving engine with a clockwork brain. Madness, utter madness."

"You've never seen this machine?"

"Of course I haven't, because it doesn't exist. How could it even be possible?"

Finn nodded. They fell silent for a time. A huge weariness washed over Finn. He had fought and fought but he had failed. There was no way out of this. Perhaps Engn would be rebuilt, and perhaps it wouldn't, but at least he'd tried. At least he'd done all he could to end the tyranny. Whatever Maeve said, he had done that. He and Connor and Diane. They hadn't just given in.

He wondered again where Diane was. She wouldn't have had far to go to escape. Back through the broken walls and away. There wasn't much else she could do. She wasn't going to come and rescue them. How could she?

He regretted asking her to come to the ruins now. Putting her through all that. She could have stayed behind in the valley as she'd really wanted, safe enough if there were no more tremors. She could have gone anywhere. Instead she'd come back with him.

He slipped into sleep then, memories of his time in the mines and of recent events twining together in confused and troubling dreams.

They were awoken by someone tugging on a grapple thrown across to them. Back on the hard surface of the ground, indistinct in the dark of the night, stood a shadowy figure.

"Diane?" She'd come for them after all.

But it was an old woman standing there when she threw back her hood. No one he knew. The torch she carried made shadows lurch about her face, as if her features were in constant flow and couldn't decide how they wanted to look. Was this it, then? Had the wreckers come to deliver their fate?

"My name is Arana," said the old woman. "Guildmaster of the Stonecarvers."

He recognized her croaking voice from the hall. "Have you come to cast us into the underworld? Or are you here to rescue us?"

The woman glanced around as if wary of being seen. She was alone. If this was an execution there'd be more of them, wouldn't there?

"What you told us in there," she said. "About Baron Rankin and Connor. I believe you. He was a great figure in our history. A good man. Any descendent of his would be as true as good stone, however its surface was carved, however it was dressed."

"Then throw a rope over," said Finn. "We can haul ourselves across to the ground. Have you got the key? We can escape without Lud knowing anything."

The woman didn't move. She looked down at the ground. "I wish I could, Finn. I do. But it isn't so simple. The world has changed, you see. In the old days it was so simple. Right and wrong, black and white. Simple battle lines. Now it's not so clear anymore. The ends justify the means, Lud says, but maybe they do and maybe they don't."

"We want to destroy Engn, and so do you," said Finn. "Surely that's simple enough?"

"Of course. Yes. And perhaps Lud is going about this the right way and perhaps she isn't. There's more than one among the guildmasters who disagree with her. But we have to remain united, don't you see? Otherwise they'll crush us. Down there in the wreckage it isn't always clear who is winning and who is losing. I do know we send down many who don't return. This is no time for factions and squabbles. We must set our little differences aside. Yes, I think we do."

From the darkness, behind him, Whelm snorted with disgust. "Great. She's come to make herself feel better. Not to actually help us."

"Let us out," said Finn. "What difference does it make? There are only two of us and the wreckage is vast. We'll be gone and no one will know."

There was a pause as she considered his words. Finally, she replied, "I'm sorry, Finn. I wish I could. But the battle lines are drawn. I wish things were different, I do. But things are as they are."

Whelm snorted again. "Great. Philosophy, too."

"Please," said Finn. "There are things we have to do there. Things Connor wanted us to do."

She paused. He thought she was going to relent. But then she pulled the cowl back over her face, turned, and hobbled into the darkness.

XXVI

Earthquakes roused him from sleep once more. Some nightmare, the details already vague, lingered in his mind. For a moment he was back at home, in bed with Diane while the house shook and danced around them.

But memory of where he really was hit him like a blow to the gut. This time the hard steel of the cage dug into his back. The cold of the night air in which they hung suspended had chilled and stiffened his muscles to useless ropes within his flesh. He was going to die. When the morning came, he and Whelm were to be hurled into the underworld, to become two more broken mechanisms among the tangled remains of Engn.

An earthquake made no sense, though. They were hanging by a chain from the wreckers' crane. How was a tremor making them rock and sway so much?

He opened his eyes. Only the faint, background glow of Engn provided illumination. The lights in the gulf beneath him were as still and indifferent as the cold stars. There was no earthquake. Then the cage jerked again.

Someone was pulling them. A muffled grapple had been thrown across, with a rope leading from it back to solid ground. Two figures stood there, hauling in the cage between them.

Their executioners had arrived. He'd though they'd be left until morning, at least, but perhaps this was what they did. Quietly throw people into the pit in the dead of night, when there was no one around to see.

"Come on, Whelm," said Finn, nudging the ex-master with his foot. "They've only sent two of them. We can fight them. Take them by surprise. Throw *them* over and get away."

Whelm groaned, then worked his way to his knees. He wasn't using his left arm at all. He stared up at Finn and then across to the two wreckers. He wasn't going to be much use in a fight. Could Finn tackle both? He could try. There was nothing to lose. The rope jerked them nearer and nearer the land. If only he had a weapon. His hand went to the spindle. It was small, but solid metal. Perhaps he could use that. Jab it into one of their eyes when they weren't expecting it.

They were over solid ground, now, three feet up in the air because of the arc of the chain. One of the figures – the taller one – pulled a key from inside their cloak and reached up to unlock the hatchway. Finn's heart pounded. He would only get one chance. He would have to take them by surprise as soon as the cage was open. He grasped the spindle in his fist, ready to lunge.

"Finn! It's okay. It's me." Diane. It was Diane. She was securing the rope around a length of iron girder jutting from the ground. She turned, slipped her hood from her head and it *was* her. Come to rescue them after all.

Finn stooped to work his way out of the cage. He dropped to the ground and limped across to embrace her. She was safe. He was safe. For that moment, nothing else mattered. Engn, the spindle, the wreckers – he didn't care about any of it.

"I thought you'd gone," he said. "I thought they'd thrown you out."

"No, I've been here. Waiting and watching."

"They just let you stay?"

She shrugged. "They truly didn't know about us. Why would they? I had to say you and Whelm had captured me to bring me here. It was the only thing I could think of."

"It was the right thing to do. I told myself you were free, but I couldn't be sure. I thought maybe she'd lied about you. That you were in another cage somewhere, or you'd already been thrown off."

"No. Nothing like that."

"That's good. That's wonderful."

Whelm was squeezing his way through the hatchway. He fell to the ground heavily with a barely suppressed groan.

The other figure who'd rescued them spoke at last. "I'll open the door in the floor of the cage before we release it. Then they'll think you decided to take things into your own hands and jump in the night. You wouldn't be the first. I think that's what they were hoping you'd do."

It was a man's voice. Another voice Finn recognized. Aelth. The tall man from the Blueprint Hill stepped forwards to shake Finn's hand. "It's good to see you again, Finn."

Finn was struggling to make sense of what was going on. Was this all some plan of Maeve's? "It's good to see you, too. But I don't understand. You were with Maeve. You're a wrecker. Why are you helping? Are you secretly working against her now?"

Aelth shook his head, looking around warily as if afraid of being overheard. "No. Nothing like that. I follow Lud, I do. It's just, what you did that night. In the Blueprint Hall. Setting fire to everything like that. It was incredible. The bravest, stupidest thing I ever saw. I couldn't just let you be thrown into the wreckage."

"I'm glad it impressed someone at least," Finn said.

Whelm climbed to his feet with an old man's groan. "What happens now? How are you going to get us out?"

"We can't get through the gates," Diane said. "I've studied them. There's no way."

"This place is a fortress," Aelth continued. "It has to be. They'd kill us all if they could. The masters and their rabble. But Diane's right. The gates are locked and guarded. I'm sorry, but the only way out is down to the wreckage."

"You can get us there?" Finn asked. "There's a way?"

"Preferably a way that doesn't involve jumping," Whelm put in from the darkness.

"There are ways," Aelth said. "We use the cages to come back up, but there are faster ways down. We use them for surprise attacks. We don't control anything down there, though. You'll be on your own. No way back up. I can't guarantee your safety."

Finn looked at Diane, who nodded, and then at Whelm, who did the same.

"We'll take our chances," said Finn. "What do we do?"

"First of all, we'll lock the cage back up," Whelm said. "Open the hatch then let it swing free again. In the morning it'll look like you jumped, and they'll forget about you."

"Won't they look for bodies?" Diane asked.

"Probably not. It's a long way down. Most likely they wouldn't be able to see in the tangle of machinery."

Aelth locked the cage up and slipped the key into a pocket. Diane released the grapple and the cage swung away through the darkness, returning a few moments later like an enormous pendulum.

"Come on," Aelth said. "We have to get to the wires." He set off, following the line of the cliff edge.

Finn caught up with him. "Aelth, I'm grateful. I mean, we're grateful. Truly. You must be putting yourself in great danger. If Maeve found out what you were doing…"

"Just because she has my support doesn't mean I like

everything she does."

"What don't you like?" Whelm asked from the darkness.

Aelth took a moment to reply. "No time to discuss it now. Lots of things. Some small, some big. In some fights you have to pick a side but freeing the two of you was something I could do, so I did it. That's all there is to it." He glanced aside to Finn. "Still, I'd be grateful if you didn't mention it to her if you do get out of this alive."

"How far are these wires?" asked Diane.

"Not far," Aelth replied. "Just past the telescopes."

"Will they be guarded?"

"Not at the top. There's no way someone could come up a wire."

"Then, they're guarded at the bottom. You didn't mention that."

Aelth didn't stop. "There's a fortified wrecker enclosure down there around the landing point. We need to be sure we're not ambushed when we go down. But they won't stop anyone from above."

"Surely they'll think it's odd in the middle of the night?" Diane asked. "Aren't they normally told who's using them?"

Now Aelth did stop. He was all but invisible in the darkness, just a silhouette against the constellations of flickering lights. "There'll be no problem, I promise. I've manned that station many times. People come down the wire at all times. Not just squads of soldiers attacking some Engn outpost, also individuals slipping down in the dead of night on some secret mission. No one will stop you. In any case, it's your only hope; it's this or go back to the cage."

"But what are these wires?" Finn asked. "How do we get down them?"

"Steel cables," said Aelth. "Anchored up here and down there. You throw over a metal chain, hold on and slide down."

"How do you stop at the bottom?" Finn asked. "Surely you'll go crashing into the ground. Or into the wreckage?"

"No, no. The wire goes over a pool at the bottom. You might get soaked, but you won't get hurt."

They were passing the bank of telescopes Aelth had mentioned. Once again, they stood at random angles, peering into the darkness above and the darkness below.

Whelm stopped. Finn thought he was going to peer through one of the telescopes, but instead he stood without moving, looking over the edge.

"What is it?" asked Finn.

"I'm not coming with you," said Whelm.

"What? Of course, you are. There's no other way."

"I can't, Finn. My shoulder's bad. There's no way I could hold onto a chain and slide down a wire."

"You'll manage somehow," said Finn.

"No. I'll only slow you down."

"But you know your way around down there," said Finn. "We'll need you." He turned to Aelth. "Is there another way?"

"The only other way is to jump."

"We'll chain you to the wire," asked Diane.

"Then I'll be attached when I hit the water," said Whelm.

Aelth's gaze darted around. He was more and more nervous at standing out in the open. "The water's not deep. You'll be okay. Finn can…"

A bell clanged in the night, ringing urgently. In a moment, another bell rang out. A third answered. Lights flickered and flared all around the wrecker island.

"The alarm," said Aelth. "You have to run. They must have spotted the swinging cage." He yanked the key from around his neck and hurled it over the edge. "I'm sorry, but you're on your own, now. If they catch me with you…" He clasped Finn's arm for a moment. "Best of luck to you, Finn Smithson. Whatever you're planning, I hope it works out." Then he was gone, sprinting off into the night.

More lights flared around the wrecker encampment. Shouts and cries filled the air. Whelm lumbering along as fast as he could, the three of them ran.

Fortunately, the wires weren't guarded. An iron frame shaped like a letter A supported two steel cables disappearing into the darkness. They looked far too thin to support someone's weight.

Diane helped Whelm onto a wooden platform. She threw a chain over one of the wires, then passed it under Whelm's arms before shackling it into a loop. "When you get to the bottom just step out of it," she said.

"But…"

"No time to discuss it, Whelm." She hurled him forwards off the platform. The wire sagged a little but held. Spinning uncontrollably, Whelm went wheeling into the darkness, sparks flying from the steel chain as it slid down the wire.

"Now you, Finn. Come on."

"We'll go down together," said Finn.

Diane threw a shorter length of chain over another wire and attached it to a steel bar for them to grab hold of. "If either of us lets go we're both dead. Ready?"

"Ready."

A shout came from nearby and an arrow whistled out of the darkness towards them. Torches were approaching. Many torches.

"Go!" shouted Finn.

They launched themselves into the night. The wind rushed at them and for a moment they were falling. Then the line went taut and the two of them were speeding together through the darkness towards the wreckage.

XXVII

Whelm was struggling to free himself from his cable, thrashing around in the pool at the bottom of the wire, as Finn and Diane thumped into him. For a moment all three went under. Finn swallowed a mouthful of gritty water. He found a slippery footing and stood. With Diane's help they hauled Whelm to his feet and lifted the wire over his head. Whelm gasped with pain as they raised his arm. Once they were all free, they splashed through the oily, rusty water to the mud of the pool's shore.

Wrecker guards were waiting for them. But as Aelth had promised, they didn't seem particularly alarmed to see three people sliding down the wire. The guards manned a line of barricades cobbled together from girders and metal plates, encircling the pool. Torches planted at random places in the walls provided a shadowy, shifting illumination. One of the guards nodded in acknowledgement at their arrival but didn't move from his post. The alarm bells from up on the surface were impossible to hear; the background thumpings and rumblings and clankings of the wreckage drowned all sound out.

Diane pulled Whelm towards a part of the barricade that looked like it might be a gate: a single sheet of iron against which girders had been angled as buttresses. She called up to the nearest guard. "Let us through. We have an urgent mission in the wreckage."

The guard peered out through a spy hole in the barricades to check no enemies were in sight, then jumped down to haul the door open.

"And release the cables from this end," Diane continued. She cast a glance at Finn, telling him to play along. "Lud's orders. The word is those ironclad devils have built a steam-powered spider that can climb *up* the wires. We're going out now to see if it's true, but until further notice the wires aren't to be used, understood?"

The wrecker guard, a lad barely older than Finn, his face pocked with angry spots, stopped what he was doing. He looked worried at Diane's words. "First we've heard about it."

Diane pressed on, sounding cross as if growing impatient with having her orders ignored. "That's because Lud has only just heard about it herself. We can't risk being overrun."

Finn thought Diane's ruse was going to work but another wrecker guard, an older woman, came over to join in the argument. "Our orders are to keep the wires open at all costs. Only Lud herself can countermand that. And who are you anyway? No one I've ever seen before." She pointed at Whelm, who was still panting and coughing from his immersion. "And he doesn't look in any state to go out on a mission in the wreckage. What's going on here?"

Finn stepped forwards to stand beside Diane. They had to hurry. Pursuers would be sliding down the wires at any moment. "Our friend here, if you must know, is the one who told us about the threat, at some cost to himself. Now open the gates and let us out. We'll leave it up to you to decide whether to ignore Lud's orders or not, but you need to be ready for attack, understood?"

The woman stood considering them, calculating. Finn expected to hear the scream of pursuers coming down the wire at any second.

The woman, too used to obeying orders, relented. "Open the gate. And hurry so we can get it closed again. Those damned ironclads could attack at any moment."

Finn, Diane and Whelm hurried through as quickly as they could, expecting shouts to call them back at any moment. Finn caught the woman's gaze as they filed past. The suspicion on her face was clear, but she didn't move to stop them.

"Good luck out there!" the lad called after them. "Show those dirty ironclads!"

Glancing back, Finn saw other wreckers were unwinding the cranks keeping the cables under tension. He wondered what would happen to anyone descending at that moment. Probably best not to think about it. Then the gate was slammed shut and they were alone in the wreckage.

"Which way?" asked Diane.

"As far from here as possible," said Whelm. "Once they straighten out what's happened, they'll come looking for us. They'll see the whole thing as an attack by the masters and retaliate. We don't want to be anywhere near when that happens."

They walked forwards in single line, Whelm leading the way. Their surroundings reminded Finn strangely of the woods back home. Instead of trees, a tangle of spars and girders and beams reached high into the sky. Crumpled skeletons of metal and mounds of rubble. Winding, forking pathways had been cleared. Through gaps in the jumble of broken machinery he glimpsed only more and more wreckage. The sky overhead was lightening a little, but darkness still lay in the abyss of Engn. On the ground, only torches and fires shining here and there provided any illumination. It was impossible to say how near or far any of them were.

"This ironclad you were supposed to take us to. Where is he?"

"I was told to take you to the clocktower."

What did that mean? Surely none of the buildings had survived; the destruction around them was absolute. "Which clocktower?"

Whelm spoke in short sentences, clearly in pain. "It's what they call one of the pillars. There's a group of masters up there trying to rebuild everything. Always wanted to go myself, actually."

"Oh really?" asked Diane. "Why is that?"

"They've scavenged a lot of machinery over the years. Valuable stuff. Worth a fortune."

"A spindle reader?" asked Finn.

"Maybe."

"So which way?"

Whelm nodded vaguely in the direction they were heading. "Towards the Great Wall. If you listen carefully you can hear the clock. We can follow the sound."

Diane glanced at Finn, a puzzled look on her face. "I can't hear anything."

"You will. They've connected it to an array of steam-powered bullhorns to blare out the sound of the ticks. Up close, it's deafening. You can hear it for miles."

"Why?" asked Finn. "Why would they do that?"

Up ahead of him, Whelm shook his head as if amused. "Trying to impose time on the world again, like the old days. Telling everyone they're still there. I didn't say they weren't crazy."

"So how do we get up?" asked Diane.

"Climb. There's a rusting ladder anchored to the stone pillar. It's a long haul. The ironclads will have plenty of time to drop things on us if they feel like it."

"But you have some way of signalling to them? Telling

them we're friends?"

"No."

"So why would they let us up?"

"Hopefully they'll see us. They have 'scopes looking down on the abyss, just like the wreckers. They'll soon hear about all the commotion. Once it's light they'll be searching for us, trying to work out who we are and what we're doing. There's a lot of watching and wondering in this war."

"You're suggesting we simply walk up to the stone pillar and climb?"

Whelm turned to face Diane. "Look, I'm sorry. That's the best I can do. By all means let's give up and flee the wreckage instead, yeah?"

"No," said Finn. "No, we'll try and reach this clock tower. See if we can climb it like you say."

Whelm turned away and carried on walking. He called over his shoulder. "If we even get that far. Plenty of other people to worry about besides the masters and the wreckers." He stopped again and, stepping off the path a short way, yanked three lengths of rusting girder from the tangle of metal. "Here. We may need to fight."

"Fight who?" asked Finn.

"Fight everyone," said Whelm.

Occasionally they heard shouts and cries in the distance as they walked, but it was impossible to say who was shouting or whether they were in pursuit. Once they heard a master's hunting horn echoing through the wreckage. They didn't stop. Sometime later, a deep explosion rumbled through the ground, sending dust and debris showering down from the rusting remains of Engn suspended above them.

"What was that?" asked Finn. He thought about the explosion they'd heard from back in the valley, just after the first earthquake.

"There are people who go around blowing bits of the wreckage up," said Whelm. "Obliterating some remnant of the machine."

"You mean the wreckers?"

"Usually lone wolves, nothing to do with Lud. People who think she's taking too long or who don't trust her."

"Then … we could find these people," said Finn. "They might be able to help us."

"Perhaps. If they don't blow us up first. Us or themselves."

As they clambered through the collapsed remains of great machines, Finn kept his eyes open for places and objects he remembered. But the machinery was so mangled it was hard to even see what each rusting mechanism had once been. Once they tottered across the rusting spoke of one of the great wheels, lying at an angle on the ground where it had fallen, half submerged in oily water. It might have been one of the wheels he'd once seen turning, but he couldn't be sure. It would never move again.

He looked out, also, for anything that might help them build a new spindle reader. It soon became apparent Whelm was right: the wreckage had been picked clean of anything valuable. They weren't going to unearth anything of use unless they were incredibly lucky. Still, he felt happier with each step they took away from the wreckers. If Lud was pursuing them, they saw no sign. They were finally in Engn, getting nearer some answers.

And his knee was holding up well; it was less swollen, and he could walk on it without too much pain. His head still throbbed a little, but it seemed to be okay without stitches. Whelm's shoulder was still a concern, though. He'd refused to let either Finn or Diane look at it, and Finn had seen him wincing more than once as he tried to swing some life into his arm. Still, the ex-master kept moving.

Thankfully, Whelm still had his wits about him, too. He stopped suddenly, head cocked on one side, then bundled Finn and Diane off the path to hide in the shadows of a collapsed and bent walkway, something like the one Finn had once taken to reach the Blueprint Hall. People were on the path, coming from behind them, making no attempt to move quietly. It was maybe midday, although the canopy of broken machinery cast everything into bars of shadow and light. Finn threw a questioning gaze at Whelm. For a reply, Whelm simply put his finger to his lips, telling them both to be quiet.

Finn expected to see a party of wreckers out hunting for them, or perhaps a troop of ironclads. Instead they watched as a woman in little more than tatters of cloth limped past their hiding place. Her eyes were wide and her breathing panicky. She moved awkwardly, as if one leg was badly hurt. Then Finn saw a chain had been locked around her ankle. A weight had been attached to the other end of the chain, making each step forwards an effort. She was followed thirty seconds later by a laughing, whooping collection of men and women carrying whips and sticks. They bashed and clanged on the wreckage around them as they pursued the woman, enjoying the pursuit of their quarry, taking their time to catch up with her as if simply out for a stroll.

As the woman turned a distant corner in the path, Finn saw what the weight attached to her ankle was: the chain ended in four or five of the self-governing valves he'd once laboured over. The mob had finally given the useless objects a grim purpose. Finn had to resist the urge to stand and confront them. The frown on Diane's face made it clear she was considering the same action. Whelm placed a hand on each of them and shook his head. They couldn't do this. They'd only get themselves killed. He was right, of course. Diane looked down at the ground as the mob racketed away.

When the path was empty, they waited ten minutes before setting off once more. "Is it like this everywhere?" Finn asked. "Is it this lawless?"

"Not all of it," Whelm replied. "These are the badlands

where anything goes. There are a few areas controlled by the wreckers, and the masters have their islands up on the pillars. In other parts people have banded together to form self-contained communities. Some of them are quite civilized, with farms and libraries and schools for the children. But they're always under threat. They're no match for a well-organized mob or an army of ironclads."

"Will we get to one of those places?" asked Diane. "Somewhere safe to sleep?"

"None round here," replied Whelm. "Not for miles around. We're on our own."

It was maybe late afternoon when the path opened out onto a wide area devoid of much wreckage. Finn recognized it immediately: the rock floor of the mines he'd laboured in. The line of stone pillars that had once supported the floor of Engn marched away into the distance. Most of the scene was lit by dappled, broken sunlight, but on the lip of the cavern the three of them stood in shadow. Up above was a sky of rusting iron: the machinery held up by its own beams and spars when the ground gave way beneath it. It sagged noticeably in several places, as if it might crash down on them at any moment.

Now Finn heard the ticking Whelm had described. In truth he'd been hearing it for a while, the steady, regular *thunks* emerging from the background hum and clank. Here the sound was suddenly clearer. Something about their deep thrum told him they were very loud but far away. They reminded him of the ticks from the clock in Connor's house, reverberating through the floor and walls. Once again, he had the weird sensation of walking through the mechanism of a clock, this one shattered, still just about ticking despite the destruction, keeping track of its own broken time.

"Which column do we have to get to?" he asked.

"In the distance. Three from the Great Wall."

"What even is this wall?" asked Diane. "I've never heard of it."

"You'll see. It's not really a wall. It's a high barricade of debris across the cavern. Word is it surrounds one of the columns, defending it, but I've never tried to map it out. Never been through it."

"Who built it?" asked Finn.

"Not sure anyone did. I think it's just the way the wreckage fell. Unless someone designed the machinery on the surface to form a barrier if the ground ever collapsed."

"Is that possible?"

"Who knows? It's not the wildest theory I've heard."

Finn started walking, but an object on the ground near his feet caught his attention. It was rusting and its handle was gone. The head of a hand-axe, like those they'd used to hack away at the rock. He stooped to pick it up, the terrible memories of those days returning.

"We need to keep moving," said Whelm. "We're too exposed out here in the open."

Finn turned the axe head over in his hands. "There's something I'd like to do first."

"What is it?" asked Diane.

"Tom. We worked together somewhere around here. I'd like to build a pyre to him."

"A *pyre?*" said Whelm. "Great. That'll really help keep us hidden."

"I wouldn't be here if it wasn't for Tom," said Finn. "He saved me. More than once. Kept me alive when I was dead on my feet. And I got away and he was crushed in the collapse."

"I'm sure he was a fine man, but there isn't time for sentiment," said Whelm. "We might be safe on top of a column. Down here we're anyone's game."

"You've always survived."

"Barely. And I've known plenty who haven't. You've seen what it's like here. It's a battlefield."

"I'm sorry," said Finn. "It won't take long, and I promised Mrs. Megrim. Just give me an hour and we can move on."

Whelm looked exasperated. Finn could see arguments and objections flashing across his features. But then he relented. Too exhausted to argue perhaps. "Fine. Have it your way. Light a fire and then stand around it thinking sad thoughts. It's not going to help us at all, but if it makes you feel better, then it's obviously worth it."

Whelm stomped off to slump against the cavern wall.

Diane put a hand on Finn's arm. "Let's search for wood and rags. Most of it is pretty damp, but we might be able to squeeze some oil from an old machine to get it going."

In the end, it took two hours to assemble a pathetic pile of splinters and cloth fragments. They built it close to the cavern wall, as out of sight as possible behind the hulk of a broken engine cylinder. Whelm had soon joined in to help them, not saying anything. It was he who lit the pyre, striking sparks into it from a flint and a square of metal he carried for the purpose. The pyre smouldered rather than burned. It gave off coils of smoke, but these meandered around on the ground rather than climbing straight upwards, as if they couldn't escape the mines of Engn, either. At the sight of the trapped smoke, Finn picked up one of the smoking scraps of wood and, cradling it with one hand, walked out into the open.

He found a spot where there was a slight draught of air. The tiny red spots of fire eating away at the wood flared brighter. Then the smoke, after thinking about it for a moment, rose upwards. For some reason that was important. It was only smoke, of course. Burning wood. Still it made Finn feel a little better, as if Tom was, in some way, finally escaping. Perhaps they'd never get out of Engn, and perhaps Mrs. Megrim would never get to hear what they'd done. Still, he'd done the right thing. He held the wood up high and watched the thin line of grey ascending to the canopy of dead machinery. It would wind its way through the latticework of holes and finally find the outside air.

"Finn."

It was Diane's voice. He could tell immediately something was wrong. He lowered the smoking stick and looked around.

People began emerging from the tangle of machinery, gathering into a mob. The wreckers, Maeve at their head. They pulled out clubs and swords as they raced towards the three of them.

XXVIII

Maeve strode forwards, a phalanx of wreckers at her back. They were all armed and armoured for war, forty or more of them, carrying blades and staves, or the bows and arrows Finn had seen in use at the wall. More wreckers emerged from the pathways, or directly out of the tangled wreckage, as if they'd been climbing through the metal boughs rather than following the paths. Quickly, they cut off all lines of escape.

"So, Finn. You run straight to the masters to tell them what you learned about us. As I knew you would."

There was no sign of Aelth behind her. Had she uncovered his part in their escape? He hoped not.

"No," said Finn. "As ever, you're wrong. We're here to finish the job we started three years ago. The job you were too busy playing your *long games* to attempt."

Maeve shook her head as if she was speaking to a child. "You don't know anything, Finn. You really have no idea what's going on here."

"You'd be surprised," said Diane. "Why don't you

carry on fighting your ancient wars, melting down the wreckage scrap by scrap, and we'll get on and do the real work, shall we? Like last time."

"Is that what you think we're doing?" said Maeve. "I assure you our plans are much bigger than that. Much, much bigger."

Understanding clicked into place in Finn's mind. How long had she known? Had this been their plan all along?

"You want to use the seismium," he said.

"*What?*" The surprise on Maeve's features confirmed Finn's suspicions. It also confirmed she had no idea Finn knew anything about the subject.

Finn pressed on. "You plan to use it to destroy Engn. That's it, isn't it? I apologize, Lud, or Maeve, or *Queen of the Desolation* or whatever you're called. I thought you were ineffectual and incompetent. Now I understand you're completely mad."

The line of wreckers stepped forwards, menace clear in their movements. Maeve stayed them with an upheld hand. She strode up to Finn, her breath warm on his face. Didn't she want her followers to hear? How many others had she told? Any of them?

She considered him for a moment. Then her hand moved. He thought she was going to strike him. He flinched. But instead she stroked the side of his face. "Connor told you the secret, did he? Shared with you the truth of what the masters have been planning all this time? So that you could help him, no doubt. And now you've come to finish what he started. I must thank you. You wouldn't be here if the time for action wasn't approaching. I think we *have* waited long enough. We will act. Rally the armies and attack. Seize the seismium and put it to good use."

He couldn't be sure how much she really knew. Couldn't afford to give anything away. At the same time, did she have any idea what she was dealing with? Perhaps, even now, she could be reasoned with.

"Look, Maeve. You're right. We have come to finish what Connor started. We've come to destroy Engn and the Hub and the seismium and everything, so no one can ever use any of it again. That's all we ever wanted to do. But the seismium isn't some little bomb you can detonate to kill a few masters and a few ironclads. It's dangerous; it will destroy everything. I told you about the effects we felt back home. The world far beyond Engn will be wrecked. All your ancient towns and cities will be gone if it's allowed to detonate. And it seems Engn might escape relatively unscathed, while everywhere else suffers. I think that's why it was built here, in the centre of the plain. Everyone knows earthquakes at worst at the mountains. That's where the faults in the rocks are." He didn't know if everyone *did* know that, but it was an idea Mrs. Megrim had spelled out to him more than once.

Maeve sounded sad when she replied. "I don't believe the seismium is anywhere near as powerful as you claim. But even if you were right, sometimes you have to destroy before you can create. A blank canvas, a clean slate. I'm sorry, Finn, but in war people die. The masters planned all along to kill us. They never should have meddled in such matters, mining the seismium and making their infernal machines. But they did, and now we will take what they did and use it against them. That's always been our intention, all these long years. I told you in the Blueprint Hall, although you wouldn't listen. We've simply been waiting for the right moment. And now here it is, when they're vulnerable and we're in charge."

"No. You'll kill everyone."

"I don't think so. But I *am* going to have to kill you, Finn. You do see that, don't you? Because of what you know about us and because you're one of them. But I'll make it quick, I promise. We're not the barbarians they say we are."

"You'll happily use their machines when it suits you?" said Whelm. "I thought you preferred to fight with sticks and rocks and quaint old technology that barely works."

"We use their own weapons against them," said Maeve. "Why shouldn't we? A final machine to destroy all the other machines. Victory over the tyranny of the clocks. Sometimes you have to use what is given to you."

"What Finn said was true," said Diane. "It doesn't matter who sets the seismium off, it will kill them and you and everyone else. And where's your victory then?"

"I assure you when the time comes, we will be far away from here. Because that's what the masters planned to do, isn't it? Send out their *clarion* call to tell their side to flee the destruction while we stay behind to be crushed and shattered. Now it will be the other way around. They'll find us gone, and understanding will come too late. The ruins of Engn and all their cities and towers will come crashing down upon them. And when it's done, we can return to rebuild what was. The brave old world."

There was no reasoning with her. She was too far gone; she was as bad as any master. Finn glanced to Diane and Whelm. He saw in their eyes they knew it too. Maeve wasn't going to be persuaded, and she wasn't going to let them live.

In a way, it was Tom that saved him once again.

"Look, may we at least have a moment to see to the pyre?" said Finn. "Before you do what you have to do. It is nearly burned out now."

Wherever in the world she came from, Maeve at least appeared to know and respect the old traditions. Quite possibly she revered such things more than Finn did. She glanced over at the pathetic pile of smouldering rags and sticks. "Who is it for?"

"Someone I worked with down here. He saved my life more than once, but he died when the end came. He was on your side. His name was Tom."

She considered. He could see the wariness in her. There were perhaps a hundred wreckers gathered at her back now, and all had weapons drawn and all looked around constantly for signs of attack. Even they were vulnerable down here in the wreckage.

"Tom Megrim?"

"You know about him?"

"I told you. We watched and waited. He was a good man. I will give you a few moments. Tend to your pyre. Remember your friend. And then it will be your turn. I'm afraid we won't have time to build pyres for you."

Finn nodded, as if accepting his fate. The three of them returned to the fire. The flames were gone now, only a few embers giving off a reluctant smoke.

"Can we escape them, Whelm?" asked Finn. "Is there somewhere we can hide?" The jungle of twisted beams and spars was nearby. It looked impenetrable. But perhaps there were pathways through.

"They know the wreckage better than me. We're only safe from them on top of one of the pillars."

"We'll never get there," said Diane. "There's no way we could outrun them all."

"So, we fight?" said Finn. "Perhaps if we can kill Maeve, they'll leave us alone." He knew they wouldn't, of course. He squatted by the pyre and stirred the ashes a little with his foot. The glow was almost gone.

"Can you summon the masters?" Diane asked Whelm. "Tell them there's a wrecker army here?"

"I'm not one of them," said Whelm. "How many times do I have to tell you? I can't just command an army of ironclads to come and rescue us."

"You said they'd be watching," said Finn. "From up there on top of the columns. They must have seen us. Seen Maeve."

"Perhaps, but it doesn't help. There isn't time for them to get across the cavern even if they wanted to."

Finn stood. "I'll tell her about the spindle. About Adage and Rankin and all the rest. Perhaps that will buy us some time."

"They hate those devices," said Whelm.

"If I tell them what images we've seen, they'll want to look. It's their history too. And I think there's a lot they don't know. Maeve would be a fool to miss the opportunity."

"Maybe. Having the spindle won't stop them killing us, though, will it?"

"They may let us live so we can build them a new reader," said Finn. It didn't sound very believable even to him. "It's all we've got."

"Worth a try, I suppose," said Whelm.

"Come on then," said Finn. "Let's give it a go."

But as he was walking back to the waiting wreckers, spindle in his hand, the ground lurched beneath him. For a moment he was falling, as if a pit had opened beneath his feet. Then the wayward rock became solid once more and he caught it up, thumping into it. He sprawled sideways, sharp pains jarring through his weak knee. As before at Connor's house, it took him a few seconds to understand what was happening. He lay on the ground as it bucked and writhed. An earthquake. Another earthquake had struck the machine.

It wasn't as powerful as those back home. Perhaps Mrs. Megrim had been right. Still, it was bad enough. Finn crawled to the lip of a ragged hole in the ground. Shouting and screaming filled the world. Nearby, he picked out Diane's voice, and Whelm's. There were many other voices. The gathered wreckers, knocked to the ground like skittles, were screaming and screaming.

It took Finn a moment to understand why. The sky was raining on them. A rain of metal spars, metal weights, metal blades. The canopy of twisted machinery on the surface was finally relenting and crashing to the floor of the caverns. The machinery exacting its revenge on those who had wrecked it.

Iron poles clanged to the ground near Finn, toppling onto him. He tried to stand but the ground shook again, throwing him sideways once more.

A hand seized him, hauling him away. Diane. He scrambled after her, following Whelm away from the falling wreckage. There was a wall of rock there, one of the old faces the miners had hewed and hacked at. Small alcoves had been cut into it, perhaps even the ones Finn and Tom had once laboured away at. They each squeezed inside one, curling up as tightly as they could while the screaming continued, and the iron rain continued to thunder.

When it was done, they had to clamber their way through the jungle of broken beams and poles that had fallen from above. The ground slept once more, but the tangle of wreckage continued to ping and clang as the last few scraps and bolts fell. There was only sky visible above now.

Eventually they pulled themselves free from the worst of the tangle and looked around. There was no sign of Maeve or any of the wreckers. A sudden mountain of broken machinery stood where they had been.

"Should we search for survivors?" said Finn.

"We have to go," said Whelm. "Get as far away as possible. Even if Maeve's gone, more will be coming. You heard what she said. *Armies*. Armies who might blame this on us."

Diane handed out fresh lengths of metal to act as crude weapons. "He's right. We have to leave now. Leave for this clocktower."

They ran as best they could then, weaving around the mounds of twisted machinery littering the cavern floor, heading for the distant rise of the great stone pillars reaching up to the living world.

The passage of the caverns took them the best part of a day. Often on the journey, Finn thought back to his previous crossing with Tom and the other prisoners. He wondered what had happened to the great wheels, the one he and Diane had escaped in. Had they tottered and crashed too? There was no sign of the river, but the En had to be here somewhere, running underground.

Once they came across another of the high walkways, this one almost intact but bent in an arch across the rubble, its back broken where it had fallen. They decided to risk using it for the speed it would give them. As they clanged across, Finn wondered if it was the same walkway. The one the ironclad had hurled him from, the one from which Rory had rescued him. It was impossible to tell now.

Finn counted the pillars as they went. Last time there'd been twenty-four, but now the line ended at eighteen. Some were mere stumps, reduced to mini-mountain ranges of rubble across the cavern floor, the machinery they'd once supported lying in rust. Others looked to be intact. From more than one, the *whump* and crash of distant machinery could be heard.

"Why one of the far columns and not one of these?" Diane asked. "There must be masters on all of them."

"Most, yes," said Whelm. "But there are masters and masters. They're not unified like they once were. The Inner Wheel doesn't sit any more, and the old guilds fight among themselves for supremacy. Most of them want to rebuild Engn, but they disagree over how, or why, or who should be in charge. Or what the point of doing so even is."

"What about this Engneer Maeve mentioned? Which pillar do people say they've seen that on?"

"They're fairy stories, Finn. They're not real."

"But which?"

Whelm shrugged. "None of these. Beyond the Great

Wall. The Engneer's column is the one the wall is protecting, so people say. If you ask me, people just like to imagine there's order in the chaos. That there's a plan, a *reason* to it all."

"Can you get through the Great Wall? Or over it?"

"I've never done it. Never heard of anyone doing it."

They clung to the shadows as much as possible, wary of being attacked from the tangled wreckage, but more wary of being spotted out in the open. They saw more than one marauding band crossing the cavern floor, but each time they managed to hide out of sight. They saw neither wreckers nor masters. In the middle of the first night, another huge *boom* shook the ground, and they fled to open ground thinking it was another earthquake. But the ground remained solid. Somewhere in the darkness, not too far away, an explosion had ripped through the ruins. Whether natural or triggered by someone, they couldn't tell.

As they neared the clocktower pillar, the titanic ticks from the tower grew oppressively loud. Before long they became deafening, hammering at them like physical blows. Finn could feel the solid weight of them on his cheekbones, thumping into his chest. Whelm handed out scraps of rag for them to stuff into their ears. It helped, a little. Beyond the pillar, and two more besides, the Great Wall of wreckage was clearly visible: a high, impenetrable forest of girders and beams and metal plates. It reached a hundred feet into the air.

The ladder Whelm had mentioned also became visible as they approached, an impossibly fine line of black leading directly up the rock. It looked a long, long climb. Above, on top of the pillar, buildings and machinery were massed, some of it clearly in ruins. But some had either survived the collapse or had been rebuilt. There was even one of the big wheels up there, sunlight flashing off it as it turned. The bullhorns could also be seen, pointing out at all angles, broadcasting the amplified seconds to the remains of Engn.

Finn felt more and more wary as they approached the pillar, expecting debris to be hurled at them at any moment. Were the masters up there looking down through 'scopes? No attack came. Perhaps they were waiting for the three of them to be completely exposed part way up. It was what he'd do.

They stopped at the base of the pillar. The vast metallic *tocks* were a little quieter there, the speakers directing the sound outwards rather than downwards. They circumnavigated the column of rock, staring up at its concave curve towering above them. The sides were smooth and the lip at the top overhung the base. Halfway round, they came across two round holes, both sealed with heavy iron grates. It took Finn a few moments to realize what they were. His memories of that day were vague and confused; he'd been overcome with fear, as well as the fumes from the burning oil. But these had to be the openings of the chutes they'd pushed him down after being condemned by the Inner Wheel. Which meant that up above, atop this column, lay that circle of twelve stone thrones.

It made sense. The masters would know where the columns were and would have sited their most important buildings on top of them. Or, rather, they would have ensured the delvings didn't undermine the most important buildings. Strange to think the pillars, seen from below, effectively mapped out all the important constructions and machines up on the surface. Something that hadn't occurred to him in all the time he'd been down there digging.

The ladder was clearly a post-destruction addition; no such escape route would have been allowed when the mines were active. Finn grasped the cold iron to see how secure it was. The uprights of the ladder were anchored to the wall by iron spikes cemented into the rock every ten yards or so, but some were loose, and the ladder swayed a little as Finn pulled on it. Still, it might hold. But even if it did, there'd be no escaping attack from above or below as they ascended.

He looked at Diane, who was peering upwards, no doubt thinking the same thoughts.

"Ready?" he said.

"Ready. The sooner we start, the sooner we can make it to the top."

Finn stepped up onto the first rung. He wondered how many there would be all together. Thousands, for sure. "Ready, Whelm?"

Whelm was standing with his back to the wide stone pillar, one hand inside his tunic exploring his damaged shoulder. "I'm sorry. I'm not coming."

"But you have to," said Finn. "They'll recognize you. They might think we're wreckers attacking them."

"You are, aren't you?"

"Well, in a way, yes. But not yet. We have to get up there and find out who sent you."

"Why aren't you coming?" asked Diane.

"My shoulder. It's too weak. I won't be able to pull myself up, or even hold on with this arm. There's nothing I can do."

Finn and Diane exchanged glances. They both knew he was right.

"What will you do if we go up?" asked Diane.

"What I always do: find somewhere to hide. I'll keep a look out for you and meet you back here when you come down again."

"But when we're up there, what are we supposed to do?" said Finn. "Who are we supposed to see?"

"I said I don't know. An ironclad. I assume they'll find you."

Diane crouched down beside Whelm. "Can I look at your shoulder? Before we go up? Perhaps I can help."

Whelm glanced up at her then looked away. "There's no need. I've had worse. A few weeks and it will be as good as new. Go up and find out what we're doing here in Engn. I'll wait down here."

Diane hesitated, wanting to say more. She clearly had her doubts about Whelm.

Finn turned away and climbed. He looked down at Diane, still hesitating with one hand on the ladder.

"I'm going up," he said.

After a moment Diane relented and followed. Whelm watched them climb a short distance, then backed away.

Finn ignored him to concentrate on the climb. As he ascended, he studied the rock face just in front of his eyes, letting his limbs settle into a rhythm of reaching and pushing. After ten minutes or so he stopped for a moment's rest, hooking an arm and a leg through the ladder to hold himself in place while his breathing calmed. His thighs were already complaining. It was going to be a long climb.

The ground was far below them, distant enough to kill them easily if they fell. "You okay?" he asked Diane, stopped just below him on the ladder.

"I'm fine. It's you I'm worried about. You're already struggling."

"Perhaps you should have gone first," said Finn, "so that I don't take you with me if I fall."

"Just make sure you don't, Finn. I'll be really cross with you if you get yourself killed."

Finn smiled, although she couldn't see. Down below, at the base of the stone pillar, Whelm was little more than a black scribble on the grey stone floor. He was heading for the twisted tangle of wrecked machinery.

"Do you think he planned this?" said Diane.

"Planned what?"

"Brought us here and then let us climb up while he stayed safe down there?"

"I'm not sure he is safe down there."

"Still, his wound is convenient, don't you think? The way he wouldn't let us look at it?"

Finn thought about it. "That iron arrow pinning him to the ground was real enough. It went clean through him. I don't think he was faking that. He's just used to looking after himself."

"Still, he might be using his wound to his advantage."

"To what advantage? He wants answers as much as we do."

"I suppose," said Diane. "Come on, keep climbing. We don't want to be doing this in the dark."

Finn reached up for the next rung, Diane's words turning over and over in his mind as he climbed.

XXIX

Halfway up the long climb, the curving side of the concave pillar stopped sloping inwards and curved gently outwards. It was immediately clear they couldn't carry on ascending as they had. It would be impossible to cling on and climb at the same time.

Finn stopped. He needed to rest. More than once he'd seen spots dancing before his eyes from the effort of their ascent. He was breathing heavily. His leg and back muscles burned, and his forearms ached from grasping the iron rungs. How long was it since he and Diane had eaten and drunk properly? He could feel the distant ground sucking at him. At the same time, it was so distant it seemed unimportant: a realm of shadows and twinkling lights, all detail gone. It was already growing dark. There was little wind down in the underworld, but awkward gusts rushed at them occasionally, threatening to pluck them off. When they came, he caught a whiff of burning oil or wood smoke from one of the distant fires in the abyss.

"We should have thought of this," Finn called down to

Diane. "The ladder slopes outwards too steeply to climb."

Diane took a moment to reply as she got her breath back. "It looks like there's room between the ladder and the rock. Climb around and go up on the inside."

She was right. It was alarming to step off the side of ladder at that height, take a hand off the rungs to reach around. Finn was acutely aware he only had to let go and he'd hurtle to his death, all his struggles over.

He made it around safely. Having the ladder between him and the gulf of air made him feel a little better. On the other hand, the drop was now in front of him, plainly visible.

Beneath him, Diane completed the tricky manoeuvre as well. The ladder swayed and jerked as she clambered around. Finn tried not to think about how precariously it was attached to the rock face. How had the masters even done it? And how did they maintain it? Probably, they didn't. He imagined the ironwork shaking free from its moorings, a moment of dizzying balance before the long plunge to the wreckage below.

He tried to put it out of his mind, tried to focus instead on the rusting metal of the ladder in front of his eyes. After a few minutes rest, they set off on the second half of the climb.

Sometime later, maybe half an hour after the turning point, Finn reached up for the next rung on the ladder to find it missing. Lost to the rhythm of the climb, he almost let go with his lower hand even as he grasped at the air. He fell against the iron ladder, banging his chin against the last of the rungs. The ladder shook and swayed but held.

"What is it?" called up Diane. She sounded utterly exhausted.

"The ladder stops."

"Are we at the top?"

Finn peered up. It was fully dark now, only the distant glow of fires down in the wreckage providing any illumination. "No, I don't think so. Looks like a section of the ladder has come loose and fallen." The ironclads clearly didn't come up this way. Perhaps they'd left the ladder in place knowing it was useless. Perhaps they'd cut the section from it deliberately. Finn hooked an arm through the top rung to give his muscles a chance to rest. His fingers were little more than frozen claws from the effort of the ascent. They'd come so far. He knew he was too spent to even think about climbing back down.

"How big is the gap?" Diane was trying her best to sound calm, but Finn heard an edge of panic in her voice.

"Let me reach and find out," said Finn. He stepped upwards so the last rung was pressed against his chest and scrabbled around in the air above his head. There was nothing. He stepped up once more, the top rung digging into his stomach. He felt very exposed as he flailed in the open air, searching for the ladder. If he reached too far, he would pitch forwards and fall. Still his fingers found only air and darkness.

"Anything?"

"No."

"Did you see any gaps in the ladder from down on the ground?"

"Obviously not. I think I would have mentioned it." He was too tired, too frightened to keep the tone of irritation from his voice.

"I'll climb up and try," said Diane.

"Why would that work?"

"Because I'm slightly taller than you. You can hold on to me while I reach up."

Diane clambered up beside him. When her face was level with his, she stroked his cheek briefly. "Come on. Hold me steady and I'll see if I can reach anything."

"Okay," Finn replied. "Sorry. Yes."

Diane climbed up past him while Finn held onto her hips, her thighs. Soon she was standing on the second-lowest rung, more or less balancing there, steadied only by Finn's grasp. He could feel her muscles shaking from the effort of what she was doing. The lurch as she overbalanced first this way, then that. He gripped her as tightly as he could, hooking his own feet through the lower rungs in case she slipped, and he had to stop her falling.

"Anything?"

"I think … yes. I touched it with my fingertips."

"Another rung?"

"I think so. I'm going to have to stand on the top of the ladder to reach it."

"I don't think I can steady you."

"We have to try, Finn. It's this or go back down. I'll step up and make a grab for it."

"If you miss, you'll overbalance. I may not be able to hold on to you."

"We'll have to try. There's nothing else to do."

She waited for a few moments, steeling herself, then thrust upwards. Finn kept a firm hold around her knees, bracing to hold her weight.

"I've got it," she called down. "There's another rung. Let go so I can pull myself up."

Her feet disappeared into the darkness above. "Does the ladder continue?" Finn called up.

"Looks like it. Come on. You'll have to do the same. I'll reach down so you don't have so far to stretch."

"Okay." Before he could stop to think about what he was doing he climbed onto the second-highest rung. Then, wobbling badly, he put one foot onto the top rung and pushed himself upwards into the darkness in a single movement.

He brushed Diane's hand, missing her grasp. But she grabbed his upper arm. She hauled him upwards. "Step up the rock face. It'll make it easier. Here. Grab the rung. Now pull yourself up."

In a few moments, they stood together on the lowest rung of the next section, arms wrapped around each other as much as the metal of the ladder. They were both badly out of breath.

"Let's hope there aren't any more gaps," said Finn.

"Yeah."

"It's a good job Whelm didn't come. He'd never have made it."

"You think he knew about the gap?"

"No. I think he would have warned us."

"Maybe," said Diane. "Come on. Let's get to the top before we run out of strength."

They resumed climbing, Diane leading the way. The ladder angled out more as the pillar curved, and they were soon crawling as much as climbing. It took huge effort. The rungs cut cruelly into Finn's shins. More than once they had to stop to lie on the ladder while shreds of strength returned.

The sounds from above became louder and louder. As well as the blaring, metallic ticks he could hear a background roar. The rock face behind him, when he reached back to lay a hand on it, was alive, thrumming with energy. He could smell burning coal and hot oil. Occasionally a cry cut through the air, though whether he and Diane had been detected he couldn't tell. At least they were protected from thrown projectiles by the overhang of the column.

Then Diane's feet, a rung above him, disappeared, as if she'd simply been sucked upwards into the sky. Finn paused, confused. Had she fallen without him seeing? Then a muffled voice called down. A man's voice. "Climb up or climb down. You decide."

After a moment's hesitation, Finn climbed up. A few more rungs and a strong hand grasped his wrist, hauling him upwards. He banged his knees hard against the lip of the rock, but in a moment, he was kneeling on solid ground. Diane was there beside him. The wind, suddenly stronger, whipped through Finn's hair. The air was bright with flames and furnaces and torches, so it took a few moments for his eyes to adjust.

Then he saw. All around them, standing unmoving,

stood a semicircle of ironclad guards.

They were nothing like the ragtag assortment that had pursued them across the plain. These might have been guards in Engn when it still stood. Their armour was uniform and polished. They all bore the same guns, small hand-sized muskets, their wide mouths aimed at Finn and Diane. He glanced at her. Relief and alarm took their turns to play across her features.

One of the guards strode forwards to haul Finn and Diane to their feet. The guard said nothing for a moment, as if studying them from behind their mask. Finn half expected to be pushed backwards, thrown off the cliff edge at any moment. It was cold at ground level, the night air chill. Finn shivered as he waited, still breathless from the long climb. The guard spoke with a muffled voice spoke. "Come with me."

The guard led them through the ring of ironclads. He was definitely a man, his voice deep. Neither Finn nor Diane struggled or objected. The farther they could get from the ladder and the pillar's edge, the better. Finn had the clear impression the other guards were uneasy, wary, but they parted to let Finn and Diane through. The other guards went back to the ring of bullhorns crowning the stone pillar. They appeared to be adjusting them, angling them down to the ground at steeper angles. The huge ticks from them continued to hammer the air.

The ironclad led Diane and Finn towards the centre of the pillar. Finn recognized where he was immediately. The shining silver walls were tarnished and marred now, the peak of the tower snapped off, but he knew the place well. The Inner Wheel, where'd he'd been brought after setting fire to the blueprints, to be tried by the assembled masters of Engn.

The ancient stone building, once completely enveloped in its modern steel spike, now lay half exposed in the open air, like the old bones of the original construction emerging through its more recent skin. The stones were worn smooth by the passage of so many years. A great crack ran jaggedly up it – an effect, presumably, of one of the earthquakes. It reminded Finn a little of Connor's home, back in the valley. The doorway to the Inner Wheel was unguarded, and the three of them passed into the shadowy, echoing space Finn recalled so clearly from the day he'd been dragged there, the day he and Connor had been heard before the Court.

The twelve stone thrones were still there, arranged in their ring around the walls. Above them, reaching up into the shadows, were the carved faces of each previous occupant of each chair. But the crack in the wall snaked also across the red tiles of the floor, right through the yellow eye circle in the middle, as if the court of twelve had been split in two.

The chairs were unoccupied. All except one. As before, Finn couldn't see the features of the person sitting there, lost as they were in the shadows of their throne. He could see only a pair of knees, wrapped in a master's cloak. A hand waved from the darkness, dismissing the ironclad, who bowed and left without saying another word.

Who was this? Someone he'd previously met in Engn? Someone with all the answers to his questions?

The voice, when it came, was a grating croak, like machinery badly in need of oil. One of the masters who'd been there last time, he thought, now sounding creakier and rustier than ever.

"You took your time to reach us, Finn Smithson."

Finn looked around, double checking none of the other thrones were occupied. "We came as quickly as we could," said Finn.

"But it's been years."

Finn looked to Diane, puzzled. "It's only been a few weeks since Whelm came for us."

"There were other signs. I'm told you ignored all of them."

"What signs?" asked Diane. "What do you mean?"

"Many, many messages were sent."

"What messages?"

The master ignored her questions. "You escaped the mines when the destruction came. It is pleasing you have finally returned to continue your punishment. No doubt that is the reason you have been summoned."

"What?" said Finn. "That's what you think is going on here? We've come back so we can to be punished?"

"Of course. I…" The master's voice collapsed into a fit of coughs. He didn't sound at all well. When he'd recovered, he continued. "I was charged to make sure you were returned to Engn, and here you are. Alas, we don't have the ironclads any more to go out and fetch people, so you were lured here instead. A few intriguing messages, a few scraps of information, and you came running."

"Was Whelm following your orders?" asked Finn.

Another dismissive wave of the master's hand. "Whelm serves only himself. We paid him to carry out our instructions. He is no longer one of us."

"You received instructions to find us? Who from?"

"Who do you think? The Director."

"This Engneer?"

"I believe so."

"So, you never met this thing? How do you even get your orders?"

"The private line-of-sight to the Hub is still active," said the master. "One or two in the Inner Wheel have always had access to it. Something the others in the Twelve know nothing about."

"And what, exactly, are you supposed to do with us? There are no mines anymore. There's only the wreckage."

"You're to go to the Hub," said the master. "No doubt suitable retribution will be meted out to you there."

"The Hub?"

"Those are my orders."

"But why?" asked Finn. "Why should this Engneer care about us?"

"The machinery is being rebuilt and all its enemies must be punished."

"You think Engn is being *rebuilt*?" asked Finn.

"Piece by piece…" The master paused again as his words became another splutter of coughing. "Forgive me. I am old and the smoke has got into my lungs. Yes. Engn has been destroyed before and reassembled, you know. All this you see is part of the great design. The other masters know nothing about it, of course. They sit atop their pillars and attempt to create Engn to their own images. Madness, pure madness. It is a long time since we've had a sitting of the full Inner Wheel. As you can see, we are somewhat reduced in number. But one or two of us at the very heart of matters have always known how things work. The Director sends us instructions and we carry them out. As has always been the case."

"You think all this, everything that's happened, was meant to be?" asked Diane. "That the destruction was all part of some great, incomprehensible plan?"

"Of course. Just because we can't understand it doesn't mean it isn't there."

It was clear this master knew nothing of what had really happened, what Finn and Diane had done, why they had returned. It was clear, also, they needed to get to the Hub. That was the heart of it. That was where the answers were. What had the old Director said to Connor about it, that day in the Control Room? *Everything comes down to this.* This, clearly, was what Connor intended all along. Somehow, he had arranged matters so these messages were sent after his death, some automated mechanism or a series of instructions left for someone else. Get to the Hub. Destroy everything, including the seismium, before the Engneer or the masters or the wreckers can use it. And, judging by the increasing frequency of the earthquakes, time was running out.

"But how are you going to take us there?" he asked. "If we try and get through the wreckage the Great Wall is in the way. Unless you have some means of flying, I don't see how your orders can be carried out."

"We'll escort you to the Wall," said the master. "Those are our instructions. From there, I assume, others will take you."

"And when will we go?"

"Immediately. I assume you won't put up a fight?"

Finn glanced to Diane. It seemed the master and the ironclads were intent on taking them where they wanted to go for once.

"We'll come along quietly," said Diane.

"Very wise."

"Tell me," said Finn, "before we go. What Guild are you from?"

"Steamwrights."

"Ah. So, you don't know anything about spindle readers?"

"What is a spindle reader?"

"They're … something like the glass orbs that used to be dotted around everywhere. But you can see old pictures in them."

"No, no. We have nothing like that. We only build weapons these days. Spend all our time fighting those damned barbarian wreckers. We…"

His words were cut off by a huge boom shaking the room, sending dust spraying down from the stone above them. Instinctively, Finn and Diane covered their heads. Finn could feel the great pillar of rock beneath them swaying. He called out through a mouthful of dust. "What was that? What's happening?"

The master stood, hands gripping the arms of this throne. He looked upwards in alarm. At the same moment, heavy feet came running. Three ironclads burst into the chamber, dust on their leather masks.

"We are under attack," one shouted. "The wreckers have come, an army of them. They have the pillar surrounded."

XXX

Outside, the first glow of dawn was already washing across the world. Groups of ironclads ran to and fro, shouting, arming muskets, wheeling large mechanisms into place at the edge of the pillar to stand beside the clusters of bullhorns.

Finn crept to the edge, wary of another explosion. No one tried to stop him. Down below, in the abyss, it was still night. But rings of flickering lights surrounded the pillar in all directions. Rank upon rank of them. As Maeve had promised, the wrecker army was attacking. Whether they thought the seismium was there, at the ruins of the Inner Wheel, he didn't know. Perhaps they planned to destroy this pillar before marching on the Hub.

It was a scene he'd seen before, from a different perspective, through different eyes. The assault on the Great Clock by Baron's Rankin's army, flickering images glimpsed in the glass orb as they huddled together in Whelm's moving engine out on the plain. And, before that, in the fading painting in Connor's old home. Perhaps everything was simply repeating as the master had suggested. A cycle of destruction and rebuilding. It was hard to see how Engn could ever rise from its current destruction, but perhaps what had been built once could be built again. And if history was repeating itself, would the pillar they were standing on fall just as the ancient clocktower had?

The contraptions the ironclads were setting up all around the edge were clearly some kind of weapon, like steam-powered slingshots. They hissed and huffed as if complaining at being moved. Ironclads shovelled coal into them, sending their furnaces flaring red, while others wound cranks and lugged boulders, rusting cogs, anything they could find, to drop into the hand-like cups on the ends of the machines' arms. At a call from someone, one of the machines was unleashed. A *whoosh* of steam and the arm unwound, sending a constellation of shrapnel into the air, throwing the machine backwards in recoil. Only heavy iron chains stopped it ploughing into the assembled ranks of ironclads.

Down on the ground other fires flared. It was hard to see what they were, but then another explosion rumbled through the ground, and another. The wreckers were firing their own explosives at the pillar. Were there ironclads down there, defending the base of the column? It was hard to be sure. More steam slingshots fired, sending more and more stone and jagged metal down onto the attackers. Other ironclads wheeled black cauldrons of sickly-smelling tar to the edge and poured the acrid liquid over. Whether it struck anyone on the ground, Finn couldn't tell. The sound of the machines all around was deafening. The bullhorns, hissing with steam, were louder than ever, battering the attackers with their ticks.

Someone touched his arm. Diane. In the confusion of the attack, no one was paying the two of them any attention. There was no sign of the master, and no ironclad stood guard over them.

"We have to get away," Diane shouted. "There's nothing for us up here."

Another huge boom rumbled through the pillar, although whether this was earthquake or explosion, Finn couldn't tell. He looked around desperately. Clouds of steam and smoke billowed around from the machinery. He could see steam winches overhanging the drop, lifts the ironclads clearly used to descend and ascend rather than attempting the ladder. But they weren't going to be able to use one of them now.

"The chutes," he called to her, putting his mouth close to her ear. "We can slide down like I did last time. We saw the openings at the bottom."

Diane looked around, calculating, worry clear on her features. She winced as another concussion shook the pillar. "How do we know the chutes still go all the way down?"

"We don't. I can't see what else to try. I don't want to climb down that ladder and have boiling tar tipped on me. We'd be shot by both sides."

"The chutes were sealed at the bottom with iron grates," shouted Diane. "Perhaps we can find some tools to lever them open or cut through them."

There were plenty of scraps of metal lying around. Finn picked up a crowbar. Diane, dodging out of the way of more running ironclads, grabbed a broken musket she'd spotted lying discarded beneath one of the wheezing steam slings. She studied it briefly.

"There's still some black powder in it. Perhaps we can use it to blow the grating open."

The thought of doing so while they were at the bottom of the chute, unable to get away, didn't appeal much. But he had no better suggestions.

"Come on," said Finn. "The entrance was underground, below the main chamber."

They ran, weaving between groups of hurrying ironclads. The ground shook again and again. Shards of metal and lumps of stone tumbled from the building housing the Inner Wheel. At one point a large ironclad barred their way. Finn thought he was going to grab them, drag them off to the edge. Instead, with a grunt, he brushed them aside and lumbered away on some other mission. Diane shrugged and led Finn onwards.

It was deserted inside the chamber. The master, whoever he was, had gone, slipping away somewhere unnoticed. A rain of dust and debris fell onto the red tiles. The crack in the floor looked wider. Finn glanced upwards one more time. Holes in the reaching walls revealed the features of the highest carved faces, those lost to the shadows when he'd first been there. Were the topmost ones those who had sat in judgement of him? Perhaps. He would probably never know.

They cut left down a flight of steps into the cramped, round room he recalled. The opening of the chute was like a well head in the centre, with only a low stone parapet to protect it. Last time he'd felt the heat from the mines blasting up at him. Now the air was cold. Distant shouts and clanging sounds echoed up at them.

"How steep is it?" asked Diane.

"Steep. It was polished steel, too. I could only slow myself down a little when it twisted around. I was pretty badly bruised when I got to the bottom."

"Perhaps it won't be so well maintained, like the ladder. It might not be as slippery."

"Let's hope," said Finn. "Try and brace yourself against the sides, especially when we get to the bottom. I remember being thrown out hard. Don't want to find ourselves crushed against the iron grate."

"I'll give you a lead," said Diane. "I don't want to crash into you if I lose control."

Finn looked around once more. Had they been seen coming down there? No one had followed them. But they would be vulnerable in the chute. It would only take one cauldron of molten tar poured down after them to burn them alive, a few dropped boulders to crush them.

He threw the crowbar down ahead of him and listened to it bang and clang into the darkness. Diane did the same with the broken musket. Then Finn squeezed himself into the narrow chute. Immediately, he slid out of control, the descent so steep he couldn't hold himself. Careering downwards, he couldn't help crying out. From somewhere up above Diane shouted after him, although if she was telling him she was following he didn't know. The chute spiralled down through the pillar of stone so that it was soon utterly dark. Again and again, he banged his head, his back, his hips against the metal.

After a few moments, however, he got the hang of splaying his hands wide to slow himself down. Wedging his feet against the walls of the chute he was able to control his descent a little more.

"Are you okay?" he called up to Diane. She was in the chute, too, judging by the crashing and clanging sounds echoing down to him. In reply all he heard was a wordless scream echoing down to him. He thought she had to be some way above him, that she'd sound nearer than she was in the confined space, but then she thumped into him, out of control. For a moment they both hurtled forwards, picking up speed all the time. The prospect of ramming hard into the iron grating at the bottom of the slide was suddenly alarming.

Then, as he had, Diane managed to slow her descent. Hands squealing on the steel slide, Finn did the same. His fingers found a crack between two of the sheets in the surface of the chute and he scrabbled at it with his fingertips, managing to stop himself completely. Diane came to a rest above him as a weight upon his shoulders.

"Well, that was exciting," she said. "Any idea how far down we've come?"

"Hard to say. It was all a blur last time. Let's go down as slowly as we can."

They crept their way awkwardly down, crab-like, more

than once losing control on some less tarnished section of steel and setting off on another flailing, crashing descent. Each time they managed to halt themselves, although always with a few more bruises to add to their arms and shoulders and legs.

The descent continued for a long time. Was it possible, somehow, this was the wrong chute? That somehow it went past the floor level of the mines, deep into the ground to who knew where? They seemed to have been sliding and clambering downwards forever. Finn was on the point of expressing his fears to Diane when he caught a faint glimmer of light from below. Wherever they were going to emerge, they were nearly there.

Three more twists and Finn found himself piling into the iron grating they'd seen from the other side. Diane arrived a moment later, throwing him hard against the grille. They were back at the base of the pillar. It was lighter now. Even so, from the narrow confines of the chute they couldn't see much. Smoke drifted across the scene before them as if it were something alive, a predator on the hunt. Occasionally, indistinct flares of flame blossomed within it, accompanied by more bangs and booms. Figures ran through the haze, although whether they were ironclads or wreckers, Finn couldn't tell. Fortunately, the smoke was too thick, and the figures were too far away for anyone to notice his and Diane's arrival.

"Can you open the grille?" Diane asked. She was above Finn, unable to see properly how the ironwork was attached to the stone.

"It's cemented in," said Finn, feeling around with his fingertips. Awkwardly in the confined space, he brought the crowbar to the grille and levered at its fixing in the stone.

"I can't budge it at all."

"Can we cut through it?"

"It's not as badly rusted as I thought. It would take a long time even if we had a good saw. Which we don't."

"Okay, so, we'll have to try the black powder from the musket. The flintlock still works so we can make a spark. But we'll only get once chance."

Finn peered out through the grille. There was still nobody near enough to see what they were doing, and the sounds of the battle should cover the detonation of the black powder.

"Hand it here," said Finn. "I'll set it off and try and turn my back before it explodes. Can you work your way back up the chute a little?"

"I'll try," said Diane. "Keep your face away from the powder. And keep your eyes shut."

Finn tipped out the powder from the musket into a little pile at the bottom of the chute, where one of the grille's two hinges was embedded in the stone. Perhaps if they could get one hinge free, they could work the other one loose by kicking at it. Fortunately, there was an inch of match cord embedded in the musket's mechanism. If he could light it with a spark from the flintlock, he would have a fuse. Enough to at least get his hands out of the way before the black powder detonated.

In the end, he had to return a pinch of black powder to the gun so he could detonate it with the flintlock mechanism and so light the match cord. In the confined space, the operation was awkward, and he had to stop repeatedly to give his cramping muscles a rest. Eventually he had it. The end of the cord glowed red. It would do.

"Get ready," he called. "I'll light it now."

Diane had managed to shuffle back up the chute a short way. Finn followed her as best he could, pressing against the sides for leverage. When he was a little way up, he embedded the dead end of the match cord into the little mountain of black powder and, turning his face away, tried to climb another foot or two farther up.

The detonation, when it came, was deafening in the narrow space. Choking smoke immediately filled the air, sucked up the chute by the flow of air.

Diane coughing and spluttered. "Did it work?"

Finn, brushing the smoke away with his hand, tried to discern what had happened. He soon saw. The stone and metalwork were blackened by the detonation, but the grille hinge remained intact, firmly embedded in the surrounding stonework.

"It's no good," he called up. "We didn't touch it."

Could they climb back up? It was surely impossible. Even if they had the strength, the slick sides of the chute were too slippery to climb.

"We'll have to shout for help," said Diane.

"Who do you hope will answer?"

"Does it matter? As long as someone does. As long as…"

An armoured hand grasped the iron grille suddenly. Someone had heard or seen them. A face, wrapped tightly in cloth so only the eyes were visible, loomed out of the smoke to peer in.

They were eyes Finn recognized. Connor's eyes.

"Are you trapped in there, Finn? Get back as far as you can, and I'll blow the grille open properly."

XXXI

Finn and Diane removed their boots and hurled them as far away as they could through the iron grille. Then, their bare feet giving them more grip on the steel slide, they worked their way twenty feet or so back up the chute.

The second explosion, when it came, was huge, deafening in the narrow space, the sound like something solid clanging off the walls. More acrid smoke billowed over them. They slid through it holding their breath. This time the grille was hanging loose, one hinge completely detached. Kicking at it, Finn knocked it loose to slide, as he had once before, out of the tunnel and onto the ground of the mines. Diane landed beside him.

Their rescuer stood over them, the same short, powerful figure Finn recalled. Except something was different, something in the way this figure, swaddled against the smoke and dust, stood and moved. It looked like Connor. It could have been Connor. And yet how could it be? Finn's childhood friend was long dead, his body mangled and lost somewhere in the wreckage of

Engn.

The figure unwrapped the cloth from his nose and mouth and Finn understood. It was Connor's father who stood there. The Baron, the man people sometimes called the King of the Valley when he wasn't around to hear. The man who'd left the valley two years back for reasons unknown. What was he doing there?

"Good job I found you," said the Baron, his voice a rumble. "You'd have been stuck there forever in your little cage."

"But how did you find us?" asked Finn, utterly confused by this unlikely meeting. All around, through the smoke, the battle raged on. The worst of the fighting seemed to be on the other side of the pillar, but cries of anger and agony rent the air from all directions. From the clash of metal upon metal, it seemed there was hand-to-hand fighting going on.

"You have unlikely friends," said the Baron. "An ex-master called Whelm. He came to find me. I have little love for the masters, but there was no ignoring his story."

"But … but what are you even doing here in Engn?"

"No time to explain now. Wrap these around your mouths and noses. You are Diane, yes? We need to get away while the wreckers and masters are busy knocking each other senseless. If someone was to pour molten oil from the top, we'd be right in the firing line."

Finn tried to get everything he'd learned about the past straight in his mind: The Temple Guilds and the Mechanical Guilds. All the details of the old Clockwork War. Connor's childhood, caught between his mother and his father. "But surely, you're on the side of the wreckers, aren't you?"

Something like amusement passed across the Baron's ruddy face. There was a sadness to his smile where once he'd laughed heartily and readily. "That bunch of idiots? Certainly not. Wouldn't trust them an inch, bad as the masters. But come. We need to put some distance between us and the pillar. We can talk later."

The Baron led them away through the roiling smoke, crouching as he ran, keeping low to the ground. As Finn followed, he saw the Baron played out a thin rope or cable from a round spool attacked to his backpack, its other end apparently secured to the base of the pillar. Was he planning to pull the pillar over by muscle power? Had he lost touch with reality just as Connor's mother had?

"What are you planning?" Finn asked as they jogged along, weaving around as they caught glimpses of wreckers or ironclads in the grey haze around them.

"You'll see," said the Baron. A huge explosion shook the ground near them, and the smoke flamed red for a moment. A shot from one of the steam-powered catapults, perhaps, fired indiscriminately into the melee. Screams of agony came through the air, and Finn was glad of the smoke, concealing the details of what was happening all around.

They reached a low outcrop of rock emerging from the floor of the wreckage. The Baron darted behind it and sank to the ground. Finn and then Diane joined him. They hadn't been seen. Three huge detonations, exploding in rapid succession, shook the ground they sat on, but not near enough to harm them.

The smoke tickled the back of Finn's throat, making him cough despite the cloth wrapped around his mouth and nose. The air tasted of dust and burning flesh but sitting nearer the ground it was a little sweeter. Diane's voice was muffled through her mask. "We need to get farther away. They could still hit us from here."

"No," said the Baron. "There's no need. And we're waiting for someone."

"Who?"

As if in answer, a figure emerged from the fog to slump down beside them.

"Ah, good, it is you," said Whelm. "You found them, then?"

"I found them," said the Baron. "Trapped like startled rabbits."

"And the charges?"

"All rigged. I've used nearly all I had. My last act of destruction but one."

"Do you think you've managed to align the charges properly?"

"We'll see, won't we?"

"Can someone please explain," said Diane, "what is going on here? We're in the middle of a battlefield. We need to *run*, not sit around chatting."

The Baron was fumbling with some mechanism he was carrying, a square metal box with a brass crank and a red button. Next to the button were two tiny electric lamps, one lit, flickering red, the other dark. The line he'd played out behind him ran directly into the box. The Baron's plan became clear. He wasn't intending to haul the tower down by simply pulling on a rope.

"We'll run soon, have no fear," said the Baron. "Would I be right in thinking you need to get through the wall of wreckage to the Hub?"

"How did you know that?" said Diane. She turned to Whelm. "Did you tell him? Did you know all along?"

"Me? Not a clue. That's something the Baron here has worked out all by himself. I just went to find him because I thought he might help."

"You know him?"

"By reputation. He's one of the lone wolves I mentioned, walking about the wreckage destroying any remaining scraps of machinery he can find. Probably him we've been hearing in the night."

"But you knew he was Connor's father?"

"I made the connection. We all saw the images in the orb, Baron Rankin of the Stonecarvers directing the battle against the Mechanicals at the Battle of the Clocktower. Finn said the likeness to Connor's father was clear."

"There," said the Baron. He was winding the crank on

the box with rapid little movements. "I think we're ready. Just need the voltaic cell to charge fully. You might all want to cover your ears."

Finn turned to look back over the lip of the rock. The drifting smoke was thinner, wispier, and there was less screaming, fewer clangs of metal on metal. Was the battle over? And if so, who'd won this time? Towering over the smoke, the great pillar of stone loomed over everything. In the distance, on the top, movement was still clear. Had the wreckers made it up there? Was someone searching for him and Diane, or had they been forgotten in the confusion? His eyes prickled as he peered upwards, trying to pick out the distant detail.

He was so engrossed he didn't notice the gang of wreckers emerging from the smoke.

There were twenty or so of them, all muffled against the fumes, but all clearly soldiers in Lud's army. All were cut and battered, and some were badly injured, blood soaking through makeshift bandages. But they all carried blades, and they'd clearly seen the four of them. They approached: wary, twitchy, glancing at each other. It was clear it wouldn't take much to trigger them into attack.

Diane's eyes were full of alarm. Whelm, next to her, tried his hardest to remain hidden. The Baron stood, his hands open in a gesture of peace. "No ironclads here, my friends. You can put down your weapons."

At the sight of the Baron, the wreckers relaxed immediately. Clearly, they all knew him, too. One of the gang members, a full-faced man with a grey beard, stepped forwards. "What are you doing here, Master Stonecarver?" To Finn's ear there was still a note of wariness in his voice.

"What I always do: destroy the infernal machinery. Find the pieces and explode them into smaller pieces, as Lud should have been doing all along."

A frown passed across the wrecker's face, but he didn't object. The Baron's heresies appeared to be well known. "Very well. We have the pillar surrounded now; we can starve them down. If you'd like my advice, you should leave. You aren't needed here anymore."

"Actually, I think I am. The job is only half done. If you'd like *my* advice, I think you should leave. Leave quickly while you still can."

Puzzle clouded the man's face. "Why? What have you done this time?"

"Isn't it obvious? I…"

The Baron stopped as a loud crack from nearby cut through the scene. The wrecker who'd been talking slumped forwards, falling like a plank to lie lifeless on the ground. On the other side of the outcrop, a phalanx of ironclads emerged from the smoke, all bearing rifles. The Baron still stood with his hands up, gaze casting between the two groups. If fighting started, Finn thought, they'd be right in the middle of it, caught in the crossfire.

"You are all enemies of Engn," said one of the ironclads. "Lay down your weapons or you will be executed where you stand."

The wreckers didn't move. None laid down their swords. Unspoken conversation buzzed in the air as the two sides eyed each other up, weighing up their chances of winning in a fight. Finn knew how it would go. One of them would move or flinch and everyone would attack, guns blazing, swords swinging. And most likely, at the end of it, none of them would be alive. As the smoke continued to clear, more detail emerged from the fog: the hard lines of the ironclads' armour, the blood stains on the wreckers' swords. It all served to make the situation seem more real, more dangerous.

Moving slowly, hands held aloft just like the Baron, Whelm stood to face the ironclads. "Perhaps you know who I am. We aren't your enemies. We aren't with them. We were traversing the wreckage when we were caught up in this battle."

"You aren't with the wreckers, but you aren't with us," said the ironclad. "That one" – he indicated the Baron with a nod of his masked head – "is well known to us. He may not be one of Lud's minions, but he is still an enemy of the great machine."

"Still, we have no part in this ancient war of yours," said Whelm. "I ask you to let us pass."

"Who is there with you, cowering behind that rock," said the ironclad. "Show yourselves."

Reluctantly, Finn and Diane stood, hands aloft, turning so both sets of soldiers could see them. From the scowls on the faces of the wreckers and from the way the ironclads took fresh grips on their rifles, it was clear both sides knew who they were.

"In a war you have to decide which side you're on," said the ironclad. "But it seems the four of you have managed to make an enemy of all of us. So be it. I propose a brief truce between our ancient guilds." He moved his gun so that it was trained on the Baron, not the wreckers. "Let us agree to dispatch these four traitors, shall we? Traitors to both sides. Then we can resume hostilities as we see fit. Do you agree?"

Words passed among the wreckers. Heads nodded. Finally, another leader emerged, a woman, her hair cropped short and her face marred by more than one brutal gash. "Very well. A brief truce, machine man. And when we are done killing them, we will kill you, too."

The ironclad made a sound that might have been a laugh. "As to that, we shall see. But first let us deal with these four. We will do it. Guns and muskets are so much easier than hacking away with sharpened lumps of metal."

The woman wrecker stepped forwards. "If your usual accuracy with those guns is anything to go by, *we'd* be in more danger if you shot at them. We will do it. They have already been condemned by Lud, and a sword is cleaner and quicker. More honest than killing someone from afar, too."

While this was going on, Finn and Diane had been looking desperately around for some means of escape, some way out. They saw nothing. They were surrounded and hopelessly outnumbered. Diane's fingers found Finn's as they stood side by side. They'd come so far and almost found the answers to their questions. But this, suddenly, was the end. At least, Finn thought, they were together. He wished she were safe, far away. But at the same time, selfishly perhaps, he was glad she was there. He squeezed her fingers tighter.

Then, down on the ground, unseen by either wreckers or ironclads, a tiny green light flickered on the metal box beside the Baron's foot. The Baron spoke again. His hands were no longer held up in the air. "In a war you must choose whose side you're on, you say. But what if you don't like either side? What if neither understands what is really going on? Or what if both are really two sides of the same coin, fighting and fighting without knowing why? Without *thinking*? Then you have to do something else. Then you have to make a side all of your own. Even if it means everyone else will hunt you down, try and kill you for fear of hearing the truth. Well. That's what I choose. That neither of you will win."

Ironclad and wrecker both moved in the next instant. But the Baron was too quick for either. He raised his foot and stamped down hard on the metal box. Upon, Finn saw, the small, red button.

And a huge explosion shook the world.

XXXII

A ball of red flame engulfed the base of the pillar, lighting up the smoke a livid red. A heartbeat later, a wall of sound crashed into them, throwing everyone to the ground. Shielded behind the outcrop of rock, Finn and the others were spared the worst of it. The armed ironclads and wreckers were less lucky.

Finn crouched with his arms over his head. He could feel the heat from the blast on the backs of his hands. After several seconds, he peeped at the scene around him through his fingers. People were staggering to their feet. Some of the ironclads had lost their masks. All their faces were vivid with shock. They lurched or crawled away, all their differences forgotten in their desperation to flee the scene of the explosion.

Finn, too, tried to rise. They had to get away. But the Baron was there, pulling him down hard, his mouth opening and closing as if he was trying to speak. The sight confused Finn for a moment.

The Baron put his mouth next to Finn's ear to repeat

his words. The explosion had done something bad to Finn's hearing. Everything had gone strangely quiet, all noise muffled. The Baron's voice sounded like it was coming from a long way away. "Wait. We're safe here. There's no need to run."

Kneeling, Finn peered over the top of the outcrop of rock. A great chunk had been taken out of the base of the pillar, like a bite from an apple. The entire column of rock swayed visibly. Tiny fragments of machinery – fragments he knew were huge machines – toppled from the top. His hearing began to return. Screaming and a deep rumbling came to his ears. The column continued to sway like a pendulum. It was easily near enough to crush them if it fell in their direction. He watched as a single stick figure, perhaps an ironclad, fell from the top, arms and legs flailing uselessly at the air.

"If it falls on us, we'll have no chance," Finn shouted.

"It won't fall on us." Connor's father kneeled beside him, watching the pillar through narrowed eyes.

"How can you be sure?"

"See."

The column swayed one more time, then reached some point of no return. Instead of swinging back, it fell. People, machinery, buildings slid from the top. The entire Inner Wheel building appeared, turning over and over as it was pitched to the ground. Finn thought he could see those ancient thrones spinning through the air, although perhaps he was imagining it. One of the bullhorns was caught mid-tick. Instead of cutting out the huge sound became a frozen wail: a mournful, falling blare as the pillar crashed towards the ground, like the death cry of some huge beast.

The column fell like a tree. As the Baron had promised, it didn't fall towards Finn and the others. Peering through the dust and smoke, Finn saw what Connor's father had done. The column was collapsing towards the Wall, towards the two other pillars standing between. Finn tried to measure the distances with his eye in that long moment of falling. The columns of rock supporting the roof of the underworld were vast. The distance between them was great, too. Was it possible the lengths were the same?

They watched in horrified fascination as the pillar crashed towards the ground. Halfway down it cracked in two, back broken by its own weight. Still, it fell towards the next column. With a thunderous boom, the top of the column crashed into the base of the next, sending it swaying in turn. Two, three pendulum swings, and then the next column fell. This, too, collapsed in the direction of the Great Wall. More machinery, more people were tipped from the top, streaming like a waterfall to the ground. The second column fell in line with the first, towards the third, and Finn finally understood what Connor's father had worked. The second pillar broke into the base of the third, and this too was toppled, falling in line. The huge stone pillar crashed into the wall of broken machinery, cutting through it with ease.

After a few moments a silence descended on the wreckage of Engn. Two huge clouds of dust billowed out from the three fallen pillars, washing over Finn and the others. When it had passed, long moments later, they stood. Everything was coated in a thick layer of grime and dust.

"There," said the Baron. "There's our pathway to the Hub."

He was right. The three pillars now lay as a single line of rock leading over the wreckage, over the Great Wall. They had only to climb up, and they could make their way into the secret heart.

"How did you do that?" Diane asked, wonder clear in her voice.

"Stonecarvers know rock," said the Baron. "We understand its grain, its cut. Before we carve, we must quarry. And in these days, I've had to do more quarrying than carving, alas. But I know where to place charges to open up rock, give me the pieces and shapes I need. This was simply a bigger scale."

"It's incredible," said Finn. He still had to shout to hear his own words.

"I didn't think you could actually do it," said Whelm. "I mean, I knew you could bring the pillar down. I didn't think you'd break through the wall, too."

"The masters of Engn have always underestimated us," said the Baron. "Just because you think big, new ideas you believe all our ideas are old and small."

"We should go," said Diane. "The wreckers and ironclads have fled. And maybe they'll assume we're all dead. But it won't be long before others use this new walkway to reach the Hub. We need to get there first."

As one, the four of them jogged towards the fallen pillar, weaving around boulders, mangled scraps of machinery and the lifeless remains of those who'd been thrown from the top. Finn tried not to look, focusing on reaching the mound of rock that would be their way into the Hub.

They had to climb up the sides of the fallen column to reach its top. A tangled section of the iron ladder gave them a start. After that, it was a matter of climbing up the curved rock face, clinging on with fingers and toes wherever they could. Diane was a good climber, lithe and quick as she wound her way up to the top. When she was there, she threw down one of the Baron's ropes to help haul Finn up. Next came Whelm. Between them they pulled the Baron up. He arrived badly out of breath, chest heaving, face red.

They set off towards the Great Wall. So far, at least, no one else was up there. In the dust-coated landscape it was hard to be sure of detail, but it appeared no one was following them.

Finn walked beside Connor's father. The Baron trudged along in silence, eyes on the distance. Until then, they hadn't spoken since the day many years ago when the people of the village gathered in the Moot Hall to hear the complaints about Matt Dobey, the old lengthsman. Even after returning from Engn, Finn hadn't spoken to Connor's father. Partly because he hadn't known what to say, how much to explain. Partly, he realized now, out of guilt at having survived when Connor hadn't.

Now at last, in this strange place, Finn found the words. "We … we tried to save him. Connor, I mean. At the end. We didn't want to leave him there. He said he'd follow us. Only, he didn't. He never came out. But what he did … it was incredible. People doubted him, but he stayed true to the end. I thought you should know."

The Baron didn't reply for a moment. Finn wondered if the man hadn't heard, if his hearing was too damaged. Then Finn saw him wiping tears from his eyes, smearing the grime on his cheeks.

"The day he was taken was the worst of my life, Finn. Worse, even, than that day in the snow when we found the two of you up that old oak tree." The Baron glanced at Finn, as if unsure how much to say. "Connor's life was difficult growing up. His mother and I tried to protect him from it. From our differences, I mean. I don't think we did a very good job. It affected him; he was torn in two by it. When he went away, I confess, I didn't know which side he'd take. I didn't want him to take either side, to have to choose. I heard word from Engn over the months afterwards, about how he was rising through the ranks, making use of his mother's connections. Even I thought, then, he'd gone to that side. That he'd rise through the ranks of the masters and become part of the machine. I was glad he was doing well but unhappy with his choices, all at the same time. I was wrong about him, terribly wrong."

"He was always on your side. He vowed to destroy Engn. He *did* destroy Engn."

"Yes. He did. But he was betraying his mother at the same time. She thinks he came here to assume his rightful position in power. It can't have been easy for him."

Connor's mother. It was only then Finn realized the Baron probably didn't know about her death. "There's something else you should know," he said. "Back home. There was an earthquake. Actually, there were quite a few, and several buildings collapsed. I'm sorry, but one was your house. Connor's mother was inside at the time. There was nothing we could do."

The look of shock on the Baron's face made it clear he had no idea. "She is dead?"

"I'm afraid so. The quakes were bad. The building was reduced to rubble."

"Ah."

"I'm sorry. I went there beforehand, tried to persuade her to leave, come to the Moot Hall. But she refused."

The Baron nodded, as if this made complete sense to him. "She never really understood what had happened to Connor. She never accepted his death. She was rather … lost in her delusions. Perhaps, in a way, that was for the best. The thought of him being gone was too much for her."

"Yes."

"These damned tremors," said the Baron, an edge of anger to his voice. "They should never have meddled. They should have left everything safely locked away in the ground."

"You know about seismium?"

"Of course. What Stonecarver doesn't? Dangerous stuff. Even minute specks of it in the rock can cause havoc. Hit the tiniest seam of it when you're quarrying, and you're in big trouble. The more there is the bigger the tremor. To collect it together, to even think about using it as some sort of weapon … it was madness. Unimaginable. Nothing is worth that. It will destroy everything, kill everyone. Like it killed Connor. Like it killed his mother."

"That's why you're not with Lud?"

The Baron nodded. "Both sides want to use it to wipe each other out. Separated from the real world here in

Engn, a madness has overcome them all. They both have to be stopped. Connor saw that. In the end, I think, he perhaps didn't take sides either, didn't choose between mother and father, new guilds and old. He just wanted to stop all the death, all the destruction. He just wanted this war to end."

"But what we did … it wasn't enough?"

"It seems not. It had to be done, but still the threat is there. Youngsters are no longer carted away to the machine, and that's good, but we're all still living under this shadow. A shadow so large many people don't even see it."

"Then, you know about the Hub? You know what Connor was trying to do?"

"Some idea. Not everything. I received certain messages hinting at what he'd unearthed, what he intended to do. And maybe I'd already guessed some of it."

"You received line-of-sight messages?"

"Word of mouth, mostly. There are older, slower networks than those 'scopes. But Mrs. Megrim passed along a few words now and then. They were always vague, of course. Guarded. Connor was in a difficult position."

"I didn't know Mrs. Megrim had done that."

"She did a lot that folks don't know about. As I think you've found out."

"Yes."

Something else occurred to Finn then. Another memory from his visit to the Baron's house. "Your wife had her own line-of-sight. Red messages rather than white, taking a different route out of the valley. Where were those messages coming from? Where did they go to?"

"That old scope? I don't think it went anywhere. I don't think the messages she imagined really existed. She used to talk about secret communications from some northern city far beyond those ringing the plain. It was like something from one of the old nursery stories. She … she didn't always have a good grasp on reality, I'm afraid."

"And this new Director. This Engneer. Have you seen it? Is it real?"

"It's real. A clockwork machine charging about giving orders, directing the ironclads to rebuild. That's what we have to destroy, I think. That's what Connor was warning us about. He must have unearthed the plans for this new work of devilry."

"Can we destroy the seismium too?"

"No one has ever amassed so much together before. The Stonecarvers have some knowledge of how to handle it. It might be possible to break the particle up into fragments, distribute them deep underground where the weight of rock can keep them in check, but it will be dangerous. No one knows exactly when the cycle will reach its end, when the detonation will occur. Could be next year, could be tomorrow. But it's obviously soon judging by all these tremors."

"So, we must acquire the particle, and make sure neither masters nor wreckers get hold of it. What do we do then?"

"Take it to Stonehavn. Our old city is in ruins now, but there are still some there that might be able to help. I think that's our only hope."

They'd reached the end of the first column, the point where it had crashed into the second. They had to climb down a steep hillside of shattered rubble to reach the fallen body of the next column. More than once they had to use the ropes. Whelm's shoulder was still giving him trouble, and Finn's knee hurt with each step. The Baron was much older than all of them and seemed to be nursing several wounds he refused to talk about. Only Diane was uninjured, and she led the way when it came to climbing.

There was still no sign of pursuit from across the floor of the abyss. But ahead, they discerned detail of the column beyond the Great Wall. It still stood intact, although to Finn's eye it was canted over at a slight angle, as if frozen in the act of falling. A visible crack ran up it, so that it was in effect two separate columns, boughs divided like the branches of a tree. The falling pillar that had crashed through the wall, held up by the line of wreckage, hadn't quite reached all the way to it.

On top, Finn picked out detail. One object, unmistakably, was the huge cube of a building he recalled from his visit with Ciara. The Hub. It stood intact. Just visible at its base, tiny ant figures were people. A line of circles climbed up the side of the pillar. A series of giant cogs, perhaps, interlocking. Some sort of lift mechanism for ascending and descending the column. Perhaps there was a moving room like the one he'd used on his previous visit to Engn. If they got that far, they might not have to climb another ladder at least.

They rested for a short time, Whelm and the Baron sharing round what water and simple, dried food they carried. Then they set off along the second fallen column. Finn wondered what part of the original machine it had supported. He tried to lay it all out in his mind, work out what each column coincided with at ground level, but he couldn't make sense of it. He'd made the journey in the opposite direction, once, speeding on the steam shuttle from Blueprint Hall to the Inner Wheel, but the details of that day were a blur.

When they set off again, Diane joined Finn and the Baron. Whelm lagged behind, glancing backwards again and again.

"You left the valley to come here?" Diane asked.

"I did. When Connor didn't come back, we both withdrew from the world. You know that. The house, the farm fell into ruin. I wanted no more to do with people. It was wrong, I know. I was grieving, I understand now. There were festivals and memorials to attend. Celebrations, such as your own arrival into the valley, Diane. But I had no energy for any of it."

"Then something changed?"

"I heard word the machine was being rebuilt. That a

new Director had started everything up again. It … gave me a purpose. I came here to put a stop to it. As perhaps I should have long ago."

His words reminded Finn of something his own father had once said. "You've been here ever since?"

"I have. Destroying any piece of the machinery I can find. Keeping my eyes open, too, trying to make sense of what's going on. At first, I joined the wreckers, the rump of the old Temple Guilds, but we soon fell out. You know why."

"You learned about the Hub?" asked Finn.

"Yes. I put a lot of thought into how I could get there with the wall protecting it. Then one day I had the idea of felling the pillars, toppling them like trees. I didn't have enough explosive for all of them, you see, but I calculated I had enough for one or two. So I thought, if I could arrange the detonations, make one pillar bring down the next like a line of dominoes, I might be able to smash through the wall, too. It took a lot of preparation. I had to pace out the distances, measure the angles, study the rock. Took a year or more to get everything ready. Then, when that master came to find me, told me what was happening, I knew it was time."

"It's incredible," said Diane.

"My father taught me well," said the Baron. "Showed me how to quarry stone for building and carving. I simply thought bigger thoughts."

Whelm jogged up to catch them, then. "We need to hurry. There are people coming."

"Who?"

"See for yourself. Wreckers coming across the cavern floor on that side of the pillars. Over there, a load of ironclads. Both armies are coming this way, converging on the gap in the wall.

"Perhaps they'll fight each other," said Diane.

"Perhaps, but they all know about the Hub. If it comes to a final battle, that's the place for it. We need to get there first."

They began to jog along, stopping only occasionally for water and food. The climb down onto the third pillar held them up again, but Finn reasoned their pursuers would be slowed when they reached the wall. They'd have to climb onto the fallen pillar to make it through. And most likely they'd be fighting each other as they went.

Crossing the third fallen column was more of a slog. It sloped inexorably upwards, its top held off the ground by the crushed wreckage of the wall. More than once, when some part of the tangle gave way or shifted, the column dropped beneath them, and they had to crouch to wait for the movement to cease.

Eventually they reached the point where the column ended in a steep drop to the floor. A hundred yards beyond, surrounded by its circle of debris, stood the cloven pillar upon which the Hub sat. They'd seen feverish activity up there as they'd neared, but no attack had come as they approached the column of rock. The people up there were too busy, so it appeared, preparing some mechanism, some defence.

Finn, Diane, Whelm, and the Baron used the ropes to clamber down from the column to the floor of the mines. The Baron went first, Diane, Finn and Whelm supporting him as he worked his way down. Whelm went next, then Finn. Finally Diane, throwing the rope down to them, climbed to reach them.

"The wreckers and the ironclads are getting near," she said. "There isn't much time."

"I'll rig my remaining explosives on the column," said the Baron. "By the look of it, it won't take much. The tremors have taken their toll. The rest of you can go up there and look for the seismium. But be warned. If those armies come, I'll have to detonate. We must be sure everything up there is destroyed. Be quick."

"Give us as much time as you can," said Finn. "All the answers are up there. The solution to all the riddles."

"Very well." The Baron held out a small lump of waxy clay, taken from his backpack. "Here. Take this with you."

"Explosive?" said Whelm.

"It's stable as long as it's kept cool. You might need it up there. Use it if you get near the Engneer. There's enough there to destroy it completely. Here are some percussion caps, too. Strike them hard and they'll trigger the explosive. Got it?"

Finn reached out to take the explosives. He, Diane, and Whelm turned and ran for the pillar that supported the Hub.

XXXIII

They reached the base of the leaning, broken pillar without being assaulted or attacked. The wheels they'd seen from afar were, as they'd thought, a ladder of interlocking cogs, each thirty of forty feet tall. The wheels were turning slowly, reluctantly, hauled around by a rattling chain from above. One wheel turned clockwise, the next anticlockwise and so forth. Welded to the front, where the 9, 18, 27 and 36 would be on a clock face, were little square platforms, big enough for one person to ride up and down.

"You think we're supposed to hop from cog to cog?" said Diane.

Finn gazed up at the towering assembly of slowly moving wheels. "Looks like it. Strange it's been left running. Strange it's not better defended."

"They usually have no need," said Whelm. "I told you; until now there was no way in or out at ground level."

"So why did they even come down here?"

"Looking for parts, like the rest of us."

"But they must have seen what we did," Finn replied.

"They must know the wall's come down."

"I guess they have more pressing things on their minds," said Whelm. "Shall we go up?"

Finn reached into his pocket to touch the memory spindle, satisfying himself it was still there. "I'll go first."

The ascent was slow and juddering. The little platforms were designed to pivot around so they were always level, but the whole contraption was poorly oiled, and the platforms squealed or even stuck completely as they turned. More than once Finn had to jump up and down to nudge a stuck platform back to level. The higher they rose, the more precarious the procedure became. Fortunately, there were welded handles to hold onto as well. The trickiest part was timing the leap between wheels. The first time he tried it he got it badly wrong. Jumping too early, he found himself tottering off-balance with nothing to hold onto. Heart pounding, he managed to find his footing and crouch on the next platform. By the time he reached the next cog he was better at it. By picking the right moment, he was able to simply step from wheel to wheel. The little platforms were slightly offset from each other to make the operation easier. Looking down as he rose into the air, he saw Diane and then Whelm were also managing to negotiate the step between the cogs.

They were soon higher than the Great Wall. The whole of the cavern opened up before him: the fallen columns and, beyond, the line of those that still stood. He also saw the massed ranks of wreckers and ironclads. They'd reached the breach at the same moment and were now attempting to climb up the round sides of the fallen column. Did they know the other army was there? It was hard to be sure. Were the ironclads rushing to defend the Hub, or were they from different pillars, different factions, with their own ideas of what Engn was supposed to be?

Slow as the cogs turned, Finn still seemed to gain height with rapidity. After only ten minutes, he was nearing the top of the column. Sounds of roaring, clanking machinery became louder and louder. The last cog rose above the lip of the pillar, taking Finn by surprise so that, instead of jumping down immediately, he rode the wheel to its very top, waiting for it to circle once more before he leapt onto the flat surface of the rock. Diane and then Whelm arrived moments later.

A squat, square building with a domed roof stood nearby. It looked to be made from the same material as the Hub itself. They loped across the ground to hide behind it.

They immediately saw one reason they hadn't been attacked. This island was now effectively two islands, the rent in the rock cutting it completely in half. All the activity, as well as the great cube of the Hub, were on the other side. So far as they could see, nothing connected the two sides except for a pair of metal rails like those the steam shuttles had once used, stretching across the void like two tightropes.

Finn, Diane and Whelm hid behind the wall of a building while they decided what to do. Many ironclads were visible across the divide, hastening to and fro. Most carried boxes and barrels to a strange contraption, a little like a moving engine but both larger and more delicate-looking than any Finn had ever seen, its body a latticework of thin metal wires. Fortunately, the machine was consuming all the ironclads' attention. They clambered all over it, pouring in liquids, making adjustments. For some reason it reminded Finn of the skeleton of some vast bird. Steam spouted from the machine. Whatever it was, it appeared to be ready for use.

Beyond them stood the great bulk of the Hub. The six vast pistons that met in the cube were idle, one sagging brokenly to the ground, another completely missing. The top ram, the one that had once pushed down from its enormous beam-engine, stood frozen in mid-action, as if the rust had come upon it suddenly to lock it in place for ever.

Next to the building stood a pole festooned with a

tangle of cables. Wires had run all through Engn in the old days, conveying timing signals and communications. Perhaps the people up there were attempting to reinstate the network. Most of the cables went nowhere, though, hanging down in short lengths, although some appeared to lead away to distant points on the ground or even other columns. Whether they were connected to anything at the other end, he couldn't tell.

"What do you think we're supposed to do?" asked Diane.

"Don't know," Finn replied. "Destroy this Engneer thing, I suppose."

"Do you see it?"

"No, must be inside the Hub. Or maybe it's already broken down."

"We'd need to get closer to use the explosive on it."

"Those rails look pretty precarious. Do you see any other way across?"

"Not from here. Let's try and get inside this building. Maybe it connects to the Hub somehow."

"Do you remember this part from your last visit?"

Finn shook his head.

They found their way inside easily enough. There were no doors, but one whole side of the building had been ripped off when the surrounding ground fell in. By stepping around the exposed edge they were able to climb within.

It had clearly been some sort of control room. Banks of rusting switches and levers took up one wall, the one overlooking the Hub. There were hundreds of dials and gauges, their needles rusted at many different numbers, their scales and units incomprehensible. A grimy window overlooked the great cube. Finn ducked down so he couldn't be seen and peeped through. Four ironclads carried something apparently very delicate to the waiting engine. They moved with great care, shuffling along slowly. The other ironclads stood back as the four passed, as if wary of what might happen.

"Finn," said Diane from the other side of the room. "Look at this."

An entire wall was taken up with a large map. It looked like nowhere Finn knew. Then it clicked: he'd had the scale all wrong. The large expanse of green was not some field or open area in Engn. It was the whole of the great grass plain, hundreds of miles across. In its very centre was a grey smudge sitting atop a thin, blue line meandering across the whole map. Engn, then, and the river En.

"It's the whole world," he said.

All around the circumference of the map were mountain ranges. More dots were marked on this circle, each with a word written beneath in carved, square letters. Finn read a few of them, touching each with his fingertip. Clockmakers ... Ironmasters ... Silversmiths ... Steamwrights ... Lensmen ... Papermakers ... Wheelwrights ... Woodturners ... Stonecarvers. These, clearly, were the city-states of the guilds. Twenty-four of them were marked in black, dotted randomly around the ring. The old Temple Guilds. But the other twelve dots – marked in red, the city-states of the upstart Mechanical Guilds – had clearly been placed more carefully, deliberately filling in the gaps between the black dots. Thirty-six cities, more or less regularly spaced around the central hub of Engn. A map of the whole world.

And Finn saw, then, precisely what the Mechanical Guilds had done. They really had imposed their time on everyone. The land had been turned into the face of a vast clock. Thirty-six numbers around its edge, and Engn at its centre. A clock he'd lived upon all his life without knowing it. He found the place where his beloved valley had to be: an unnamed smudge of green mid-way between the cities of the Clockmakers and the Stonecarvers.

His home looked so tiny, so insignificant. He stepped back to take in the scale of the whole. Someone, he saw, had drawn a wavy red line right around the edge of the map, beyond the thirty-six cities, cutting through the mountains. He thought he knew what that line might be. The extent of the land that would be destroyed if the seismium was allowed to detonate. The scale of it was incredible. He wondered who had drawn that line, made that calculation. Someone hoping to let the seismium explode, or someone trying to prevent it?

"Finn!"

The alarm in Whelm's voice snapped him out of his reverie. "What is it?"

"We've been seen."

Finn raced back across the room to the window. "The ironclads?"

"Not just them. The Engneer, too. It's there. By the stairs. It's … Finn, you really need to see this. I had no idea. I truly had no idea."

The note of shock in his voice sent alarm hammering through Finn. He peered through the window, smearing a circle in the grime to see better. There, a short way away across the crack separating the two halves of the pillar, was something like one of the moving engines. It had four spoked wheels and steam billowed from the machinery propelling it forwards.

But it wasn't simply a machine. It was like a carriage for someone badly injured, or who had lost the use of their legs. A person sat in the midst of it, hands on levers, body propped by spars as if they were unable to hold themselves upright. It was hard to tell for sure where the person ended, and the machine began. But there was no mistaking who it was sitting there.

There wasn't a new Director after all. The old one had survived, despite terrible injuries. Across the divide, Connor, the real Connor, looked back at them.

XXXIV

"Why, Finn? Why have you only come now when it's too late?" Connor's voice sounded hoarse, croaky, as if a part of the machinery had lodged itself in his throat. He didn't look well, his skin pallid, his head slightly slumped to one side, held up by a cap of metal mesh.

Finn stood on one side of the divide. Connor, nestled within the steaming, hissing machinery that carried him around, on the other. An array of ironclads and silverclads stood behind Connor, many holding muskets and grappling irons. All of them were aimed at Finn, Diane and Whelm.

"We came as quickly as we could," called Finn across the rift. "We didn't know what we had to do."

A whoosh of steam blasted from Connor's carriage, as if it were angry at Finn's words. Connor tilted his head to address the guards standing behind him. "Get back to the engine. Get it up to temperature. These three pose no danger to us."

When the four of them were alone, Finn relaxed and

grinned at his boyhood friend. An image flashed through his mind of that long-ago day when the two of them had weathered an avalanche in the arms of an oak tree. It was wonderful and impossible Connor should still be alive. He'd clearly suffered terrible injuries, but he'd survived.

Finn spoke in a lower voice, so they wouldn't be overheard. "What happened to you?"

"This contraption? Isn't it obvious? My legs were crushed in the collapse. I was pulled out barely alive. They gave me a wheeled chair at first, and pushed me around when I needed to move, but it was too slow, too frustrating. My right arm is also badly damaged. I had them build this steam carriage, modifying a moving engine so I could get around."

"You've got them obeying your orders."

He'd imagined Connor dropping his guard too, setting aside the role he'd been playing. But his expression didn't change at all as he replied. "Some are loyal, some aren't. I've had to weed out the latter. I needed people I could trust."

"But what's going on?" said Diane. "We've come all this way. What do you need us to do? And why is it too late?"

"We've come for the seismium," said Finn. "That's what it's all about, isn't it?" Connor scowled, but maybe Finn wasn't reading his expressions properly. Maybe his old friend's face and voice no longer worked too well.

Finn pressed on. "We thought we had to destroy *you*. We thought you were some sort of machine, a failsafe mechanism woken up to reconstruct Engn. It is good to see you again, Conn."

Connor's engine rocked backwards and forwards slightly, as if it was preparing itself to leap across the chasm at them. "You came here to kill me and take the particle?"

"We didn't know what we had to do," said Diane. "All we had were a few cryptic messages and suggestions. The spindle, the line-of-sight transmissions. How were we supposed to know about any of this?"

"No," said Connor. "You had all the answers all along. I told you everything, showed you everything. All this time I needed you, and you didn't come. In the end, I had to send Whelm to find you. Have you had a happy time, the two of you? I hear you share a house now, old Mrs. Hampton's. Have there been celebrations and parties? Food, drink, and long walks through the woods? Do you want to know what my life's been like all this time?"

"It isn't like that," said Finn. "We didn't know. We thought Engn lay in ruins and you were dead. If you'd wanted us to come and help, we would have. You know that. The vow still stands. Why didn't you just tell us? Why be so damned secretive?"

More steam hissed from the machine. "I had to be secretive, Finn, because I was alone and surrounded by enemies. I told you plainly enough what I needed you to do."

"Look, we're sorry," said Diane. "We didn't know, truly. We'll come over the fissure. It's ridiculous talking like this."

Connor rocked to and fro some more, then backed away a yard or two to give them space to cross. Finn and Diane took a rail each, holding hands for balance. The iron rails sagged as they stepped across, flexing like old wood. The drop on either side fell away alarmingly. Finn could feel the heat coming from Connor's moving engine. When they reached him, Diane went back and helped Whelm to cross, too.

Behind Connor, the ironclads continued to work away, clustering around the other machine, climbing beneath it to make adjustments or simply polishing its smooth surfaces.

"The explosions we heard," said Diane. "Was that because of all this? Because of what you're doing here?"

"We've had accidents," said Connor. His voice hadn't

lost its grating edge. "Bad accidents. Moving the seismium is dangerous. When we took it down the other day, the tremor was enough to split the column in two. Two of our high-pressure engines exploded into the abyss. You probably heard that; the detonation was deafening. Although you probably didn't hear the screams that went with it."

"We had no idea," said Finn. "Truly. Tell us what we need to do. Is that engine over there going to destroy the seismium somehow? Is that what you've been doing?"

"Destroy the particle?" said Connor. "Did you even bother to listen to what I told you on the spindle? There is no known way to destroy it, not safely, not now. Perhaps, if you'd come earlier, there might have been time. Now there's only one thing we can do: take the seismium away to construct new machinery around it, machinery that actually *works.*"

"No."

"Yes. I'm taking the particle away to a new Engn. It is fortunate there are enough ironclads and masters still loyal to me. Fortunate, also, that two years ago I uncovered the likely whereabouts of the Gargantua engine, along with the plans drawn up by Adage, my mother's forebear. It is far away, beyond the plain and the ring of city states. I don't know how much of it still stands, or how much of it was even built in the first place, but I have to go and find out."

"We can come with you, help you."

"There is room for only one. In truth the machine can barely manage that. And no one must know where I'm going; the risk of the cycle repeating is too great."

"Connor, please, don't do this. We can help. Somehow, we can destroy the seismium."

"It's too late, Finn." A shrill whistle sounded from his machinery. It was a signal to the guards. A troop of ten of them came clanking over.

"Lock these three in the Hub," said Connor. "Don't harm them, but make sure they can't escape."

Finn backed away, conscious of the great crack in the rock behind him. "Connor, what are you doing? This makes no sense. You want to build a new Engn? After everything we've done? That's madness."

"Want, Finn? You think I *want* to do this? Why do you never understand anything? I'm doing this because I must, because no one else will. The poison's been let into the world and all we can do is live with it. *Contain* it. Perhaps if you'd been here, we could have worked out another way, but you weren't, were you?"

The ironclads ran to surround them. With the fissure to their back, Finn and the others could do nothing. Diane tried to charge through the guards, scurry between two of them. They caught her and pinned her arms behind her. Others grasped Finn and Whelm to march them towards the Hub. Finn shouted wordlessly, but it was no use.

A rusting sign next to the Hub door said, simply, *Engn*. They were thrown to the ground inside. The ironclads hauled the door shut.

Connor was wheeling off, his steam-powered carriage wheezing steam. But then he stopped and turned back. Something like his old, boyish expression was back on his features. "Finn, I … I'm sorry to have to do this to you. Since the accident, since I was crushed in the collapse, I haven't always been myself. I know that. But this is the only way."

"We can still fix everything," Finn shouted through the door. "We can destroy the particle, Connor. The Stonecarvers can dismantle it, put it back in the ground. Then once we're done, you can come back home and everything will be like before."

The youthful expression on Connor's face slipped away again. "The Stonecarvers?"

"Yes. Your father. He's…"

Another shrill whistle from the moving engine silenced Finn.

"What do the Stonecarvers know? What do any of

them know? Masters and wreckers, Temple Guilds and Mechanical. It's their fault, all of them. One side built the weapon to kill the other. The other plans to steal it and use it as well. They'll slaughter us all. You really think it's so simple? You think this story will have a clean, happy ending, and we can all go home?"

"We can help, like before."

"No. No one must know where I'm going."

"But your father, he's here, at the foot of the pillar. He believes you're dead."

That stopped Connor, but only for a moment. "You see? That is why I must go. The longer I stay, the more I put those I love in danger. You two, and what's left of my family. I don't want any of you to end up crushed beneath the wreckage like I was. My father didn't know me that well towards the end, but perhaps he'll understand what I'm doing if you explain it to him."

"Connor, I…"

Another whoosh of steam billowed from Connor's carriage. He shouted to the ironclads. "Enough! We're out of time. Lock these doors and lift me into the other engine. We have to do this now."

XXXV

"Let's try and break down the door," said Finn. "We have to stop him."

He set about barging into the door with his shoulder. It gave a little but held. From outside he could hear the thunder of a steam engine turning at high speed. There were shouts, words he couldn't make out, then a scraping sound. The engine roared even louder, sounding like it was being pushed to its limits. Then the sound dropped away sharply to be replaced by a low thrum. Finn stood unmoving, looking into Diane's eyes while they both listened.

"What's going on?" she said.

"I don't know. I don't understand."

They tried again to barge down the door, hitting it together. It refused to budge. After several minutes of trying, Finn sank to the ground. The door was solid. He looked around. The steel rams he recalled pressing with all their might on the dice-sized cube of seismium lay limp and useless now. A rickety tower of scaffolding had been erected in the centre of the space, giving the ironclads access to the point where the tapering rams met.

"Finn, Diane. Look what I've found."

Whelm had been exploring around the edge of the Hub, looking for another way out. In one corner there was a jumble of boxes and metal cases and tables. Cables reached upwards through holes punched in the Hub wall, the point next to the pole they'd seen. Whelm had pulled aside some metal sheets and found, attached to one of the cables, a mechanism with a glass orb on top, like those Finn had seen in the Directory control room. A spindle reader.

Finn rose and raced over as quickly as his knee would let him. "Is it functioning? Can you make it work?"

"It has power, but everything's so rusted." Whelm put his face near the mechanism and blew sharply to dislodge the dust. He tweaked something within the contraption and then, when it refused to spark into life, banged it hard with the flat of his hand. On the second strike a red light flickered within it. There was a smell of burning dust and, after a moment, a faint grey light glowed from the orb.

"Can you see anything in it?" asked Diane. "Is it connected to anywhere?"

"Doesn't look like it," said Whelm. "I'm just seeing noise."

"But is there a slot for a spindle?" asked Finn. He was studying the machine, looking for somewhere the sliver of metal could slide in, trying to remember how they worked.

"Down here," said Whelm. "It's a recorder, but it should be able to play, too. But what's the point? I told you, we can't get any more from that spindle of yours, it's encrypted. And it's too late now."

"Why did Connor say we had all the answers all along?" asked Diane. "What did he mean? He couldn't understand why we hadn't acted, as if we'd have no trouble seeing the pictures. He sounded like we'd betrayed him."

Finn shook his head. It made no sense.

"Go over everything that happened," said Whelm. "When he gave you the spindle, he must have given you the key as well."

"I'm telling you he didn't," said Finn. "We don't have time for this. Connor's obviously gone mad. Perhaps his brain was damaged when the machinery fell. Or perhaps" – it was the first time he'd admitted the idea, even to himself – "perhaps he was never really on our side. Perhaps this was what he intended all along. Perhaps he's his mother's son rather than his father's after all. Plus, there are two armies about to attack and the Baron's going to blow up the column of rock we're standing on. We have no time."

"We have to," said Whelm, half shouting. "This is why we've come. You must have missed something. Think. Everything could depend on this. There has to be an answer."

After a moment Finn relented. "There's not much to say. We'd already set off the collapse, disrupted all the timing signals. Engn was imploding around us. And he gave me the spindle and told me to take it."

"He must have said why."

"No! He just said it would be useful. Nothing more."

"Useful how?"

"He didn't say!"

"Okay, look, just repeat everything that was said, as well as you can remember it."

The scene was etched on Finn's memory. He'd replayed it over and over often enough, looking for what he'd missed. "Connor gave me the spindle and said, 'It will come in useful.' I said, 'What do I do with it?' and he replied, 'It'll be obvious. But remember what it was all for. Why we did this. Promise me. You must remember what it was all for.' And then he went back to the controls and we left."

"He was obviously giving it you for a specific reason,"

said Whelm. "It was clearly really important. He wouldn't have stopped and said all that otherwise, with Engn falling down around your ears."

"I know! But that's all he said."

A look of surprise and then understanding burst across Whelm's face. "By the stars," he whispered to himself.

"What is it?" said Finn.

Whelm's voice was quiet when he replied. "He must have been afraid someone was listening. Or perhaps he was just so used to keeping everything secret."

"What? What is it?"

"Don't you see? He told you the encryption key. He said it very clearly. *Remember what it was all for.* But he didn't just mean that, he was telling you the key was *all fours.* Twenty fours. He repeated it to be sure you heard. It's as simple as that. A key so obvious we didn't even bother trying it."

"It … it can't be that simple."

"Try it," said Diane. "Dial the number in and try it."

Whelm worked away feverishly, setting up the device, turning the little brass wheels used to set the encryption key. When he was done, he stood back and closed a circuit by turning a small lever.

The familiar fuzz and fog filled the orb. They leaned in closer, their breaths misting the glass. Then the image of Connor appeared, just as they'd seen him the first time they'd read the spindle back in the valley. Connor in the Control Room, wary, afraid of being overheard or caught.

His voice was strangely mechanical when it came from the machine, but it was clearly him. "Finn. There isn't much time. This spindle will explain everything. Everything you have to do. I'm told you're here in the Directory now. You'll understand it all when you see. We had it so wrong, Finn. I mean, we were right, of course, but we knew nothing. Everything depends on this, Finn. On you and Diane. *Everything.* What we're going to do is just the start. Engn is…"

The images skipped. This was where they'd cut out before, the start of the encryption. But this time, after a scribble of fuzz, the pictures settled down and continued.

"…a weapon. A terrible weapon. That's what it's been all along. A machine for destroying the world. And it's so terrible they had to keep it a secret while they built it, while they waited for the right time. You'll see it all when you look at these images I've collected.

"The defeated masters of the Mechanical Guilds plotted to get their revenge in the Clockwork War by destroying everything, levelling the land and starting again. But the reason got lost. The secrets were too well kept, and Engn became this insane, self-perpetuating machine no one understood any more. It was just *there*, something so big most people didn't question it. What we need to do, what we vowed to do that day – we were right. Engn is a cruel, brutal place. We do have to destroy it. But that's only the start. It won't solve anything because the real problem is the particle, and the war, and history. You'll see. Look at these images. The machine was just there to contain the seismium, and now the machine's useless. We must build a new one. A new Engn to contain the particle. There's an alternative machine we can use as a start, built long ago in secret. We'll do it differently, of course. We won't have ironclads dragging people off to slave away for no reason or any of that. But we *have* to do this.

"I don't know if I'll survive the destruction. I don't know if you or Diane will. But if even one of us does, they must come back here and start again. I don't know how, but we have to try. The machine will fight us. The old ways will resist; one side or the other will want to stop us. If I'm still here, come and find me. Come as soon as you can. I'll need you. I don't know for sure how much time there is before the cycle reaches its end, but we may not have long. Come and help build the new Engn with me. Please."

The images in the orb faded out, to be replaced by a different scene. One they didn't recognize, a gathering of a group of cloaked masters somewhere.

Whelm turned the lever to switch the machine off. He turned to Finn and Diane. "No need to sit through the rest of it now."

"It's incredible," said Finn. "All this time. Connor's been working away on his own. Badly injured, trying to save the world. He must have known we'd survived. He must have been puzzled we didn't come to help. And then, later, angry. Finally, he got the line-of-sight network back and sent us messages. Used the same encryption key, I suppose. He must have wondered why we weren't coming. He was ready to act. There were more and more earthquakes and explosions, and still we didn't come. How could I have been so stupid not to see it?"

He looked to Diane. "We failed him."

She put a hand on his arm, grasping him. "We're here now. We can still help, if we can get to him."

"No," said Whelm. "I don't think we can."

"What do you mean?"

"Don't you see? He's building a new Engn, yes. But not here. He's taking the seismium away. That moving engine we saw them loading things into, it must be the flying machine we saw from the wrecker cage. That's what he's been doing. Using his position as the Director to create his own moving engine so he could get around, and then the flying engine so he could escape. This Engn is lost and broken, riven by wars and rusting away, rendered useless by its own secrecy and complexity. He's going to start again somewhere else, build this other machine he mentioned."

From outside, the thrum of the steam engine they'd heard roared back to life. The pitch climbed again, the speeding machinery sounding like it was on the point of imminent explosion.

"We have to get out there," said Finn. "We have to go with him."

There were shouts from outside, then a scraping sound

of something heavy moving over the ground. The engine screamed even more shrilly. There was one more shout – and then the sound of the engine dropped away, its note falling as it plummeted from the pillar. The sound ceased. No one spoke. Finn, Diane and Whelm stood in silence, ears pressed to the door.

Then, after long moments, the sound of the machine returned. Distant, now. Steadier.

Slowly it grew quieter as the flying engine carrying Connor and the seismium steamed away into the sky.

XXXVI

"He's going to do it, isn't he?" said Diane. "All alone, he's actually going to try and get a new Engn working."

"Yes," said Finn. "He is."

"And then, sooner or later, it will all happen again. All the secrecy and misery. The masters and the ironclads. Everything that's happened. Because sooner or later someone will want to use a weapon like that, and others will want to defend it, keep it for themselves."

She, Finn, and Whelm stood on the lip of the rock pillar. In the distance, a dot that might have been a bird at first glance, the flying engine was just visible in an unblemished grey sky. They'd escaped eventually, smashing down the Hub door with a length of rusting steel shaft. Too late to stop Connor. Too late to escape with him.

"Perhaps it will be different this time," said Finn. "Connor will … make sure it isn't like before. He'll make sure people aren't taken and used. He's been hurt, clearly, but I trust him still."

"And perhaps it will be no different at all," she said. "A generation or two and things might end up just as they were, the truth lost."

"Where do you think he's even gone?" said Whelm.

"It seemed to me he turned north," said Finn. "That must be where this other machine is. Or perhaps he's going to try and find the Lords of the High Ice, see if they even still exist."

"Perhaps he's simply taking the seismium as far away from civilization as possible," said Diane. "Find somewhere so remote it can't harm anyone, can't destroy any more lives. Apart from his."

Finn thought about the map he'd studied in the control room. It covered a vast area, but it stopped at the mountains circling the great grass plain. How much bigger was the world? What lay beyond, off the edge of the charts? He sighed. The wind from the north was sharp on his cheeks, making his eyes water. The flying machine was gone, lost to the distance. "Perhaps. One final act of sacrifice. It would be like him."

Whelm said, "According to the spindle, the seismium has a period of three hundred and seventeen years and that it needs to be contained when it's at its most active. All the earthquakes mean we must be getting close. There might not be time to get a new Engn running."

Finn nodded. Behind them, the ruined bulk of the Hub lay in darkness. The ironclads were leaving, descending the cogs to join in with the battle down below. They'd started by trying to defend the pillar, keeping the wreckers away. Now it looked like the two sides were simply intent on destroying each other. Even from their great height, Finn could hear shouts of rage, screams of agony. But there were fewer of them all the time. The fighting was coming to an end. It didn't look like either side had won. He wondered what had happened to Connor's father. Was he down there still, waiting for the moment to set off the explosives?

"What should we do now?" Diane asked.

"Be absolutely sure the Hub is destroyed," said Finn. "That's the one thing we can do. Even with the seismium gone, people might carry on trying to rebuild it. People who never even knew what the machine was for in the first place. But with the Hub gone there can be no Engn."

"And then?" asked Diane. She was looking at Finn rather than Whelm as she asked. Her meaning was clear. Was Finn going to be content with that? Was he done? Or was he going to head off into the north, try and track down Connor and his flying engine and the seismium. He wished he could give her an answer. He wished he knew. Was the story over or not?

"Let's make sure it's destroyed," he said. "Make sure the machine can never threaten us again. And then … then we'll see. Perhaps we'll hear something more from Connor and we'll know what we need to do."

"We need to give our wounds time to heal, your head especially. That wound still looks bad."

"Then I suppose we head home, for a time at least. There's nothing left for us here."

"And if another earthquake strikes? Or another cryptic message comes through?"

He put an arm around her, holding her close against the cold. "We'll worry about it when it happens, okay?"

She didn't look completely convinced. But she nodded in agreement.

A shiver went through the ground they stood on, then, as if the pillar of rock was trying to shake them loose, throw them to the ground.

"We should get down," said Whelm. "Who knows how long this rock will stand. The tremors have weakened it badly."

"Yes. But give me a few minutes. I want to use this explosive Connor's father gave me."

"On what?"

"The Hub, obviously."

They ran back into the carcass of the huge cube at the centre of everything. The seismium was gone, of course. The Hub was rusting and quiet, could never be used again. Still, it felt good to be committing this act of destruction. Climbing onto the scaffolding, Finn gently squeezed the explosive into the gap between the rams. It oozed around the sides as he packed it together. Finally, he embedded a percussion cap in it and stood back.

"That's not actually going to achieve anything," said Whelm when Finn joined back on the ground.

"It will make me feel better," said Finn.

Diane had found a charged musket and she handed it to Finn. They backed away ten or twenty yards, then Finn fired his blunderbuss shot at the explosive, spattering the whole area with shot and shrapnel. One piece, at least, hit the percussion cap. The explosive detonated in a roar of flame and sound, wrenching the rams out of line, sending one of the four horizontal ones see-sawing to the ground with a thunderous clang.

"There," said Finn when it was done. "We can go now."

They worked their way back across the rails, then stepped onto the clanking cogs, still turning away, to descend to the underworld one last time.

They found the body of Connor's father at the foot of the column. He lay near the bundle of explosive he'd been strapping to the base of the tower. His chest was a mess of blood and purple flesh. Some scattershot musket fire, Finn thought, an ironclad seeing a wrecker and killing him where he stood. He'd died without knowing his son was still alive. In that moment it seemed unbearable. He'd been so close. Connor's mother had died believing her son still lived. It turned out she'd been right after all.

After a moment, Whelm studied the charge the Baron had set, the wires running from it.

"This is ready to blow," he said after a moment.

"We should complete his work," said Diane. "Destroy

the Hub for good."

They took the spool of wire the Baron had carried and let it unravel behind them as they picked their way through the battlefield. The fighting was over now. The two armies had clashed and, it seemed, all but wiped each other out. The wreckers had outnumbered the ironclads but the ironclads, better armed, had held their own. Now, by the look of it, most on both sides were dead. Dead or dying.

No one attacked them or tried to stop them. One or two people were picking their way among those still alive, bandaging wounds, doing what they could for the injured. Finn saw an ironclad, helmet discarded, tending to the mangled leg of a wrecker. Perhaps, he thought, perhaps the Clockwork War was finally over.

They joined in with helping carry the wounded away from the Hub. People stood atop the fallen column, lowering ropes to haul the injured up. Finn, Diane and Whelm joined in, carrying the wounded on makeshift blanket stretchers. Whelm winced each time they lifted one of them, his shoulder still giving him trouble. He didn't say anything about it.

When it was done, and no one living remained around the Hub, they climbed the ropes themselves. Finn and Diane, hands clasped together, pressed the red button on the Baron's detonator. A cloud of smoke and dust billowed from the base of the column. The ground shook as the huge sound of the explosion hit them. The pillar stood a moment longer, defying them even then, then sagged to one side. Finally, it crashed into the abyss, the Hub a useless tangle of metal and stone. Finn could taste its dust in his mouth.

"We did it then," said Finn. "We finally destroyed it."

"Let's go," said Diane. "Let's go home."

A day later, Whelm led them to a place where they could climb out of the underworld. One of the walkways had crashed to the ground, but its other end was still tethered to the surface, giving them a steep slope they could ascend. Ropes had been set up for people to haul themselves upwards, like lines up a rock face.

Diane went first, followed by Finn. After a few yards, he realized Whelm wasn't following. He looked back down.

"Are you coming?"

"No."

"Why?"

Whelm looked around, running his hand through his hair. "There are still columns standing. I know a bit about explosives, about how Connor's father rigged them. I'm going to complete his work. Make sure it's all gone. If there's nothing left of the original ground level, if none of the old buildings and machines still stand, then it will truly be destroyed. People can pick over the wreckage all they like, but that's all it will be. Wreckage."

Finn looked down at him, then up at Diane. They were both waiting for him to speak.

"When you've finished," he said, "will you come and find us in the valley?"

"You think I'd be welcomed back?"

"I know you would."

"Then, if I survive, I will."

"Good," said Finn. "Make sure you do."

Together, he and Diane climbed from the wreckage of Engn, back into the light.

ABOUT THE AUTHOR

Simon Kewin was born on the misty Isle of Man but now lives deep in the English countryside. He writes fantasy, science fiction and some things that can't make their minds up. He is the author of over 100 published short stories as well as a growing number of novels.

To find out about his other books, go to:

www.simonkewin.co.uk

Sign up for his newsletter and you'll be the first to know when he has new books out. There are some fine sci/fi and fantasy books to download for free as thanks.